Raves for Robert Goddard's

HAND IN GLOVE

"DAZZLING IN ITS DECEPTIONS. . . . *HAND IN GLOVE* HAS METICULOUS CONSTRUCTION, A TWIST OF PERSONALITY FOR EVERY STOCK CHARACTER AND A DASH OF HONOR WHERE YOU WILL LEAST EXPECT IT. . . . *HAND IN GLOVE* IS THE PERFECT FIT."

—*Detroit News & Free Press*

"Filled with denouement and witty characterization. . . . Even the minor characters, all of whom are skillfully and attentively drawn, have surprises to offer."

—*Boston Globe*

"A PAGE TURNER THAT DISHES UP SURPRISE UPON SURPRISE."

—*Chattanooga Times*

"A MASTERFUL TALE. . . . Goddard delivers complex adventure, emotional insight, and finely wrought prose. Highly recommended."

—*Library Journal*

"*HAND IN GLOVE* WILL BRING YOU INTO ITS SHIMMERING PLOT AND MENAGERIE OF INTRIGUING CHARACTERS THE MOMENT YOU TURN TO PAGE ONE. . . . This dark and dramatic trail of dark events will appeal to your sense of adventure and love of a good, honest, hard-hitting mystery-rich novel."

—*Macon Beacon*

"IT'S THAT TRICKY, INGENIOUS PLOT THAT GENERATES . . . *HAND IN GLOVE*'S CONSIDERABLE SUSPENSE. . . . matching wits with the devious Goddard guarantees some surprises."

—*Orlando Sentinel*

"A DARKLY ROMANTIC THRILLER TO RIVAL THE WORK OF P. D. JAMES."

—*New Woman*

Also by Robert Goddard

Past Caring
In Pale Battalions
Painting the Darkness
Into the Blue
Debt of Dishonour

HAND IN GLOVE

ROBERT GODDARD

WSP

WASHINGTON SQUARE PRESS
PUBLISHED BY POCKET BOOKS

New York London Toronto Sydney Tokyo Singapore

This book is a work of fiction. Names, characters, places, and incidents are either the product of the author's imagination or are used fictitiously. Any resemblance to actual events or locales or persons, living or dead, is entirely coincidental.

WSP

A Washington Square Press Publication of
POCKET BOOKS, a division of Simon & Schuster Inc.
1230 Avenue of the Americas, New York, NY 10020

ISBN: 0-671-89037-9

First Washington Square Press trade paperback printing October 1994

10 9 8 7 6 5 4 3 2 1

WASHINGTON SQUARE PRESS and colophon are registered trademarks of Simon & Schuster Inc.

Printed in the U.S.A.

Originally published in Great Britain by Bantam Press

HAND IN GLOVE

PART ONE

ONE

THERE IT WAS: THE same sound again. And this time she knew she was not mistaken. Sharp metal on soft wood: the furtive, splintering sound of the intrusion she had long foreseen. This, then, was the end she had prepared for. And also the beginning.

She turned her head on the pillow, squinting to decipher the luminous dial of the clock. Eight minutes to two. Darker – and deader – than midnight.

A muffled thump from below. He was in. He was here. She could no longer delay. She must meet him head-on. And at the thought – at the blurred and beaming clock-face before her – she smiled. If she had chosen – as in a sense she had – this would, after all, have been the way. No mewling, flickering fade from life. Instead, whatever was about to follow.

She threw back the covers, lowered her feet to the floor and sat upright. The drawing-room door had been opened – cautiously, but not cautiously enough to escape her. He would be in the hall now. Yes, there was the creak of the board near the cupboard under the stairs, abruptly cut short as he stepped back in alarm. 'No need to worry,' she felt like calling. 'I am ready for you. I will never be readier.'

She slid her feet into their waiting slippers and stood up, letting the night-dress recover its folds about her, letting the frantic pace of her heart slacken. There was probably still time to pick up the telephone and call the police. They would arrive too late, of course, but perhaps . . . No. It was better to let them believe she had been taken completely by surprise.

He was on the stairs now, climbing gingerly, keeping to the edges of the treads. An old trick. She had used it herself in times gone by. Another smile. What use was reminiscence now, far less regret? What she had done she reckoned, on the whole, she had done well.

She reached out and picked up the torch from the bedside cabinet. Its barrel was smooth and cold in her grasp, as smooth and cold as . . . She set off across the room, concentrating on action to deflect any doubts that these last moments might bring.

She had left the door ajar and now, raising it fractionally on its hinges, swung it open in absolute silence, then stepped out on to the landing. And froze. For he was already rounding the bend near the top of the stairs, a black hunched shadow visible only because she had known he would be there. Her heart pounded in her throat. For all the preparation – for all the rehearsal – she was frightened now. It was absurd. And yet, she supposed, it was only to be expected.

As he reached the landing, she raised the torch, holding it in both hands to stop it shaking, and pushed the switch with her thumb. And there, for an instant, like a rabbit in a headlamp, he was caught, dazzled and confused. She made out jeans and a black leather jacket, but could not see his face clearly past the object he was holding up to shield his eyes. Not that she needed to, because she knew very well who he was. Then she recognized what he had in his hand. One of the candlesticks from the drawing-room mantelpiece, his fingers entwined in its brass spirals. It was upside-down, with the heavy sharp-rimmed base held aloft.

'Hello, Mr Spicer,' she said in as steady a voice as she could command. 'It is Mr Spicer, isn't it?'

He lowered the candlestick an inch or so, struggling to adjust to the light.

'You see, I knew you were coming. I've been waiting for you. I could almost say you were overdue.'

She heard him swear under his breath.

'I know what you've been paid to do. And I know who's paid you to do it. I even know why, which is more, I suspect, than—'

Suddenly, time ran out. The advantage of surprise expired. He launched himself across the landing and seized the torch from her grasp. He was stronger than she had supposed and she was weaker. At any rate, the disparity was greater. As the torch clattered to the floor, she realized just how frail and helpless she really was.

'It's no good,' she began. 'You can't—' Then the blow fell and she fell with it, crumpling to the foot of the balustrade before the lance of pain could reach her. She heard herself moan and made to raise her hand, dimly aware that he was about to strike again. But she would not look. Better to focus on the stars she could see through the uncurtained window, scattered like diamonds on jeweller's velvet. Tristram had died at night, she recalled. Had he glimpsed the stars, she wondered, as death closed in? Had he imagined what would become of her without him? If he had, this would surely not have been it, for this he could never have anticipated. Even though the makings of it were there, beside him, as he died. Even though—

TWO

'Hello?'

'Charlie? This is Maurice.'

'Maurice? What a lovely surprise. How—'

'Not lovely at all, old girl. I've got bad news. It's Beatrix.'

'Beatrix? What—'

'Dead, I'm afraid. Mrs Mentiply found her at the cottage this afternoon.'

'Oh, God. What was it? Her heart?'

'No. Nothing like that. It seems . . . According to Mrs Mentiply, there'd been a break-in. Beatrix had been . . . well . . . done to death. I don't have any details. The police will be there by now, I imagine. I'm going straight down. The thing is . . . Do you want me to pick you up on the way?'

'Yes. All right. Yes, perhaps you could. Maurice—'

'I'm sorry, Charlie, really I am. You were fond of her. We all were. But you especially. She'd had a good innings, but this is . . . this is a God-awful way to have gone.'

'She was murdered?'

'In the furtherance of theft, I suppose. Isn't that how the police phrase it?'

'Theft?'

'Mrs Mentiply said there were things taken. But let's not jump the gun. Let's get there and find out exactly what happened.'

'Maurice—'

'Yes?'

'How was she killed?'

'According to Mrs Mentiply . . . Look, let's leave it, shall we? We'll know soon enough.'

'All right.'

'I'll be with you as soon as I can.'

'OK.'

'Have a stiff drink or something, eh? It'll help, believe me.'

'Perhaps you're right.'

'I am. Now, I'd better get on the road. See you soon.'

'Drive carefully.'

'I will. 'Bye.'

'Goodbye.'

Charlotte put the telephone down and walked back numbly into the lounge. The house seemed even larger and emptier than usual now this latest sadness had come to add its weight to the silence. First her mother, with lingering slowness. Now, with sudden violence, Beatrix too. Tears filled her eyes as she looked around the high-ceilinged room and remembered them gathered there, in paper hats, to celebrate one of her childhood birthdays. Her father would have been present too, of course, grinning and tickling and casting animal shapes on the wall with the shadows of his clenched fingers in the firelight. Now, thirty years later, only her shadow moved as she turned towards the drinks cabinet, then stopped and slowly turned away.

She would not wait. She had done enough of that over the years, more than enough. Instead, she would leave a note for Maurice and drive herself to Rye straightaway. No doubt there was nothing to gain by it, except the relief that mobility might bring. It would stop her moping, at all events. That is what Beatrix would have said, in her brisk no-nonsense way. And that, Charlotte supposed, was the least she owed her.

It was a still June evening of hazy sun, mocking her grief with its perfection. A sprinkler was swishing on the neighbouring lawn as she went out to the garage, a dove cooing in the trees that screened the road. Death seemed preposterously remote in the perfumed air. Yet death, she knew, was here to dog her steps once more.

As if to outrun it, she drove with reckless speed down across the Common and out along the Bayham road, past the cypress-fringed cemetery where her parents lay, south and east through the somnolent woods and fields where she had played and picnicked as a girl.

She was thirty-six years old, materially better off than she had ever been in her life, but emotionally adrift, assailed by loneliness and barely suppressed desperation. She had given up work – one could hardly call it a career – in order to nurse her mother through her final illness and thanks to what she had inherited did not need to resume it. Sometimes, she wished she were not so independent. Work – however humdrum – might introduce her to new friends. And economic necessity might force her to do what she knew she ought: sell Ockham House. Instead of which, since her mother's death seven months before, she had departed mournfully for a long holiday in Italy and had returned from it none the surer what she wanted from life.

Perhaps she should have asked Beatrix. After all, she had seemed happy – or at least content – in her solitude. Why could Charlotte not be the same? She was younger, of course, but Beatrix had been her age once and even then had been a woman alone. She overtook a tractor and trailer, calculating as she did so in what year Beatrix had been thirty-six.

Nineteen hundred and thirty-eight. Of course. The year of Tristram Abberley's death. A young man of artistic temperament carried off by septicaemia in a Spanish hospital, little realizing the fame posterity would heap upon him or the fortune it would confer upon his heirs. Behind him, in England, he had left a young widow, Mary – of whose subsequent remarriage Charlotte was the issue; a one-year-old son, Maurice; a solitary sister, Beatrix; and a slender body of avant-garde poetry destined to be enshrined by the post-war generation in A level syllabuses up and down the land. It was Tristram Abberley's posthumous royalties that had set up Charlotte's father in business, that had paid for Ockham House and Charlotte's education, that had left her as free and friendless as she currently was.

For this, she realized with a sudden drying of the throat, was what Beatrix's death represented: the loss of a friend. She was old enough to have been Charlotte's grandmother and in the absence of a real one had happily filled the role. During her schooldays, Charlotte had spent most of every August with Beatrix, exploring Rye's cobbled alleyways, building castles on Camber Sands, falling asleep to the strange and comforting mew the wind made in the chimneys of Jackdaw Cottage. All so long, so very long ago. Of late – especially since her mother's death – she had seen little of Beatrix, which now, of course, she could do no more than bitterly regret.

Why, she wondered, had she taken to avoiding the old lady? Because Beatrix would not have hesitated to tell her she was wasting her life? Because she would have said guilt and grief should never be indulged lest they take too strong a hold? Perhaps. Perhaps because she did not wish to confront herself, and knew Beatrix Abberley had the discomforting knack of obliging one to do precisely that.

When Charlotte arrived, the day-trippers and souvenir-hunters had left and Rye was settling into a drained and drowsy Sunday evening. She drove up the winding cobbled streets to St Mary's Church, where a few worshippers were still wandering away after Evensong. Then, as she turned towards Watchbell Street, she was confronted by a trio of police cars, one with light flashing, a cordon of striped tape round the frontage of Jackdaw Cottage and a huddle of idle onlookers.

She parked in Church Square and walked slowly towards the cottage, remembering all the hundreds of times she must have come this way knowing she would find Beatrix waiting – tall, thin, keen-eyed and intent. But not this time. Not this time nor ever again.

The constable who was on duty directed her inside. There she found, seemingly in every doorway, plastic-gloved men in boiler suits, armed with powder and tiny brushes. In the drawing room stood one man distinct from the rest, grey-suited and frowning, picking his way through the tea cups and sugar bowls displayed in one of Beatrix's glass-fronted cabinets. He glanced up at Charlotte's approach.

'Can I help you, miss?'

'I'm a relative. Charlotte Ladram. Miss Abberley's—'

'Ah, you'd be the niece. The housekeeper mentioned you.'

'Not a niece, exactly. But never mind.'

'No. Right.' He nodded wearily and made a visible effort to summon a greater degree of attentiveness. 'Sorry about this. Must be a dreadful shock.'

'Yes. Is . . . Is Miss Abberley . . .'

'The body's been removed. Actually . . . Look, why don't you sit down? Why don't we both sit down?' He shooed a stooping figure away from the fireplace and led Charlotte towards one of the armchairs on either side, then sat down in the other one. It was Beatrix's, as Charlotte could easily tell by the jumble of cushions and the crooked pile of books on the floor beside it, where the old lady's questing left arm could easily reach. 'Sorry about all these people. It's . . . necessary.'

'I quite understand.'

'My name's Hyslop. Chief Inspector Hyslop, Sussex Police.' He looked about forty, with thinning hair combed forward in a style Charlotte disliked, but there was a winning edge of confusion to his features and a schoolboyish clumsiness about his dress that made her feel it should be her putting him at his ease, not the other way about at all. 'How did you hear about this?'

'Maurice – Maurice Abberley, that is, my half-brother – telephoned me. I gather Mrs Mentiply found . . . what had happened.'

'Yes. We've just sent her home. She was a bit upset.'

'She'd worked for Miss Abberley a long time.'

'Understandable, then.'

'Can you tell me . . . what you've learned?'

'Looks like a thief broke in last night and was disturbed while helping himself to the contents of' – he pointed across the room – 'that cabinet.'

Turning, Charlotte saw for the first time that the glass-fronted cabinet in the corner was empty and that its doors were standing open, one of them sagging on its hinges.

'Full of wooden trinkets, according to Mrs Mentiply.'

'Tunbridge Ware, actually.'

'I'm sorry?'

'It's a special form of mosaic woodwork. The craft has long since died out. Beatrix – Miss Abberley – was an avid collector.'

'Valuable?'

'I should say so. She had some pieces by Russell. He was just about the foremost exponent of . . . Ah, the work-table is still here. That's something, I suppose.'

In the opposite corner, beside a bookcase, stood Beatrix's prize example of Tunbridge Ware: an elegantly turned satinwood work-table complete with drawers, hinged flaps either side of the leather-covered top and a silk work-bag beneath. All the wooden surfaces, including the legs, were decorated with a distinctive cube-patterned mosaic. Though it was not this but the array of mother-of-pearl sewing requisites kept in the pink silk-lined drawers that Charlotte remembered being fascinated by in her childhood.

'The effect is produced by applying a veneer of several different kinds of wood,' she said absently. 'Highly labour-intensive, of course, especially on the smaller pieces. I suppose that's why it died out.'

'I've never heard of it,' said Hyslop. 'But we have an officer who specializes in this kind of thing. It'll mean more to him. Mrs Mentiply said the cabinet contained tea-caddies, snuff boxes, paper-knives and so forth. Is that your recollection?'

'Yes.'

'She agreed to draw up a list. Perhaps you could go over it with her. Make sure she leaves nothing out.'

'Certainly.'

'You say this stuff is worth a bit?'

'Several thousand pounds at least, I should think. Possibly a lot more. I'm not sure. Prices have been shooting up lately.'

'Well, we can assume our man knew that.'

'You think he came specifically for the Tunbridge Ware?'

'Looks like it. Nothing else has been touched. Of course, the fact he was disturbed may account for that. It would explain why he left the work-table behind. If he was in a panic to be away, he'd only have taken what was light and portable. And he would have been in a panic – after what happened.'

Charlotte gazed around the room. Aside from the empty cabinet, all else seemed intact, preserved in perfect accordance with her memory of so many tea-time conversations. Even the clock on the mantelpiece ticked to the same recollected note, last wound – she supposed – by Beatrix. 'Where did it . . .' she began. Then, as her glance moved along the mantelpiece, one other change leapt out to seize her attention. 'There's a candlestick missing,' she said.

'Not missing, I'm afraid,' said Hyslop. 'It was the murder weapon.'

'Oh, God. He . . . hit her with it?'

'Yes. About the head. If it's any consolation, the pathologist thinks it must have been a quick exit.'

'Did it happen here – in this room?'

'No. On the landing upstairs. She'd got out of bed, presumably because she'd heard him down here. He seems to have climbed in through one of these windows. None of them would have given a professional burglar much trouble and that one there' – he pointed to the left-hand side of the bay – 'was unfastened when we arrived, with signs of gouging round the frame, probably by a jemmy. Anyway, we can assume he heard her moving about upstairs, armed himself with the candlestick and went up to meet her. He probably didn't intend to kill her at that point. She had a torch. We found it lying on the landing floor. Perhaps he panicked when she shone it at him. Perhaps he's just the ruthless sort. There are a lot of them about these days, I'm afraid.'

'This was last night?'

'Yes. We don't know the exact time of death yet, of course, but we reckon it was in the early hours. Miss Abberley was in her night-dress. The curtains in her bedroom, in the bathroom and down here were all closed. They stayed that way until Mrs Mentiply arrived at half past four this afternoon.'

'What made her call? She doesn't usually come in on Sundays.'

'Your – half-brother did you say? – Mr Maurice Abberley. He'd telephoned his aunt several times and become concerned because there was no answer. She'd told him she'd be in, apparently. He lives quite some way away, I believe.'

'Bourne End. Buckinghamshire.'

'That's it. Well, to put his mind at rest, he telephoned Mrs Mentiply and asked her to look round. I'll need to confirm her account with him when he arrives, of course. You live somewhat nearer yourself?'

'Tunbridge Wells.'

'Really?' Hyslop raised his eyebrows in sudden interest.

'Yes. I suppose that's why I know so much about Tunbridge Ware. It's a local speciality. There's a very good collection in the—'

'Does the name Fairfax-Vane mean anything to you, Miss Ladram?'

'No. Should it?'

'Take a look at this.' He opened his pocket-book, slid out a small plastic bag enclosing a card and passed it to her. Set out boldly across the card in Gothic script was the heading THE TREASURE TROVE and beneath it, in smaller type: COLIN FAIRFAX-VANE, ANTIQUE DEALER & VALUER, 1A CHAPEL PLACE, TUNBRIDGE WELLS, KENT TN1 1YQ, TEL. (0892) 662773. 'Recognize the name now?'

'I know the shop, I think. Hold on. Yes, I do know the name. How did you come by this, Chief Inspector?'

'We found it in the drawer of the telephone table in the hall. Mrs Mentiply remembered the name as that of an antique dealer who called here about a month ago, claiming to have been asked by Miss Abberley to value some items. But Miss Abberley hadn't asked him, it seems. She turned him away, though not before Mrs Mentiply – who was here at the time – had shown him into this room, giving him the chance to run his eye over the Tunbridge Ware. Now, how do you know him, Miss Ladram?'

'Through my mother. She sold some furniture to this man about eighteen months ago. As a matter of fact, Maurice and I both felt she'd been swindled.' And had bullied her remorselessly on account of it, Charlotte guiltily recalled.

'So, Fairfax-Vane is something of a smart operator, is he?'

'I wouldn't know. I've never met the man. But certainly my mother . . . Well, she was easily influenced. Gullible, I suppose you'd say.'

'Unlike Miss Abberley?'

'Yes. Unlike Beatrix.'

'You don't suppose your mother could have told Fairfax-Vane about Miss Abberley's collection?'

'Possibly. She knew of it, as we all did. But it's too late to ask her now. My mother died last autumn.'

'My condolences, Miss Ladram. Your family's been hard hit of late, it appears.'

'Yes. It has. But— You surely don't suppose Fairfax-Vane did this just to lay his hands on some Tunbridge Ware?'

'I suppose nothing at this stage. It's simply the most obvious line of inquiry to follow.' Hyslop made a cautious attempt at a smile. 'To expedite matters, however, we need a definitive list of the missing items with as full a description as possible. I wonder if I could ask you to find out what progress Mrs Mentiply has made.'

'I'll go and see her straightaway, Chief Inspector. I'm sure we can let you have what you need later this evening.'

'That would be excellent.'

'I'll be off then.' With that — and the chilling thought that she was glad of an excuse not to go upstairs — Charlotte rose and headed for the hall. She turned back at the front door to find Hyslop close behind her.

'Your assistance is much appreciated, Miss Ladram.'

'It's the least I can do, Chief Inspector. Beatrix was my godmother — and also somebody I admired a great deal. That this should happen to her is . . . quite awful.'

'Sister of the poet Tristram Abberley, I understand.'

'That's right. Do you know his work?'

Hyslop grimaced. 'Had to study it at school. Not my cup of tea, to be honest. Too obscure for my taste.'

'And for many people's.'

'I was surprised to find he had a sister still living. Surely he died before the war.'

'Yes. But he died young. In Spain. He was a volunteer in the Republican army during the Civil War.'

'That's right. Of course he was. A hero's end.'

'So I believe. And yet a more peaceful one than his sister's. Isn't that strange?'

THREE

THE EMPLOYMENT OF AVRIL Mentiply had represented Beatrix's principal concession to old age. It was, as she had often explained to Charlotte, a substantial concession, since Mrs Mentiply's standards of cleanliness were less exacting than her own. Nevertheless, the relationship had endured, far longer than initial reprimands and threats of resignation had suggested it might. Indeed, it had eventually blossomed into something not far short of friendship. Consequently, upon arrival at Mrs Mentiply's house that evening, Charlotte had not been surprised to find her strained and tearful, with the promised list of missing Tunbridge Ware far from complete.

She lived with her taciturn husband in a strangely sunless pebble-dash bungalow on the Folkestone road – one of the few parts of Rye to which tourists never strayed. It was not a setting in which Charlotte would have wished to linger. Yet linger she had, as Mrs Mentiply offered her cup after cup of stewed tea and poured out her distress at Beatrix's death.

'I know she was old, my dear, and frailer than she'd care to admit, but she always had an . . . indomitable look . . . that made you think she was indestructible. But she wasn't, was she? No more indestructible than any of us would be if we were attacked in our own home like she was. What's the world coming to, I should like to know, when that kind of thing can happen to a respectable old lady?'

'Could have been worse,' put in Mr Mentiply, whom Charlotte had hoped might take one of several hints and leave the room but who had instead remained slumped in his chair by the flame-effect gas fire. 'At least it wasn't one of those sex maniacs. Just a straightforward burglar.'

'Have some respect for the dead, Arnold,' retorted Mrs Mentiply. 'Miss Ladram doesn't want to hear talk like that.'

'Only facing facts.'

'Well, facts are that if he'd been a *straightforward burglar* he wouldn't have murdered Miss Abberley, would he?'

'She should have stayed in bed. Left him to it. Then she'd have come to no harm.'

'How do you know?'

'Stands to reason, doesn't it? He was only after her knick-knacks. You said so yourself.'

Seeing that Mrs Mentiply was once more close to tears, Charlotte decided to intervene. 'It's certainly the Tunbridge Ware the police want to know about. Let's just read through this list and make sure we've left nothing off, shall we?'

'Very well, my dear.'

'A tea-caddy with a view of Bodiam Castle on the lid. Two cake baskets. A cube-patterned tray. Two other marquetry trays. A thermometer stand. A solitaire set. Three paper—'

At the first ring of the telephone in the hall, Mrs Mentiply was out of her chair and bustling from the room. Charlotte took a deep breath and set the list aside. Then Mrs Mentiply reappeared. 'It's your brother, Miss Ladram. He wants to speak to you.'

Charlotte smiled and made her way to the telephone. 'Hello, Maurice?'

'I'm at Jackdaw Cottage, Charlie. Chief Inspector Hyslop's been putting me in the picture. And a depressing one it is.'

'I know. I'm drawing up a list of the missing items now with Mrs Mentiply.'

'So I understand. The Chief Inspector wants me to go with him to the mortuary. To identify Beatrix.'

'Really? He never—' Charlotte stopped. Hyslop had probably thought it a kindness not to ask her to perform such a duty. 'Will you go straightaway?'

'Yes. But there'll be a sergeant here to take the list when you've finished it. It's probably best to get the identification done as soon as possible.'

'Of course.'

'Afterwards, well . . . I was wondering if I could spend the night at Ockham House.'

'Certainly. You don't need to ask.'

'There'll be umpteen formalities to see to tomorrow. Registrar, solicitor and so forth. And I can't say I fancy driving all the way back to Bourne End tonight.'

'All right. I'll see you later.'

As she put the telephone down, Charlotte realized what a relief it would be to let Maurice take charge of the whole sad affair. Since her father's death, he had become the calm and efficient organizer of family business. He had assumed control of Ladram Aviation, her father's barely solvent flying school, and turned it into Ladram Avionics, an internationally successful company. He had negotiated the contracts relating to his own father's poetical works from which her mother — and subsequently she — had handsomely benefited. And he had consistently shown himself able to offer his half-sister a helping hand without trying to run her life. Now, once more, he would come to her rescue. And, as she walked slowly back into the Mentiplys' sitting room, she acknowledged to herself that the sooner he did so the happier she would be.

The list at last completed and delivered, Charlotte drove back to Tunbridge Wells. It was pitch dark by the time she reached Ockham House and cold enough for the warmth of the day to seem a distant memory. At all events it felt cold, though whether the temperature was to blame — or Mrs Mentiply's account of how she had found Beatrix — Charlotte was uncertain.

'He'd hit her with one of those heavy brass candlesticks. Several times, I should say. I hardly recognized her at first. Her hair all matted with blood. And this terrible wound in the side of her head. They told me it must have been quick and I hope to God they're right. But it won't fade quickly from my mind, I can tell you. I shan't ever forget going up those stairs and finding her huddled in the corner of the landing. Not ever.'

Charlotte turned on more lights than she normally would and lit a fire, then poured herself the stiff drink Maurice had recommended earlier. As the fire gained a hold and the chill left her, she went in search of the family photograph album and found in it the last picture taken of Beatrix. Longer ago than she would have expected, it dated from a party thrown in honour of her eightieth birthday. There, on the lawn at Swans' Meadow — Maurice's home beside the Thames at Bourne End — the family had staged a rare and photographically commemorated gathering.

Beatrix was, naturally enough, the centre of the septet. Unusually tall for a woman of her generation, she had also remained resolutely straight-backed with the passage of time. Newly coiffured and barely smiling, she projected even greater self-possession in the picture than she had in life. Mary, Charlotte's mother, standing to Beatrix's left, could, indeed, have been the same age rather than twelve years younger. Hunched and peering, contriving somehow to frown and smile simultaneously, her appearance produced in Charlotte a surge of grief and guilt that was so intense she slammed the album shut. Then, after a swallow of gin, she reopened it.

Only to confront herself to her mother's left, grinning fixedly at the camera. She had worn her hair too long then and favoured shapeless dresses intended to disguise her weight. Not that she need have worried on that score. Five years later, bereavement had achieved what a dozen different diets never had. Yet this image of herself reminded her why she had always, even as a child, sought to avoid being photographed. Not because of superstition or shyness, but because the camera could force her to do what she least desired: to see herself as others saw her.

On Charlotte's left, unbalancing the group by standing a foot or so to the rear, was Mary's brother, Jack Brereton. At the sight of him, red-faced and clearly more than slightly drunk, Charlotte chuckled. Uncle Jack, thirteen years his sister's junior, was the free and infuriating spirit that she was sure every family needed. Witty when sober and offensive when not – which meant at least half the time – he was as unreliable as he was lovable. As a result of their parents' early death, he had lived with Mary even after her marriage to Tristram Abberley. Later, during the war, they had all lived with Beatrix in Rye and from those crowded years in Jackdaw Cottage Uncle Jack had culled a vast fund of anecdotes with which to entertain those – like Charlotte – who had never had to endure him on a daily basis.

The three figures to Beatrix's right were Maurice, his wife Ursula, and their daughter Samantha. They were a family within the family, the one branch of it where convention and continuity seemed assured. Each of them was strikingly good-looking and seemingly happy to proclaim an easy-going affection for the other two. Hence the casual way in which Maurice had put his arm round Ursula's waist. And hence the unthinking readiness with which Samantha held her mother's hand.

Even at fifteen, Samantha's clear-skinned beauty had not been in doubt, although the figure with which she was subsequently to turn many a head had yet to fill out. Ursula and she could just about – Charlotte reluctantly conceded – be taken for sisters, so lightly and elegantly had Ursula coped with motherhood and early middle age. They both had naturally wavy hair and an instinctive finesse of bearing, although it was an awareness of their own superiority – conveyed by the way they held their chins, the manner in which they met the camera's gaze – that had always set Charlotte's teeth on edge.

As her eyes moved to Maurice – calm, debonair and jauntily grinning – she heard a crunch of car tyres on the gravel of the drive that told her he was about to arrive in the flesh. Suddenly, without understanding why, she knew she did not wish to be found studying an old photograph in which two of the subjects were now dead. Accordingly, she closed the album and hurriedly put it away, allowing just enough time to compose her features in the mirror before opening the front door.

'Hello, old girl.' He greeted her with a hug and a weary smile.

'Hello, Maurice.' Stepping back from their embrace, Charlotte caught herself comparing him for an instant with his photographed image.

His hair was marginally thinner, perhaps, the smudges of grey at his temples more extensive. Otherwise, he was at fifty what he had been at forty-five: lean and craggily handsome, with a reassuring blend about him of strength and sincerity. He inspired trust even – perhaps especially – in those who did not know him. As for those who did, occasional descents into petulance were easy to forgive when set against his undoubted generosity.

'I could use a drink, Charlie, I really could.'

'I'll pour you one. Come in and sit by the fire.'

He followed her into the lounge and subsided into an armchair. By the time she had returned from the drinks cabinet with a large scotch and soda, he had loosened his tie and was massaging his forehead. 'I'm glad you lit this,' he said, nodding at the blazing logs. 'Those mortuaries chill your blood, I can tell you.'

'I can imagine.'

'Be grateful that's all you need to. Do you remember the last time I had to visit one?'

'For Dad.' She remembered well enough. She was never likely to forget. One foggy afternoon in November 1963, her father had crashed his light aeroplane in Mereworth Woods, killing himself and his passenger. It was at that point in their lives that Maurice had emerged from Ronnie Ladram's jovial shadow and imposed his personality upon the family. Charlotte often suspected he had been secretly relieved at his step-father's death, if only because it meant he could bring some order to the chaotic affairs of Ladram Aviation. Though even now, more than twenty years later, he would never allow himself to admit as much.

'I spoke to Ursula on the car phone. She sends her love – and her sympathy.'

'That's kind of her.' Charlotte took her glass back to the drinks cabinet, recharged it, then returned to the fireside. Maurice had lit a small cigar and, when he offered one to Charlotte, she surprised herself by accepting.

'The police were asking about Fairfax-Vane,' he said after a moment of silence.

'I know. They think he may be behind the break-in. But I hardly—'

'You didn't meet him, Charlie.' It was true. Maurice had been the one delegated to visit Fairfax-Vane's shop and attempt to buy back the furniture Mary had sold him. Without success, as it had turned out.

'Did he strike you as worse than just a con-man, then?'

'He struck me as slippery enough for anything.'

'Even murder?'

'I don't imagine he intended it to go that far. I don't even imagine he broke into the cottage himself. Probably some young tearaway he hired who panicked.'

'So, Beatrix was killed for a few thousand pounds' worth of Tunbridge Ware?'

'More than a few thousand. Do you realize what that stuff fetches these days?'

'Not really.'

'A lot, believe me.'

'Oh, I do. But, even so, it seems . . . such a sad and pointless death.'

'I agree. Though perhaps Beatrix wouldn't.'

'What do you mean?'

'Well, she was never one to knuckle under to anything, was she? The idea of dying in defence of her possessions might have appealed to her. She *was* eighty-five. Perhaps it was better than . . . whatever would have happened to her eventually.'

'Perhaps.'

'It's about the only consoling thought I can come up with, I'm afraid.'

'Then we'd better cling to it, hadn't we?' Charlotte sighed and gazed into the fire. 'In the absence of any other.'

FOUR

EVENTS THE FOLLOWING DAY moved faster than Charlotte had anticipated. Thoughts of Beatrix — and the circumstances of her death — had kept her awake until the small hours. Then, when exhaustion had finally gained the upper hand, she overslept. When she came downstairs in mid-morning, it was to find Maurice engaged in a lengthy telephone conversation with his secretary at Ladram Avionics. He had already, it was to transpire, made an appointment for them to see Beatrix's solicitor in Rye that afternoon, pressure of work obliging him to push matters forward with some vigour. For this he apologized, though Charlotte did not think he needed to. As far as she was concerned, the formalities of death were best conducted speedily. If Maurice had displayed the same attitude after their mother's death — rather than trying to cocoon her from the reality of it — she would, she now thought, have been grateful.

Over a late breakfast, they discussed their last meetings with Beatrix. Charlotte had not seen her since Christmas, though she had spoken to her by telephone on several occasions, most recently on her eighty-fifth birthday. Maurice, by contrast, had been entertained to tea at Jackdaw Cottage less than a month ago, on the Sunday before Beatrix's departure for her annual fortnight with Lulu Harrington in Cheltenham. The two had been at school together and with sudden dismay Charlotte realized that Lulu had yet to be informed of her old friend's death.

She had no sooner begun contemplating the dismal task of contacting her than the telephone rang. It was Chief Inspector Hyslop's sergeant, requesting that they call at Hastings Police Station as soon as possible. He declined to say why, but, since the urgency of his request seemed manifest, they agreed to set off straightaway.

*   *   *

Hyslop could scarcely disguise his satisfaction when they arrived. He escorted them to a room where, on one long table, were arranged the items of Tunbridge Ware Charlotte and Mrs Mentiply had listed as missing the previous evening.

'You recognize them, Miss Ladram?'

'Why, yes. These are the contents of Beatrix's cabinet. There's no question about it.'

'So we thought. They match your descriptions exactly.'

'You've recovered all of them?' put in Maurice.

'Yes, sir.'

'Where did you find them?'

'A store-room at the rear of the Treasure Trove, Fairfax-Vane's shop in Tunbridge Wells. The premises were searched early this morning.'

'And Fairfax-Vane?'

'Under arrest. Presently unable to account for his possession of these items.'

'My congratulations, Chief Inspector. You've made excellent progress.'

'Thank you, sir. If I could ask you, Miss Ladram, to make a statement formally identifying them as Miss Abberley's property . . .'

'Gladly.'

'Then I'll be free to return to my questioning of Mr Fairfax-Vane. Though perhaps I ought to say just Fairfax. We gather "Vane" is a purely professional handle.'

'Even his surname's a fraud, then?' asked Maurice.

'Yes, sir.' Hyslop smiled. 'As you say.'

Charlotte should have been more pleased than she was by the news of Fairfax-Vane's arrest. To her mind, the rapid solution of the crime only heightened its pointlessness. Theft and murder were bad enough, she reflected, without being compounded by incompetence.

After she had made her statement, they visited the Registrar's office nearby. The provision of a death certificate took longer than seemed necessary, but was eventually accomplished. They were, indeed, only a few minutes late for their three o'clock appointment in Rye with Beatrix's solicitor, Mr Ramsden. He was a dull and deferential man of middle years to whom Beatrix's straightforward requirements must have seemed utterly unexceptional. He offered his condolences, then proceeded to explain the provisions of the will he had drawn up for his client some years previously.

'I believe you are aware, Mr Abberley, that Miss Abberley appointed you her executor?'

'Indeed.'

'Then it will suffice for me to summarize how her estate is to be disposed of. There is a bequest of ten thousand pounds to Mrs Avril Mentiply and a gift of five thousand pounds to the East Sussex Naturalists' Trust.'

'Lame ducks of all species were her speciality,' said Maurice.

Ramsden glanced from one to the other of them, clearly discomposed by this shaft of humour. 'To proceed. Jackdaw Cottage, which she owned outright, goes to you, Miss Ladram, along with its contents, including all Miss Abberley's personal possessions.'

'Good heavens. I'd no idea.' Nor had she. Insofar as she had considered the point, she had assumed Maurice, as Beatrix's nearest blood relative, would inherit everything.

'She told me some time ago, old girl,' said Maurice, patting her hand. 'You were her god-daughter, after all.'

'But . . .' It was futile to explain how such generosity only increased the guilt she felt for avoiding Beatrix in recent months. She fell silent.

'The residue of her estate', Ramsden resumed, 'devolves upon you, Mr Abberley. That comprises such capital as may be left after bequests and inheritance tax and such royalties as may continue to be due under the estate of Miss Abberley's late brother, Mr Tristram Abberley. Copyright in his works expires, I believe, at the end of next year.'

'Except for the posthumously published poems, that's correct,' said Maurice. 'Perhaps it's as well she never had to get used to doing without the income.'

Perhaps Maurice was right, thought Charlotte. He had Ladram Avionics, after all, in which the investment of Abberley royalties had paid a handsome dividend. And she had her own substantial share-holding in the company, inherited from her mother. But Beatrix was likely to have given away as much as she had saved over the years. Though poverty would never have threatened her, the necessity to economize might have. That she had been spared the experience represented a meagre form of solace.

*   *   *

27

Ramsden's office was only a few doors from the premises of Rye's principal undertaker. There Charlotte and Maurice were received with doleful solicitude and gently guided through the maze of funerary alternatives. Beatrix had not specified in her will whether she wished to be buried or cremated and neither Charlotte nor Maurice could remember her ever expressing a view on the subject. Her neat and unsentimental nature suggested, however, that cremation was the choice she would have been likely to make and on this they settled.

Outside, the streets were crowded with shoppers and tourists. Their loud voices and gaping faces seemed to magnify the warmth of the afternoon to a single burning pitch. All Charlotte wanted was to be done with the business that had brought them to Rye, free of the commitments Beatrix had wished upon her. But to want, as she well knew, was not necessarily to achieve.

'Do you think we should go up to the cottage?' asked Maurice. 'The police will have finished by now and we could easily collect the key from Mrs Mentiply.'

'I'd rather not. It's too soon to start sorting through Beatrix's possessions. I should feel she was there all the time, looking over my shoulder. Perhaps after the funeral.'

'As her executor, I'm not sure I can wait that long. I'll need to find her cheque books and bank statements for probate purposes. See if there are any unpaid bills about the place.'

'Of course. I hadn't thought of that.' It was typical of Maurice to take his responsibilities seriously. Fortunately, she did not have to. 'Can't you go alone?' she asked, in a tone that urged him to say he could.

'I can, Charlie, yes. With your permission. You are the new owner, remember.'

'Don't be silly. Of course you have my permission. Go ahead. I'm only grateful I don't have to take the task on myself.'

'Very well. I'll come back tomorrow and try to sort everything out. If that's what you want.'

'It is. Definitely.'

Maurice suggested they eat out that evening and Charlotte agreed enthusiastically, hoping good food and drink consumed in pleasant surroundings might lift her spirits. Before they set off, however, there was one duty to be performed which she knew she could neither postpone nor avoid. Lulu Harrington had to be told.

Charlotte had never met Lulu, even though she and Beatrix had been friends from schooldays. She had taught at Cheltenham Ladies' College for forty-odd years and now lived in a flat in the town, enjoying what Charlotte imagined to be a fittingly demure retirement. When she answered the telephone, she did so in text-book style, stating the exchange as well as the number and pronouncing all three syllables in 'Cheltenham'.

'Miss Harrington?'

'Yes. Who is that, please?' She sounded frail and a touch querulous. Charlotte's heart sank.

'My name's Charlotte Ladram, Miss Harrington. We've never met, but—'

'Charlotte Ladram? Oh, of course! I know who you are.' Her tone was warmer now. 'Beatrix's niece.'

'Not her niece exactly but—'

'Good as, I rather thought. Well, forgive me, Miss Ladram. May I call you Charlotte? Beatrix always refers to you as such.'

'Of course. I—'

'It's a great pleasure to speak to you at last, I must say. To what do I—' She broke off abruptly, then said: 'Is Beatrix all right?'

Suddenly fearful that Lulu would guess before she could tell her, Charlotte blurted out: 'I'm afraid she passed away yesterday.' Then she regretted her abruptness. 'I'm sorry if it's a shock. It was for all of us.' But only silence followed. 'Miss Harrington? Miss Harrington, are you still there?'

'Yes.' She sounded calm and sombre now. 'May I . . . That is, what happened . . . exactly?'

She would have to know of course. There was no way of pretending Beatrix had slipped away peacefully. As she explained the circumstances, Charlotte sensed how brutal and unfair they must sound to one of Beatrix's own age who also lived alone. But the circumstances could not be altered.

When she had finished, there was another momentary silence. Then Lulu said simply: 'I see.'

'I'm really very sorry to have to break such news to you.'

'Pray don't apologize, my dear. It's good of you to have called.'

'Not at all. You were Beatrix's oldest friend, after all.'

'Was I?'

'Of course you were. She always said so.'

'That was good of her.'

29

'Miss Harrington—'

'Call me Lulu, please.'

'Are you sure you're all right? This must have come as a terrible shock.'

'Not really.'

'What?'

'Forgive me. I mean simply that at our age – Beatrix's and mine – death can never be regarded as a surprise.'

'But this is different . . . This was not . . .'

'Not natural. Quite so, my dear. The difference does not escape me, I assure you.'

'Then how . . .' Charlotte stopped herself. The old lady was clearly wandering. It would be charitable to disregard whatever she said. 'Will you wish to attend the funeral, Lulu? It's to be held next Monday, the twenty-ninth. It's a long way for you to come, of course, but I could offer you overnight accommodation if that would help.'

'Thank you. That's very kind of you. But . . . I will think about it, Charlotte. I will think about it and let you know.'

'Of course. Of course. Do that. Now, if you're certain you're all right—'

'Absolutely. Goodbye, Charlotte.'

'Good—' The line went dead before she could finish. And left her staring at her own puzzled frown in the mirror above the telephone.

FIVE

'FAIRFAX.'

'Good morning. Is that Mr Derek Fairfax?'

'Speaking.'

'My name's Dredge, Mr Fairfax. Albion Dredge. I'm a solicitor, representing your brother, Mr Colin Fairfax.'

Derek felt the blood rush to his face. It had happened. What he had dreaded ever since Colin's arrival in Tunbridge Wells. A reversion to type, some might say. A stroke of bad luck, Colin would undoubtedly protest. A problem, unquestionably, that Derek did not need. 'Representing him in what, Mr Dredge?'

'I regret to have to tell you, Mr Fairfax, that your brother was arrested yesterday by the Sussex Police and subsequently charged with serious criminal offences.'

'What were the offences?'

'Handing stolen goods. Conspiracy to burgle. Aiding and abetting murder.'

It was worse than he had imagined. Far worse. 'Murder, you say?'

'An elderly spinster was found battered to death at her cottage in Rye on Sunday afternoon. You may have seen a report of it on the local television news.'

'No. I don't think so.'

'Then let me explain.' As Dredge did so, Derek felt a clammy foreboding rise about him. Colin would have no truck with violence. That was certain. But he had never been scrupulous about the provenance of what he bought and sold. He habitually sailed close to the wind. Sometimes too close, as the affair in St Albans proved. Could he have gone so far as to commission a burglary in order to obtain a collection of Tunbridge Ware? If he knew he could make enough out of it, the answer had to be yes, especially if his finances were in a more than usually parlous state. Murder, of course, he would never have countenanced. Nor strong-arm tactics of any kind. But if he had misjudged his associates, if he had trusted to luck and the good sense of those who had none, then the consequences could be precisely what the police had alleged. 'He is currently being held at Hastings Police Station,' Dredge concluded. 'And will appear before the magistrates tomorrow morning.'

'Does he . . . deny the charges?'

'Unequivocally.'

'Then . . . how does he account for the Tunbridge Ware being in his shop?'

Dredge sighed. 'He assumes it was planted there.'

'You sound doubtful.'

'I'm sorry. I didn't mean to. It's simply . . . well, in the perception of the police, it's exactly what he would say, isn't it?'

'He hasn't suggested *they* planted it, has he?'

'Mercifully, no.'

'Then who . . . why should . . .'

'Mr Fairfax, I don't wish to be abrupt, but such questions are perhaps best considered at another time. My purpose in telephoning you today is to ask whether you would be prepared to act as surety in the event that the magistrates grant bail. If granted, the figure involved is likely to exceed your brother's means.'

Derek could have told Dredge that himself. Colin's means had never to his knowledge kept pace with his expenditure. Too often in the past, indeed, Derek had been obliged to bail him out, literally as well as metaphorically. And each time he had sworn it would be the last. So had Colin, come to that. 'What sort of figure are we talking about?' he asked defensively.

'It's hard to say. The police will oppose bail. The question may not arise.'

'But if the question does arise?'

'Then it will be a substantial sum.'

'How substantial?'

'I would imagine . . . somewhere between five and ten thousand pounds.'

A woundingly large portion of Derek's savings, then, to be forfeited in the event that Colin decided a moonlight flit to an extradition-haven was in order. Even as Derek considered the possibility, he caught himself reflecting at the same time that it might almost be worth losing such a sum if it meant Colin could never again ask him for help.

'Your brother indicated you were the only person likely to be willing to assist.'

'No doubt.'

'And are you . . . willing to assist?'

'Yes. I suppose I am.'

'Can you attend the court tomorrow morning?'

Derek glanced at the diary that stood open on his desk. Wednesday the twenty-fourth of June contained nothing that could not be rearranged. 'Yes. I can be there.'

'The magistrates' court is in Bohemia Road, Hastings. Proceedings commence at ten thirty.'

'Very well. I'll meet you there.'

Derek put the telephone down, lifted off his glasses and began rubbing the bridge of his nose. When he closed his eyes, the present – his sombre suit, his desk, his office, his glazed vista of Calverley Park, his every proof and appanage of age and status – floated away like gossamer in the breeze. In their place, he and Colin were children again in Bromley, Colin six years the older, as fly and daring as Derek was shy and timid. Derek had often in those days taken the blame for his brother's antics and covered his tracks and falsified his alibis. And now he knew – if he had ever doubted it – that nothing had really changed.

He rose and crossed to the window. Tunbridge Wells was looking its best in the quiet midsummer weather, the pale façades of Regency villas dotted amidst the greenery, the hazy air seeming to weigh down still further the heavy-leafed horse chestnuts in the park. He had lived here for seven years now, seven good if scarcely glorious years of steady progress at Fithyan & Co. Barring catastrophes, a partnership lay within his grasp. But might not Fithyan consider his connection with a corrupt antique dealer – or worse still a murderer – just such a catastrophe? What would the clients say? What would the other partners think?

How he wished Colin had never settled in Tunbridge Wells. It had only been intended as a temporary move in the first place, a way of easing him back into the outside world. Instead he had found the Treasure Trove and a swift road back to the profession that had already undone him. And now, it seemed, it had undone him again, with a vengeance that might be visited upon his brother as well as himself.

Maurice had set off early for Rye and was to return to Bourne End direct. For the first time since Beatrix's death, Charlotte was left to her own thoughts and devices. A morning of energetic gardening having failed to cure her restless mood, she went out in the afternoon, scouring the shops for half a dozen things she did not need.

As the working day drew towards a close, she found herself halfway down the High Street and realized with faint surprise that she was heading in the direction of Chapel Place. She could easily have turned aside and taken a more direct route back to her home in Mount Ephraim. But she did not. Curiosity – or something more complex – overcame squeamishness and she pressed on towards what she now knew was her destination: the Treasure Trove.

It was a narrow-fronted emporium with peeling paint around the windows, squeezed between a photographic studio and a second-hand bookshop. The Gothic script in which the name had been rendered over the door matched the style on the card Hyslop had shown her. To one side there was a separate doorway with a bell labelled simply FLAT. The interior of the shop was unlit and seemed cavernously dark by contrast with the brightness outside. There was no sign proclaiming opening hours and Charlotte, who had assumed that somebody would be standing in for the proprietor, felt slightly cheated.

Stepping closer, she shaded her eyes and peered through the window. Several bookcases and sideboards revealed themselves amidst the gloom. She glimpsed some shadowy oil paintings and dangling brasswork, a pine chest and a cheval-glass towards the rear. Then, stacked in a tall corner cabinet, she noticed the Tunbridge Ware. Small pieces for the most part, Fairfax's legitimate collection – if it was legitimate – looked thoroughly unremarkable. Perhaps, thought Charlotte, that explained—

Suddenly, there was a movement close behind her, reflected in the cheval-glass. Glancing across to it, she saw a man standing almost at her shoulder, staring into the shop. He was of medium height, lean with thinning hair, dressed in a brown somewhat rumpled suit and wearing gold-framed spectacles on which the sunlight flashed. She would have taken him for a disappointed customer but for the intensity of his expression. There was in his face a look almost of agony. He did not shift his ground as she watched, merely gazed past her, apparently struck motionless by something he had seen or thought.

Charlotte turned and smiled at him. 'I'm afraid it's closed,' she said.

At first he did not respond. Then, as if her words had only just reached him, he looked at her and opened his mouth, but did not speak.

'It's closed,' she repeated.

Still he said nothing. Then, abruptly, he swung on his heel and started back towards the High Street, walking with unnecessary speed, almost, it seemed to Charlotte, as if he wanted to run.

Derek reached the George & Dragon a few minutes after opening time. He was known as an occasional if scarcely regular customer, but was too distracted to do more than smile stiffly in response to the barmaid's welcome. Taking his beer into the garden, he sat at a table and took several quaffs of it. He did not drink much as a rule, but he had every intention of breaking that rule tonight.

The first thing he must do, he told himself, was to stop behaving like the criminal his brother might not even be. Thanks to Colin's use of the name Fairfax-Vane, nobody was likely to realize Derek was related to the proprietor of the Treasure Trove. In court, of course, and in newspaper reports of the case, they would insist on using Colin's real name, but until then he was completely safe. The idea that the junior staff of Fithyan & Co. were already conducting a whispering campaign against him was therefore absurd. Though the idea that they might yet, he supposed, was not.

He swallowed some more beer, shaking his head at the thought of what the young woman outside the Treasure Trove was likely to have made of his conduct. He should never have gone there and did not really know why he had. She had only been trying to be helpful, after all.

Silently, he cursed Colin. What a strange thing brotherhood was. They had nothing in common save an ever more distant past. They did not even like each other. And yet they were bound together by something stronger than either love or friendship, something irresistible and indissoluble. Derek did not understand it, but he knew he could not overcome it. Tomorrow, reluctantly and with an ill grace, he would stand by his brother.

SIX

MAURICE HAD TELEPHONED CHARLOTTE upon his arrival home to report what he had learned from Chief Inspector Hyslop: that Colin Fairfax had been charged and would appear before Hastings magistrates in the morning. The appearance would be a brief one, with the case adjourned until a later date. All that was likely to be settled was whether Fairfax would be remanded in custody – as Hyslop hoped – or granted bail. Accordingly, Maurice had decided not to attend, feeling that two days away from Ladram Avionics were quite enough.

Charlotte, however, had taken a different view. She wanted to see the man who was responsible for Beatrix's death. Doing so might satisfy her curiosity where peering into the window of the Treasure Trove had not. And so the morning found her at Hastings Magistrates' Court, joining the throng of worried clients and harassed lawyers in its cheerless outer hall.

There was no sign of Hyslop and, with ten-thirty drawing near, she decided to enter the court. It was a small, modern, airless room of laminated wood and plastic-coated metal in which little of the law's gravitas seemed detectable. There were several officials already present and, near the front, two men urgently engaged in a whispered discussion. One of them was a short rotund fellow in a dark three-piece suit, a sheen of sweat visible on his high domed forehead. The other was taller and leaner, with his back turned so that Charlotte could not see his face. She thought they might both be solicitors.

'The Crown Prosecutor's solicitor has just told me he'll be opposing bail in the strongest possible terms, Mr Fairfax,' said Albion Dredge.

'So,' Derek replied, 'I've wasted my time by coming, have I?'

'Not at all. Not at all. There's always a chance.'

'How good a chance?'

'In view of the gravity of the charges – and your brother's previous conviction – not very.'

Derek sighed. He had no wish to see Colin behind bars, but at least it would relieve his anxiety over whatever bail he might have to put up. 'How long before the case comes to trial?'

'Six months or so.'

'*Six months?*'

'At least. The courts are inundated these days. Of course, there's some possibility the Crown Prosecution Service may drop the aiding and abetting charge. They know it's much the weakest of the three. It's also the most serious. As it's intended to be.'

'What do you mean?'

Dredge lowered his voice still further. 'Between you and me, Mr Fairfax, I think the police added it to the list to put pressure on your brother. If he'd say who sold him the Tunbridge Ware, they might well drop it. And that might alter the situation over bail.'

'But Colin denies buying the stuff.'

'Exactly.'

'You mean he'd have to plead guilty to the other charges?'

'To handling, at all events.'

'Which he isn't prepared to do?'

'Not yet, no.'

'I see. OK, Mr Dredge. Thanks very much for putting me in the picture.' Derek stood upright and turned to resume his seat in the row behind. As he did so, his eyes met those of a woman sitting another three rows back who had not been there before. Instantly, he coloured and looked away. It was the woman he had encountered outside the Treasure Trove the previous afternoon. And this time he could not walk away.

*   *   *

Who was he? Why was he here? Charlotte had scarcely begun to ponder the questions when a general hubbub signalled the start of proceedings. The desks at the front of the court filled rapidly. Hyslop nodded to her in acknowledgement as he joined the latecomers. Then a clerk bade them all rise and three magistrates took their places on the bench.

With less ceremony than Charlotte had expected, the case was called. A policeman led the defendant in through a side-door and escorted him to the dock. He stood with his hands resting on the rail before him, no more than twenty feet from Charlotte. Since his attention was focused on the bench, she had no need to worry that her scrutiny of him would be noticed.

He was tall and broadly built, with a flushed and rather puffy face, brown hair worn too long, greying at the sides and thinning on top. He wore a dark blue blazer, fawn trousers and an open-necked striped shirt that was stretched taut over a substantial paunch. There was a red handkerchief spilling flamboyantly from the breast pocket of his blazer and an oversized signet-ring on the little finger of his left hand. She had not expected to like him. On the contrary, she had expected to be repelled by him. And so, in a sense, she was. A ladies' man going to seed, a smooth-talking fraudster running out of time and luck, grown old and careless enough to have set this squalid crime in motion. That is what she thought of him. And somewhere, on a level of which she was only partially aware, she wished he was younger and more blatantly charming. She wished there was more in him to detest.

Suddenly, she realized she had failed to keep pace with the business of the court. The charges had been read and the defendant had stated his full name – Colin Neville Fairfax. But he had not been asked to plead guilty or not guilty and this rather confused Charlotte. As did the speed with which the magistrates seemed to be moving towards an adjournment. 'We will fix a full hearing for a month's time,' announced the chairman. 'Any objections?' None appeared to be forthcoming. The chairman craned forward to consult his clerk. 'Is Friday the twenty-fourth of July acceptable to all parties?' Various heads nodded. 'Very well. The twenty-fourth of July it is. Mr Dredge, you are appearing for the defendant?'

'Yes, sir.' As Fairfax's solicitor bobbed up, Charlotte recognized him as the person to whom the mystery man from the Treasure Trove had been talking earlier. 'My client will be disputing all the charges and therefore wishes to apply for bail.'

'Mr Metcalfe?' The chairman raised his eyebrows at the Crown's solicitor.

'We oppose bail, sir. These are very serious charges. The police believe there is a strong likelihood that the defendant will not present himself for trial. In this regard, I should draw your attention to his previous conviction, details of which I have placed before you.'

'Ah, yes.' The chairman looked down at some papers in front of him. 'Mr Dredge?'

'I would point out that my client was granted bail prior to that conviction, sir, and complied fully with the conditions imposed.'

'Quite so.' The chairman scratched his nose, then said: 'Are you thinking of bail on the defendant's own recognisance, Mr Dredge?'

'No, sir. The defendant's brother, Mr Derek Fairfax, is prepared to stand as a surety.'

'And is Mr Derek Fairfax present?'

'He is, sir.' Dredge turned and extended his hand towards a figure in the row behind him, who half rose in response. And so at last Charlotte discovered who he was: Colin Fairfax's brother.

'I see,' said the chairman. 'Well now, I think we will retire for a moment.' At that he and his two colleagues rose and left.

Murmured conversations sprang up in their absence. Dredge moved across to the dock and began a whispered exchange with his client. Derek Fairfax did not join them, but looked in their direction and once, as Charlotte watched him, seemed about to glance towards her. But he did not.

Then the magistrates returned. After a general shuffling in seats and clearing of throats, the chairman said: 'In view of the nature and gravity of the offences involved in this case, we have decided to refuse bail.' He looked across at the defendant. 'You are remanded in custody, Mr Fairfax, and will reappear before us on the twenty-fourth of July. This case is now adjourned until that date.'

Derek was looking at Colin when the chairman announced he would not be granted bail and knew precisely what his crumpled wince of disappointment signified. It was the expression with which he had greeted life's reverses from childhood, a weary acceptance that, through no fault of his own, his plans had gone awry. What followed was also characteristic. He raised his eyebrows, puffed out his cheeks and slowly shook his head. Then the policeman who had brought him in touched his elbow and he descended from the dock. At the last moment, before turning towards the side-door, he looked across at Derek and winked. In response, Derek could do no more than feebly raise one hand.

After Colin had vanished, Derek remained where he was, waiting for the court to empty. Dredge lingered for a moment, talking to his opposite number. When they had finished, he motioned for Derek to join him. Then, together, they moved slowly towards the exit.

'As I feared, Mr Fairfax, your brother's previous conviction told against him.'

'You did your best, Mr Dredge. Where will Colin be held?'

'Lewes Prison.'

'Will I be able to visit him?'

'Of course. But I should leave it a couple of days. Let him settle in.'

Abstinence of all kinds would be his greatest hardship, Derek suspected. Alcohol, food, conversation and women. Despite Colin's reputation as a Don Juan, that was probably the correct order. Last time, it had to be said, he had emerged looking fitter and healthier than when he had gone in. But he was older now, less resilient, less tolerant of discomfort, less than the man he had once been. 'Do I take it from what you were saying earlier, Mr Dredge, that you'll be encouraging him to plead guilty, at least to the handling charge?'

'I'll be explaining the consequences of not doing so, certainly.'

'And they are?'

'Potentially serious. The Crown can show he knew where the Tunbridge Ware came from. Therefore they can show he must have known it was stolen. Complicity with the thief is contestable. Knowledge that he *was* a thief isn't.'

'So Colin has no defence?'

'Only his contention that the goods were planted, which no jury will swallow. And judges tend to reward what they see as perverse or mischievous pleas with heavy sentences.'

'What sort of sentence could we be talking about?'

'The maximum for handling stolen goods is fourteen years.'

Fourteen years would take Colin past sixty and the world into a new millennium. It suddenly seemed to Derek an unimaginably long time. 'What about the other charges?' he murmured.

'Conspiracy to burgle carries the same maximum.'

'And aiding and abetting murder?'

'Is unlikely to stick.'

'But if it does?'

'Then the same as for murder itself. Life.'

After a brief conversation with Hyslop on the steps of the court building, Charlotte made her way back to her car, wondering why she felt so disappointed by what she had witnessed, why she could not summon up more indignation on Beatrix's behalf. Colin Fairfax was not, of course, the man who had actually bludgeoned her to death, but he was responsible for it having happened. That seemed certain. Why then could Charlotte not hate him as she should?

She reached her car, climbed in and wound down the window. Birds were singing in the bushes behind her and somewhere music was playing on a radio. Beatrix would have forgiven Fairfax, of course. That was the irony of it. *'Clearly the man meant me no harm,'* Charlotte could imagine her saying. *'If I had realized how badly he wanted the Tunbridge Ware, I would have given it to him.'*

Charlotte shook her head in bemusement and slid the key into the ignition. As she did so, a figure appeared round the corner of the building and began walking towards her. It was Derek Fairfax, bowed and frowning, one hand fumbling in his jacket pocket. He did not glance in her direction and at first she thought he would walk straight past without noticing her. But his car, it transpired, was the one next to hers. As he turned into the narrow space between them, he looked up and saw her.

For an instant he seemed about to smile, then the anxious frown reasserted itself. Did he know who she was? Charlotte wondered. If he did, she must avoid speaking to him at all costs. There was no time to analyse why, merely to yield to the instinct. She started the car and saw him step back a pace in surprise. Then, accelerating too hard, she skidded out of the bay, regained control and swerved towards the exit, resisting all temptation to glance in the rear-view mirror.

According to Dredge, the woman they had seen talking to Chief Inspector Hyslop was Beatrix Abberley's niece, Charlotte Ladram. She it was who had identified the Tunbridge Ware found in Colin's shop. Thus had Derek learned why she should have been both at the Treasure Trove and Hastings Magistrates' Court. What she had thought as she peered into the gloomy interior of the shop or gazed

40

at Colin, rumpled and forlorn in the dock, he had, of course, no way of knowing. Had they spoken on either occasion, he would naturally have offered his condolences. There was nothing else he could have offered. Perhaps, therefore, it was as well that they had not spoken.

Such thoughts were in his mind as he looked up and saw her, sitting at the wheel of the car next to his. Their eyes met, then parted. He hesitated, uncertain what to do. It would surely be ridiculous to ignore each other. After all, she knew who he was now. There was no point pretending any more. And yet—

Suddenly, she started her car, skidded forward, slowed momentarily, then swerved towards the exit. He fell back against the wing of his own car, aware that she had come close to hitting him in her eagerness to escape. To escape *him*. That was it, of course. That was the true measure of the contempt she held him in on his brother's account. She could not bear even to speak to him.

SEVEN

DEREK DECIDED IT WOULD not be politic to take any more time off that week. Thursday's edition of the local newspaper reported Colin's court appearance, but if anybody at Fithyan & Co. knew they were related – as he was sure some did – they said nothing about it.

On Saturday afternoon, he drove to Lewes and presented himself at the prison gates amidst a ragged band of wives, girlfriends and children. They were admitted, after considerable delay, to a large bare-walled room with chairs and tables arranged in rows. Seated at the tables, looking variously eager, ashamed and indifferent, were the husbands, boyfriends and fathers, rendered indistinguishable by their blue-grey prison fatigues.

This was the first such visit Derek had ever embarked upon. Colin had been granted bail last time and had specifically asked to be left alone during his subsequent confinement. It was a request Derek had been happy to comply with. But there could be no such embargo now. There were things to be said and this was the only venue in which they could be said.

Colin was sitting at the far side of the room, staring blankly into space. He did not seem to see Derek until the last moment, then started violently, made to rise, thought better of it and subsided into his chair with a sigh.

'Hello, Derek. Pleased you could make it.' He smiled weakly.

'Hello, Colin. How are you?' As Derek sat down and examined his brother, he suddenly regretted the question. Such an enquiry was always platitudinous, but now it seemed downright insensitive as well.

'Wonderful,' said Colin. 'This place is like a health farm, only a damn sight cheaper.'

'I . . . er . . . I was sorry they refused you bail.'

'Pull the other one. You were relieved. *I* would have been in your shoes.'

Derek laughed nervously and glanced around. At the tables on either side, inmates and visitors were trying inarticulately to pretend they understood each other, while behind them a warder paced gloomily around the room and cast bored glances up at the clock on the wall.

'Thanks for trying anyway,' said Colin. 'I might not show it, but I am grateful.'

'Least I could . . .' Derek sat forward in his chair, resolving to say what had to be said without further prevarication. 'Dredge thinks you should plead guilty to the handling charge.'

'Dredge is an old woman.'

'He's your solicitor, Colin. And he has your interests at heart.'

'Maybe. I wouldn't know. I used him when I bought the lease of the Treasure Trove and he made heavy enough weather of that.'

'Why are you using him now, then?'

'Because he was the only solicitor I could think of when the police said I could call one. Now I find he thinks I'm guilty just like they do. The question is, Derek, what do you think?'

Derek took a deep breath. 'You tell me.'

'What do you mean by that?'

'I mean you denied everything last time as well.'

'And?'

'And it wasn't true, was it? You were in it up to your neck.'

Colin frowned, started to say something, then stopped and grinned. 'You're right. I lied. I make a habit of it. You should know. You of all people.'

'Exactly.'

'But I'm not lying this time.'

'How am I to know that?'

'Because you know me. I'm a liar and a bit of a rogue and a worse brother than you deserve. But I'm not a fool. Never have been. Agreed?'

'Agreed.'

'Then would I really leave my calling card at a house I intended to break into? As clues go, it's a pretty glaring one, isn't it?'

'I gather from Dredge the police don't think you were the person who actually broke in.'

'No, they don't. They think I paid some young tough to do it. Or agreed a price for the Tunbridge Ware with somebody who I knew *would* do it. Either way, they think I'm behind it. But they've as good as told me they'll drop the aiding and abetting charge if I'll name my accomplice. Dredge reckons I might wriggle out of conspiracy as well on that basis. And be looking at no more than five years for handling *if* they can nail somebody else for burglary and murder.'

'But you're not willing to do it?'

'I *can't* do it, because I didn't have an accomplice. Do you seriously imagine I'd stay silent to protect somebody who's prepared to stave an old lady's head in? Not on your life. Especially not if the police were offering me good solid reasons for making a clean breast of it. Which is precisely what they are doing.'

'So the stuff really was planted?'

'Put it this way. The first I knew about any of this was when the police came hammering on the flat door at seven o'clock on Monday morning brandishing a search-warrant. I wasn't happy to see them, but I was happy to let them into the shop, because I knew there was nothing there. When I saw the Tunbridge Ware, standing in a cardboard box on the table in the back-room, well, you could have knocked me down with a feather.'

'How do you think it got there?'

'Somebody must have broken in during the night and put it there. One of the panes in the window next to the back door was knocked out. And I'd left the key in the lock. I'm careless that way.'

Derek did not doubt his brother's carelessness. But he knew the police would. They would have viewed the broken window as a clumsy attempt by Colin to cover his tracks. 'You heard nothing in the night?'

'Not a thing. But I'd been hitting the scotch. It would have taken a bomb to wake me. Which reminds me . . .' He leaned forward. 'I haven't had a drink since then. You didn't have the good sense to smuggle in a half-bottle, did you?'

'No, I certainly did not.'

Colin grimaced. 'A pity. But not a surprise. You always did have too much respect for rules and regulations.'

'If you had the same amount, we wouldn't be here now, would we?'

'Maybe not.' Colin forced a grin. 'Let's call a truce. When I took the police into the shop, the back door was locked, with the key in it. Simple enough for an intruder to arrange by reaching through the missing pane after he'd left, of course. But the police weren't interested. They had the Tunbridge Ware. And they had me. So they were satisfied. As they were intended to be.'

'Intended by whom?'

'I don't know. That's the whole point. Nobody hates me enough to go to so much trouble. I've put a few noses out of joint over the years, admittedly, but not *that* far out. Besides, if they were prepared to kill *and* had it in for me, why not go the whole hog and stave *my* head in?'

'Well?' Derek could tell by the twinkle in Colin's eyes that he had an answer.

'I've thought it through, step by step. I've had plenty of time to think this past week, believe me. And I've come to the conclusion that I'm not what all this is about. I'm just the fall guy, the shady antique dealer who takes the blame.'

'So . . . what are you saying?'

'I'm saying the police are looking at it the wrong way round. They see burglary as the objective, murder as the result. Whereas I reckon murder was the real objective. The stolen Tunbridge Ware – and me – were just camouflage.'

For a second, Derek seriously entertained the possibility. Then scepticism got the better of him. 'Isn't that rather far-fetched, Colin?'

'Listen to what happened. Then tell me whether it's far-fetched or not.'

'All right. I'm listening.'

'About six weeks ago, I had a telephone call from a woman who gave her name as Beatrix Abberley. She said she had some Tunbridge Ware she wanted valued with a view to disposal. We agreed I'd call a few days later and take a look at the stuff. The address was Jackdaw Cottage, Watchbell Street, Rye. When I asked how she'd heard of me, she said she had relatives in Tunbridge Wells and often went there. She'd seen my display of Tunbridge Ware in the window and had remembered the name of the shop. Well, I wasn't arguing. Off I went to Rye. She'd been specific about the time I was to arrive. Ten-thirty on Wednesday the twentieth of May. I was there on the dot. A housekeeper answered the door. She said she didn't know anything about the appointment, but she showed me into the drawing room and went to fetch Miss Abberley. I was giving the Tunbridge Ware the once over when the lady came in. As soon as I saw her, I knew something was wrong. The woman who'd phoned me was much younger. And she'd had a twang to her voice, like a faint American accent. Or one being disguised. But Miss Abberley was an old refined English spinster. And she was adamant she hadn't called me. Well, I knew she was telling the truth. That was obvious. But what was I supposed to do? Say it had all been a ghastly mistake? Since I was there, I reckoned it was best to try and brazen it out. The Tunbridge Ware was a nice collection. Very nice. I tried to negotiate a price. But she wasn't interested. Not a bit. So, I decided to call it a day. I gave her my card in case she ever changed her mind and left with fulsome apologies. As to the 'phone call, I wrote it off as a misunderstanding. Maybe I'd misheard the name or the address. Or both. I knew I hadn't, of course, but no amount of speculation on my part was going to explain what had happened. So, I forgot all about it.'

'Until the police arrived on your doorstep?'

'Not quite. That's where it gets odder still. About a week later, Miss Abberley – the *real* Miss Abberley – telephoned me. I thought for a moment she must have reconsidered my offer. But no. She simply wanted me to tell her why I'd visited her. Well, I'd already done that. But she wanted more: everything I could remember, in fact, about the original telephone call. The woman's voice. Her exact words. Every detail I could recollect.'

'She believed you?'

'Yes. Strange, isn't it? It's the sort of story I might have made up just to get over the threshold. But it happened to be true. And she believed it. She hadn't when I'd called at the cottage. She'd made that obvious. But now she did.'

'Why the change of mind?'

'She wouldn't say. She simply thanked me for the information and rang off. And that was the last I heard about it. Or expected to hear. Until Monday.'

'Did you tell the police all this?'

'Of course. But I was wasting my breath. They had their solution. They had their suspect. And they weren't going to be deflected by anything I said.'

'It's understandable.'

'Maybe. But they don't need your understanding. I do.'

Derek looked away for an instant. Almost everything he knew about his brother constituted grounds for doubt. Except for the fact that he could never have been stupid enough to incriminate himself in the way the police alleged. Colin's version of events made more sense than any other Derek had heard – and was the more disturbing because of it.

'Would you do something for me?' asked Colin.

'What did you have in mind?'

'Contact Beatrix Abberley's family. Try to persuade them I'm telling the truth. They must want the real murderer caught as badly as I do. And they must know what his motive was, even if they're unaware of it at the moment.'

Derek thought of Charlotte Ladram speeding out of the car park in Hastings. 'I don't think they'd welcome such contact.'

'You can win them over. I know you can. Diplomacy's always been your forte.'

'I'm not so sure. Didn't you have a dispute with them last year over the price of some furniture? The police think that's how you got to hear about the Tunbridge Ware.'

'They're wrong. I'd forgotten all about it. I didn't know the woman I bought the furniture from was related to Miss Abberley until the police told me.'

'Maybe not. But the family obviously think otherwise. And it's bound to prejudice them against you.'

Colin sat back in his chair, stared intently at Derek for a moment, then said: 'I don't underestimate the difficulties. I'm only asking you to try.'

'All right. I'll see what I can do. But it may not be much.'

'Anything's better than nothing. And nothing is what I have to go on at the moment. Apart from this.' Colin reached into his pocket, took out a scrap of paper and slid it across the table. On it was written, in pencilled capitals, TRISTRAM ABBERLEY: A

'What's this?'

'Beatrix Abberley was the sister of Tristram Abberley, the poet. Heard of him?'

'Vaguely.'

'I'm reading his collected works at the moment, courtesy of the prison library.'

'You? Reading poetry?'

'I've not much else to do, have I? Being accused of aiding and abetting his sister's murder has done wonders for my poetic sensibility. Unfortunately, I can't follow his kind of stuff any better now than when I was at school. But biography's a different matter. The library doesn't hold a copy, but the librarian favoured me with these details.'

'You want me to buy a copy for you?'

'No. I want you to buy a copy for both of us. It's bound to say something about his family, isn't it? It'll give you the background you need. Maybe even a clue. Or maybe nothing at all. We won't know until we try, will we?'

'It seems a bit of a long-shot.'

'It's the only kind of shot we have.'

Derek shook his head doubtfully and reached forward to pick up the piece of paper. As he did so, Colin stretched across the table and pressed his hand over Derek's. 'I'm relying on you. You know that, don't you?'

'Yes.'

'I won't say you owe it to me to do this, because it wouldn't be true. But there's no one else I can turn to. Not a soul.'

'Is that what I am, then? Your last resort?'

Colin smiled. 'I suppose so. But isn't that what brothers are for?'

EIGHT

BEATRIX'S FUNERAL WAS CONDUCTED with the chilling seemliness reserved for such occasions. On a pluperfect summer's day, a score of mourners gathered at St Mary's Church, Rye for a short but eloquent service and were then conveyed by a flotilla of gleaming limousines to Hastings Crematorium for the conclusion of the ceremony.

Mrs Mentiply wept openly. One or two of Beatrix's neighbours dabbed at their eyes. Otherwise, the affair passed off with a lack of emotional display of which Charlotte was sure Beatrix would have approved. Lulu Harrington did not attend, having sent Charlotte a brief note explaining that she did not feel equal to the journey. But there was a full turn-out of family members, Samantha having arrived home for the summer from Nottingham University the day before and Uncle Jack having done his best to sober up as well as smarten up for the occasion.

Eyeing her relatives across the crematorium chapel, Charlotte caught herself thinking what a typically English amalgam they were of restraint and indifference. As soon as she had decided to exempt Maurice and herself from this charge, however, she realized how unfair she was being. Why should Ursula and Samantha express more than they felt at the death of an old and not always companionable woman? The manner of her death was not their fault and could not be altered by any amount of conspicuous grieving.

Besides, they played the parts allotted to them with commendable diligence. Ursula assumed her decorous place beside Maurice in the garden of remembrance, shook hands with all the mourners and thanked them for coming. Jack refrained from cracking a single joke. And Samantha's distant expression could easily have been taken for pent-up emotion, so winsomely affected did a black dress and hat make her appear.

Afterwards, the family adjourned to Ockham House for tea. At first, it was clear that none of them knew whether to strike a note of sorrow or of celebration. Had Beatrix died in her sleep, her age and mental alertness would have been counted as reasons to take comfort from her passing. As it was, one violent moment cast its shadow over a lifetime of serenity. At all events, Charlotte supposed Beatrix's life had been serene, although the truth was that nobody had known her well enough to be absolutely certain.

For once, Jack's waggish ways were welcome. He it was who prompted Charlotte to offer the scotches and gins everyone was silently craving and, from that point on, conversation and affectionate reminiscence flowed. The need to function as a group faded as the stilted mood of the funeral ebbed away. Jack began to monopolize

Samantha's attention with his lubricated and faintly lecherous wit. Ursula drifted out on to the lawn to smoke a cigarette. And Maurice sought to reassure Charlotte about his stewardship of her inheritance.

'I think I can safely claim to have put everything in order, Charlie. Not that it was difficult. Beatrix ran her affairs very efficiently.'

'I'm sure she did.'

'A formidable lady, in many ways. I shall miss her.'

'We shall *all* miss her.'

A peal of laughter from Samantha floated across to them and Maurice smiled. 'Well, you and I will, certainly.' He grew more serious. 'I leave for New York tomorrow. Life – and business – must go on.'

'Of course.' Maurice seemed to spend half his time in the United States these days, which was not surprising in view of Ladram Avionics' steady expansion in the American market. 'And how is . . . business?'

'Is that a polite enquiry or a shareholder speaking?' He grinned. 'Either way, the answer's the same. Never better.'

'Then, either way, I'm glad to hear it.'

'But it means I shall have to leave you in the lurch where Jackdaw Cottage is concerned.'

'You've done more than I could reasonably have expected already, Maurice. It's high time I took a hand.'

'What do you think you'll do with the place? Sell?'

'I suppose so. That is . . . What else can I do with it? It's what I should do with this house as well, come to that.'

'Yes, it is. I've told you so often enough. It would fetch a good price. And it might help you to . . . start afresh, so to speak.'

'You're right. I know. But knowing and doing are two—' She broke off at the sudden realization that her voice was the only sound in the room. Jack's guffaws had ceased. Samantha's giggles had died. Turning, she saw they were both looking towards the open French windows. Ursula was standing there. With a stranger beside her.

Derek left Fithyan & Co. early that afternoon and toured the book-shops of Tunbridge Wells in search of two copies of *Tristram Abberley: A Critical Biography*. He found only one and the assistant looked puzzled by his request to order a second, but she assured him that it would take no more than a couple of weeks to obtain.

Sitting in his car, he unwrapped the book and gazed at the face that stared up at him from the cover. According to what he had read on the back while standing in the shop, Tristram Abberley had died of wounds incurred while fighting in the Spanish Civil War. Derek was not surprised therefore by the martial air of the photograph, clearly taken in Spain some time before the poet's death. He was a slim good-looking man of about thirty, with short and already receding hair above a clear and square-jawed face. His uniform was dusty and ill-fitting, the ruined wall against which he was leaning sun-baked and crumbling. But none of that mattered. The nonchalant angle at which he held a cigarette between the first and second fingers of his left hand; the disdainful arching of his eyebrows; the casual pose he struck against the wall: all these captured and conveyed the personality of one whose self-confidence could survive any adversities.

Derek was about to open the book when he caught sight of one of his clients approaching along the pavement. Instantly, he felt he must not be seen. Not with *this* book at *this* time. Hastily, he pushed it out of view beneath the dashboard, started the car and turned into the traffic.

The roads were busy. The afternoon was hot. As he trailed and braked his way up across the Common towards Mount Ephraim, he began to think about Charlotte Ladram and how he might best approach her. He had looked up her address in the telephone directory earlier and had recognized Manor Park as the name of one of Tunbridge Wells' many quiet residential side-roads lined by tree-screened villas. The directory had listed the subscriber as Mrs M. Ladram. Her mother, perhaps? If so, she must have been the woman Colin bought the furniture from last year. But the police had told Colin she was dead. The discrepancy was easily explained, since the directory was a two-year-old edition, but it left open the possibility that Miss Ladram no longer lived there. In that event, Derek would be reduced to asking Dredge for information, something he had hoped to avoid.

It was the thought of explaining himself to Dredge that finally decided the issue. Much more deliberation, he knew, would undermine his resolve completely. He took the next turning on the right, paused to consult his street-map, then set off again, arriving a few minutes later in Manor Park. There he left his car and began to walk, checking each house name as he went. It was a neighbourhood of such heavy-curtained quietude that he felt reluctant even to clear his throat, but the trees which denied him a view into most of the gardens at least ensured he could not be seen from within.

Ockham House disclosed itself as a glimpse of stolid gabling behind a high thorn hedge. A gravelled drive curved out of sight beyond the entrance and, as he started up it, Derek felt intensely conscious of the crunching noise his shoes made at every step.

Then, rounding a screen of rhododendrons, he came upon a flower-bordered lawn, with the house set above it on slightly higher ground. It was a stuccoed villa of modest proportions, bay-fronted and high chimneyed, with little in the way of architectural elaboration. Derek felt strangely encouraged by its lack of grandeur and quickened his pace.

As he approached the front door, he saw that the lawn curved round to the side of the house. There, seated on a wicker chair in a sunny corner, was a woman in a dark dress, smoking a cigarette. He could not tell whether she had seen him, nor whether she was Charlotte Ladram, but he felt it would seem odd to ignore her, so he walked slowly towards her across the lawn.

As he drew nearer, it became apparent that her dress was not merely dark but black, as were her stockings and the shoes she had kicked off in front of her. She was definitely not Charlotte Ladram, being taller and slimmer, with fashionably short blonde hair. And he could be sure she had not seen him, because she had her eyes closed. She was leaning back in her chair, savouring the sunlight and each lungful of smoke. Beside her, on the grass, was a narrow-brimmed black hat. It was the hat that removed the last doubt in Derek's mind about why she was dressed as she was. But even as he decided to turn and walk away, she opened one eye, then the other, and looked at him.

'Good afternoon.' Her voice was clipped and husky. 'And who might you be?'

'I . . . I'm sorry . . . My name . . . That is, I was looking for Miss Charlotte Ladram.'

'For Charlie?' She smiled. 'She hasn't told us about you. Is this a recent acquaintance?'

'No. She doesn't . . . Is she in?'

'Oh, yes. She's in.'

'Well, perhaps this isn't . . . the right time.'

'No, no. The more the merrier, you might say. Let me show you the way.'

'There's really no—'

But it was too late. She rose, stepped into her shoes and beckoned for him to follow her towards the house. He had no choice but to comply, certain though he now was that he had arrived at the worst possible time. A short flight of steps led up from the lawn to some open French windows. The woman paused as she reached them and waited for him to catch up. In the room beyond her, he could see four figures turning to look in his direction. They too were wearing black.

It was Derek Fairfax. As Charlotte recognized him, a shaft of anger lanced through her. What could the man be thinking of? To arrive at such a time was either crass insensitivity or a calculated insult. If he thought such an approach would aid his brother's cause, he was much mistaken.

'A visitor for you, Charlie,' said Ursula. 'I'm afraid I didn't catch the name.'

'A friend of yours?' murmured Maurice.

'No. He's Derek Fairfax. Colin Fairfax's brother.'

'Good God. What—'

'I'm sorry.' Fairfax stepped into the room. 'I really am sorry to intrude like this. I had no idea . . . that the funeral was . . .'

'Fairfax?' said Jack with a frown. 'Isn't that . . . the name of . . .'

'The man responsible for Beatrix's death,' said Charlotte. 'I can't imagine what brings you here, Mr Fairfax.'

'I came to express my condolences.'

'You could have done that by letter if you thought it appropriate.'

'Yes. But—'

'Have you come for some other reason?'

'Well . . . In a sense. But perhaps I could call back another—'

'I'd rather you didn't.'

'If you have something to say,' put in Maurice, 'why don't you say it?'

Fairfax's eyes flashed around the room. He was licking his lips and there was a trickle of sweat at the side of his brow. In other circumstances, Charlotte might have felt sorry for him. But these were not other circumstances. She watched him struggle to compose himself. Then he said: 'My brother assures me he had nothing to do with the break-in at Miss Abberley's cottage.'

'He would, wouldn't he?' remarked Ursula, stepping past him to reach an ashtray.

'But I believe him. And if you heard what he had to say I think you might as well.'

'Unlikely,' said Maurice. 'My mother was swindled out of some furniture by your brother last year. And I subsequently had the dubious pleasure of meeting him. Untrustworthy would be to put it mildly.'

'But not a fool. That's the point. Only a fool would do what the police claim he did.'

'Am I to take it,' said Charlotte, 'that your real purpose in coming here is to protest your brother's innocence? If so, I can't see how we can help you.'

'He thinks – and so do I – that the real motive for the break-in was to murder Miss Abberley.'

'Oh-ho,' said Jack. 'The plot thickens.' He grinned, but nobody else seemed to find the situation amusing.

'The Tunbridge Ware was stolen,' said Maurice. 'And found in his shop. How does he explain that?'

'Planted by the murderer to cover his tracks.'

'Oh, come on! He can't be serious.'

'Besides,' said Ursula, 'why should anyone want to murder Beatrix?'

'I don't know. But I thought . . . perhaps you . . .'

'Might be hiding something?' snapped Charlotte.

'No. Not hiding. Just not realizing the significance of . . . of something . . .'

'Perhaps you think *we* murdered her. For her money.'

'Of course I don't.' He looked at her imploringly, urging her to yield just enough ground for him to take some kind of stand. But she would not.

'My sister and I are the principal beneficiaries under Beatrix's will, Mr Fairfax,' said Maurice calmly. 'For my own part, I am the chairman and managing director of Ladram Avionics, an internationally success-ful company of which you may have heard. My means are considerable. Do you really think I care about a modest bequest from my aunt?'

'No. I never suggested you did.'

'Charlie is also well provided for, as you can see. She owns this house. And a substantial shareholding in the company.'

'There's no need to tell Mr Fairfax our business, Maurice,' said Ursula.

'My point is that by no stretch of the imagination can we be said

53

to have needed what we gained by Beatrix's death. And nobody else gained anything.'

'I thought there was a nest-egg for Mrs Mentiply,' remarked Jack.

'Do be quiet, Jack,' said Ursula.

'Oh, well, all right.' He assumed a contrite expression. 'Only trying to help.'

Fairfax was still looking at Charlotte, still silently pleading with her to be reasonable. And she was still determined not to be. 'Miss Ladram,' he said falteringly, 'I'm not accusing anybody of anything, least of all you. I'm only trying to establish the truth of what happened. Don't you want to do the same?'

'We already have,' she replied. 'The only service you can render us is to identify your brother's accomplice.'

'He didn't have one.'

'If that's what you think, I'm sure we'd all be grateful if you left – and didn't come back.'

Maurice put a protective arm round her waist. 'I'll second that. Time you left, Mr Fairfax. Bother me if you really must. But leave my sister alone.'

Ursula moved across to Fairfax's shoulder. 'Cue to depart,' she murmured.

'What?'

'Shall I show you out?'

Ursula's smile and her condescending gesture towards the garden completed Fairfax's defeat. He stepped back and looked away, seeming to shrivel before them. Suddenly, Charlotte regretted their implacable show of unity. Perhaps, after all, he had meant well. But it was too late to find out. Already, he had turned and was hurrying towards the French windows. Ursula swayed out of his path with a little wave of dismissal.

'Goodbye, Mr Fairfax. So good of you to have called.'

'There's no need for that,' said Charlotte.

'Well, I'm sorry, my dear. I thought you wanted rid of him.'

'I did. But not—' She broke free of Maurice and hastened into the garden. Derek Fairfax had reached the drive and was walking fast towards the gate. To recall him now – even had she wished – would have been pointless.

'What's wrong, old girl?' said Maurice, coming up behind her.

'Nothing. I just . . .'

'Don't worry. He'll give us no trouble.'

'Perhaps we should have been less abrupt.'

'He was the one who was abrupt.'

'Even so, he's not responsible for his brother's actions, is he?'

'Then he shouldn't try to excuse them, should he?'

'He didn't. Not really.'

Maurice's arm once more encircled her. 'Let's forget him. And his brother. Let's forget all about the squalid crime that ended Beatrix's life and remember instead the many happy years she had before Mr Fairfax-Vane crossed her path. She'd want us to, you know.'

'Yes. She would.' Fairfax was out of sight now. Charlotte told herself to put him out of mind as well. 'Come on, Maurice. Let's go in and have another drink. I could do with one.'

'That's my girl.' With a beaming smile, he ushered her back to rejoin the others.

NINE

DEREK FELT SO ASHAMED by how he had managed – or mismanaged – his visit to Ockham House that for several days afterwards he could not think of the event without physically flinching. Colin had praised his diplomacy, but what would he say when he heard just how undiplomatic his brother had been?

Further contact with the Abberley family was, for the time being, out of the question. Derek's only immediate hope of learning more about them was to read Tristram Abberley's biography. This, with guilty zeal, he proceeded to do over the next three evenings.

The book was the work of an American academic, Emerson A. McKitrick, first published in 1977. Derek, whose taste in literature seldom led him beyond the realm of light detective fiction, was surprised by how absorbed he rapidly became in the life-story of an avant-garde pre-war poet. Perhaps he should not have been, however, since *Tristram Abberley: A Critical Biography* had assumed for him the characteristics of a convoluted whodunnit. The only real difference was that, in this case, the mystery did not begin until long after the book had ended.

From the first, Derek found himself sharing McKitrick's evident frustration. Who was Tristram Abberley? What manner of man was he? Sportsman; idler; intellectual poseur; spendthrift; communist; homosexual; womanizer; traveller; wastrel; husband; father; soldier; poet. He had apparently been all of these and more. Yet, at the end of his life, it was possible to believe that he had been none.

He was born at Indsleigh Hall, near Lichfield, in Staffordshire, on 4 June 1907, the third and youngest child of Joseph and Margaret Abberley. The other children were Lionel (born 1895) and Beatrix (born 1902). Joseph Abberley was a partner in a Walsall soap manufacturing business, Abberley & Timmins. He was a man of humble origins who had risen, thanks entirely to his own efforts, to considerable prosperity. His aspirations for his children were that they should enjoy all the social and educational opportunities he had been denied. But what they made of those opportunities was, as such men often find, not what he had anticipated.

For this — and most other insights into Tristram's early years — McKitrick was indebted, as he made clear, to the poet's sister, Beatrix, the only living witness to many of the events he described. The thought that she too was now dead struck home at Derek. It transformed what must have been mere reminiscence when related to the author into a fixed and final historical statement. No more than what it told could ever now be told.

Lionel Abberley was, according to Beatrix, a young man of exceptional sporting and intellectual prowess. Destined for a place at Oxford in the autumn of 1914, he enlisted instead in the Army at the outbreak of the First World War and was killed early the following year. His mother, devastated by the loss, entered a physical and mental decline that ended in her death in November 1916.

How these two blows affected the character of young Tristram was not certain. What was certain was that his father invested all his hopes for the future in his remaining son and that Beatrix was obliged to assume a maternal role in the family despite her tender years.

Tristram followed in his brother's footsteps at Rugby without ever quite fitting them and went up to Worcester College, Oxford in the autumn of 1926. He had till then displayed neither poetic vocation nor political conviction, but both were soon to blossom. Oxford in the late twenties was, of course, an ideal environment for this to happen in and McKitrick went to great lengths to demonstrate how Tristram was influenced by and associated with such contemporaries as W.H. Auden and Louis MacNiece. Excessive lengths, Derek felt, since actual links between them appeared to have been few.

Joseph Abberley's reaction to the publication of Tristram's first full-length poem, 'Blindfold', in the anthology *Oxford Poetry* in 1928 was said by Beatrix to have been mixed, revealing as the work did a socialist sentiment to which the old man was bound to object. He objected even more to the friends Tristram invited to Indsleigh Hall, suspecting that those who were not communists were homosexuals and that many of them were both. Predictably, McKitrick looked for evidence of homosexuality in Tristram's behaviour at this time, and claimed to find some. If he did, it was not in the testimony of Beatrix Abberley. She maintained that what misled her father was merely a dandified pose on her brother's part.

After leaving Oxford, Tristram lived for a year in London with assorted friends, writing sporadic but unpublished verse. He continued to accept a generous allowance from his father, who cherished the hope that he would eventually return home and take over the reins at Abberley & Timmins.

In the summer of 1930, Tristram embarked on a European tour to which his father had agreed only as prelude to his settling down to some kind of career. At Joseph Abberley's insistence, Beatrix accompanied her brother. In the course of the next year, they visited nearly every country in Europe, including Russia, Germany, Italy, France – and Spain. Tristram's exposure to the widespread economic distress they saw, coupled with a rosy-hued view of Stalin and an aversion to Mussolini, completed his conversion to socialism, though it was never to extend to a formal acceptance of Communism. What was to emerge from the rash of poems inspired by the tour was a coolly controlled anger at the abuse of political and economic power coupled with a keen sympathy for the underdog. Tristram Abberley struck many of those who met him in the early thirties as a witty pleasure-loving young man, but beneath this image – as the poems proved – a robust and articulate mind was at work, analysing humanity on a grand as well as a minor scale. Yet he seemed also to crave personal involvement in the events of the day, a craving rooted, as McKitrick saw it, in his presence in Madrid at the time of the anti-monarchist riots of May 1931, when he became convinced that only concerted action by the common people could achieve genuine political change.

Back in England in the autumn of 1931, Tristram at last complied with his father's wishes and accepted a junior managerial position at Abberley & Timmins. It was a disastrous move. Within a few months, he had put his socialist principles into practice by encouraging the workforce to resist a pay cut. A complete rift between father and son ensued. Tristram was dismissed and his allowance cancelled. Beatrix sided with her brother and was similarly disowned. They moved to London and lived together in straitened circumstances, Tristram scraping along as a journalist with various left-wing weeklies.

Tristram's first collection of verse, *The Brow of the Hill*, was published in October 1932. Although it made little impact at the time, it contained what McKitrick categorized as his best and most heart-felt poems, including the frequently anthologized 'False Gods'.

The sudden death of Joseph Abberley early in 1933 transformed his children's finances. Tristram was able to abandon journalism and take up a free and easy existence in London society, whilst Beatrix left London to settle in Rye. Brother and sister drifted apart from then on and, at this point in the book, McKitrick was obliged to resort to more varied sources of opinion about his subject's development.

The general view was that Tristram was a hedonist with an uneasy conscience. The wealth he had inherited from his father enabled him to lead an extravagant and irresponsible life, indulging his enthusiasm for travel, fast cars and beautiful women. The poems he wrote served to assuage the guilt he felt at such activities. And all the while a basic inclination towards socialism, apparent in his verse if not in his behaviour, ensured that he could not ignore the problems of the age.

After spending much of 1934 in the United States, he returned to England to put the finishing touches to his second collection of verse, *The Other Side*, published in the spring of 1935. This collection met with widespread critical approval, even though, in McKitrick's judgement, the poems generally failed to match the originality and immediacy of his earlier work.

That spring also saw his engagement to Mary Brereton, a twenty-one-year-old secretary at his publisher's offices, a girl far removed from the female company he had lately been keeping. Her description of their courtship, as recorded by McKitrick, conjured up a strangely simple image of the poet: loyal, generous and more contented than the nature of his verse suggested. They married in September 1935 and, for a while, Tristram filled the role of doting husband as easily as he had that of the free-thinking socialite.

When the Spanish Civil War broke out in July 1936, he seemed at first reluctant to become involved. By the autumn, the International Brigades had begun recruiting volunteers to fight for the Republican cause, but he made no move to join them. He expressed his support for the Republic when the periodical *Left Review* conducted a poll of English writers, but that was as far as he went. McKitrick attributed his reticence to domestic considerations. He had a young and by now pregnant wife to support, along with her orphaned brother. They had to come first. And, since he could give no practical assistance to the cause, he decided to refrain from empty rhetoric on its behalf.

As the Civil War continued, and the Republic's plight worsened, his inaction began to gnaw at his conscience. The conflict between the Republic and Franco's Nationalists distilled for him, as for many others, the conflicts of a whole decade. It was a heaven-sent opportunity to take a stand in defence of his principles. The birth of his son, Maurice, in March 1937, freed him of at least one domestic preoccupation and in July he accepted an invitation to attend an International Writers' Congress in Spain. He set off claiming that he wished merely to discuss intellectual attitudes to the war, but McKitrick contended that he had already resolved to take an active part in the hostilities. A desire to emulate his dead brother's heroism and to recapture the exhilaration he had felt during the riots in Madrid six years before combined to override all reservations. When the congress ended, he did not return home.

The first Mary Abberley knew of her husband's decision to fight was when she received a letter from him announcing his acceptance of a commission in the British Battalion of the Fifteenth International Brigade. She was horrified. But she would have been even more horrified had she realized she would never see him again.

Tristram committed himself to the Republican cause just as others were beginning to abandon it. By the summer of 1937, the International Brigades were a weary and disillusioned force, with most of their best and brightest recruits killed in earlier fighting. But, to those who recollected his arrival for McKitrick's benefit, Tristram Abberley had come as living proof that all was not lost. They spoke of his energy and his generosity, his contagious belief in the justice of their struggle, his ability to restore a sense of purpose even to the most disaffected. The final and most contradictory of all the phases of his life – that of the selfless warrior – had begun.

But it was not to last long. Lieutenant Tristram Abberley first saw action – and distinguished himself by his bravery – on the Fuentes del Ebro front in October 1937. Then, in January 1938, his battalion was called in to the gruelling Battle of Teruel. He suffered a serious leg-wound during a rifle engagement outside the city on 20 January and was subsequently evacuated to hospital in Tarragona. Amputation was not considered necessary and he appeared to be well on the road to recovery when a blood infection set in. He died on 27 March 1938 and was buried in Tarragona the following day.

Tristram Abberley's career as a poet did not end with his death. Indeed, in many respects, it was only then in its infancy. His experiences in Spain had prompted a last outpouring of verse, sent back to his widow among his personal effects and not published until 1952, when it emerged under the title *Spanish Lines*. This revived interest in the whole body of his work, which during the 'fifties and especially the 'sixties grew steadily in popularity and esteem. By the time of McKitrick's research for his book in the mid-seventies, he was regarded as one of the most significant English poets of his generation.

Wisely, McKitrick did not attempt to reconcile the conflicting aspects of his subject's life and personality. The poems, he thought, were what would ultimately be remembered about Tristram Abberley. Though the biographer could explain *how* they had come about, he could not penetrate to the secret of *why*.

Derek's despondency deepened as he neared the conclusion of the book. He had hoped, for no good reason, that something – anything – in the life and death of Tristram Abberley would come to his rescue. Instead, he was left as empty-handed as he had feared he would be. The Beatrix, Mary and Maurice he had read about might as well have been different people for all the insight he had gained into their more recent lives. If there was a secret buried in their collective past that explained what had happened, it was not to be found in the words and actions of a long-dead poet. If it was to be found at all, Derek would have to look elsewhere. But in what direction he did not know. He had been running towards a dead end all along. And now he had arrived.

TEN

EIGHT DAYS HAD PASSED since Beatrix's funeral when Charlotte decided she could postpone a visit to Jackdaw Cottage no longer.

On a cool breezy morning, she drove down to Rye, collected the key from Mrs Mentiply and entered what was now her property but still seemed indelibly to belong to another.

Thanks to Mrs Mentiply, the cottage was spotlessly clean. It was as if she regarded her bequest as a retainer and meant to discharge her duties more assiduously after her employer's death than before. The effect was to suggest Beatrix had merely gone away for a few days. All was as she might expect to find it when she returned. Except that she would not return.

Listlessly, Charlotte wandered from room to room, reliving in jumbled order her visits down the years. In her memory of them, she fluctuated between childhood and her present age, but Beatrix never varied. Always she was the same: kindly but not indulgent, generous but not playful. She had treated Charlotte as an adult long before she was one and retained to the end an independence of mind which some found disconcerting but which Charlotte had come more and more to admire.

But an end had come to all that and to preserve Jackdaw Cottage as some kind of museum was surely not what Beatrix would have wanted. As she gazed from the window of what had often been her room out across the small patch of garden towards the sea, Charlotte knew that the wisest solution was the swiftest: sell up and have done.

Yet Beatrix would surely also have wanted her to have a memento of their times together, something that would remind her of her godmother whenever her eye fell upon it. Ironically, she would have chosen one of the smaller pieces of Tunbridge Ware, but they lay bagged and labelled in a police station basement, awaiting Colin Fairfax's trial. The only remaining item of Tunbridge Ware was the work-table in the drawing room and, as soon as Charlotte had thought of it, she realized how appropriate it would be, since it combined practicality and elegance in a manner close to Beatrix's heart.

Without further ado, she carried it out to her car, went back for some blankets to wrap it in for the journey, then briskly took her leave. Tomorrow she would contact an estate agent and put the sale of Jackdaw Cottage in hand. Tomorrow nostalgia would be cast aside.

'So, what you're telling me,' said Colin, 'is that you've drawn a complete blank.'

'Yes,' Derek replied, averting his gaze towards the bare wall of the visiting room. 'I'm afraid I have.'

61

'The family have nothing to say?'

'Not to anybody associated with you.'

'And there are no clues to be found in Tristram Abberley's biography?'

'None. Read it yourself and see.'

'I intend to.'

They eyed each other warily for a moment, Derek sensing the silent accusation of failure that hung between them. Colin would think he had lost his nerve, misplayed his hand, blown his chance. And the worst of it was that he would be right.

'Where do we go from here?'

'I don't know.'

'Well, I do. At least, I know where *I* go. Down for a long stretch. Dredge keeps pushing me to do some kind of deal with the police. And I would if I could. But I can't. They all think I'm holding out on them. They mean to make me suffer for that. And suffering isn't my favourite occupation. But it seems I may have to get used to it.'

'I'm sorry, Colin. If there was anything—'

'Find something!' Colin nearly shouted the words, drawing a sharp glance from the warder. 'Just keep trying, brother,' he murmured through a fixed grin. 'You're my only hope.'

At Ockham House, Charlotte was in the process of selecting a suitable place for Beatrix's work-table when the telephone rang. It was Ursula.

'Hello, Charlie. Maurice asked me to call you.'

'Really? I thought he was still in New York.'

'He is. But we spoke last night. He wanted me to find out if you could have lunch with us next Sunday.'

'Next Sunday? Well, yes, I'd be delighted. But . . .'

'Is there some problem?'

'No. No problem at all. I'm just surprised Maurice should make a transatlantic phone call simply to invite me to lunch.'

'Well, it appears he's bringing somebody back with him from New York who wants to meet you, so he asked me to make sure you were free.'

'To meet me? Who is this person?'

'I don't know. Maurice wouldn't say. "*Very keen to make your acquaintance.*" That's all I know. A secret admirer, perhaps.'

'In New York? I hardly think so.'

'I shouldn't be too sure.'

'You know who it is, don't you?'

'Absolutely not. Guides' honour. Anyway, the mystery will be solved on Sunday. You will come, won't you?'

'Don't worry. I'll be there. With an incentive like that, how could I stay away?'

ELEVEN

THE FORCED JOLLITY OF a midsummer Sunday lay in wait for Charlotte throughout her journey to Bourne End. Every pub car park was full, every picnic-spot clamorous with children and dogs. Why she should be forever excluded from the communal pleasures of humanity at play she did not know. Sometimes she was glad to be excluded. Sometimes she suspected it was an insult devised by the world for her and nobody else. And sometimes she simply did not care.

The Thames was clogged and noisy with crafts of all description. Charlotte crossed it at Cookham and turned, with some relief, into the unmarked road that led to an exclusive handful of riverside residences, among them Swans' Meadow.

It was a house, she often thought, ideally suited to its owner's personality. Visible from the other side of the river and therefore an object of admiration, it was also aloof and secluded. Though large and lavishly appointed, it did not flaunt its architectural wares, but blended discreetly into the affluent landscape behind weeping willows and well-clipped hedges. Maurice had bought it twenty-one years ago as a glamorous new home for his glamorous new wife and he remained conspicuously proud of both acquisitions, as eager to protect them as he was to be envied on their account.

Aliki, the Cypriot *au pair*, answered the door and directed Charlotte to the garden, where the family — and their mysterious guest — were relaxing while she prepared lunch.

They were sitting on canvas chairs beneath a silver birch tree, with a tray of drinks standing on a table close at hand. Behind them the lawn, its flower-borders awash with colour, stretched to the bank of the river, where the weeping willows stirred serenely in a gentle breeze. Maurice, a smiling figure in panama and cravat, waved to Charlotte as she approached. To his right sat Ursula in a polka-dot dress, coolly remote behind dark glasses and cigarette smoke. Next to her, just outside the shadow of the trees, sat Samantha, stretching her legs and holding an iced glass against her cheek as she absorbed the heat of the sun. She was wearing an abbreviated pink swimsuit and an expression of calculated languor. To Maurice's left sat their guest, enjoying – as Charlotte felt sure he was intended to – a spectacular view of Samantha's bronzed and shapely limbs. He was square-shouldered, with a shock of dark hair and a beard, informally dressed in a pale green shirt and trousers. He rose as she drew near, shot her a flashing smile and extended his hand.

'Hi. My name's Emerson McKitrick.' He spoke in a subdued American accent and by the time she had released his hand, Charlotte had realized who he was.

'Tristram Abberley's biographer.'

'The very same. We never did meet while I was researching the book, did we?'

'No, we didn't.' It was twelve years ago – whilst Charlotte had been away on an ill-fated holiday in the Greek islands – that McKitrick had interviewed her mother. She had spoken afterwards of a polite and good-looking young man and Charlotte could see that this had been a considerable understatement. 'What an unexpected pleasure, Mr McKitrick.'

'It's *Doctor* McKitrick, Charlie,' put in Maurice.

'Oh, I—'

'So why don't you call me Emerson and solve the problem that way?'

'Sit down and have a drink, Charlie,' said Ursula. 'We've left a chair for you – and a glass.'

Charlotte found herself seated next to McKitrick, aware that she was blushing for no good reason. 'What . . . er . . . What brings you here . . . Emerson?'

'Research. Same as last time.' He did have a winning smile. There was no question about it. And enough laughter-lines at the edges of his eyes to suggest he was no dry and cloistered academic. But he was altogether too tanned and muscular for that to be plausible anyway. Charlotte caught herself guessing his age and settled on forty. 'My teaching schedule at Harvard means this is about the only time of year I can get away.'

'And what are you researching?'

'Something I'm kind of hoping you can help me with.'

'*Me?*'

'That's right. You in particular.'

'While Emerson explains,' said Ursula, 'I really must go and see how Aliki's coping in the kitchen.' She rose and smiled at McKitrick. 'Do excuse me.'

'Sure.'

Turning towards her daughter, Ursula said: 'And it's high time you put some clothes on, young lady. Unless you're thinking of lunching in your swimsuit.' Then she headed towards the house, leaving Samantha to grimace at the others before following. It really was, as became apparent when she left her chair, an extremely brief costume, cut as revealingly high at the hips as it was scooped daringly low at the back. McKitrick did not seem to mind Charlotte seeing him watch her curvaceous retreat across the lawn.

'A beautiful wife *and* a beautiful daughter. You're a lucky man, Maurice.'

'Are you married yourself, Emerson?' asked Charlotte.

'No.' He grinned. 'Except to my work.'

'Which you think I can help you with?'

'Perhaps I'd better come clean. My publisher's been pressuring me for a few years now to produce a new edition of *Tristram Abberley: A Critical Biography*. I've been stalling them, mostly because I don't enjoy going over old ground. But there's a chance now of finding some fresh material that would make a new edition worthwhile.'

'How so?'

'The chance arises from your godmother's recent death. As soon as I heard about it – from a friend at Oxford who passed through Harvard at the end of last month – I tried to contact Maurice. When I found out he was in New York, I fixed up a meeting with him.'

'And I told him the whole sad story,' said Maurice.

'It is sad,' said McKitrick. 'She was a feisty old lady. I liked her.'

'So did we all,' said Charlotte. 'But I still don't see—'

'I met with Beatrix twelve years ago, when I was doing the original research for the book, and got a whole mass of valuable information from her about Tristram's early years. In fact, she was pretty well my only source for his life before and immediately after Oxford. Up to about 1933, that is. But it was oral stuff. Straightforward recollection. She had no papers that Tristram left behind. None, I should say, that she was prepared to let me use.'

'Well,' said Charlotte, 'it was always my understanding that none existed. Apart from the poems themselves, of course. And a few letters. But surely my mother showed you those.'

'She did. But when I was speaking with Beatrix about Tristram's last few months, in Spain, she told me he'd written to her regularly from there – right up to his death. And that she'd kept the letters.'

'Really? Mother never mentioned such letters to me.'

'Nor to me,' put in Maurice.

'No. Because Beatrix didn't tell her. She evidently didn't want Mary to be jealous. It seems Tristram wrote more often to his sister than his wife. That could have been hard for a young widow to accept.'

'And it would have been typical of Beatrix to want to protect Mother from any unnecessary pain,' said Maurice.

'Right,' said McKitrick. 'That's how I saw it. And she was still protecting her nearly forty years later. So, I had to go along with it. I tried to persuade her to let me see the letters, but it was a waste of effort. You two know better than me she couldn't be shifted once she'd made up her mind. I had no choice but to go ahead without the material. And, anyway, she didn't leave me completely empty-handed. She said she'd give the letters to Maurice before her death on the understanding that, when Mary died, they could be made public. She was assuming, naturally enough, she'd die before Mary. And she was assuming, I reckon, she'd have plenty of time to set her affairs in order. As it is, Mary predeceased her. If I'd known, I'd have contacted Beatrix straightaway, as you can imagine. But, instead, the first I heard was of Beatrix's own death. That's why I was so anxious to get in touch with Maurice. To find out what arrangements she'd made for the letters.'

'I had to tell him she'd made none,' said Maurice. 'Maybe she thought she could postpone facing me with it. After all, she was in excellent health. Maybe she just forgot what she'd promised. Either way, she never breathed a word to me about it.'

'I don't quite understand,' said Charlotte. 'If these letters exist, they'll be stored somewhere at Jackdaw Cottage. Surely that's obvious.'

'Exactly,' said Maurice. 'And as I explained to Emerson when we met in New York, it means they're your property, under the terms of Beatrix's will.'

'Which is why I said I needed your help.' McKitrick smiled at her. 'Whether we look for the letters – whether I use them if we find them – is down to you, Charlie. You and nobody else.'

Lunch was more enjoyable than Charlotte had expected. McKitrick's ready wit and wide-ranging opinions kept everyone amused and involved. He had the ability to uncover people's particular enthusiasms and to talk entertainingly about them. Academic life, the aviation industry, equestrian sport, Cypriot cuisine, even Tunbridge Ware. It seemed he could speak divertingly and intelligently on virtually any topic. And he was, as Samantha remarked when she passed Charlotte on the stairs, 'a gorgeous hunk into the bargain'.

Nothing more was said about the letters until the party had returned to the garden. Then, without seeming to engineer the situation, McKitrick walked to the river's edge with Charlotte and watched a squadron of swans pass majestically by before remarking: 'A researcher's always a bit of a mendicant. Begging access. Borrowing quotations. I guess there'd be no more biographies if we weren't so shameless.'

'There's no need to beg in this case. If Maurice is happy for you to look for these letters, so am I.'

'I appreciate it, I really do.'

'I'm only surprised he didn't come across them himself.'

'He wasn't looking for them. It makes all the difference.'

'I suppose it does. When do you want to visit the cottage?'

'When could you show me round?'

'Oh!' She caught herself blushing again. 'You want me to come too?'

'I was hoping you would. Whatever we find is your property, remember. And it'll be for you to say what we do with it. Besides, a treasure hunt is more fun when there are two.'

'A treasure hunt? Is that what this is?'

'In a sense. Academic research is a lot like prospecting for gold. You're always hoping to hit a rich seam, but you hardly ever do. When shall we find out if this is to be an exception to the rule?'

His smile was conspiratorial and contagious. And Charlotte was powerless to do other than smile back. 'Tomorrow,' she said. 'I don't honestly think I could wait any longer.'

TWELVE

CHARLOTTE DID NOT CARE to admit to herself just how excited she was by the prospect of assisting Emerson McKitrick with his research. To have done so would have been to admit how drab her life had become and how desperate she secretly was for some small measure of romance and adventure.

The signs were there, however, clear and incontrovertible. She slept poorly. She took exaggerated care over her hair and make-up. She chose to wear a more flattering outfit than the occasion warranted. And she broached a bottle of Chanel perfume that had stood untouched in a cupboard since Christmas.

Emerson travelled to Tunbridge Wells by an early train from London, where he was staying, and Charlotte drove him on to Rye. They reached Jackdaw Cottage a little after ten o'clock. And there – bar a short break for lunch – they remained all day, proceeding methodically from room to room, checking carefully the contents of bureaux and bookcases, cupboards and cabinets. Every piece of paper in every drawer was examined, every book opened in case a letter had been slipped between the pages, every nook and cranny penetrated in search of a hidden bundle. The task, though time-consuming, was not difficult, for Beatrix had never been able to abide untidiness. Though she had accumulated a good deal in the course of a long life, she had always been strict and orderly in her domestic arrangements. Such papers and documents as she had preserved were stored in the obvious places. Even in the loft, to which Emerson ascended in mid-afternoon, discipline prevailed. Nowhere was a bulging suitcase or battered despatch-box to be found. Nowhere, indeed, were any caches of letters – let alone the ones they sought – waiting to be unearthed. No billets-doux from long-dead beaux. No birthday cards from years gone by. And nothing at all – neither scrap nor jotting – from Tristram Abberley.

At six o'clock, they abandoned the task and retreated to the Ypres Castle Inn on Gun Garden Steps, where they sat with their drinks in the small garden and gazed out across the harbour towards the sea. They were tired and despondent, though Charlotte was aware that Emerson was merely disappointed at having found nothing, whereas she was also fearful that their failure would bring an abrupt end to their association.

'I can't understand it, Charlie. I was so sure they'd be there, so confident.'

'Because of what Beatrix told you?'

'Yuh. She didn't have to hide them. There was no need.'

'But she appears to have done precisely that.'

'I'm not sure. The housekeeper hasn't touched anything. Maurice has removed nothing apart from bank statements, cheque-books and a couple of bills.'

'And all I've taken from the cottage is a Tunbridge Ware worktable. It contains thimbles, needles and a few buttons, but no papers of any kind.'

'Right. And we're sure – because Maurice has already checked it out as her executor – that she didn't deposit any packages with her bank or solicitor.'

'Yes. Which appears to leave us back at Jackdaw Cottage.'

'Empty-handed. We've searched the place as thoroughly as we can short of lifting floorboards or climbing up the chimney. There's nothing there. Like I say, she had no need to hide the letters. Nobody but me knew they even existed.'

'So what do you think? Did she destroy them?'

'Her dead brother's last letters? No. Nobody would do that. Besides, she'd promised me she wouldn't. And she wasn't a lady to break her word.'

'Then what did she do with them?'

'I don't know. Unless—' He broke off and frowned thoughtfully.

'What is it?'

'Unless she was afraid they'd go astray. Be overlooked after her death. Trashed before anybody realized what they were. Is it possible she left them with somebody for safe-keeping? A friend, perhaps?'

'Of course it's possible. But why would she trust a friend with the letters if she wouldn't trust Maurice or me with them?'

'Because she might have wanted to use a neutral party – somebody outside the family. Not that I'm saying it's what happened. I'm just trying to cover every eventuality. Hell, I don't even know if she had such a friend.'

'Oh, but she did!' Suddenly, Charlotte smiled. 'You're right. It's obvious. Her oldest friend of all. She was the neutral party. Lulu Harrington.'

They drove back to Tunbridge Wells, Charlotte having to restrain herself from exceeding all known speed limits, so impatient was she to put her theory to the test. Her first action on entering Ockham House was to seize the telephone and dial Lulu's number. Relief swept over her when it was answered in Lulu's familiar tone.

'Lulu? This is Charlotte Ladram.'

'Charlotte? What a delightful surprise. How are you?'

'Fine, but—'

'I really was so very sorry to miss Beatrix's funeral. I trust my wreath was safely delivered?'

'Yes. Yes, it was. Forgive me, but this call is rather urgent. I'm hoping you'll be able to help me.'

'I'll be happy to, if it lies within my power.'

'I think it may. Tell me, did Beatrix ever leave anything with you for safe-keeping? A parcel or packet of some kind?' She paused and waited for an answer, but there was none. 'Lulu?'

'Yes, my dear?'

'Did you hear what I said?'

'Yes. I heard. A parcel or packet. What makes you ask?'

'That's a little difficult to explain.'

'I see.' She sounded pensive, almost apprehensive.

'So what's the answer?'

'Are you phoning on somebody else's behalf?'

'No.'

'Not perhaps on your sister-in-law's?'

'You mean Ursula?'

'She will have to accept I did not know what it contained. And that I was bound by a solemn promise. What else could I do?'

'Lulu, I don't know what you're talking about.'

'But you must.'

'You still haven't answered my question.'

'No. No, I haven't, have I?'

70

'Are you going to?'

There was no reply. Charlotte thought she could hear Lulu's slightly wheezy breathing at the other end and decided this time to let her choose when to break the silence. At last she said: 'I think we must meet, my dear. This matter has been preying upon my conscience. And I can think of no one better than you to confide in. There is no one else, indeed, in whom I *could* confide. So, let us meet. The sooner the better. I see now that I must make a clean breast of what I have done. Without further delay.'

THIRTEEN

TO CHARLOTTE, CHELTENHAM SEEMED like a less hilly version of Tunbridge Wells. There was the same abundance of Regency architecture, the same bustling but well-ordered gentility. She arrived in the heat of early afternoon and spent an uncomfortable half hour locating Park Place, where Lulu lived among the many similar tree-lined residential roads south of the centre. She had come alone, having persuaded Emerson that his presence might alarm Lulu. Indeed, though she had not told him so, she did not propose to mention his interest in Beatrix's affairs. She did not even know yet whether she would relay to him everything Lulu had to say. Their telephone conversation had left her confused and uncertain about what to expect of her visit. Vapid anti-climax or astounding revelation. Either was possible. And, to tell the truth, she was not sure which she was hoping for.

Courtlands was one of a terrace of white-rendered Regency dwellings where, according to the array of bells at the entrance, Miss L. Harrington occupied the ground floor only. Charlotte had barely time to remove her finger from the buzzer when the door opened and a tiny white-haired old lady with twinkling blue eyes smiled out at her.

'Charlotte?'

'Yes. I . . . I'm sorry if I'm late.'

'You're not, my dear. Do come in.'

Lulu led her down the hall and into a high-ceilinged drawing room crowded with books, paintings, photographs, figurines and a seemingly limitless number of different tea-sets displayed in glass-fronted cabinets. It would be difficult, Charlotte felt, to cross to the fireplace without accidentally kicking a china rabbit or upsetting a pile of knitting patterns. And what looked like the most comfortable armchair was occupied by the dormant mound of a huge Prussian blue cat. Of cats and clutter in general Beatrix had never approved and it seemed odd to think of her spending a contented fortnight there every year.

Lulu bustled about preparing tea and Charlotte followed her into the kitchen to help. The window looked on to a well-kept garden where two teenage boys were playing with a frisbee. Seeing Charlotte glance out at them, Lulu said: 'They live in the first-floor flat. I have tenants above and beneath me. To be honest, I am glad of their company. We schoolmistresses like to have the young about us even in our dotage, you know.'

'How long have you lived here?'

'Since I retired from teaching. Twenty years ago this month. How time does fly. The College had accommodated me till then. I was a housemistress, you understand. What I should have done afterwards without Beatrix's help I cannot imagine. It would certainly have been beyond my means to buy this house.'

'You mean Beatrix lent you some money towards it?'

'Not lent. *Gave*. Beatrix was, as you must know, exceedingly generous. Too generous, I sometimes thought.'

'Yes. She was.' Suddenly, Charlotte flushed. 'I'm sorry. I didn't mean—'

'It's perfectly all right. I know exactly what you meant. She was generous *and discreet*. I felt sure she would never have mentioned the assistance she gave me to anybody else. I only mention it now because it has, in some sense, a bearing on what has occurred.'

'And what *has* occurred?'

'Come into the drawing room, my dear. Drink some tea and humour me by eating some cake. Then I'll explain everything.'

Before Lulu offered any explanations, Charlotte was obliged to offer one of her own. Meeting the old lady's mild but perceptive gaze across the tea-tray, she had the impression that the lie she had prepared was no longer sufficient. But it was too late to prepare another.

'Beatrix once told Maurice and me she had letters from her brother, sent to her from Spain in the months before his death, that should not be made public while my mother was alive. We were puzzled we couldn't find them at Jackdaw Cottage and thought she might have left them with you for safe-keeping.'

'She may have done. It *is* possible.'

'I don't understand.'

'Neither do I. But you are about to, where as I may never.' Lulu smiled. 'Forgive me. I do not mean to tease. But am I to take it you did not telephone me at the request of Ursula Abberley?'

'You are. Ursula doesn't even know I'm here.'

'Extraordinary.' She shook her head in evident bemusement. 'Beatrix and I met at Roedean, as I'm sure you're aware. More than seventy years ago. A very long time. Long enough, you might think, for me to know her mind better than anyone. Well, if I do, it means nobody knew her mind at all. For I did not, I freely confess. She was and is to me an enigma.'

Lulu fell silent, but Charlotte could sense it was only an interval to collect and marshal her thoughts. She resumed without need of prompting.

'Beatrix was considerably more intelligent than me. She had a faculty for seeing to the heart of things which could be quite disarming. You must know that, of course. What I mean is that she had such a faculty even as a child. Her father withdrew her from Roedean after her mother's death. Had she remained, she could easily have surpassed my academic achievements. I went on to Girton College, Cambridge, and came here to teach at the Ladies' College in 1923, but we never lost touch. I often went to stay with her at Indsleigh Hall and later at Jackdaw Cottage.'

'You must have met Tristram, then?'

'Oh, yes. On several occasions. But he had little time for a dowdy schoolmistress like me. I can hardly claim to have known him. An impulsive young man, certainly, as I suppose the manner of his death proves. So far as letters to Beatrix are concerned, she never mentioned receiving any, but, then again, there is no reason why she should have. Our friendship was never intimate, you must understand. We enjoyed each other's company, but I was never her confidante.'

Once again, Lulu paused, frowning as if it was difficult to frame what she had to say. But the difficulty was soon surmounted.

'I was, of course, immensely grateful to Beatrix for the help she gave me in buying this house and when she asked me to help her, I saw it as partial repayment of what I owed her. Not that Beatrix looked upon it in that light. She would, I do not doubt, have accepted a refusal to co-operate as no more than my right. But I did not refuse. Not even when, as recently, what she asked of me seemed so . . . so very strange.'

'What did she ask of you?'

'Initially, my participation in a harmless fraud.'

'Fraud?'

'Yes, my dear. You see, Beatrix has come to stay with me every June for as long as I have lived here. You know that, of course. And you think she spent a fortnight with me on each occasion. But the truth is that she spent no more than a couple of nights at either end of the fortnight under this roof. Every year, for the intervening ten or twelve days, she was elsewhere.'

'*Elsewhere?*'

'It was a regular arrangement. She would arrive and, within a day or so, depart.'

'But . . . to go where?'

'I don't know. She wouldn't say. Somewhere, clearly, that she did not wish you or any other member of the family to realize she visited. That is why she always returned here before going home, in case there had been any messages for her. In the event of one of you insisting on speaking to her or actually presenting yourself on the doorstep, I was to say she had gone away unexpectedly – and certainly for the first time. But the situation never arose. For twenty years, we practised our little deception without once coming close to being discovered.'

'You mean . . . last month . . . and every other June . . . she wasn't here at all?'

'Not for more than a few days, no.'

'I just can't believe it.'

'I sympathize. It must seem incredible. Yet it is true. I grew accustomed to it. I even enjoyed the element of risk associated with it. And I could see no harm in it. If Beatrix considered it necessary – for whatever reason – why should I stand in her way?'

'But . . . surely . . .' Into Charlotte's mind floated the recollection of all the postcards she had received from Beatrix during her annual fortnight in Cheltenham. '*Arrived safely. Lulu well. Cheltenham as beautiful as ever.*' 'What . . . What about the postcards? She sent me one every year. Maurice too.'

'Written by Beatrix, but posted by me, after her departure for her other destination.'

'And you don't know where that was?'

'I have no idea. She arrived by train. She left by train. It could have been anywhere in the country. I was curious at first, of course, but later I ceased to wonder. It was none of my business. After what Beatrix had done for me, the least I could do in return was respect her privacy — and drop a few postcards into the pillar-box at the appropriate time.'

Charlotte watched the cat stir and reposition itself in the armchair next to Lulu's. Slowly, the true significance of what had been said was becoming clear to her. The deception was one thing, its purpose quite another. For twenty years, Beatrix had been somewhere and done something in total secrecy. If it was innocent or inconsequential, why cover her tracks so carefully? What could warrant such an elaborate lie? 'Why tell me now, Lulu?' she asked at length. 'Why not keep her secret for ever?'

'Because of the additional request she made of me this year. A request with which I complied rather against my better judgement.'

'What was it?'

'Beatrix arrived here on the first of June and left the following day. All seemed the same as usual, although she struck me as somewhat preoccupied. She returned on Wednesday of the following week and remained until Friday. It was on Thursday, sitting where you are sitting now, that she told me quite calmly over morning coffee that she thought her life was in danger.'

'What?'

'At first, I assumed she meant she had some medical problem. But she rapidly disabused me of the notion. What she meant was quite specific. It was possible, indeed probable, she said, that she would die in the near future. If she was not ill, I asked, had she had some premonition of death? No. Facts which had come to her attention had convinced her of its imminent likelihood. She was not prepared to disclose what those facts were, nor to suggest how she might die. She did not, indeed, expect or ask me to believe her. All she wanted was my agreement to perform a simple task in the event of her being proved right. She had four large padded envelopes with her, sealed and addressed with type-written labels. As soon as I heard she had died, I was to take them to a postal district other than Cheltenham and despatch them. I was not to open them or to pass them on to any third party.'

'You agreed?'

'Yes. Initially, I tried to reason with her, to persuade her either to justify her prediction or to withdraw it. But I soon realized I was wasting my breath. Beatrix was not easy to shift once she had made up her mind about something and, clearly, she had made up her mind about this. When she added that I was the only person she could ask to do such a thing – and that it was imperative it be done – I felt I could not refuse. Besides, I consoled myself I would never be called upon to do it, since she was clearly mistaken, labouring under some appalling misapprehension. But I should have known better. I had seldom known Beatrix to be mistaken about anything. And events were to show she was not mistaken about this either.'

'So you posted the letters?'

'Yes. From Gloucester, the day after you telephoned to report Beatrix's murder.'

Lulu's strange remarks during that conversation now made sense. At the time, Charlotte had attributed them to shock, and shock of a kind had indeed been responsible. But it was the predictability of Beatrix's death, not – as Charlotte had supposed – the exact reverse, which had taken Lulu aback. 'Who were the letters to?'

'Beatrix asked me on my honour neither to record nor to memorize the names and addresses.'

'*You don't know?*'

'I tried to obey Beatrix to the last. I had never known her to act unwisely. I assumed she had her reasons and that they were good and sound. But of course I saw what was on the labels. I could hardly not. And I could not will myself to forget what I saw. I did not memorize the information. Nevertheless, I remember some of it. One letter was to your half-brother's wife, Ursula. Mrs Abberley, as it was typed, at an address in Buckinghamshire.'

'Swans' Meadow, Riversdale, Bourne End?'

'Very likely.'

'She's said nothing about it. Not a word. Even to Maurice. I'm sure he'd have told me.'

'You must take that up with her. Of course, I have no idea what the envelope contained. She may not have realized its origin.'

'And the others? Who were they to?'

'People I have never heard of. Mr Griffith, at an unpronounceable address in Wales. Llan-something, Dyfed. Miss van Ryan – I think – at a high number in Fifth Avenue, New York. And Madame – a surname beginning with V – at an address in Paris.'

The name Griffith meant something to Charlotte, though what she could not recall. For the rest, she was as much in the dark as Lulu. 'Is that all you can remember?'

'I fear so. Since we agreed to meet, I have racked my brains for more – and found nothing. The news of Beatrix's death quite overwhelmed me. I travelled to Gloucester in a daze and did what had been asked of me without considering the consequences. At the time, it seemed to me that the most important thing was to do what I had promised Beatrix I would do. To do it and to forget it. But, in the weeks that have followed, I have been unable to put it out of my mind. Who are these people? What have I sent them? Was I right or wrong to obey my friend? Should I, for instance, have told the police she foresaw her death? I decided in the end there was nothing to be gained by doing so except a reputation for senile delusions. After all, it seems clear enough that this man Fairfax was behind her murder. As far as their investigations were concerned, I could add nothing to what they already knew. Nevertheless, I continued to fear that my actions would rebound on me. Which is precisely what I thought had happened when you telephoned. I felt sure Ursula must have traced the letter back to me. Even when you denied it, I remained uncertain. All I knew was that I could no longer keep this knowledge to myself. I had to share it with somebody. Who better than Beatrix's god-daughter? I had tried to avoid the issue by absenting myself from the funeral. But your telephone call convinced me I could avoid it no longer.'

Charlotte leaned back in her chair and tried to assimilate what she had heard as coolly and rationally as possible. Beatrix had foreseen her death. That must mean she had guessed or calculated that Fairfax-Vane would not take 'no' for an answer. If so, her real concern seemed not to have been for her own safety, rather for what would happen after her death. Hence the carefully made arrangement with Lulu. But what was she trying to prevent – or bring about – by sending the letters? What was it she could not risk being stolen, found or simply overlooked? And why could neither Maurice nor she be trusted with the information? Some old letters from Tristram Abberley could hardly be the answer, even though their absence from Jackdaw Cottage suggested they might be. What, then? What in the wide world could have been her purpose?

'I am sorry to inflict this mystery upon you, my dear,' said Lulu. 'But do not let it sully Beatrix's memory. She knew what she was about, I feel sure. Perhaps, after all, we should defer to her judgement. Perhaps we should simply leave matters as they are.'

'You don't really mean that, Lulu, do you? If you did, you'd never have told me about it.'

'For my own part, I think I do mean it. But I am also sure it is not for me to say. You must decide.'

'I already have.'

'Yes.' Lulu smiled. 'I rather thought as much.'

FOURTEEN

CHARLOTTE SPENT THE NIGHT at an hotel in the Cotswolds. She could have pressed on back to Tunbridge Wells, but then Emerson might have telephoned her and she knew she should speak to Ursula before telling him what she had learned from Lulu. Another advantage was that she could time her arrival at Swans' Meadow to ensure Maurice had left for the office whilst Ursula would still be at home.

As it was, she nearly misjudged matters. When Ursula opened the door, she wore the faintly harassed air of somebody verging on being late for an appointment.

'Charlie! What a surprise!'

'Can we have a brief word, Ursula? I'm sorry to have given you no warning.'

'Of course. But we must talk on the hoof. I'm due at the hairdresser at ten o'clock.' She set off at a clip back into the house, Charlotte following. 'It's not about the letter, is it? Have you had one too? If so, you'd do better to talk to Maurice.' She turned into the downstairs cloakroom and began applying mascara in front of the mirror. 'I'm not sure what he intends to do about it.'

Charlotte did not know how to react. The last thing she had expected was that Ursula would guess the reason for her visit. She saw her own slack-jawed frown of puzzlement, reflected in the mirror over Ursula's shoulder.

'Something wrong?'

'What . . . What was in the letter?'

'Ingratiating twaddle from that brother of Fairfax-Vane. Are you saying you haven't had one? We thought he must have written to you as well. In fact, Maurice tried to phone you last night. Where were you? Out on the town with Emerson? He's a real dish, isn't he?'

'I don't understand. Is this . . . Was this recently?'

Ursula turned round and stared at her. 'What *is* the matter, Charlie? You're not making any sense. Fairfax has written to Maurice apologizing for making an exhibition of himself at the funeral and asking if we can think of any reason why somebody should want to murder Beatrix. Other than his own brother, of course. The letter arrived yesterday. We assumed he'd sent one to you as well.'

'No . . . That is . . . I'm not sure. He may have done. I've not been home since then.'

'*Not home?*'

'I went to see Lulu Harrington in Cheltenham and stayed in the area overnight.'

'Beatrix's friend? What did you want with her?'

Charlotte thought for a moment. Then she said: 'Is there anyone else here?'

'No. Aliki's shopping. And Sam's gone to London for the day. Why?'

'Can we sit down in the lounge? There's something I need to ask you. It's very important.'

'But I'll be late, Charlie.'

'Please. It really is imperative I discuss this with you as soon as possible.'

Ursula glared at her, then sighed, wound her lipstick back into its barrel and dropped it into the make-up bag beside her. 'All right. Let's go through.' She marched impatiently past Charlotte towards the lounge and was already seated, head cocked in expectation, when Charlotte reached the room herself.

She sat down on the edge of the chair opposite Ursula's, composed herself and said: 'Lulu claims to have posted a letter to you on the Tuesday following Beatrix's death – at Beatrix's prior request. Is it true?'

Ursula frowned. 'What does she say was in the letter?'

'She doesn't know. Beatrix left it with her, to be dispatched in the event of her death. It was one of four to which the same conditions applied.'

'Who were the others to?'

79

'Strangers. Nobody she or I know.'

'I see.'

'You haven't said yet whether it's true. Did you receive such a letter?'

'Where did she send it from?'

'Gloucester.'

'On the twenty-third of June?'

'Yes.'

'In a padded envelope?'

'Yes. How did—'

'Then it *is* true, Charlie. I did receive it.'

'But . . . you've never said . . .'

'A word about it? For good reason, I think you'll agree. I didn't know it was sent by Lulu. Or that Beatrix had anything to do with it. I know nobody in Gloucester. The address was typed. And there was nothing inside to identify the sender.'

'What was inside?'

'Six sheets of paper. All blank.'

'Blank?'

'Yes. Bizarre, isn't it? I took it for some weird practical joke. I never imagined – never would have – that Beatrix was behind it. Are you sure about this?'

'Lulu is.'

'Well, I don't know the lady, of course, but couldn't she be misleading you? It's easy to blame the dead. They can't deny anything.'

'What would be the point?'

'I haven't the least idea. Have you?' Ursula smiled in a thin-lipped signal of disbelief.

'I'm certain Lulu's told me the truth.'

'No doubt you are, but you've always been too trusting, haven't you?' The smile tightened, conveying more than mere disbelief. There was now about it the hint of a warning.

'Did you keep the letter?'

'No. Why should I have?'

'Or show it to Maurice?'

'Certainly not. I didn't want to worry him with such nonsense.'

'You think he would have been worried, then?'

'Perhaps.'

'But you weren't?'

'It would take more than an envelope full of blank sheets of paper to unsettle me, as you should know. I put it out of my mind. Frankly, I advise you to do the same.'

'I'm not sure I can.'

'Well, that's your choice, isn't it?' Abruptly, Ursula rose to her feet. 'I really can't dally any longer, Charlie. Would you mind awfully if I threw you out?'

All the way to Tunbridge Wells, Charlotte struggled within herself to find reasons to believe what Ursula had said. But there were none. It was as inconceivable that Lulu had sent the letter at her own initiative as it was that Beatrix had wanted to send blank paper to her nephew's wife after her death. Besides, Ursula had only described the contents of the envelope after establishing that Lulu did not know what they were. If she had intended to lie, Charlotte had given her the perfect opportunity to do so.

But to what purpose? Beatrix's carefully laid plan defied analysis so long as the nature of her posthumous communications remained unknown. A Welshman; a New Yorker; a Parisienne; and Ursula. Surely fifty-year-old letters from Tristram Abberley could not connect them. Yet something did. And blank paper was not it.

FIFTEEN

Dear Miss Ladram,

I have thought long and hard before writing this letter, but I have decided it is the only way to put certain points to you which I strongly feel, on my brother's behalf, need to be addressed. I greatly regret what happened when I called on you two weeks ago and I hope, by writing, to avoid any of the misunderstanding which arose on that occasion.

The first thing to be said is that my brother, though something of a rogue, is not the sort to involve himself in—

Charlotte thrust the letter impatiently back into its envelope. She could spare neither time nor attention for Derek Fairfax's protestations of his brother's innocence. Indeed, had she been certain that the letter was from him when she found it, lying between a credit inducement and a card from her dentist on the doormat at Ockham House, she might not even have bothered to open it. There was more urgent business to be attended to. Far more urgent.

Yet in its commission she immediately encountered an obstacle. When she rang Emerson's London hotel, it was to be informed that he was out. All she could do was to leave a message asking him to call her.

She retreated to the lounge and sat down, feeling suddenly tired, drained by the long drive and her fruitless efforts to untangle Beatrix's intentions. Idly, she reopened Derek Fairfax's letter.

> The first thing to be said is that my brother, though something of a rogue, is not the sort to involve himself in any kind of violence. He may well have paid your mother less for her furniture than it was worth, but he would never be a party to burglary, let alone murder. It is simply not in his nature.
>
> The second thing to be said is that he is not a fool. Yet only a fool would leave his calling card at a house he intended to burgle *and* stress his interest in the object of that burglary in front of witnesses. I just cannot believe he would behave so stupidly.
>
> My brother thinks — and so do I — that he is merely the fall guy for Miss Abberley's murder, that the purpose of the break-in was to kill her, not to steal her collection of Tunbridge Ware. That is why I am writing to you, to appeal for your help in—

Charlotte dropped the letter on to the coffee-table beside her chair and leaned back against the cushions. The house was silent, gripped by the immobility of a windless summer's day. She had not yet opened a single window and, until she did so, no sound could intrude upon her thoughts. Was it possible that Fairfax was right? Was it conceivable that somebody had wanted Beatrix dead for a reason of which the police had no inkling? If so, Beatrix had known the reason. The letters had represented her insurance against murder. They had not protected her. They had not even been intended to. But they had served a significant purpose. That Charlotte could not doubt. A Welshman; a New Yorker; a Parisienne; and Ursula. Beatrix had spoken to each of them from beyond the grave. And it would have been unlike her to speak in vain.

*   *   *

Time passed. Charlotte closed her eyes. And became a child again. She was at Jackdaw Cottage, dressed for the beach. But she could not set off till she had found Beatrix. And though Beatrix was there, calling to her, she could not tell which room she was in. Every room she went to, upstairs and down, seemed the right one as she approached. Then, as she entered, she realized Beatrix's voice was coming from somewhere else. As she searched, she became more anxious, fearful that she would never find her at all. Then there came another sound. It was the ringing of a telephone. She ran into the hall and picked it up. But the line was dead. And the ringing went on.

Suddenly, Charlotte was awake. She jumped up and hurried to reach the telephone before it stopped ringing, struggling to order her thoughts as she went.

The caller was Emerson McKitrick, as she had guessed, eager for news. She apologized for not having been in touch sooner and explained why. In her account of her visit to Lulu, she omitted nothing, but, in relating what Ursula had told her, she studiously avoided any implication of what she had already concluded: that Ursula was lying.

'This beats me,' said Emerson when she had finished. 'I mean, Jesus, *blank paper*? What the hell's the point?'

'I don't know. I was hoping you might.'

'Do you think that's what all the letters contained?'

'Again, I don't know. None of it makes any sense.'

'We should ask the other recipients, I guess.'

'But who are they? Lulu's only absolutely certain of one of their names.'

'You mean Griffith?'

'Yes. But it's a very common surname in Wales. We don't even have an initial.'

'I reckon I can supply that.'

'What?'

'It has to be Frank Griffith, doesn't it? Haven't you heard of him?'

'Frank Griffith?' Now, at last, she remembered. Frank Griffith had fought with Tristram Abberley in Spain. He had sent Tristram's possessions back to Mary after his death. And he had visited Mary after returning to England to describe how Tristram had died. Charlotte had heard her mother describe the visit on several occasions. 'Of course. Tristram Abberley's comrade-in-arms. You must have come across him when you were researching your book.'

'I only wish I had. But I couldn't trace him. He'd cut himself off from the veterans' association completely. The general consensus was that he was dead. But Beatrix seems to have known better. It looks like she was holding out on me.'

'Then we're none the wiser. Dyfed's a big county. And every other settlement must begin with "Llan".'

'We might be able to get round that.'

'How?'

'Can you take me to Rye again tomorrow? There's something at Jackdaw Cottage I need to check out. It may help.'

'Of course. But what is it?'

'I'd sooner say nothing till I'm sure. But, if I'm right, there might be a way to track Mr Frank Griffith to his lair.'

SIXTEEN

IT WAS THURSDAY MORNING and Derek had calculated that this was the first day when he might hope for a reply to one of his letters. Accordingly, he delayed setting off for Fithyan & Co. in case the postman brought some response from either Maurice Abberley or Charlotte Ladram.

As he waited, the thought crossed his mind that they might simply ignore his appeals altogether. What would he do then? The prospect of another unsolicited visit to Ockham House appalled him, yet, without the help of those who had known Beatrix Abberley, he could gain no glimmer of an insight into why she had been murdered. Without that, Colin's cause was lost. And Derek, though not threatened with imprisonment, stood to lose something only slightly less important than his liberty. For he believed Colin was innocent. And Colin was relying on him to prove it. If he failed to do so, no excuses would suffice. If he could not save his brother, he could not save his self-respect either.

At that moment, the rattle of the letter-box announced the arrival of the post. He hurried into the hall to find nothing but a flimsy card lying on the mat. He grabbed it up and read:

Dear Mr Fairfax
The book you ordered – *Tristram Abberley: A Critical Biography* – is now to hand and awaiting your collection. Please bring this—

Derek screwed the card into a tight ball in his hand and let it fall to the floor. Another day was bound to pass now with nothing achieved. Another day would be wasted when every moment was crucial.

Emerson McKitrick refused to tell Charlotte what he hoped to find at Jackdaw Cottage until they arrived there later that morning. Then he led the way to the bureau in the drawing room.

'Beatrix kept some maps here, Charlie, remember?'

'Yes. What of it?'

'Here they are.' He slid four Ordnance Survey maps out of one of the pigeon-holes. 'It struck me as weird when I first saw them. But it didn't seem important till you told me about Frank Griffith. See?' He laid them out across the flap of the bureau.

'I don't understand,' said Charlotte, staring down at their unremarkable pink covers.

'Three of them are local, right? Sheet 189 covers Rye, Sheet 188 Tunbridge Wells, Sheet 199 Eastbourne and Hastings. But look at the fourth. Sheet 160 is the odd one out.'

'The Brecon Beacons,' said Charlotte, reading the title.

'You got it. Central Wales. Why should Beatrix want a map of that area?'

'Because it's where Griffith lives?'

'That's what I reckon.' He unfolded Sheet 160 and spread it out on the floor. Crouching over it, Charlotte saw no obvious clues, merely the bunched contours and green polygons of an afforested upland landscape. But Emerson saw rather more. 'This is the Dyfed boundary, look.' He traced a line of dots and dashes across the left-hand side of the map. 'We can ignore everything east of that.'

'Even so—'

'I reckon Beatrix went to see Frank Griffith during her fortnights with Lulu. Cheltenham's a handy staging post on a journey from Rye to Dyfed, wouldn't you say?'

'Yes. I suppose it is.'

'OK. And we know she travelled by train. So, where's the railroad?'

'There.' Charlotte pointed to a firm black line snaking across the north-west corner. She was excited now, sure that Emerson was right. 'And the biggest settlement served by the railway is—'

'Llandovery.' Emerson grinned at her. 'I think we've found him, don't you?'

SEVENTEEN

THE FOLLOWING MORNING FOUND Charlotte driving fast along the main road that skirts the northern fringes of the Brecon Beacons, with Emerson McKitrick navigating in the passenger seat beside her. They had arrived in Wales the previous evening and had stayed overnight at a country house hotel north-east of Brecon. Emerson, it appeared, was used to the best and had insisted that his newly recruited assistant should travel in style. Charlotte, for her part, had not cared to analyse too closely the exhilaration she felt. Was it the thrill of the chase or the glamour of the company? To be entertained to dinner in a candlelit restaurant by a handsome American was for her a novel and intoxicating experience. To assume the role of equal partner in his endeavours — however briefly — raised in her mind more alluring possibilities than she felt able to cope with.

Emerson was the perfect gentleman, as charming as he was considerate. Entranced by his gallantry, Charlotte was also confused by it. Was he merely humouring her? Or was he, perhaps, growing to like her as much as she was growing to like him? He was such an altogether grander type of man than those with whom she had previously been entangled. Not that there was any question of entanglement where she and Emerson were concerned. To let her frail hopes and fragile emotions run away with themselves would be, she knew, the sheerest folly.

And yet, when she had been dressing for dinner, and had glanced from the window of her room and seen him, strolling in the hotel garden, champagne-glass in hand, she had allowed herself to imagine for a few heady moments what it would be like if they were there for no reason but the pleasure each could give to the other. And what she had imagined she blushed now to recall.

Llandovery was a grey huddle of a town occupying a wedge of flat land where three rivers met beneath rolling mountain slopes. The beauty of its setting was in stark contrast to the grim reality of its three principal streets, where none of the passers-by seemed willing to reciprocate Charlotte's smile.

Emerson, however, was undaunted. In every shop they came to, he enquired after Frank Griffith and seemed able to extract more helpful responses than Charlotte had expected. There were, it transpired, several Griffiths known to the proprietors, but none of those in their seventies was called Frank.

As noon approached, they decided to try the pubs. Of these there were far more than the size of Llandovery appeared to justify and most of them were as cheerless and unwelcoming as Charlotte had feared. They had treated the landlords of half a dozen similar establishments to various tipples – and learned precisely nothing – when they entered the inaptly named Daffodil Inn, bracing themselves to consume yet more mineral water they did not want. But this time their efforts were not to be wasted.

'Frank Griffith?' said the man behind the bar. 'Oh, yes, I know him. Seventy if he's a day, I should reckon. He comes in here most market days. Farms a few sheep, see, up at Hendre Gorfelen, beyond Myddfai. If you've a map, I can point it out for you. What would you be wanting with him, might I ask?'

'We're distantly related,' said Emerson. 'I thought I'd track him down while I was in the country.'

'Well, well. That will be a surprise for him, won't it? Perhaps it'll put a smile on his face. He seldom enough wears one.'

After a frugal lunch, they drove up into the foothills of the Brecon Beacons. The day was overcast and clammy, the air still and watchful. Through the twisting switchback terrain they slowly wound, like two predatory creatures – Charlotte suddenly and irrationally thought – running their quarry to earth.

Halfway between Myddfai and Talsarn, they turned down a rutted track that looped round the side of a hill, marking the boundary between enclosed pasture and open moorland. The track descended briefly to cross a gurgling stream, then rose again, rounded another

87

hill and ran down through an open gateway to its destination.

Hendre Gorfelen comprised a small slate-roofed farmhouse of whitewashed stone, two barns and several ruinous byres. An old and rusting Land Rover stood in the corner of the yard and beside it a trailer. Some chickens were pecking listlessly at a scatter of straw in the mouth of one of the barns but, otherwise, there were no signs of life.

Emerson climbed out of the car and walked towards the house. Charlotte followed more cautiously, the secluded atmosphere reinforcing her earlier supposition that somebody as old and reclusive as Frank Griffith would not welcome visitors. Emerson, however, did not seem to share her misgivings. He rapped on the door with the heavy knocker, then, when there was no immediate response, stepped across to peer in through one of the windows.

'Out – or lying low,' he announced as Charlotte drew near.

'Well, he *is* a farmer. He could be anywhere on the hills.'

'What do we do, then? Wait for him to come back? That might not be till sundown.'

'We could drive around, I suppose, in the hope of spotting him.'

Emerson sniffed unenthusiastically and walked to the end of the building, where a crooked wicket-gate gave on to a small and overgrown garden. He glanced around for a moment, then shrugged his shoulders, stalked back to the door and tried the knocker again.

'I don't think he's in there, Emerson.'

'Reckon not. But you can never—' His hand had strayed to the knob and, as he turned it, the door swung open on its hinges. 'Well, well, well.' He grinned at her. 'Open sesame.'

'It's not so surprising. In these parts, they probably don't need locks and bolts.'

'Everybody needs locks and bolts, Charlie. But I'm not complaining if friend Griffith thinks he's an exception. Why don't we take a look inside?'

'What if he comes back and finds us? We don't want to antagonize him.'

'He won't be back for hours. Probably pulling a lamb out of a gully somewhere. Come on.' He led the way, stooping to clear the low lintel, and Charlotte followed.

Ahead of them, a short flagstoned passage ended in a narrow flight of stairs. There was a door on either side of the passage, the one on their right closed, the one on their left standing open. Stepping through the open doorway, they found themselves in a small and sparsely furnished dining room. A large stout-legged table filled most of the space, bestriding a threadbare rug. There were two chairs drawn up beneath the table and a settle in one corner. The walls were bare and the window uncurtained. For all that it was a hot day, it seemed cold to Charlotte and she felt a shudder run through her.

'Homely, right?' said Emerson.

'I can't imagine Beatrix staying here. It's so austere.'

Emerson opened the door on the other side of the room. It led to a kitchen, where a range, a sink, assorted cupboards and a view of the garden contrived to lighten the atmosphere. Everything was certainly clean enough, Charlotte noted. There were no frying-pans full of congealed fat, no breadboards deep in crumbs. Frank Griffith was evidently neither a sloven nor a sybarite.

They returned to the passage and Emerson pushed open the other door. Charlotte followed him into the room expecting more of the stark and barren same. What she found instead was so different that she stepped back in surprise.

The room was warm and welcoming, two of its walls lined to the ceiling with crammed bookshelves. The window was curtained and the floor decently carpeted. A thick rug occupied the hearth, flanked by comfortable armchairs. Logs and kindling stood ready and inviting in the fireplace. Above them, on the mantelpiece, was a mellow-toned clock and, beside it, a vase filled with freshly cut marigolds. In one corner stood a broad old desk and, behind it, a chair with buttoned-leather seat and back.

As Charlotte moved towards the desk, her eye was taken by a wooden stationery box positioned at one end. It was Tunbridge Ware, a fine example too, decorated with a butterfly on the lid. Was it one of Nye's? she wondered. Whoever the craftsman, she could not doubt who had given it to Frank Griffith.

'This could only have come from Beatrix,' she said to Emerson.

'It's as we suspected, then.' He was standing by one of the floor-to-ceiling bookcases, running his eye along the titles. 'He's a well-read sheep-farmer, isn't he? But not an agricultural work to be found.'

'What, then?'

'History and politics by the look of it. Biased to the left, as you'd expect of an old Brigader. Hill. Hobsbawm. Orwell. Carr. Symons on the General Strike. Thomas on the Spanish Civil War. And – Jesus! – my own book. *Tristram Abberley: A Critical Biography*. Well,

I reckon that's some kind of compliment, don't you? I wonder—'

He stopped in the same instant that Charlotte heard a low growl from the doorway. They turned to find a black-and-white sheep-dog eyeing them menacingly, crouched as if ready to attack, its teeth bared. And behind the dog stood Frank Griffith.

Charlotte knew it was him immediately. He was the right age and had just the warily alert expression she had somehow expected. He was short and narrow-shouldered, wearing shabby tweeds and a Connaught hat. In his right hand he held a stick, raised at a threatening angle. His grip on the shaft was tight, his hands disproportionately large. For all his slightness of build, he conveyed an impression of sinewy strength, of trained and tempered physical resources. His face was thin and prominently boned, the skin browned by wind and sun and wrinkled like a rhino's. His lips were compressed, his deep-set eyes trained unblinkingly upon them.

'Mr Griffith?' Charlotte said nervously. 'My name is Charlotte Ladram. You may have heard of me . . . from Beatrix.'

He did not so much as nod in acknowledgement, but he muttered something to the dog, at which it stopped growling and fell back on its haunches.

'This is Doctor Emerson McKitrick, the writer. You know his work, I believe.'

Emerson grinned. 'Sorry to barge in like this. The door was open.'

'But that's no excuse,' said Charlotte. 'We really are extremely sorry, Mr Griffith. It was unforgivably rude of us. But we were anxious to contact you . . . to find out where you were.'

'I tried to track you down twelve years ago,' said Emerson. 'All your old comrades said you must be dead. Glad they were wrong.'

'We need your help, Mr Griffith. Beatrix was a friend of yours, wasn't she? She was my godmother. Perhaps you know that.' A disturbing thought flashed across her mind. 'I suppose . . . you do realize . . . Beatrix is . . .'

'Dead.' Griffith had spoken for the first time, but his expression had not altered. 'I know.'

'You admit you were friends, then?' said Emerson.

'*Admit?*' Griffith raised one eyebrow just enough to signal his disgust at the choice of word.

'Pardon me,' said Emerson. 'Why don't we come clean? We know Beatrix came here at least once a year, using visits to Lulu

Harrington as cover. And we know she left a letter with Lulu this year, to be mailed to you in the event of her death. All we're trying to find out is what was in the letter.'

Griffith stepped past the dog and walked across to join them by the bookcase. Emerson was still clutching the copy of his biography of Tristram Abberley. Griffith lifted it gently from his grasp and slid it back into its place. 'Researching for another book, are we?' he murmured.

'Maybe. I know Beatrix kept some letters Tristram had sent her from Spain, which she wouldn't show me twelve years ago. Now they're missing.'

'Are they?'

'Did she have Lulu send them to you, Frank?'

'My friends call me Frank, Doctor McKitrick. Most of them are dead. And you were never one of them.'

'There's something I should explain, Mr Griffith,' said Charlotte, trying to strike a conciliatory note. 'Beatrix bequeathed all her possessions to me. You could argue that anything she left behind is rightfully mine.'

'Could you, indeed?'

'But there's more to it than that. Beatrix was murdered and she seems to have known she was going to be. Surely you can understand my wish to find out what lies behind her death. I owe it to her to do everything in my power to learn the truth. As her friend, won't you help me?'

He stared at her for a moment, then replied. 'I've always acted according to my conscience, Miss Ladram. I'm not going to stop now.'

'Then . . . will you help?'

'I'll do what I think best. That doesn't include satisfying your curiosity.' He nodded at Emerson. 'Or your friend's.'

'See here—'

'I've a question for you, Doctor McKitrick.' Griffith tapped Emerson on the chest with his stick. 'What makes you think Tristram Abberley wrote to his sister from Spain?'

'She told me so.'

'Is that a fact? Did she tell you as well, Miss Ladram?'

'Well . . . No.'

Griffith glanced from one to the other of them. Then he grunted, as if some point had been confirmed to his satisfaction. 'I read about

Beatrix's murder in the papers. They said an antique dealer had been arrested and charged. Seemed certain he was guilty. You agree, Doctor McKitrick?'

'Open and shut, far as I know.'

'And you, Miss Ladram?'

'I'm not sure. Fairfax-Vane may be a scapegoat.'

'Who for?'

'I don't know. It's one of the reasons why I wanted to speak to you.' Previously, Charlotte would have said no such thing. Now, confronted by just one of the secret figures in Beatrix's life, she realized it was true: the explanations she had hitherto accepted were no longer sufficient. 'How long have you lived here, Mr Griffith?'

'What's that to you?'

'It's just I wondered if . . . You do own this farm, don't you?'

'I'm nobody's tenant, if that's what you mean.'

She decided to back her judgement. 'Did Beatrix help you buy the place?'

His eyes widened slightly, but he displayed no other reaction. He looked at Emerson, then back at Charlotte. 'A scapegoat, you reckon?'

'It's possible.'

'Many things are.' He turned, walked to the window and gazed out into the yard. 'Many things.' He seemed lost in thought, hunched slightly beneath the burden of whatever he was hiding. Then, without turning round, he added: 'I need to think about what you've said. I need time, you understand?'

'Of course. We're staying locally. There's no hurry.'

'Write down the 'phone number for me.'

Emerson exchanged glances with Charlotte, then took his notebook from his pocket, tore out a page and handed it to her. She picked up a pencil from the desk and recorded the number. 'I'll leave it here, shall I?' she asked.

'Do that. Then go. Both of you.'

'How do we know you'll call?' put in Emerson.

'You don't.' Still he did not turn to face them. 'I may not. It's up to me, not you.'

'But we can't just—' Charlotte's raised hand and shake of the head silenced him. Bluff and bluster would not help their cause. Of that she was certain.

'All right, Mr Griffith,' she said. 'We're going. Think about what I said.' She hesitated, in case he was moved to respond. Then, when it had become obvious he would not, she led Emerson from the room and out into the yard. When they reached the car and she glanced back at the window, Frank Griffith was nowhere to be seen.

EIGHTEEN

OVER DINNER THAT EVENING, Charlotte and Emerson discussed their visit to Frank Griffith and wondered if they would hear from him. Whether or not he made contact, Emerson agreed that Charlotte's had been the correct tactics.

'I reckon he may trust you, Charlie, whereas reading my book doesn't seem to have given him a very high opinion of me. Perhaps he thinks I got Tristram Abberley all wrong and, who knows, maybe I did. His last months in Spain, anyway. But then, if I did, Frank Griffith could put me right, couldn't he? *If* he wanted to. Beatrix knew where he was, but she didn't tell me. He must have wanted to stay hidden even then. Why? Why so badly? That's what I can't understand.'

'So he could forget about Spain — and what he did there?'

'But he hasn't. That's the point. He hasn't forgotten a damn thing. All those books. All those memories locked up in his head. Everything's there — if only I could prise it loose.'

'You think he knows something valuable about Tristram?'

'Maybe. He was there — beside his bed in the hospital at Tarragona — when he died. And he was the one Tristram trusted to send back his last poems to your mother. Nobody else was so close to him at or near the end.'

'But that doesn't explain why Beatrix should help him buy Hendre Gorfelen — as I'm sure she did — or visit him there every year.'

'No. It doesn't. But the letter Lulu mailed to him might. And he might be willing to tell you what it contained. What you said about discovering the truth behind Beatrix's death got to him, I'm sure of it. It was a clever ploy.'

'It wasn't just a ploy.'

'But this guy Fairfax was caught red-handed according to Maurice.'

'So he was.'

'Then where's the room for doubt?'

'I don't know. Perhaps there isn't any. Let's wait and see what Frank Griffith has to say.'

'If anything, you mean.'

'Yes. *If.*'

Charlotte fell asleep that night rehearsing in her head all the ifs and buts and maybes Beatrix's death had led her into. If Fairfax-Vane was innocent, as his brother claimed . . . But how could he be . . . ? Maybe, just maybe, he was telling the truth . . . If he was, Beatrix had been murdered for an altogether different reason than they thought . . . But what reason . . . ? Maybe, just maybe, Frank Griffith knew the answer . . .

Early the following afternoon, Derek Fairfax faced his brother across a bare table in the grim and echoing visiting room at Lewes Prison. Colin was nearing the end of his fourth week in custody and had visibly deteriorated since Derek had last seen him. There were dark bags under his eyes and his face had lost its normal high colour and acquired instead a grey and clammy pallor. More worrying still was the faint but detectable tremor in his hand as he rubbed at his unshaven chin.

'You don't look well, Colin.'

'I might perk up if you brought me some good news.'

'I only wish I could. But so far my letters have been ignored.'

Colin snorted. 'Bloody letters! Of course they've been ignored.'

'Well, if you've a better idea . . .'

'Maybe I have. Give it up, Derek. I'll be committed for trial next week. Just let it happen. Wash your hands of the whole thing.'

'You can't mean that.'

'Unless you already have. Is that it?' Colin's tone had altered now, self-pity giving way to sarcasm. 'Perhaps you're just stringing me along. Telling me you're straining every sinew on my behalf when in reality you're sitting back and rubbing your hands with glee at the thought of being rid of me for good and all. Well, don't worry. You'll get your wish. Ten or more years in this or some other hell-hole will be the finish of me, no question.'

'Colin, for God's—'

'Why not come out and say it? You don't much care whether I'm guilty or innocent. Either way, you think I deserve what I've got coming. Just like everybody else.'

Derek knew hardship and frustration were what had driven Colin to throw such accusations in his face. But the knowledge did not make them any easier to bear. 'This is ridiculous,' he protested. 'I'm doing everything I can to help you.'

'Is that a fact? Well, you could have fooled me.' Colin leaned forward across the table, fixing Derek with his bloodshot eyes. 'Or perhaps it's just that help from you is indistinguishable from hindrance.'

Derek flinched. 'Is that what you really think?'

'Yes. It really is.'

In Wales, Charlotte's day passed listlessly, with no word from Frank Griffith. By the evening, she and Emerson had agreed they could leave matters in his hands no longer. They would return to Hendre Gorfelen next day, invited or not. Emerson's argument was that, if Griffith intended to co-operate, they would already have heard from him. If not, they had nothing to lose.

Charlotte was less certain. Griffith was not a man to be rushed or crowded. He had laid down the terms on which he might be approached. To disregard them was to court failure. Yet they could not wait indefinitely. Somehow, at some time, the issue had to be forced.

And so it was, but not by them. When Charlotte returned to her room after dinner, the telephone rang before she had even closed the door.

'Hello?'

'Miss Ladram?'

'Mr Griffith. I thought you'd never call.'

'So did I. But we were both wrong, weren't we? Are you alone?'

'Yes.'

'Can you be here at seven o'clock tomorrow morning?'

'*Seven o'clock?*'

'Too early for you, is it?'

'No. Not at all. We'll be there, Mr Griffith, rest assured.'

'You misunderstand. I mean just you, Miss Ladram. Not Doctor McKitrick. I'll talk to you alone – or not at all.'

'But—'

'I'm not open to argument. Take it or leave it.' He paused, then added: 'Should I expect you?'

Charlotte hesitated only momentarily before answering. 'Yes, Mr Griffith. You should.'

NINETEEN

DRIVING ALONE THROUGH THE green and empty heart of Wales
early that summer Sunday, Charlotte felt as if the world had been
newly made and revealed to her. The colours of sky and grass were
clarified, the sounds of birdlife and running water magnified, till
nothing beyond the hills where Frank Griffith had found and made
his home seemed real any longer.

At Hendre Gorfelen, the dog sat waiting in the yard, snapping at
stray flies that floated in the sunshine. It pricked up its ears when
Charlotte drove into sight and barked twice, but did not stir even
when she climbed from the car and walked towards the house.

The door opened before she reached it and Frank Griffith stepped
out to meet her. He was bare-headed, his grey hair thin and crew-cut,
and he was smoking a pipe, holding it oddly by the stem a little short
of the bowl. His shirt and trousers were ironed and pressed, as if in
honour of her visit, and she felt quite touched by the smartness of
his appearance. But he was not smiling. Indeed, looking at him, she
could scarcely imagine a smile crossing his lined and wary face.

'You came, then,' he said neutrally.

'Surely you knew I would.'

He nodded. 'And McKitrick?'

'I'm alone, as you can see.'

'Good.'

'Why didn't you want me to bring Emerson?'

'Because I don't trust him.'

'But you do trust me?'

'Yes.'

'Why?'

'Because Beatrix said I could. Quite a compliment, isn't it?'

'Yes . . . I . . .'

'How did you know she helped me buy Hendre Gorfelen?'

'It was just a guess. She helped Lulu Harrington in a similar
way.'

'And others too, no doubt. She was a fine woman. And a foul-
weather friend: the best kind.'

'She came here every year?'

'Yes. Every year since I bought the place. Since *we* bought it, I should say. That was in 1953. How she explained her trips before the arrangement with Lulu I don't know.' He glanced up at the sky, then said: 'It's going to be a grand day. Will you step up to the top with me? You'll enjoy the view, I think.'

Instructing the dog to stay where it was, he led Charlotte up a narrow path adjoining the entrance to the yard. It wound up between stone walls to a stile in the corner of a steeply sloping field, where sheep were busily grazing. Griffith set off across the field at an angle, setting a pace Charlotte found difficult to match. 'Did you . . . farm before you . . . came here, Mr Griffith?' she panted.

'No. I'm a Swansea boy, born and bred. The first time I came to the mountains was on a steelworks outing. I knew then it was where I wanted to end up. Never thought I would, though. Never would have, come to that, but for Beatrix. It was a better cure for what ailed me than a dozen doctors had prescribed.'

'And what . . . did ail you?'

'People. People and what they do to each other.'

'Is that why . . . you didn't want anybody . . . to know you were here?'

'In part. Beatrix understood. I don't expect you to.'

'How did you . . . first meet her?'

They arrived at another stile on the farther side of the field. Here Griffith stopped and waited for Charlotte to catch her breath. The land fell away sharply behind them, a tumbling succession of stone-walled fields dotted with sheep and interspersed with thickly wooded coombes, all bathed in sharp morning sunlight. The mountainous horizon to the west created the illusion that this landscape was limitless, that nothing save ever-rolling hills lay between it and infinity. Griffith re-lit his pipe and gazed about him, Charlotte's question apparently forgotten.

'It's a lovely spot,' she ventured.

'It is that.'

'I was asking . . . wondering, that is . . .'

'When I came home from Spain in December 1938, I called on your mother to tell her how her husband had died. I'd written to her previously, enclosing his few papers and possessions, but it seemed only right to pay my respects in person. I'd admired Tristram Abberley long before I met him, on account of his poems. A copy of

97

The Brow of the Hill was one of the few items of luggage I took to Spain. To find myself fighting alongside him was a great honour. So, naturally, I did what I could for him after his death. I visited your mother. And then I visited Beatrix. She insisted I stay with her at that little cottage in Rye for a week or more while she fed me up and listened to me talking about her brother. God knows what the neighbours thought.' He paused, then added: 'Not that there *was* anything for them to think.'

Was that true? Charlotte wondered. Had she stumbled on an old and secret love affair? Beatrix had always seemed immune to such emotions, but she had also been adept at concealing what she really thought or felt. 'You don't have to explain yourself to me, Mr Griffith.'

'No? I rather thought I did.' He sucked at his pipe for a moment, then said: 'Well, let that pass. When I left Rye just before Christmas, 1938, I never expected to see Beatrix again. She urged me to keep in touch – to let her know if I ever needed any help – but I no more took her offer seriously than I envisaged having to take her up on it. I intended to go back to Swansea, find work and forget everything about Spain.'

'Was fighting there such a disillusioning experience?'

'Fighting anywhere's a disillusioning experience. But that's no bad thing. The illusion is to believe it can be enough merely to fight. I see that now. Now I'm too old for it to matter. I went to Spain because I was as short of money as I was of patience with a rotten, raddled system. Marked down because I was self-educated, well-read and not about to say "thank you very much" when a cigar-sucking manager told me I had to take a pay cut in the interests of the company's shareholders. Betrayed by so-called socialists like Ramsay MacDonald. Punished for the ultimate sin of not knowing my place. To men like me, communism represented the best – the only – hope for the future. A stand had to be taken. Against capitalism. Against fascism. Against the entire class system. That's why I went to Spain. And that's why I was sickened by what I found there. Because it was no more a crusade than any other war. Because settling old scores and winning internecine squabbles mattered more to the Republican rag-bag of an army than ensuring the defeat of fascism. Which is why, of course, it wasn't defeated. And why my faith in my fellow man finally was. They gave us a farewell parade in Barcelona. And, when we reached Victoria station, they cheered us to the rafters.

But they were nowhere to be seen when I returned to Swansea. Cold shoulders and dark looks were the only welcome I had there – from family and from friends. I was an embarrassment to one and all. I'd not only been stupid enough to go to Spain. I'd been inconsiderate enough to come back alive.'

'What did you do?'

'Survived as best I could. Served in the Army during the Second World War. Did my little bit to kill off fascism, in Germany and Italy if not in Spain. Afterwards, I drifted. I must have had a dozen different jobs in a dozen different towns before . . .' He tapped his forehead. 'Before something snapped here and I fetched up in a mental hospital, trying to glue it back together again. I mentioned Beatrix's offer to one of the doctors, apparently. I can't remember doing it. But he wrote to her on my behalf and she responded. She became a regular visitor. And eventually she became a friend. The farm was her idea for when I was well enough to leave hospital. And it was a good one. Out here, I don't have to listen to lies or breathe polluted air or swallow my principles. Sheep don't pretend to be clever, you see. They're just grateful for the life they lead for as long as they lead it. And so am I.'

'Was it you or Beatrix who wanted to keep your friendship a secret?'

'It was both of us. Beatrix because she didn't want her family to think her gullible or sentimental. And I because I didn't want people like Emerson McKitrick beating a path to my door looking for tit-bits of knowledge about Tristram Abberley's last days.'

'What did Beatrix do here?' Charlotte hesitated as the impudence of the question dawned on her. 'I'm sorry. I didn't mean to—'

'She tramped the hills. She cooked meals for me. We reminisced. We laughed. We quarrelled. We spent time together.'

'Every June – for more than thirty years?'

'Yes.'

'And was this year different in any way?'

Griffith's gaze narrowed. 'In retrospect I see it was. She was distracted, often to the point of irritability. I blamed old age, which only irritated her the more.' The ghost of a smile crossed his lips. 'She said nothing about fearing for her life. If she had— Well, let's just say I had no inkling of any such thing.'

'How did you hear of her death?'

'By her own hand. The letter Lulu sent me made it clear its despatch meant she had died suddenly and unnaturally – as I subsequently confirmed.'

Charlotte could hear her own heart beating rapidly as she asked: 'What was in the letter?'

'A note from Beatrix and a sealed package. The note told me what I've just told you – and asked me to burn the package without opening it. She said it contained letters from Tristram—'

'From Tristram? Then Emerson's right. She did keep them.'

'Presumably.'

'*Presumably?* Surely you didn't—'

'Burn it?' He looked directly at her. 'What else do you think I did? It was Beatrix's last request. I owe her the peace I enjoy here. How could—' He turned away and his voice faltered. 'How could I not do as I was asked?'

Charlotte stared at him for a moment, then up into the sky above their heads, where a bird of prey was circling slowly in the void. Had Beatrix stood here a few short weeks ago, she wondered, and planned all this? A paper-chase in which the prize could never be found. Blank pages for Ursula. An unopened package for Frank Griffith to burn. And who knew what else besides? 'Were you aware she left three other letters with Lulu?'

'I was not.'

'One to Ursula, Maurice's wife.'

'I know who she is.'

'Well, would you like to know what her letter contained?'

'No.'

'Not even to satisfy your curiosity?'

'I'm not curious.' He looked back at her. 'I know and understand as much as Beatrix wanted me to. That's enough.'

'But why should she want you to destroy her brother's letters?'

'If I could tell you why, there'd have been no point to her request, would there? Can't you simply accept that she had the right to decide how they should be disposed of?'

Faced with such a direct challenge to her inquisitiveness, Charlotte fell silent. Beatrix's wishes deserved to be respected. There was no disputing that. Yet they were so inextricably bound up with the mystery of her death that to obey them blindly was also to conspire at a suppression of the truth. Just as to defy them was to be disloyal to her memory. Neither choice was beneath contempt and neither wholly honourable.

'Have you had any breakfast, young lady?' asked Griffith with disarming gentleness.

'What . . . ? Well, no, I . . .'

'Come down to the house and I'll cook you some. You look as if you need it.'

TWENTY

THE AROMA OF BACON, mushrooms and tomatoes sizzling in a pan reminded Charlotte of breakfasts she had had in her childhood, mopping up the molten fat on her plate with a soldier of bread whilst her father grinned and winked at her across the kitchen table. '*Be good, squirt,*' he would say, rising hurriedly to go after a glance at the clock. A lock of his hair would always flop on to her forehead as he stooped to kiss her and he would invariably add in an artificial growl: '*See you later . . .*'

'Alligator,' she murmured, more than twenty years on from the last time she had finished his sentence.

'What was that?' Frank Griffith frowned across at her from the range, spatula in hand.

'Nothing.' She shook her head, as if to dislodge what she had remembered. 'Nothing at all. I'm sorry.'

'No need to apologize to me. I talk to myself all day long. It's a hazard of living alone.' He began distributing the contents of the frying-pan on to plates. 'You have lived alone, haven't you, since your mother died?'

'Yes. How did—' She broke off, then added: 'Beatrix would have told you, of course.' Breakfast was placed before her. Griffith sat down with his own on the other side of the table. 'Thank you. It's rather strange, I must say, to meet somebody for the very first time and to find they've known all about you for years.'

'Beatrix didn't tell me *that* much.'

'Just enough?' She smiled, but he did not respond. They ate in silence for a moment, then she said: 'And you're quite certain you don't know who the other two recipients of Beatrix's letters are?'

'Beatrix never mentioned a Miss van Ryan in New York or a Madame V in Paris.'

'Do you think they might also have known Tristram?'

'Old girlfriends, you mean? Or mistresses?'

'Perhaps. You spent several months with Tristram in Spain. He might have said something . . . let a similar name slip one day . . .'

'He might have. But he didn't.'

'How well would you say you knew him?' There was no reply and the pointed way in which Griffith went on eating made it clear there was not about to be. 'I'm sorry,' she said. 'Am I asking too much?'

He glanced up at her. 'That's not the issue, is it?'

'Then . . . What is?'

He pushed his plate aside and poured some tea into their mugs. Then he lit his pipe – a lengthy process in itself – and leaned back in his chair, still apparently considering Charlotte's question. 'I knew Tristram Abberley as a comrade-in-arms,' he began between puffs of smoke. 'And I thought I understood him as a poet. When he first joined our company of the British Battalion, in the summer of 1937, I was suspicious of him. I was afraid, I suppose, that my literary idol would turn out to have feet of clay. And I was afraid the principles he stood for would bring us into conflict, because by then I was sick of the whole damned business and just wanted to be free of it, whereas he was newly arrived, with every illusion about the struggle for liberty and democracy intact.'

'Why did you stay? Surely, as a volunteer—'

'You could volunteer *in* but not *out*. Our passports were confiscated – if you had one, that is. I'd left England in November 1936 on a weekend excursion ticket and if I'd tried to go back without permission I'd have been arrested by the Republican authorities as a deserter and probably shot. Requests for home leave were always denied, of course. They knew you'd never come back. Not once you'd seen through the lie you were fighting for – the lie that there was actually a Spanish Republic to defend. There wasn't. The Republic was a sack full of snakes, each one more concerned with biting the other occupants than uniting against Fascism. The Basques and the Catalans struggling to break free. The Anarchists and the Communists vying for supremacy. And the Russians clutching the strings that held the sack shut, doling out arms and ammunition according to ideological prejudice rather than military logic, manipulating and deciding everything on instructions from Moscow.'

'Did Tristram see it that way too?'

'Eventually. But he didn't let it drag him down. In a strange kind of way, he didn't seem to care. I think it was enough for him that one small band of men should fight honourably together for what they believe in, even if their beliefs have long since been betrayed. The attack on Saragossa in October 'thirty-seven, Tristram's first action, was a typical cock-up. Russian tanks were used to break through the enemy lines, with our company among the infantry following. But the tanks went too far too fast and were cut off, leaving us stranded in no man's land, exposed to machine-gun fire. Three of us found a poor kind of cover in a ditch. Me, Tristram and a Spaniard called Vicente Ortiz. Most of the battalion's reinforcements were Spaniards by then and Vicente was a case in point. We had to lie there till nightfall before we could even try to get back to our lines, with bullets whining overhead and screams of agony floating across from wounded men nearby. We could do nothing for them, of course. We could do little for ourselves. Except keep our courage up. And I don't think we'd even have managed that without Tristram. He sustained us with jokes and stories of what we'd do in Madrid the first night of victory. And then he led us back to safety under cover of darkness. But for him, I'm not sure Vicente and I would have made it. We agreed afterwards that he'd probably saved our lives.'

'Were you with him when he was wounded?'

'Yes, though I didn't see it happen. That was at Teruel. The worst . . .' His voice took on a distant tone. 'The worst of all.' Then he seemed to regain his concentration. 'Teruel must be the coldest and grimmest city in Spain. To launch an offensive against it in mid-December was plain lunacy. But it's what we did. And all for no strategic advantage I could understand. Later, I found out the whole battle – and every life lost in it – was just to persuade the Republican government's paymasters in Moscow that the army they were funding and equipping could still fight. Well, we certainly fought. And died.'

He seemed to slip into a reverie, puffing at his pipe and staring into the middle distance. 'What happened?' Charlotte prompted him.

'What happened?' He looked up sharply, then relaxed. 'Our battalion wasn't called in until the Republican forces who'd taken the town found themselves besieged and in danger of being cut off – as we'd all predicted they would be. We had to dig trenches under three feet of snow. I still dream sometimes of feeling as cold as I felt that winter on the heights above Teruel. Still, cold or not, we held the line, at least for a while. There was a lot of grumbling in the ranks. A good deal of dissent. Even reports of mutineers being shot. Spirits were low. Except Tristram's. He blazed with some inner light of certainty and confidence. But it didn't protect him when it mattered. He was hit by rifle-fire during an operation to recapture some hills from which the Nationalists were threatening to cut off the Canadian Battalion. It was a nasty leg-wound, but I never thought for a moment he wouldn't pull through. In fact, I envied him for being evacuated. Told him so to his face. The next time I saw him, in the hospital at Tarragona, he was dying of some infection he'd picked up there. I regretted my words then, I can tell you.'

'How did you get back to Tarragona?'

'By the skin of my teeth. And the self-sacrifice of another.'

'Who?'

'Vicente Ortiz. He was a cross-patch little anarchist from Barcelona who you'd curse for his pessimism one day and praise for his determination the next. Our battalion abandoned Teruel in late February and withdrew to the Aragon hills. We were still licking our wounds when Franco launched a new offensive early in March. The effect was devastating. The Nationalists pushed back the entire front as easily and quickly as if they were rolling up a rug. It turned into a headlong retreat. We were too weary and short of ammunition to fight, too afraid of summary execution to surrender. It was just a mad scramble to escape, in which you could easily fall behind and find yourself overtaken by the enemy advance. That's what happened to Vicente and me. We were resting in a ruined barn in the hills, waiting for darkness, when a Nationalist patrol stopped nearby. Vicente could hear them debating whether or not to search the barn. It was odds on they would, which we knew would be the finish of us, because the Nationalist commander on that part of the front, Colonel Delgado, was notorious for having prisoners shot.'

'How did you escape?'

'Vicente suggested that if one of us went out to meet them and surrendered, he could make them think he was alone. Then they might not bother to search the barn. Since I didn't speak more than a few words of Spanish, only Vicente stood any chance of pulling if off. He realized it had to be him – and so did I – the moment he came up with the idea.'

'And he went?'

'Yes. He went. I wish I could tell you I tried to stop him, but I didn't. I bit my tongue and let him go because I knew it really was the only chance we had and because I was glad – yes, truly glad – I wasn't the one who had to do it. I can see him now, stumbling down the rocky slope towards them, hands above his head, gabbling out some abject words of surrender. And it worked. Whatever story he told must have satisfied them, because they trussed him up and started back with him straightaway, while I watched helplessly from the barn. Gratitude was all I felt at first, though it didn't last long. Then came guilt for what I'd let him do. And that's never left me.'

'Do you think they killed him?'

'I'm sure they did. They or whoever he was handed over to. I hope for his sake it was quick. If I could have that day over again, I'd tell him to stay in the barn with me. If they'd come to search it, we could have put up a fight. At least we'd have died together.' A long sigh escaped him and he shook his head, as if in response to some thought he had not spoken. 'I pressed on after dark and had got ahead of the Nationalists again by dawn. How I carried on after that I don't really remember, but eventually I caught up with what was left of the battalion. I was in such a bad way they sent me on to Tarragona to rest up and recover. I knew I'd see Tristram there and I was dreading having to explain what had happened to Vicente. They'd become good friends over the months. When I saw the state he was in, I realized he couldn't last long. I don't suppose I'd have told him the truth if he hadn't asked me about Vicente point blank. Then I recounted the whole story. I felt better for getting it off my chest. Tristram didn't reproach me. He knew I'd be reproaching myself for the rest of my life. But the news seemed to depress him more than any of the other deaths I had to report. There were plenty of them, God knows. And soon there was Tristram's as well.'

'You were with him at the end?'

'Yes. I was. I did what I could for him – which was very little. He was anxious his papers and keepsakes should be returned to his wife – your mother – and I promised him they would be. After he died, I parcelled them up and took them to the British Consul. When he heard they'd belonged to Tristram Abberley the poet, he left no diplomatic stone unturned to make sure they reached their destination. I didn't know then whether I'd ever make it back to England myself. Frankly, I doubted it.'

'But you did, didn't you?'

'Yes. I was still alive come the autumn, when the Republic decided it no longer wanted the International Brigades. The outcome of the war was certain by then. We marched out of Barcelona two months before Franco marched in. All we left behind were futile memories – and the bodies of men like Tristram Abberley.'

'Have you ever been back?'

'Never. Under Franco it would have been unthinkable. Now it's too late. It was probably always too late.' He propped his pipe against the teapot, gathered up their plates and mugs and carried them to the sink. 'Most of those who were there just want to forget. It's the only form of healing they know.'

Charlotte watched him as he began rinsing the crocks, his back turned to her so that he was unaware of her scrutiny. It was strange to reflect on how much this lonely old man had witnessed in a life destined to end where now he stood, in hiding from the world. Had he really burned Tristram's letters without opening them? Had he burned them at all? She could not ask him again. It was too pointed, too heedless of the tragedy he had recounted. He had said it and he had meant it. Or had he? *What else do you think I did?* They had been his words. *How could I not do as I was asked?* How indeed? After what she had just heard, Charlotte was beginning to doubt whether that was the question at all.

TWENTY-ONE

DEREK REACHED RYE SHORTLY before noon. Stung by Colin's scornful remarks, he had decided to approach Beatrix Abberley's housekeeper in an attempt to learn whether she was holding back any vital information. He did not think it likely, but at least the exercise would prove he was still trying to do something on his brother's behalf.

At Colin's request, Albion Dredge had sent Derek copies of the statements made by the prosecution witnesses. These had included their addresses, in Mrs Mentiply's case The Dunes, New Road, Rye. The name had led Derek to expect a seaside setting, but the reality was stubbornly landlocked. The Dunes was a hedge-shrouded bungalow on the eastern outskirts of the town, whose only hint of the ocean was a bedraggled seagull perched on the apex of the roof.

Derek opened and closed the creaky front gate in a furtive manner which he knew would arouse the suspicion of anybody watching from the house but which he was powerless to control. He would have given a great deal to be able to turn back there and then, but the recollection of Colin's sneering expression drove him on to the sunburst front door and a reluctant stab at the bell-push.

Two loud rings brought no response. Squinting through the frosted glass, Derek could see nothing beyond a blurred and empty hallway. Mrs Mentiply was clearly not at home. He would have to try again later – or abandon the whole idea. He turned to go. Only to pull up instantly at the sight of a man watching him from the corner of the house.

'Oh!' said Derek. 'Hello.'

The man nodded. He was a thin, grey, mournful-looking fellow in a tattered warehouse coat. Both the coat and his hands were smeared with dirty oil. In one hand he held a spanner, in the other a cigarette.

'Er . . . I was looking for Mrs Mentiply.'

'The Missus is at church.'

'Ah. When is she likely to be back?'

'When the vicar runs out of things to say. But what do you want with her?'

'Well . . . Mr Mentiply . . . I . . .' Derek moved towards the man, smiling nervously. 'My name's Derek Fairfax.'

'Fairfax? No relation to the bugger they got for doing in Miss Abberley?'

'My brother, actually.'

'Is that a fact?' Mentiply grinned mirthlessly. 'Well, the Missus won't thank you for dropping by, I can tell you. She worshipped the old girl.'

'I only wanted to ask her a few questions.'

'What about?'

'About whether anything unusual happened in the weeks prior to Miss Abberley's death.'

'Anything not involving your brother, you mean?'

'Well . . . Yes.'

Mentiply took a drag on his cigarette and coughed expectorantly. 'You can wait for her if you like.'

'Thanks.'

'But you're wasting your time.' With that, he turned on his heel and vanished from sight.

Belatedly, Derek realized he was meant to wait on the doorstep, not inside. After shifting awkwardly from one foot to the other for a minute or so, he made his way to the corner of the house. There was a garage between it and the boundary hedge, at the end of a cinder track. A battered old car was standing half in and half out of the garage, with its bonnet raised and Mentiply stooped over its filth-encrusted engine. Derek walked up to him.

'Still here?'

'Yes. I thought . . . since your wife's not back yet . . .'

'You thought what?'

'Well, perhaps you know something.'

'About Miss Abberley and her high-and-mighty family? What would the likes of me know?'

'I believe my brother's innocent, you see.'

'Do you? That's nice for him.'

'It's the week or so after his visit to Jackdaw Cottage on the twentieth of May I'm particularly interested in. It's possible something happened during that period to worry Miss Abberley – something which could hold a clue to the identity of her murderer.'

'Doesn't your brother know who he hired to do it, then?'

'He didn't hire anybody.'

'No?' Mentiply abruptly gave up trying to shift a stubborn nut with a muttered, 'Sod the thing' and stood upright, wiping his oily hands in an equally oily rag. 'Are you just shooting a line, son? Why that week especially?'

Mentiply's sarcasm about the Abberleys and his sudden curiosity heartened Derek. 'Because Miss Abberley telephoned my brother a week or so after his visit and said she accepted he hadn't called on her under false pretences.'

'Says who?'

'The point is, Mr Mentiply, did something happen? Your wife might know without being aware of it.'

'Doubtful.' He frowned. 'Would that week have included the bank holiday?'

'Er . . . Yes. Yes, it would have. The last Monday in May. Why?'

'Oh . . . Nothing.'

Derek willed himself to stay silent. It was the best way to encourage Mentiply to say more.

'Except . . .' He scratched his chin. 'Funny, really. It was on the bank holiday. The pub was open all day. That's how I remember. I'd seen him before, a couple of times, when Maurice condescended to pop round for a word with the Missus. But he'd been fired long since, I was told, and he certainly didn't come from round here. So, it *was* odd. And it was him all right. I'd recognize him even without his uniform.'

'Recognize who?'

Mentiply took a last draw on his cigarette, then flicked the butt past Derek's chin on to the cinder track. 'Maurice Abberley's chauffeur. Used to drive him down here in his I'm-rich-and-you're-not Bentley. Until he was given the order of the boot, some time last winter. Too fond of the bottle to drive for a living, according to the Missus. I suppose that tallies with where I saw him. Public bar of the Greyhound, bank holiday Monday afternoon.'

'What was he doing there?'

'Drinking.'

'In Rye, I mean.'

'Couldn't tell you.'

'Didn't you ask?'

'Oh, I asked. But he pretended he didn't know me from Adam. Denied being Maurice's chauffeur. Denied being anybody's chauffeur. Suggested I was too pie-eyed to recognize my own mother. Bloody nerve!'

'It does seem strange. What's his name?'

Mentiply frowned. 'Can't for the life of me remember. Couldn't at the time. If I had, I wouldn't have let him get away with it so easily. What beats me is—' He broke off at the sound of the gate being opened. 'That'll be the Missus,' he said. '*Avril!*'

Mrs Mentiply materialized at the corner of the house, plump and matronly in her Sunday best.

'*Oh!*' *she said.* '*You've got a visitor, I see.*'

'*No. You have. Name of Derek Fairfax.*'

'*Yes.*' *Derek smiled awkwardly.* '*I . . . er . . . I'm Colin Fairfax's brother.*'

Mrs Mentiply coloured ominously. '*Then you're not welcome here.*' *She glared at her husband.* '*I should have thought that was obvious.*'

'*Don't take on, Avril. I've just been trying to remember the name of Maurice's chauffeur. The one he sacked for drunkenness.*'

'*Why do you want to know?*'

'To help out this young fellow.'

'Help him out? I can't imagine what you're thinking of, Arnold, I really can't. As for you, Mr Fairfax—'

'I'm sorry,' put in Derek. 'This is all my fault. Why don't we—'

'Spicer!' exclaimed Mentiply. 'That was the bugger's monicker.' He grinned triumphantly at Derek. 'Mr Spicer, as Miss Abberley would have called him.'

TWENTY-TWO

MAURICE'S CAR WAS PARKED at a boldly nonchalant angle in front of the hotel. What its owner might be doing there Charlotte could not imagine. Suddenly, her thoughts were plucked away from Frank Griffith's sombre reminiscences and deposited in the here and now of difficult questions and side-stepped doubts. She had anticipated having to explain herself to Emerson, but Maurice's presence posed additional problems which transformed a delicate task into a formidable one.

They were in the lounge, relaxing over pre-lunch drinks. Neither displayed any sign of anxiety. Indeed, as Charlotte entered the room, they were laughing uproariously, like two old friends exchanging a joke. Then they saw her.

'Charlie!' said Maurice, jumping to his feet. 'We were beginning to worry about you.'

'There was no need.'

'I expect you're wondering what I'm doing here, aren't you?'

'Well . . .'

'I phoned him last night,' put in Emerson. 'Thought I ought to bring him up to date.'

'And I decided to join you here,' said Maurice with a grin.

'I was going to tell you this morning,' Emerson continued. 'But you'd already gone by the time I came down for breakfast.'

'I left a note for you.'

'By which we're both greatly intrigued.' Maurice's grin declined into the faintest of smiles. 'What did this Griffith fellow have to say for himself?'

'Quite a lot. Everything we wanted to know, in one sense.'

'Does he have the letters?' asked Emerson.

'No. Not any more. Why don't I explain over lunch?'

'Do put us out of our misery first,' said Maurice. 'What has he done with them?'

'He destroyed them. At Beatrix's request.'

Emerson swore loudly and instantly apologized. 'I'm sorry. News like this is a real body-blow to a biographer.'

'I'm sorry too.'

'Destroyed them,' said Maurice musingly. 'Well, well, well.' Then he looked quizzically at Charlotte. 'How, exactly?'

'He didn't say. Burned, I suppose.'

'But you do believe him?'

'Yes.' Charlotte knew she should meet Maurice's gaze as she replied, but something prevented her, something that turned what should have been a confident assertion into a stubborn protestation. 'I believe him.'

Nothing Maurice and Emerson said during lunch implied that either of them doubted Charlotte's account. They were both disappointed, of course, especially Emerson, for whom it represented a frustrating end to his quest for further insights into the mind of Tristram Abberley. But Charlotte suspected anything beyond disappointment existed only in her over-sensitive imagination. She was also aware that Maurice was even more awkwardly placed than she was. Since her visit to Swans' Meadow, Ursula had been obliged to tell him about Beatrix's letter. Whatever he really thought, he had to sound as if he believed her, which is exactly what he did. In the circumstances, his loyalty was admirable and Charlotte's heart went out to him.

In the final analysis, however, burnt letters were as unsatisfactory as blank pages. They hid their secrets with terrible certainty. Which left those unwilling to abandon the search with little alternative but to sustain it for its own sake. In Charlotte's case, the reluctance to give up had more to do with Emerson McKitrick than Tristram Abberley. But the effect was the same. When Maurice cast around for other avenues they might yet explore, she responded eagerly.

'I'm off to New York again on Thursday,' he announced as they awaited their coffees on the sun-dappled terrace behind the hotel. 'And I'll see if I can track down a Miss Van Ryan in Fifth Avenue while I'm there, though, with no number, I'm not optimistic.'

'Will you go too, Emerson?' asked Charlotte.

'Reckon not. Maurice has generously invited me to stay at Swans'
Meadow for a spell and there's some unrelated research I want to do
in Oxford.'

'I've also suggested, Charlie,' said Maurice, 'that you might be
willing to introduce him to Uncle Jack.'

'Uncle Jack? Well, certainly. But why?'

'Because he was living with Mother and me when Tristram died
– and when Frank Griffith came to see her. I was just a babe in arms.
But Jack was in his early teens, nosing into everything. So, it's just
possible he might be able to shed some light on what Tristram did
or didn't send back from Spain.'

'I can't see how. The real question, surely, is what he sent to
Beatrix. And you didn't go to live with her until after the war broke
out.'

'True enough. Maybe it's not worth inflicting the old bore on
yourselves after all.'

'My training says otherwise,' put in Emerson. 'Check every loose
end in case it's a thread leading to the truth. That's how we academics
get by. I'll risk being bored by Uncle Jack if you will, Charlie.'

Charlotte smiled more broadly than she had intended. 'I can't
refuse then, can I?'

Later, when Emerson went to summon their bills, Maurice dropped
his affable guard for a moment and said to Charlotte, without any
preamble: 'I don't suppose you believed Ursula's story, did you?'

'I . . . Of course I did.'

'I wouldn't have, in your shoes. It seems too utterly fantastic. That's
one of the reasons why I came here. To reassure you. It *is* true. The
letter contained nothing but blank pages. I saw them myself.'

'You saw them? But Ursula said—'

'She hadn't shown me the letter? I know. That's true too. I came
across it in her bedside cabinet while I was trying to find some
cuff-links. I just couldn't resist taking a peek inside. Well, I didn't
know what to make of it, as you can imagine. But I couldn't ask
Ursula. She'd have thought I was spying on her. She must have
thrown it away shortly afterwards, because it wasn't there next
time I looked. Of course, I had no idea it was from Beatrix. I
still can't begin to imagine what she meant by it.' He glanced
round to make sure Emerson was not bearing down on them, then
added: 'The thing is this, Charlie. Ursula doesn't know I ever saw

the letter and I don't want her to – for obvious reasons. So, can I rely on you to keep it to yourself?'

There was a conspiratorial gleam in his eye, a hesitant edge to his smile. Suddenly, Charlotte realized she had been outmanoeuvred again. By agreeing to stay silent, she was also agreeing to accept Maurice's version of events without question. Yet to refuse was inconceivable. 'Of course,' she said, expunging every trace of reluctance from her tone. 'Your secret's safe with me.'

Emerson travelled in Maurice's car when they left the hotel that afternoon. It was only sensible, since he would be staying at Swans' Meadow henceforth, but it meant Charlotte had to face the long drive back to Tunbridge Wells alone. Initially, the prospect depressed her. But, after setting out, she began to think it was probably for the best. With Emerson for company, she might have let slip some unguarded remark hinting at what she was beginning more and more to suspect: that everybody she had questioned about Beatrix was holding something back; that all of them, in one way or another, were lying.

TWENTY-THREE

DAVID FITHYAN, SON OF the founder of Fithyan & Co., was a ruddy-faced sandy-haired man in his mid-forties who devoted what little time he could spare from playing golf and flirting with the office girls to ensuring that none of the company's more significant clients had cause for dissatisfaction. The moment Derek had been summoned to see him, he had known his error-strewn audit of Radway Ceramics was going to be the subject under discussion and so it had inevitably proved.

'George Radway cornered me at the club last night and gave me a real earful, I can tell you.' For which, Derek did not doubt, he would be made to suffer. 'I had a word with Neil this morning and according to him this isn't the only example of slipshod work by you recently.'

'There have been . . . one or two problems.'

'That's putting it mildly. Most of your accounts have fallen behind schedule. Hardly a week goes by without you taking a day or two off.

And when you are here you seem too distracted to be of much use.'

'I'm very sorry if . . . well . . . if I haven't been pulling my weight.'

'Sorry's not good enough, Derek. What I want to know is what you propose to do about it.'

'You have my assurance there'll be no repetition of the difficulty with Radway's.'

'Do I? Do I really?' Fithyan sighed and smoothed down his hair with an elaborate elbow-cocked movement of his left arm, designed, Derek suspected, to expose his wristwatch beneath his cuff so that he could check if their encounter had yet exceeded its allotted span. 'Is all this . . . this inefficiency . . . because of your brother, may I ask?'

Derek flushed. 'Ah. You know about that, do you?'

'Of course I know, man. Everybody knows. You didn't seriously expect to keep it dark, did you?'

'Well . . . No. No, I suppose not.'

'You have my sympathy. It can't be pleasant to find your brother's a criminal.'

'He . . . um . . . hasn't been convicted yet, actually.'

'No. But he will be, won't he? At least, so I'm told.'

'Told? By whom?'

Fithyan frowned. 'Not by anybody specifically. It's just . . . common knowledge.'

'Ah. I see.'

'Now, Derek, what it comes to is this. We can't afford passengers at Fithyan & Co. We all have to *compete* and *perform*.' He stressed the two words as if by emphasis alone he could do both himself. 'We realize members of staff are bound to have personal problems from time to time. We're not heartless or unfeeling. But we can't allow those problems to affect the company's reputation. You appreciate that, I'm sure.'

'Of course.'

'Very well. So, can I assume you'll be putting this . . . preoccupation . . . this . . . this embarrassment . . . behind you?'

'Yes.' Derek tried to inject some eagerness into his response. 'Yes. I honestly think you can.'

Fithyan smiled clammily. 'Splendid, splendid.' He glanced at his wristwatch. 'Sorry I've had to wield the big stick, Derek. It's for your own good, really it is.'

'Yes. I know.'

'After all, none of us is our brother's keeper, as the poet said.'

'It wasn't a poet, actually. It's in the Bible. As a question. Am I . . . my brother's keeper?'

Fithyan's grin crumpled into puzzlement, then became a glare. 'Really? Well, whatever, the point is made.' And their interview, his expression declared, was at an end.

Derek returned to his office as to a haven. There he could close a door against the world, at least for a while, and ponder the disarray to which his life had lately been reduced. Through no fault of his own, of course. Through no fault of Colin's either. Yet it had happened. And Fithyan had served notice that it could not remain so for much longer.

Derek subsided into the chair behind his desk and noticed three messages left for him on separate pieces of paper, all in the huge childlike hand of his secretary, Carol. *Please ring Mr Hamlyn, VAT Office. Please ring Ann Nicholson, Radway Ceramics. Please ring . . .*

Maurice Abberley, Ladram Avionics. Derek gaped at the words for several seconds before he found it possible to believe that they were what he thought. Maurice Abberley had contacted him. Of his own volition. Of his own choosing. Why – and especially why now – Derek could not imagine. Neither did he try. Obedient to the instinct of the moment, he picked up the telephone and tapped out the number.

A blandly polite receptionist; then a honey-toned secretary; and then, with bewildering suddenness, Derek found himself talking to Maurice Abberley in person.

'Mr Fairfax. Thanks for calling back.' He sounded neutral, almost affable, as if he were conversing with a business acquaintance.

'Mr Abberley, I . . . I was somewhat . . .'

'Surprised to hear from me? I thought you might be. I suppose you wrote to me more in hope than expectation.'

'Er . . . Yes . . .'

'Some recent developments have made me think you may have a point, however. About your brother being less guilty than he appears, I mean. Perhaps not guilty at all, if it comes to it.'

'Really? Well, I'm—'

'Why don't we meet and talk about it, Mr Fairfax? Compare notes, so to speak.'

'Yes. Yes, I'd like to.'

'I have to fly to New York on Thursday. So, how would tomorrow suit you?'

Another absence from Fithyan & Co. so soon after a reprimand would be to invite serious trouble, as Derek well knew. Yet how could he refuse? This was the Abberley family's first gesture that could not be called implacably hostile. 'Yes. Tomorrow would be fine. When and where?'

'Four o'clock. Here at my office.'

'Fine. I'll be there.'

Derek put the telephone down and leaned back slowly in his chair, too confused by the turn of events to summon a reaction. Just as he had despaired of being able to pursue the mystery of why Maurice's former chauffeur should have been in Rye a few days after Colin's visit to Jackdaw Cottage, a way of doing so had obligingly presented itself. Just as he had virtually agreed to abandon his brother to his fate, it had become impossible not to make one last effort on his behalf. The ironies and contradictions persisted. And he was helpless to resolve them.

TWENTY-FOUR

JACK BRERETON HAD BEEN a wastrel and a parasite all his life. He had tried to deflect criticism for this by remaining perpetually good-humoured, with jokes, anecdotes and racing tips forever on tap. And he had succeeded, for his sister, Mary Ladram, had always been generous to him, ensuring his later years were not dogged by poverty and its close companion, squalor. He had worked with Ronnie Ladram in his younger days, but, since Maurice had eased him out of the business, had become a full-time idler. He rented a small flat in Earl's Court, which served as an ideal base for his daily wanderings between pubs, clubs, casinos, betting shops and a stubbornly loyal handful of blowzy girlfriends. If not the black sheep of the family, he was certainly its grubby and disreputable old ram. He seldom left London and Charlotte, when she went there, never visited him. Yet he had expressed no surprise at her request to bring Emerson McKitrick to see him. It had merely confirmed his opinion of himself as somebody everybody wanted to meet, however often they tried to deny it.

Even if Jack's flat had been large enough for cat-swinging, which it was not, his standards of housekeeping would have ruled out the entertainment of guests. Accordingly, he escorted Charlotte and Emerson round the corner to one of his homes from home, a tiny mews pub full of polished wood and smoked glass, where he was greeted with sarcastic familiarity. Installed in a corner with a double scotch and a packet of Senior Service cigarettes, he proved as talkative as Charlotte had anticipated. The difficulty, indeed, was confining him to what they were interested in, for his reminiscences tended to jumble together different people, places and times with little sense of sequence or relevance.

'Tristram was hero-material, all right, no question about it. Not my type, though. Give me Compton and Edrich any day. We lived in Knightsbridge then. Handy for the park, if not for much else. Tristram took me up to Speakers' Corner sometimes. He liked listening to the fanatics ranting about the millennium and the dictatorship of the proletariat. Not my idea of fun, I can tell you.'

'About his death, Uncle Jack . . .'

'Mmm? Oh, I can't remember much. A letter from the British Consul in Tarragona broke the news. His belongings followed later. Mary was pretty cut up, as you'd expect. Can't say I was. Beatrix came up from Rye to comfort her. Beatrix herself took it on the chin. Well, that's the sort she was. They don't make them like her any more. Just as well, perhaps, eh? I remember her giving what-for to a gypsy once who tried to curse her because she wouldn't buy any lavender. My God, but that was a set-to. You should have—'

'What about Frank Griffith?' put in Emerson. 'Recall anything of his visit? It would have been December of 'thirty-eight.'

'No sense quoting dates at me, old son. As far as I'm concerned, they come boxed at Christmas and no other way. There *was* some grim-faced Taff who turned up on the doorstep one day, it's true. But he wasn't the only one. When he came, whether it was before or after the Spaniard—'

'What Spaniard?'

'Haven't I ever told you about him, Charlie? Not exactly the Spaniard who blighted my life, but he looked like he'd blighted a good few others. About seven foot tall, thin as a shadow, with a hooked nose you could open a soup-tin on. Mary was frightened of him and I don't blame her. He put the wind up me too. He wasn't what you'd call the playful kind. Beatrix did most of the talking, as I—'

'Beatrix was there as well?'

'Of course. This was at Jackdaw Cottage. We spent a few weeks there during the summer holiday. The summer before the war, it must have been, because we were installed there for the duration come 1940.'

'Can we be clear?' said Emerson. 'Frank Griffith visited you and your sister in Knightsbridge in December nineteen thirty-eight?'

'If you say so, old son. Winter it certainly was. And Tristram hadn't been a year dead.'

'Then a Spaniard came to see you while you were staying in Rye in the summer of nineteen thirty-nine?'

'That's it.'

'What did he want?'

'Couldn't tell you. I made myself scarce. He *seemed* to have known Tristram. Fought with him, perhaps. On the other hand, well, he was nothing like your Welsh friend. In fact, he was so *unlike* him – so arrogant, so icily courteous – you could easily have taken him for somebody who'd fought *against* Tristram. It struck me there was a touch of the Nazi to him.'

'You mean he was a Fascist?'

'Could have been. No Commie, that's for certain. But I don't really know. He was closeted with Mary and Beatrix for an hour or more. Neither said much about it afterwards. I think they were just glad to see the back of him. So was I. The temperature dropped by about six degrees while he was on the premises.'

'What was his name?'

'If he gave it, I wasn't listening. Aren't they all called Gomez?'

'Not Ortiz, by any chance?' asked Charlotte. 'Vicente Ortiz?' She noticed Emerson glance sharply at her and instantly regretted the enquiry. The man Jack had described did not sound anything like Frank Griffith's *'cross-patch little anarchist from Barcelona'*.

'Don't think so. In fact, definitely not.'

'What sort of age?' asked Emerson.

'Oh, fortyish I suppose. I'd have said sixty at the time, but you know how any adult looks ancient to your average twelve-year-old boy. I asked Mary later if he was some admirer Beatrix had picked up on her travels. She wasn't amused. Fetched me such a clip round the—'

'What travels?'

'Didn't I mention them? No, I suppose I wouldn't have. Well, Beatrix was never a stay-at-home, was she? Except during the war, when she had no choice. She'd been to the French Riviera – or it could have been the Swiss Alps – or it could have been both – for a good couple of months that spring.'

'The spring of nineteen thirty-nine?'

'Yes. That's right. When she announced she was off, I was hoping she'd insist we all go with her. A jaunt to lay Tristram's ghost, so to speak. I wouldn't have minded missing school. And Mary might have met some handsome Frog to take her out of herself. But no. It was never suggested. Beatrix went alone. And we stayed put, with little Maurice screaming fit to burst his lungs every night and Mary mooning about and staring soulfully at Tristram's photograph. Not a jolly time, I can tell you. In fact, I counted it as pretty mean of Beatrix to swan off on her own and leave us to stew. I suppose it was unfair of me, because she never was mean, was she? No doubt she had her reasons.'

But what were they? Charlotte wondered. An aimless sojourn among the flesh-pots was so uncharacteristic of Beatrix as to be completely implausible. With the example of her annual fortnights with Lulu in mind, it was easier to imagine a different destination and a secret purpose. Glancing at Emerson, she could see that the same thought had crossed his mind.

'She always did have, didn't she?' Jack continued. 'A law unto herself and a mystery to everybody else, our Beatrix. You know, I've often suspected she objected to publishing Tristram's Spanish poems. May even have delayed it happening. Mary said she'd never thought of doing anything with them until the early 'fifties and I don't suppose there'd have been much of a market for them during or immediately after the war, though God knows we could have used *any* income, however meagre. His other two collections were out of print and we were all living in that flat in Maidstone where you were born, Charlie. Mary, Squadron Leader Ronnie, Maurice, me and you, of course. The Sardine family, Ronnie used to call us. A real card, he was. But money slipped through his fingers like sand, so I don't know why it took them so long to think of pushing out *Spanish Lines*. I'd have suggested it myself years before if I'd known the poems existed, but Mary never said a dicky bird to me about them. She'd been pretty protective where Tristram's effects were concerned and I'd had my head bitten off too many times to pry, I can tell you.

Besides, I had to watch my step after Ronnie taxied on to the scene. He might have persuaded Mary they should chuck me out and make me shift for myself. I couldn't have—'

'Why do you think Beatrix should have objected to publication, Uncle Jack?'

'Can't begin to imagine. Not sure she did. But, if she didn't, why wait so long?'

'Mother always said that, until she met Dad, she'd have found it too painful to rake over Tristram's memory.'

Jack sniffed and toyed with his whisky. 'Maybe,' he muttered.

'You don't buy that?' said Emerson.

Jack shook his head. 'Can't say I do. You see, there were umpteen family conferences about it before it was ever announced, even to me. Pow-wows behind closed doors between Mary, Ronnie and Beatrix. My impression – hardly more, I grant you – was that Beatrix had the ultimate say-so, that she could have vetoed the whole idea – and very nearly did.'

'I don't understand,' said Charlotte. 'Surely, as Tristram's widow, Mother had the right to do as she pleased with any poems he sent her.'

'Nail on the head,' said Jack, winking and pointing an unsteady forefinger at her. 'My point exactly. What did it have to do with Beatrix? Why did they need her consent? Not just want her to agree, I mean, but absolutely have to persuade her. I've often wondered.'

'Didn't you ever ask?' said Emerson.

'You bet, old son, but little good it did me. They closed ranks. Reckoned I was making something out of nothing. Maybe I was. We'll never know now, will we? Not now they've all gone to a better place. One where I don't anticipate ever meeting them.' Jack grinned at his own joke. When neither Charlotte nor Emerson could summon even the weakest of smiles, he shrugged his shoulders and said: 'Please yourself.'

'I'm sorry, Uncle Jack,' said Charlotte. 'We're grateful for all this information. Unfortunately, it's inconclusive. It leaves us—'

'At another dead end,' put in Emerson.

'Never promised it wouldn't, did I?' protested Jack. 'And talking of dead ends, my scotch reached one a thirsty few minutes ago. Any chance of a refill?'

TWENTY-FIVE

LADRAM AVIATION BEGAN ITS commercial existence in a Nissen hut on a disused RAF station halfway between Maidstone and Tonbridge. Its corporate successor, Ladram Avionics, was run from a trapezohedron of blue glass and tempered steel amidst the reservoirs and dual carriageways of south Middlesex. Here, shortly before four o'clock on a still and muggy afternoon, Derek Fairfax arrived for his appointment with Maurice Abberley. Less than an hour before, he had abruptly abandoned an auditing commitment in Sevenoaks knowing that David Fithyan, when he heard what he had done, would be enraged. But, to Derek's surprise, Fithyan's likely reaction meant nothing to him. Nothing, at all events, whilst Maurice Abberley's motives in asking to meet him remained so tantalizingly uncertain.

The interior of Ladram Avionics was as plush and sleekly modern as the exterior suggested it would be. Most of the staff looked as if they modelled in their spare time and the furnishings were ergonomically futuristic. A lift nearly as large as Derek's office at Fithyan & Co. bore him smoothly and swiftly to the top floor, where Maurice's pneumatic secretary was waiting to greet him.

The chairman and managing director's office, to which she led him, was a suitably vast expanse of deep-piled carpet, with the letters L and A elaborately interwoven in the pattern. One entire wall was of tinted glass, through which the serpentine tangle of London's road network looked as remote and serene as the canals of Mars. Maurice's crescent-shaped desk was positioned so that this Olympian perspective met his gaze every time he glanced up, as he now did at Derek's entry.

'Glad you could come, Mr Fairfax,' he said, striding across the room with hand outstretched and smile conjured from nowhere. 'And so punctual too. I like that.' He was elegantly dressed in a dark suit and monogrammed tie and his voice seemed to fill the empty spaces of the room. Everything about him – his tone, his appearance, his awareness of his own authority – made Derek feel shabby and inadequate by comparison.

'Would you like some tea?'

'Er . . . Yes. Thank you.'

'India or China?'

'Well . . . I . . . I don't mind.'

'Lapsang then, I think, Sally,' said Maurice to the secretary, who nodded and withdrew so silently Derek did not even hear the door close behind her. 'Come and sit down, Mr Fairfax.' He motioned towards two leather armchairs.

'Thank you. You . . . er . . . have a splendid view.'

'I do, don't I? I find it helps me keep a sense of proportion.'

'I suppose we all . . . need that.'

'Oh yes. We do. Undoubtedly. In fact, you could say it's why we're meeting this afternoon.'

'Really?'

'In the immediate aftermath of a death, particularly a violent one, there's little scope for mature reflection. That's why your visit to Ockham House was so untimely.'

'I realize it was now. I'm sorry. I should have known better. I was anxious to do something – anything – to help my brother.'

'It's understandable. I hope you agree our reaction was also understandable.'

'Of course.'

'So, let's not misunderstand each other on this occasion. I have no liking for your brother and no confidence in his innocence. But certain recent developments have undermined my confidence in his guilt to the extent that I think it only proper – only fair – to inform you of them. As you said in your letter, it's in all our interests to establish the truth about Beatrix's death. If your brother *was* responsible, you will just have to accept the fact. If not, I want to find out who the culprit really is.'

'Those are my views too, Mr Abberley. I'm only—'

'Ah,' interrupted Maurice. 'Here's tea.'

Tea was delicately served in wafer-thin Spode, Maurice beaming irrepressibly whilst his secretary ministered to them. When she had left them alone again, he leaned forward, as if a greater degree of intimacy were suddenly called for.

'Charlotte thinks we should leave well alone, Mr Fairfax. So does my wife. In fact, none of my family seems to share my misgivings. They wouldn't approve of my talking to you. So I think it would be best if we kept this to ourselves, don't you? It would only lead to pointless recriminations otherwise. Can I rely on your discretion?'

'Yes. Absolutely.'

'Good. What I'm about to tell you may mean nothing. I must warn you of that. I wouldn't want you to jump to any conclusions. A mystery conceals trifles more often than riches.' He smiled, then said: 'My aunt was a very private person. I never regarded her as secretive because I never thought she had anything to be secretive about. She belonged to a different generation, one less accustomed than we are to parading our emotions. I'd always supposed that accounted for her reticent nature. Now . . . I'm not so sure.'

'No?'

Maurice sipped at his tea, then reclined in his chair, swivelling it slightly to face the window. 'It's an odd business. Confoundedly odd. As I say, it may amount to nothing at all. On the other hand, it seems to me you should know about it. Then you can judge for yourself. And act accordingly.'

Derek listened attentively as Maurice continued. Beatrix Abberley, it appeared, had concealed for many years a friendship with a man called Frank Griffith, who had fought with her brother in Spain. She had also concealed certain letters sent to her by her brother from Spain and these she had arranged to be sent to Frank Griffith after her death with a request that he destroy them unread. This he claimed to have done. Nobody could suggest any reason why Beatrix should have gone to such lengths to prevent the letters coming to light. Nor could they credit the notion that she had been killed because of them. Yet the fact remained that she had foreseen – even expected – her death. It seemed as if she had known her life was in danger and had prepared herself accordingly.

'It's hard for me to believe she was murdered on account of some fifty-year-old letters from my father, Mr Fairfax, very hard indeed. If my mother was still alive, I'd think Beatrix had been trying to keep something from her. A love affair Tristram had in Spain, perhaps. But my mother died last year, so that can't be it. Equally, it's hard now to believe Beatrix was murdered simply for a few antiques. There are too many other unexplained circumstances. If she thought her life was being threatened – by your brother, for instance – why didn't she go to the police? Or tell me about it? Why do nothing at all to protect herself? And how did she know anyway? What made her so certain something was going to happen to her?'

'I may be able to point you towards an answer,' said Derek, suddenly eager to share his half-formed conclusions. 'Your aunt's conviction that she was going to be murdered fits with some information I've uncovered.'

Maurice's gaze intensified. 'What information?'

The sequence of events Derek sketched out was part known, part conjectural. Yet the force of its logic could not be denied and his belief in it strengthened as he spoke. When Colin visited Jackdaw Cottage on 20 May, Beatrix regarded him as a foot-in-the-door confidence trickster whose explanations were a tissue of lies. But, a week later, when she telephoned him, she clearly believed his story and wanted to hear every detail of it. Only a few days afterwards, she travelled to Cheltenham, en route for Wales, firmly convinced her murder was already being plotted. Whatever convinced her must therefore have occurred during the days immediately following 20 May. And the only unusual event reported during that period was a sighting in Rye of Maurice's former chauffeur, who had been anxious to deny—

'Spicer?' exclaimed Maurice. 'Spicer was in Rye on the twenty-fifth of May?'

'Arnold Mentiply is adamant it was him.'

'Strange.' Maurice frowned. 'Very strange.'

'I gather you dismissed him because of drunkenness.'

'I had no choice. He was a good driver, but he couldn't be relied upon to remain sober. I let him go at Christmas.'

'Do you know where he works now?'

'No. In the circumstances, I could hardly give him a reference. And I've heard nothing more of him. He lived in a flat in Marlow while he was with me. But I doubt he's still there.'

'What contact would he have had with your aunt?'

'Minimal. The odd word perhaps. He drove me down to Rye whenever I visited her.'

'He had no connections with the area?'

'None I was aware of. I simply can't account for him being seen there. Unless he works in the locality now, of course.'

'If he does, why would he pretend to Mentiply he was somebody else?'

'I don't know. But for that, I could regard it as a pure coincidence.'

'One of rather too many, surely?'

'Yes. That's the point, isn't it?' Maurice thought for a moment, then said: 'Spicer was a rough diamond in many respects. It's possible he could be involved in criminal activities. I can't deny it.'

'But you don't know where he is?'

'No. No idea at all.' He rubbed his chin reflectively. 'But I could ask around. His landlady in Marlow. The pub he used. He might have told somebody what his plans were.'

'I'd be very grateful if you could make some enquiries,' said Derek, detecting a pleading note in his voice as he spoke. 'I've done just about as much as I can on my brother's behalf.'

'I'll see what I can find out as soon as I return from New York,' Maurice replied. 'Meanwhile, however, I should have thought there *was* something you could profitably do to help your brother.'

'What?'

'See Frank Griffith. Establish whether he's telling the truth.'

'You think he might be lying?'

'I don't know. I haven't met him, remember. Charlotte certainly believes him. But to destroy Tristram's letters, without even reading them first . . . I'm not sure I can believe anybody did that.'

'But . . . if he didn't . . .'

'He may still have them. Either way, he may know what they said.'

'And that might tell us why Beatrix was murdered.'

'Exactly.' Maurice looked Derek intently in the eye. 'I promised Charlotte I wouldn't bother Griffith. And I doubt I'd learn anything even if I did. But you're free to do as you please. And maybe — just maybe — your brother's predicament will persuade Griffith to reveal what he knows, where Charlotte's curiosity didn't.'

'It's certainly worth a try.'

'Yes.' Maurice smiled. 'I rather think it is.'

TWENTY-SIX

'IS IT REALLY A dead end?' asked Charlotte. 'To your research, I mean?' She had driven Emerson back to Swans' Meadow and they were standing together by the bank of the river, while behind them on the lawn Samantha lay prostrate on a sun-lounger, insulated against the world with dark glasses and Walkman.

'Looks that way.'

'But it seems so . . . unsatisfactory.'

'It is, Charlie. You're right. But what can we do? Your Uncle Jack's reminiscences are intriguing, but they lead us nowhere. Beatrix seemingly didn't want anybody to read Tristram's letters. Well, Frank Griffith has made sure nobody will. And we don't have any way of knowing what was in them.'

Charlotte was suddenly tempted to contradict Emerson and tell him she was not sure Frank Griffith had destroyed the letters. But she knew why she was tempted, as well. Because, if Emerson's research was at an end, so was all hope of their acquaintance blossoming into something more. To betray Frank's trust on an emotional whim would be unforgivable. Therefore she must hold her tongue. 'When will you go back to Harvard?' she asked lamely.

'Why? Do you want to get rid of me?'

'Of course not.' She blushed. 'You know I don't.'

'I've been one hell of a nuisance since I arrived, haven't I? Dragging you all over the country. Cross-questioning you at every turn.'

'I've enjoyed it. Really.'

'So have I.' He smiled. 'Matter of fact, I was wondering whether I could persuade you to join me on a couple more trips while I'm here.'

'What sort of trips?'

'No more research, I promise.' He let his gaze engage hers for a playful instant. 'Purely for pleasure, this time.'

Charlotte's own smile was as much one of relief as of eagerness. 'I'd love to,' she said.

'Then why don't we start with dinner this evening? Restaurant of your choice.'

'It sounds wonderful.'

'Great.' He lowered his voice and nodded towards Samantha's recumbent form. 'But don't tell Sam, eh? It's possible she might feel jealous.'

Derek did not return to Tunbridge Wells that afternoon. Instead, he drove on to the motorway and headed towards Wales, intent on pursuing the hope Maurice Abberley had planted in his mind. Their second encounter had been infinitely more encouraging than their first. Maurice struck Derek as a man willing to confront unpalatable facts even when they flew in the face of his own prejudices. Derek did not delude himself into believing there was any real affinity between them. All that united them was a desire to learn the truth, in Maurice's case in order to avenge his aunt, in Derek's in order to exonerate his brother.

He stopped for the night at a pub near Abergavenny and sat alone in a corner of the bar, plotting how best to approach the unapproachable Frank Griffith. To plead? To demand? To reason? His choice might be crucial, yet it could not be made until he had met and taken stock of the man. Even then, it might be in vain. Griffith could easily prove immovable or genuinely unable to help. He could—

There Derek stifled the last of his speculations. They were as pointless as they were dispiriting. And, tomorrow, he would have no need of them.

Charlotte dined in vastly different circumstances at an award-winning restaurant beside the Thames. She was a stranger to such extravagance, not because she could not afford it, but because she had never seen any purpose in spoiling herself. Her boyfriends – such as they had been – would not have displayed any of Emerson McKitrick's social accomplishment, nor would they have attracted – as he did – admiring glances from ladies at other tables. Charlotte was elated by the thought of being envied on his account, by the host of unspoken possibilities that clustered around their ever greater familiarity with each other.

'How come you've never married, Charlie?'

'I've never been asked.'

'I can't believe that.'

'It's true. What's your excuse?'

'Indecisiveness, I guess.'

'I can't believe that either.'

'Well, it doesn't necessarily mean not being able to make up your mind. It can also mean not taking risks with your emotions.'

'In that case, I know the feeling.'

'I thought you might. It doesn't pay in the long run, does it?'

'I'm not sure.'

'Don't wait to be sure, Charlie. Not every time. If you do, you'll just go on waiting.'

'Will I?' Their hands touched and briefly engaged. And Emerson's only answer was a smile.

Later, with their meal over and the restaurant emptying, they strolled down to the river's edge and watched the dining room lights shimmer on the black surface of the water while a restless moorhen splashed and clucked among the reeds on the opposite bank. Charlotte was to sleep at Swans' Meadow that night, but she was reluctant for them to return there, knowing that, once they had done so, Emerson's company would no longer be exclusively hers. She was reluctant, indeed, to break in any way the spell under which she had fallen. The silk of her dress felt cool against her skin, the clasp of his arm warm around her waist. When he kissed her, she was neither prepared nor surprised. It had been bound to happen. Only her self-doubt had made her think it might not.

'Nothing's ever wasted, Charlie,' he whispered. 'On a wild goose chase, you may find a swan.'

'Don't flatter me too much. I might come to expect it.'

'Why shouldn't you – when you deserve it?'

'But I don't.' She was going to tell him. She knew that now. It was too late not to. 'I've deceived you.'

'I don't believe it.'

'It's true.' Too many years of loneliness and vulnerability were stored within her for judgement or deliberation to stand a chance. She wanted to surrender herself to Emerson, body, soul, secrets and all. She did not want to be alone any more. 'I don't think Frank Griffith really destroyed those letters. I think he still has them at Hendre Gorfelen.'

'So do I.'

'What?'

'So do I, Charlie.' She made out his smile in the darkness. 'I just wanted to hear you say it.'

'You've known all along?'

'Suspected.'

'He won't give them up. I'm sure of that.'

'So am I.'

'Then what—'

Another kiss silenced her. 'Then it doesn't matter, does it?' he murmured. 'We'll keep Frank Griffith's secret. You and I. Together.'

'Together?'

'Don't you want to take one of those emotional risks we were talking about?'

'Yes.' She lowered her head against his shoulder. 'I do.'

TWENTY-SEVEN

AT SEVEN O'CLOCK THE following morning, Derek telephoned
Fithyan & Co. and recorded an apology for his absence on the
answering machine. Any risk of having to explain himself to David
Fithyan was thereby avoided, or at any rate postponed. Two hours
later, he was in Llandovery, seeking directions to Hendre Gorfelen.
By half past nine, he was driving along the curving hillside track
towards the farm. Within a few minutes, he had arrived.

He stopped the car in front of the house and wound down the
window. He could hear a distant bleat of lambs and, closer to hand,
a susurrous movement of tree-tops in the breeze, but no sound to
suggest Frank Griffith was nearby. He climbed from the car and
looked around, relieved no dog had yet hurled itself from a barn.
None of the windows of the house were open. This, and the fact
that anybody inside would have heard him arrive, convinced Derek
nobody was at home. Nevertheless, he walked up to the door and
knocked. There was no response.

He retraced his steps to the car and sat back in the driving seat.
Although Griffith might be away for some time, he would eventually
return, whereas to scour the hills in search of him carried no guarantee
of success. There was nothing for it, then, but to sit tight.

Derek sighed and closed the window. Idly, he reached across
to the glove compartment and took out his copy of *Tristram Abberley:
A Critical Biography*. In the index, *Griffith, Frank* warranted just
one entry. Derek turned to it and ran his eye down the page
until he came to Griffith's name.

When Abberley died, semi-conscious and probably too delirious
to be in much pain, in the early hours of Sunday 27th March,
a sergeant from his own platoon, Frank Griffith, was loyally in
attendance. It was the same man who, shortly after the poet's
perfunctory funeral in Tarragona Cemetery, delivered his papers
to the British Consul for onward transmission to his widow. It
was a simple and no doubt unconsidered act, yet, had Griffith not
carried it out, the whole corpus of Abberley's Spanish poetry might

easily have been lost. As it was, the belief commonly held for many years after Abberley's death, that he had written no poems at all whilst in Spain, was shown to be a fallacy when, in 1952—

A sudden rap on the glass reverberated in Derek's ear. He started so violently that the book slipped from his grasp. When he turned, it was to see a face staring in at him, a lined and expressionless face which, even though Maurice Abberley's description had been second-hand, he recognized instantly.

'Good morning,' he ventured, as he wound down the window. 'Frank Griffith?'

'And you would be?'

'Derek Fairfax.' He opened the door an inch or so, which was all Griffith's position made possible. 'Let me . . . er . . . introduce myself.' Now, late enough to have made some kind of point, Griffith stepped back, allowing Derek to climb out. 'You may have heard of my brother, Colin Fairfax.' He grinned uneasily. 'Also known as Fairfax-Vane.'

'You're right. I *may* have.' There was nothing in Griffith's gaze to encourage communication of any kind, let alone discourse. 'What do you want?'

'I understand . . . Well, that is . . . Perhaps we could discuss this indoors.'

'We could not.' He glanced into the car and Derek wondered if he could see what he had been reading.

'I'm told you have some letters, Mr Griffith, sent to Beatrix Abberley from Spain in the 'thirties by her brother, the poet, Tristram Abberley.'

'Told by whom?'

'I . . . I'd rather not say.'

'Then maybe I'd rather not answer your questions.'

'I'm here to appeal to you on my brother's behalf. I wouldn't be prying – or even curious – but for the position he's in. He may go to prison for something he didn't do. Perhaps for a long time. He's not a young man. I—'

A touch of Griffith's stick on Derek's shoulder silenced him. 'If the letters you referred to existed – if I had them – what difference could they possibly make to whether your brother is convicted or not?'

'I don't know. But Beatrix Abberley was anxious to make sure they didn't fall into the wrong hands, wasn't she? If we could find out why—'

'What would you say if I told you I'd burned the letters – without reading them?'

'I wouldn't believe you.'

Griffith's eyebrows twitched up, his first facial reaction of any kind. 'I can't help your brother, Mr Fairfax.'

'Can't or won't?'

'Is there a difference?'

'I think so. All I'm asking you to do is show me the letters – or tell me what they contain that could make his sister a target for murder.'

'You're asking more than you know.'

'You admit you know what's in them, then?'

'I admit nothing.'

'Are you prepared to stand idly by and let an innocent man be sent to prison?'

Griffith did not reply. Instead, he wedged his stick in the handle of the car door and pushed it wide open. 'This is my farm. I'd like you to leave it.'

'Mr Griffith—'

'Leave me alone!' His voice was raised to a sudden bellow. A dog barked and loped into view round the end of the car. 'That's all I ask.' His tone had reverted to normal now. He turned and signalled the dog to sit, then looked back at Derek. 'There's nothing for you here, Mr Fairfax. Not a thing.'

'What about my brother?'

'Exactly. *Your* brother. Not mine.'

'You fought in the Spanish Civil War, didn't you? Wasn't that for universal brotherhood?'

'Some thought so. Some still do. I don't.'

'Isn't there anything—'

'No. There isn't. I paid my dues a long time ago. I'm not paying any more. Get into your car. Drive back to your own world. Leave me in mine.'

Griffith's gaze reached Derek as if he truly was peering out at a world he had renounced. His mouth was set in a firm line. He was breathing quickly but steadily. His shoulders were braced. His

determination not to yield – not to reveal any part of the secret he
had promised to keep – was palpable. And Derek realized in that
instant that against it he was helpless.

'Goodbye, Mr Fairfax.'

TWENTY-EIGHT

IT HAD BEEN A morning of departures at Swans' Meadow: Maurice,
soon after dawn, bound for New York; Emerson, somewhat later,
travelling to Oxford for the day; Ursula, later still, destined for an
appointment with her beautician in Maidenhead; and lastly Charlotte,
setting off back to Tunbridge Wells shortly before noon.

Only Samantha was there to see her off and she did not supply a
cheerful farewell. Charlotte found her consuming a laggardly breakfast, downcast and *déshabillé*, in the lounge.

'Not dressed yet, Sam? Your mother will not approve.'

'She doesn't approve of very much at the moment, does she?
Why should I be the exception?'

'I'm not sure I know what you mean.'

'Haven't you noticed the prickly atmosphere round here? Mum
and Dad have been stalking each other for days like two alley-
cats who can't decide to strike first.'

'You're imagining it.'

'No. You're just too dazzled to have noticed.'

'Dazzled? By what?'

'By who, you mean. Did he take you somewhere swish last
night?'

Charlotte leaned close to Samantha's ear and whispered: 'Mind
your own business.'

Samantha blushed, then giggled. 'I'm sorry, Charlie. You're right.
What's it got to do with me? Emerson's a gorgeous guy. I wish you
luck.'

'Thank you,' said Charlotte with a sarcastic curtsy.

'But tell me, do you know what's gnawing at Mum and Dad?
Something is.'

Charlotte could easily have guessed. Perhaps Ursula had told
Maurice what was really in Beatrix's letter. Or perhaps she had

not. Either way, the fact of it could not be wished away. How they coped with that knowledge was their affair. One Charlotte was too preoccupied to concern herself with. 'I really don't know what you're talking about, Sam. And now I must be going.'

Derek reached Tunbridge Wells in the middle of the afternoon. He was tired and dispirited, filled with a sense of his own inadequacy. To go home was as unthinkable as a late appearance at Fithyan & Co. He was a fugitive lacking direction as well as purpose. And so, with a kind of logic he thought Colin might applaud, he found himself at the Treasure Trove, repository for much else that was worthless and unwanted.

He let himself in with the key Colin had given him and gazed around at the dust that had settled on every horizontal surface. The place had always been somewhat down-at-heel. Now the stale air of neglect was there to compound the effect. The gilt-framed hunting scenes; the Hogarth prints; the antique maps; the horse-brasses; the bust of Cicero; the grandfather clock; the stuffed bear; the elephant's foot; the *chaise-longue*; the cheval-glass; the pine chest; the sparsely filled cabinet of Tunbridge Ware: all bore the same grey blur in testimony to their owner's absence.

Derek leaned back against a table and surveyed the scene. Beyond the window, no passers-by paused to peer into the shadowy interior. The Treasure Trove was closed and was not expected to open. Tomorrow, Colin Fairfax-Vane, proprietor, would be committed for trial on charges he could not hope to rebut. Tomorrow, the hollowness of his last pretence would be exposed. And his brother would watch it happen. There was nothing else he could do. Nothing, at all events, that a stuffed bear and a dead Roman could not match.

Charlotte had only been back at Ockham House a few minutes when the doorbell rang. Answering it, she found a girl standing on the step with an enormous bouquet of flowers: lilies, dahlias, carnations and chrysanthemums, riotously coloured and scented in a haze of gypsophila.

'Miss Ladram?'

'Yes. But there must be—'

'For you.' The girl lowered the bundle into Charlotte's arms. 'There's a note attached.' She smiled and turned to go, leaving Charlotte to close the door and carry the flowers to the kitchen before she could spare a hand to open the tiny envelope pinned to the cellophane.

There was nothing on the card save Emerson's Christian name, signed with a flourish. But there did not need to be. Leaning back against the sink, Charlotte could fill her lungs with the heady aroma of a future she had never till these last few weeks anticipated. Out of Beatrix's death might come her happiness. And the possibility dispelled all sense of irony, let alone of doubt. She raised the card to her lips and kissed it.

TWENTY-NINE

MIDNIGHT. AND AT THE twelfth stroke of the clock, Frank Griffith stirred wearily in his chair. He had delayed long enough, he knew. If he delayed any longer, he might never do it at all. Yet do it he must. To have held back when he first received Beatrix's letter was understandable. To stay his hand once more when Charlotte found him was excusable. But now understanding and excuses had run out. Fairfax's visit had proved what he should have recognized all along: that Tristram's secret would not be safe until his letters to Beatrix were destroyed.

Frank leaned forward to tap out his pipe against the fender, then rose and rubbed some of the stiffness out of his lower back. In front of him, dimly reflected in the clock-glass, he could see his lined and hollow-cheeked face. He had been strong and lithe and handsome once, striding the cobbled streets of Swansea while white horses rode the bay and factory hooters blared out their summons. So young and confident of his place in the world, with a tireless body and an inexhaustible mind, hard as the steel he forged, bright as the sun on the hills. All that was gone and wasted now, shed and shattered in dole queues and hunger marches, sloughed like a flayed skin on the snowy heights above Teruel.

This should have been done years ago. They should have been buried with Tristram in Tarragona. Or consigned to flame somewhere far back along the road that ended here, in his old age and solitude. But they had not been. So now, as the new day inexorably advanced, he would have to ensure that at long last they were.

He made his way to the kitchen, moving slowly and quietly so as not to rouse Bron. There he put on his boots and a jacket and took down the torch from its nail beside the range. He opened the back door and stepped out into the garden, pausing to let his eyes adjust to the moonlight. He shivered and chuckled faintly at how frail he had grown. He felt cold even on a balmy midsummer night, whereas once—

Stifling such futile thoughts, he walked round to the wicket-gate and let himself into the yard, raising and lowering the latch with punctilious care, for he saw no sense in taking any risks, even if in truth there were none to be run. He gazed about him and breathed deeply. All was still and silent. The wind had died with the day, leaving the moon to preside in pale and ghostly splendour over the empty black gulfs of field and moor. He knew them all. He knew them well. Every peak and slope, every rain-hewn cleft. Every boulder, every blade. This was home. This, he supposed, was where, one day not far off, he would die. And at least, after this night's work, he would die with a clear conscience.

Old age craves reassurance as well as rest. He waited longer than necessary for certainty to creep upon him through the chill. Then he marched across the yard and entered the barn, slipping in through the half-open door. And there he stopped once more. The darkness was absolute, but silence did not impose itself until a fraction of a second after his entrance. No matter. The scratching had been unmistakable. It was a dormouse. Nothing more and nothing larger. It would not move again while he remained. And he would not remain long.

He switched on the torch and ran its cone of light along the upper half of the left-hand wall, counting the trusses as he went. There was the ladder, propped against the wall. And there, he knew, wedged between the fifth beam and the thatched roof, was what he had come for. Tristram's letters from Spain and fifty years ago. His confessional. His apologia. His secret.

Frank stepped across to the ladder and moved it to a position just short of the fifth beam. Clutching the torch in his right hand and trailing its light on to his feet, he began to climb, placing both feet on each rung before moving to the next. Five rungs took him to within reach of the hiding-place. Raising the torch, he shone it into the gap and made out the familiar shape and metallic sheen of the biscuit tin he had used. It had once contained shortbreads, a Christmas present from Beatrix. Now it contained a fragment of his own past, and the lie of another's, preserved in ink and paper, bound in string and secrecy.

Transferring the torch to his left hand, he reached out with his right and picked up the tin, then started back down the ladder. So light his burden, so simple his task: soon it would be safely done. The next rung was the last. Then it only remained—

He was pulled off the ladder so suddenly and violently that he hit the straw-scattered floor before he was aware of what was happening. The torch had fallen to his left, the tin had slipped from his grasp. As he tried to rise, he was dazzled by the brilliance of some more powerful torch than his own, then his head was jerked aside by a gloved hand. There was a movement above him, a stumble, an oath, a stooping form faintly discernible, black moving against black, an arcing flash of light, then a scrape of metal on stone. Whoever he was, he wanted the tin and what he must know was inside. And now he had found it.

Frank propped himself up on one elbow and saw the man crouching a few yards away, with something clutched against his chest. It was happening too fast for him to intervene. It was happening and he was losing what he should never have preserved. Cursing his age and his indecision, he began to struggle to his feet. 'Stop!' he bellowed. 'Stop, damn you!'

Suddenly he was blind, assailed by white glaring light. He could see nothing and hear less. He tried to turn, to escape for the moment he needed to understand where he and the man and the door were in relation to each other. But it was too late. After all the moments he had frittered away since the letter arrived, another was too much to ask. He knew that. It was the only thing he did know.

Something struck him in the chest with such force that he was thrown backwards off his feet. There was a falling plunging instant, too brief for him to form a single thought beyond the burning shame of his stupidity. Then he hit the wall. And broke through into oblivion.

PART TWO

ONE

Dear Sis,

Well, I did it, didn't I? It's what you suspected I was going to do all along, I know, even though you never said so. But we don't need to speak in order to communicate, do we? Not you and I. We understand each other. We always have and we always will. Even if sometimes we don't like what we understand.

The Writers' Congress was a bigger farce than I'd anticipated, which is saying something. The usual caravanserai of windbags and wineskins swapping insults and exhortations, gesturing with clenched fists and feeble minds. If I hadn't been planning to enlist when I came out, I think their intellectual posturings would have convinced me I should. I can't tell you what a relief it was to leave them to it and make the only gesture that means a damn thing in this tortured country. I should have volunteered for the International Brigade last autumn. Would have, but for Mary and the boy. Well, better late than never, I suppose.

I won't pretend this outfit isn't amateurish and inefficient. I certainly won't claim I'm being adequately trained or am likely to find myself properly armed and equipped when the time comes to fight. But that isn't the point, is it? The point is simply to do something – anything – rather than sit idly by and let the Fascists do as they please. All the reasoning – all the temporizing – in the world won't stop them. Maybe nothing will. I don't give a lot for our chances and that's a fact. But at least we have a chance – a fighting chance. It's the only kind that really matters.

I know what you'll be thinking. I know because I often think it myself. Am I trying to live – or die – up to Lionel's example?

Am I trying to prove a point to those who reckon I'm just another high-sounding nothing? Well, maybe. Maybe and why the hell not? I'm not Byron or Brooke or Cornford. Not yet, anyway. If I end up being killed out here, it will be a kind of immortality, judging by their examples, but then poets ought to die in battles rather than bathchairs in my opinion!

What do you say to that, Sis? After all, your opinion's worth more than mine. It always has been, ever since you first planted the idea in my mind. When was that, do you remember? Nine years ago, or ten? A long time, anyway. Too long, some would say, to be living a lie. And I'd agree with them. Even though the lie has often seemed more like the truth than those burrs to the spirit we call facts. It can't continue. I know that. But how to end it? How and when? Perhaps by coming here I'm trying to run away from the answer. You wouldn't have run, I know. You'd have consented to whatever I decided. But you're stronger than me and you haven't had to carry this pretence as I have all this time, like an invisible ball and chain round my feet, pulling me back, weighing me down, reminding me that every accolade is hollow, every triumph a defeat in disguise. How apt that my poetic début should have been entitled *Blindfold*, since a blindfold is what my readers have unwittingly worn over the years. I wonder if it will ever be removed.

The boy is the problem, Sis. Maurice Tristram Abberley. Just four months old and already I feel he's reproaching me. Friends, lovers, critics, poets and the whole great gullible reading public were fair game. Even Mary's starry-eyed trusting nature doesn't seem to have troubled my conscience. Not half as much, anyway, as having a son who will one day grow to be a man and want to know the truth about his father.

The truth for the moment is that I'm doing my bit for Spain, for which read the lost cause of socialist brotherhood, and am proud of what I'm doing. Fear, anger, frustration and disillusionment are no doubt queuing up outside even as I write these words, but they haven't battered down the door yet and, when they do, I can be sure of facing them without feeling like an impostor.

Don't worry too much about your little brother. Spare any sympathy you have for Mary, who deserves more of it than I do. I shall probably be back sooner than I expect, shame-faced and resentful at the premature end of my preposterous adventure.

You can tell me then what a fool I've been. Or maybe *I'll* tell *you*.

I'll write again as soon as I can.

Much love,

Tristram.

TWO

CHARLOTTE'S DROWSY IMPRESSION WAS that the doorbell had been ringing for some time when she finally woke. It was just after seven o'clock according to her alarm clock and therefore too early even for the postman. Clambering from bed and struggling into a dressing-gown, she crossed to the window and parted the curtains, peering out through the gap to see who her caller could possibly be.

It was Frank Griffith. She recognized his Land Rover, parked in the drive, even before she saw him standing below, stabbing impatiently at the bell-push. For an instant, the incongruity of seeing him there overwhelmed her reactions. Then she pulled back the curtains, raised the window and leaned out.

'Frank!'

His head jerked up. As it did so, a white patch of bandaging became visible beneath the rim of his hat, along with a pale smear of grey stubble on his chin. He looked weary and unkempt. There was a glimmer of something akin to desperation in his eyes.

'What . . . What on earth are you doing here?'

'Don't you know?'

'Of course not.'

He took a long deep breath, as if to calm himself, then said: 'Can I come in?'

'What's wrong?'

'I'll tell you inside.'

'Very well. Can you wait while I put some clothes on?'

'I'll wait.'

She opened the front door to him a few minutes later. At closer quarters, he looked even more ragged and distraught, with dark shadows beneath his eyes and a sheen of perspiration on his face.

He had removed his hat and was holding it awkwardly, crumpled in his hands. The bandage encircled his head and was stained brown with dried blood behind his right ear.

'What's happened to you?' she asked.

'Not an accident.'

'Then . . . what?'

'You said we could talk inside.'

'Of course. I'm sorry. Come in.'

She stood back and he stepped past her into the hall. As he did so, the thought struck her that he must have started from Hendre Gorfelen well before dawn to have arrived so early.

'Would you like . . . some tea . . . or coffee?'

'Water, if you can spare some.' There was no trace of sarcasm in his voice, but his tone had unquestionably altered since their last meeting. Some of the layers of suspicion had been restored and she could not understand why.

'Come into the kitchen.' She led the way and poured him some water, which he gulped down in three swallows. 'Tell me what this is about, Frank. Please.'

'The letters have been stolen.'

'What letters?'

Anger flashed across his face for an instant, then he set his glass down and said: 'I didn't destroy them. You knew that all along. Didn't you?'

'Suspected, yes. Or hoped. But . . . you say they've been stolen?'

'I had a visit from Derek Fairfax yesterday.'

'Fairfax? How did he—' As Frank glanced reproachfully at her, she broke off. 'I didn't tell him anything. As God's my witness.'

He stared at her for a moment, then said: 'Fairfax made me realize how foolhardy it was to keep the letters. Last night, I went to fetch them from their hiding-place in the barn. I was going to burn them, as I should have done the day they arrived. But somebody was waiting for me.'

'Who?'

'I never saw their face. They took me by surprise. Threw me against the wall.' He pointed to the bandage round his head. 'I must have been knocked out for a few seconds. When I came to, they'd gone. And so had the letters.'

'Oh, God.' Charlotte put her hand to her mouth, struggling to come to terms with what Frank had said. Tristram's letters existed after all. And were important enough for somebody to resort to violence in attempting to steal them. As perhaps they had before. Looking at Frank, she saw it was not mistrust that had overtaken him, but shame. Then she noticed the bloodstain on the bandage again. 'Have you seen a doctor?'

'No.'

'You must. You may be concussed. At the very least, you should have the wound—'

'There's no time for that!' he shouted, so loudly that Charlotte fell instantly silent. Then, seeing her shocked reaction, he added: 'I'm sorry. I drove straight here after cleaning myself up.'

'Because you thought I'd arranged the theft?'

Their eyes met and contended for a moment. Then he said: 'No. But I thought you must have told somebody – or led them to believe – that I still had the letters.' As soon as the words were out, Charlotte flushed and looked away, wincing at the thought of how her stupidity could have led to this. 'It seems I was right,' said Frank.

'No . . . That is . . . I told Derek Fairfax nothing.'

'Who did, then?'

'I don't know.'

'Maurice?'

'Impossible. Besides . . .'

'McKitrick?'

'No. He wouldn't. They don't even—' She looked back at Frank, insisting to herself that she must remain calm and logical. 'I told Maurice and Emerson what you'd told me. It's possible they didn't believe you'd destroyed the letters. I didn't myself. As for Derek Fairfax, I've no idea how he heard about them.'

'From one of you three.'

'I suppose so. It just doesn't seem . . .' She shook her head. 'Whoever told him, I find it hard to imagine he attacked you.'

'So do I. But somebody did. Somebody who wanted those letters very badly. Fairfax because he thought they might help his brother. McKitrick because he couldn't stand to be denied the insight they might give him into Tristram Abberley's mind.'

'What insight would they give him?'

'One that would wreck his carefully worked out—' Frank stopped abruptly, mouth open, staring straight ahead.

'You read them, then?' Charlotte stepped closer. 'What was in them, Frank? What was it Beatrix went to such lengths to hide?'

He looked at her. For a moment, she was sure he meant to tell her. Then his jaw set in a determined line. 'All I want to know is how to find Fairfax and McKitrick.'

'I can't help you if I don't understand.'

'What makes you think I understand? If I did, I'd have taken Beatrix at her word and burned . . . burned . . .' The sentence stumbled to a halt and Frank leaned back heavily against the work-top behind him. He had suddenly grown pale. His hand, as he raised it to his temple, was shaking.

'What's the matter?'

'I don't . . . don't quite . . .' He shook his head and blinked several times. 'I'm sorry. I felt dizzy for a moment. But . . . it's passed now.'

'You need medical attention. Let me drive you to the hospital.'

'No. I have to—' He took a step across the room, then pulled up and bent his head forward, grimacing as if in pain. It was as he began to sway on his feet that Charlotte hurried across to support him.

'You're going to the hospital. Now.'

'I can't . . . can't . . .' The grimace faded. He raised his head and seemed to recover some of his colour. But still he was unsteady, his arm trembling as Charlotte held it. 'Oh, God, I wish I was younger.'

'Please let me take you to the hospital, Frank. All this can wait until you're feeling better.'

'Can it?'

'It'll have to.'

She could see the outward signs of his inner turmoil: the twitch-ings of his face, the darting of his eyes. But she could also sense the sudden weakness that was eroding his resolution. 'All right,' he murmured. 'Have it your way.'

Charlotte led him out through the door. As they moved slowly down the hall, he shook his head several times and once said 'Sorry' for no particular reason. Charlotte did not reply. She had the impression there was no need, that Frank Griffith's apology was directed not at her, but at somebody else altogether, somebody who was no longer alive to receive it.

THREE

COLIN FAIRFAX'S SECOND APPEARANCE before the Hastings magistrates was, if anything, more perfunctory than his first. He spoke just once, to confirm his own name. But for his position in the dock, he might otherwise have seemed uninvolved in the proceedings, a mere disgruntled observer of what was in reality another vital stage in his devourement by the law. He resembled the victim of some giant python, swallowed whole and helpless, conscious of his predicament yet aware that his every act of resistance only bears him further down to where the digestive juices wait.

Glancing across at him, Derek reflected on how quickly and easily he had forgotten all he had suffered at this man's hands over the years. The lies, frauds and deceptions. The ingratitude, mockery and condescension. They did not matter now. They had vanished and taken with them the bluff and bluster beneath which Colin Neville Fairfax, defendant, was simply one more weak and squirming human unable to comprehend his fate. As well as being, of course, Derek's only brother.

The charges were read. The Crown's solicitor requested summary trial, which Albion Dredge did not oppose. A bundle of statements was handed over. Reference was made to seventeen exhibits, namely the stolen items of Tunbridge Ware, which were standing on a side-table. And thereupon Colin was, in the words of the chairman of magistrates, 'committed to stand trial before a judge and jury at Lewes Crown Court.'

Before Derek had properly absorbed this development, Dredge had reapplied for bail in pessimistic tones and been refused. Colin was led away, the court rose and Derek found himself trailing out of the room amidst a clutch of lawyers and policemen. He had the vague impression that Dredge was trying to avoid him. Certainly the fellow showed no inclination to break away from a smiling conversation with his opposite number to speak to him. After lingering nearby for a few moments without catching Dredge's eye, Derek decided to leave him to it. He turned and made his way to the exit.

As he pushed the main door open, he noticed – without paying her much attention – a woman standing at the foot of the short flight of steps. She glanced up as he began his descent and, in that instant, he recognized her. It was Charlotte Ladram.

He pulled up. 'Miss . . . Miss Ladram,' he said lamely, struggling to identify what it was about her that was so different from his recollection of their earlier meetings. She was less elaborately dressed, it was true, in trousers and a plain blouse, and was wearing dark glasses, where before her large, brown, faintly startled eyes had been clear to see. But something else had altered too, something, much less obvious but, it seemed to him, far more profound. 'I . . . I didn't . . .'

'Hello, Mr Fairfax.' She removed her glasses and looked directly at him, but did not smile. 'Could you spare a few moments, please?'

'Of course.'

'Perhaps we could talk in my car.'

'Certainly.'

She turned and began walking briskly towards the car park. He had to hurry to catch up with her.

'Is this . . . about my letter?'

'Not exactly.'

'Then what?'

She countered the question with one of her own. 'I take it your brother's been committed for trial?'

'Yes. He has.'

'No last minute evidence was produced to save the day?'

'No.' He frowned. 'How could it be?'

'I gather you've been making efforts to unearth some.'

Suddenly irritated by her tone, he snapped back: 'Why shouldn't I?'

She glanced round at him, too briefly for him to read the thoughts behind her expression, then said, pointing ahead: 'Mine's the Peugeot.'

They reached the car and Derek moved to the passenger door. Charlotte gazed at him momentarily across the roof, then turned her key in the lock. They climbed in alongside each other and Derek was about to fasten his seat-belt when he remembered they were going nowhere. Self-consciously, he slid it back into its harness.

'I meant what I said in the letter . . . you know.'

'No doubt.'

'All I'm trying to do is—'

146

'Who told you about Frank Griffith?' The question fell like a blade across his words.

'I . . . don't know what—'

'You visited him yesterday at Hendre Gorfelen and asked about Tristram's letters to Beatrix, didn't you?'

'Well . . . yes.'

'So, who was the source of your information?'

Late, but not too late, his thoughts caught up with his reactions. 'Why should I tell you anything – when you tell me nothing?'

Her head drooped slightly. He heard her sigh, though whether from weariness or exasperation he could not judge. 'I'm sorry,' she said in a softer tone. 'I've no right to interrogate you. Besides, I think I know the answer before I ask the question. You didn't steal the letters, did you?'

'Steal them? You mean they really do—'

'Exist? Yes. Unless the thief has already destroyed them.'

'Then what . . . what do they contain?'

'I don't know. Frank Griffith arrived at my house early this morning in a bad state. He'd been attacked. It happened last night, while he was removing the letters from their hiding-place. Your visit had prompted him to burn them as Beatrix had originally asked. But he didn't get the chance. He's in the Kent and Sussex Hospital now, suffering from concussion. He hasn't told me what's in the letters or why Beatrix should have wanted them destroyed, partly because he thinks I'm to blame for what's happened, as in a way I am.' She had rested her hands on the steering-wheel and now, as Derek watched, her grip tightened. 'He trusted me and I betrayed that trust. Which is why I'd like to know who your informant was.'

'I promised not to reveal his identity.'

'It was Emerson McKitrick, wasn't it?'

'Who?'

'*Emerson McKitrick.*' She turned round and stared at him.

'But . . . you mean . . . Tristram Abberley's biographer?'

Incredulity was legible in Charlotte's expression. 'Are you saying it wasn't?'

'Of course I am. I've never met him. I've read his book. But that's all.'

Charlotte frowned. 'Then . . . it must have been Maurice.'

Whilst Derek was still debating whether to lie or not, he realized that to do so was pointless. His incapacity to deceive was never more evident within himself than now, when somebody whose trust he badly wanted to win defied him to throw away his chance.

'It was, wasn't it?'

'Yes. He asked me up to Ladram Avionics on Wednesday and told me all about Frank Griffith and the letters.'

'Why? What reason did he give?'

'He said he was no longer certain my brother was guilty, but couldn't do anything about it without arousing family opposition.'

'From me, you mean?'

'I suppose so. Among oth—'

'That's ridiculous!' She slapped the steering-wheel in irritation. 'Ow!'

'What's wrong?'

'Nothing.' She winced and shook her right hand, then inspected it. 'Well, a bruise perhaps. I probably deserve it for letting Maurice think I wouldn't—' She broke off, then resumed in an altogether different vein. Derek had the disquieting impression that she was talking more for her own benefit than his. 'Other than you, only Emerson McKitrick had a compelling reason to steal those letters. That's true whether or not Maurice put you up to visiting Hendre Gorfelen. And I was the one who told Emerson I believed Frank had hidden them there. So, either way, I'm still to blame. For letting him make a fool of me. For breaking my word. For—' She stopped and leaned back in her seat, massaging the heel of her hand as she stared out through the windscreen of the car.

'Miss Ladram, if there's anything I can do . . . to help, I mean . . .'

'There is.'

'What?'

'Go and see Frank Griffith. Tell him what you've told me. Tell him that if Emerson McKitrick does have the letters, I . . . Well, just say I shall find out for certain today, one way or the other.'

'How?'

'Leave that to me.' She looked at him and, a second later, past him. He was aware of wanting to say much more than he either could or should, conscious and resentful of how marginal his own concerns were to Charlotte's. 'I must go now,' she added, in a tone bordering on impatience. 'I really must.'

FOUR

NOT TILL SHE HAD driven across the bridge at Cookham and
turned in to Riversdale did Charlotte's resolution falter. Till then,
indignation had blotted out her shame. But now, when confrontation
with Emerson McKitrick was imminent, her mood changed. She
halted at the roadside several driveways short of Swans' Meadow and
twisted the rear-view mirror round to reflect her own face, then stared
at it intently, at the puffy eyes, the flushed cheeks, the quivering lips.
About her neck and nose and forehead there was a sheen of perspiration
and, when she withdrew her hand from the frame of the mirror, she
could see that it was trembling.

She wound the window down and took several gulps of air. But
all that was cool and fresh had been crushed out of the afternoon
and replaced by a hazy and oppressive stillness. Whatever courage she needed she must find within herself. That at least was
clear.

Yet nothing in Charlotte's life had prepared her for an occasion
such as this. A sheltered childhood and an unadventurous youth had
left her ill-equipped to understand her emotions, let alone command
them. It was not the probability that Emerson had deceived her that
wounded her, so much as the growing certainty that she was to
him merely a means to an end, as uninteresting and unappealing
as she had long feared she truly was.

She glanced up at her reflection and saw the tears brimming
in her eyes, swallowed hard and climbed abruptly from the car.
If she delayed any longer, she would be in no fit state to continue. And continue she must. She began to walk fast towards
Swans' Meadow, clenching her teeth as she went, rehearsing in
her mind all that might be said and done when she stood before him and scanned his face for the glistening snail's trail of a
lie.

There was no answer to the doorbell. It was the last eventuality
Charlotte had anticipated. Peering through the bull's-eye window
into the hall, she could see no movement within, yet she could

not bring herself to believe there would continue to be none. It was scarcely credible that everybody was out. She had supposed Emerson might well be, but had assumed one or all of the others would be there to let her in. She pressed the doorbell again and waited. Still there was no response.

Turning, Charlotte looked back up the drive and knew, if she had ever doubted it, that to return to Tunbridge Wells with nothing accomplished was out of the question. If she did, what would she say to Frank Griffith? What, for that matter, would she say to herself? No. She must remain where she was for as long as necessary. She must not let Emerson McKitrick elude her.

She walked round to the side of the house and entered the garden through the honeysuckle arch, wondering if she would come upon Samantha, recumbent on the lawn despite the lack of sun. But the lawn was empty. There was no sign of Samantha or of anybody else.

She walked over to the gazebo and reached up into the shadowy recess above the entrance. Sure enough, the reserve house key was hanging in its place on a nail. She took it down, retraced her steps as far as the kitchen door and let herself in. Dropping the key on one of the work-tops, she carried on towards the lounge, reckoning that would be the best room in which to wait.

It was as she reached the hall that an awareness of something amiss – some discrepancy in the atmosphere – stopped her in her tracks. A second later, just as she was about to dismiss the sensation as a symptom of her anxiety, she heard from above a sound more like a slap than anything else, then a cry that was also a laugh, and then . . . the voices of Emerson and Ursula, neither raised nor muted, pitched as naturally and casually as those of two people who believed they were alone were likely to be.

'Come back to bed,' said Emerson. 'Whoever it was has given up and gone.'

'Yes,' replied Ursula, her tone buoyed up by the residue of a giggle. 'You're right.'

'I'm always right.'

'About what a woman like me really wants, you mean?'

'That especially.'

'Then I'm surprised you should suggest going back to bed.' There was a pause, filled by the hint of a kiss, though not, Charlotte sensed, of mouth on mouth. 'It's cooler here, by the window.'

Charlotte gazed up the stairs at the empty landing and caught a glimpse of shadows moving against the wall. She clutched at the newel-post for support, unable to retreat or advance, compelled by the acoustics of the house to listen as the very worst she had feared was eclipsed by events.

'You really are insatiable, aren't you, Emerson?'

'So are you.'

'Just as well.'

'Get down.'

A second passed, then another, then Ursula moaned: 'Oh, God, that's good.'

'There's better to come.'

'Spare me . . . your Harvard puns . . . but . . . nothing else . . .'

Their words petered into panting breaths, rising steadily together towards what Charlotte was as powerless to prevent as she was to evade. She stood where she was, struggling to keep from her mind the images conjured by what she could hear. The pleasure they took from each other was undeniable and somehow worse than the knowledge of what they were doing. Just as the sound of their coupling was worse than the sight of their joined and naked bodies could ever be.

Then the climax, the groaning and the falling, the clammy un-ravelling of their sweat-soaked limbs, the moist and meaningless kisses, the husky heartless laughter.

'Better?' asked Emerson.

'Than Maurice could ever imagine.'

'And Charlie?'

'You're too good for her. Far too good.'

'But not for you?'

'Oh, no. I deserve the best. And I appreciate it.'

'Yuh.' Emerson sniggered. 'Reckon you do.'

Two impulses wrestled for mastery in Charlotte's mind. To walk upstairs and confront them where they lay. Or to turn and creep away. She did not have enough courage for the first, but she did have enough to resist the second. She walked back into the kitchen, paused to compose her face in the mirror beneath the clock, then opened the door to the garden and slammed it with enough force to set the glasses singing in the cupboard.

Absolute silence reigned for the first time since she had entered. It lasted for as long as it took her to return to the hall. Then, as she looked up, Emerson appeared at the head of the stairs, fastening a towelling bathrobe about his waist. He was barefoot and breathless, his eyes narrowing above the falsest of smiles.

'Charlie! Did you ring the bell? I was taking a shower and couldn't hear much above the spray.' But his hair was dry. As if aware of the contradiction, he began to tidy it with his hand. 'How did you . . . er . . . get in?'

'There's a spare key kept in the gazebo.'

'Oh . . . right.' He began to descend.

'Where is everybody?'

'Oh . . . er . . . Sam's visiting friends, I think. And Aliki has a long weekend.'

'What about Ursula?'

He reached the foot of the stairs and looked straight at her, his performance growing more accomplished with every second. If she had really just walked in, she would have been fooled − once more. 'Ursula?' he said with a smile. 'I don't know. Out somewhere, I guess.'

'It doesn't matter. It's you I wanted to see.'

'You look kind of worried. What's wrong?' He reached towards her and must have been surprised by the speed with which she withdrew. 'Charlie?'

'Don't touch me.'

'What?'

'You heard.'

'I don't . . .' Momentarily, his gaze threatened to shift to the landing. Was he afraid that Ursula had appeared, négligéd and casually grinning? If so, he stifled the fear with aplomb. 'I don't know what this is all about, Charlie. Why don't you tell me?'

Tristram's letters were more important than the anger and humiliation churning inside Charlotte. She knew that, but the knowledge made her task no easier. 'Frank Griffith was robbed last night.'

'Robbed?'

'The letters were stolen.'

'You mean Tristram's letters?' Was he a good enough actor to fake the quiver of shock that passed across his face? Charlotte could not be sure.

'You took them, didn't you?'

He shook his head. 'No.'

'You wined and dined and flattered and flirted with me until you were sure he still had them, hidden at Hendre Gorfelen.'

'No.'

'Then why else did you spend time with me? Not for the pleasure of my company. I know that now – as I should have known it all along.'

'What do you mean?'

'Why don't you admit you have them? There's nothing I can do about it.'

'Because I didn't take them. Maybe I would have if I'd known where they were – or been sure they existed. Either way, if I had, I'd be on a plane back to Boston by now, wouldn't I? Not waiting here for you to brand me a thief.'

It was a valid point and, for the first time, Charlotte began to consider the possibility that somebody else altogether had been responsible for the theft, somebody who had also murdered Beatrix, somebody whose name and motive she was a long way from discovering.

'Has Frank Griffith admitted keeping the letters?' said Emerson.

'Yes.'

'And has he told you what they contain? What big secret Beatrix wanted him to keep?'

She looked at him and saw then how completely the biographer's curiosity had taken him over. His expression was more animated than she had ever known it and at last she felt she understood him. Everything he had done since arriving in England had been geared to learning the truth about Tristram Abberley. Nothing else had mattered. Toying with Charlotte's emotions had meant as much as seducing Ursula. And that was precisely nothing. 'What did you hope to learn from her?' she said as she stared at him.

He frowned. 'From whom?'

Charlotte stepped closer to him and lowered her voice to a whisper. 'I know Ursula's upstairs. And I know why. I heard everything. Every word.' She closed her eyes, then reopened them. 'Every sound.'

Incredibly, Emerson smiled. 'Right,' he whispered back. 'I understand.'

'Is that all you can say?'

'She doesn't mean a damn thing to me, Charlie. Believe me.'

'I do. That's what makes it so contemptible.'

'OK. Maybe it does. But listen. Do you know what was in the letters?' His smile remained, rueful and cynical, not one whit abashed or ashamed. 'I have to find out.'

She stepped back, certain now that he was innocent of what she had suspected, just as she was certain of his guilt on almost every other count. 'You disgust me,' she snapped.

He shrugged. 'It's an occupational hazard.'

'Get out of my way.' She moved towards the front door, but he stepped into her path and she pulled up. Still he was smiling, with a sparkle of duplicity in his deep brown eyes.

'Shall I tell you what really disgusts you, Charlie?'

'If you must.'

'Still wanting me.' He stretched out his hand and, before Charlotte could stop him, slid it down over her breast. 'Perhaps wanting me even more now you know what's available.'

It was the faint trace of truth in his remark – the incontestable stirring of desire she had felt whilst standing there and listening to what he had done to Ursula – that gouged the deepest. Why did he have to be so loathsome and yet so close to understanding her?

'What's in the letters? You wouldn't regret telling me. I guarantee it.'

She pushed his hand away and stared at him. 'I'd regret telling you anything. That *I* guarantee.'

'Harsh words, Charlie.'

'But meant. Sincerely meant. Unlike a single one of yours. Now, may I leave please?'

'Sure. I'm not stopping you.' He raised his palms in a gesture of surrender. 'Go right ahead.'

And she did, through the door and up the drive, walking fast without looking back, steeling herself neither to flinch nor falter, holding back the tears till she had reached the privacy of her car and could hold them back no longer. Then, amidst her sobs, she took from her handbag the florist's card he had sent her that bore his flourishing signature. The first large ominous drops of a cloudburst were falling as she wound down the window and cast out the torn fragments. Then she started the engine and accelerated away.

FIVE

ALL THE STRENGTH AND self-assurance Frank Griffith had seemed to possess when encountered on his home territory had vanished in the antiseptic surroundings of the Kent and Sussex Hospital. Looking at him, Derek saw only a frail and wizened old man, propped up on a bank of pillows with deckchair-striped pyjamas fastened stiffly round his neck, barely distinguishable in fact from the dozing and dribbling occupants of the other beds in the ward. His eyes had grown dimmer, his voice more gravelly, since their last encounter.

'I didn't steal the letters, Mr Griffith.'

'I know.'

'Or pay anybody else to.'

'I know that too. If you had, you'd have realized by now they couldn't help your brother.'

'Maybe so. I only hope something can.'

'Why? Why do you care?'

'Because he *is* my brother, come what may.'

'I thought I had brothers once. Hundreds of them. Thousands.' Griffith's gaze moved past Derek and beyond, it seemed, even the wall behind him. 'I should have known better.'

'But blood's thicker than water.'

'Not at my age. Not at any age if—' He broke off and looked back at Derek. 'What did you say you do for a living?'

'I'm an accountant.'

Griffith nodded. 'Balancing the books.'

'Sometimes.'

'Not these books though. They're long past balancing.'

'Not necessarily.'

'They are. Believe me.'

'How can I, when you won't tell me what I need to know?'

Griffith fell silent for a moment. A gurgling coughing fit came and went further down the ward, as it had done twice before. Then he said: 'What kind of a man is your brother, Mr Fairfax?'

'Colin? He's an antique dealer, as you know. A bit shady, I suppose. I shouldn't care to be responsible for his accounts.'

'But what kind of a *man*?'

'Charming. Entertaining. Plausible. Lovable, in a way. Also vain, untrustworthy and thoroughly unreliable.'

'But still you try to help him?'

'Who else would if I didn't?'

'Would he do the same for you?'

'I don't know. The situation's never arisen. Except . . .'

'Except?'

'When we were boys, in Bromley, back in the forties, our father built a swimming-pool in the garden. He thought we should both learn to swim. And so we did, though I never much took to it, whereas Colin . . . Well, one day, when Mum and Dad were both out, it must have been the summer I was five, I fell in while larking about on the edge and knocked my head on the side. I must have lost consciousness, because I can't remember anything after hitting the water. Colin was climbing a tree at the bottom of the garden. A big old oak, it was. He saw what happened, saw me floating face down in the pool, must have realized I was going to drown. So, he scrambled down, raced up the garden, jumped in and pulled me out. He saved my life. But for him, I wouldn't be here now.'

'So, you see this as repayment of a debt?'

'No. I don't. That's not it. I'd be doing this whether or not—' A change of expression on Griffith's face – a twitch of his eyes to the left – halted Derek in mid-sentence. When he looked round, it was to see Charlotte Ladram walking slowly down the ward towards them. Her face was flushed and even to Derek's eyes it was obvious she had been crying. 'Miss Ladram,' he said, rising to offer her his chair, 'what's—'

'Emerson McKitrick didn't take the letters,' she said in a flat and strangely matter-of-fact tone.

'Can you be sure?' asked Griffith.

'Absolutely.' She subsided into the chair whilst Derek fetched another for himself. 'Please don't ask me to explain.'

'He's still here, then?' said Griffith. 'In England?'

'Yes.'

'Then I agree. He can't have taken them, can he?'

'No. If he had, he'd have gone straight back to Boston. He said as much himself.' She sighed. 'I'm sorry, Frank. Really I am.' Then she sighed again. 'How are you feeling? They tell me they're only keeping you in as a precautionary measure.'

'For observation.'

'That's right.'

He grunted. 'I don't like being observed.'

'And you won't like what I'm about to say. But it has to be said.'

'What is it?'

Derek saw her hands tighten into fists and guessed she had rehearsed this speech long and hard. 'I will do everything in my power to help you recover the letters, but unless you tell me what they contain – what Beatrix's secret was – then there is nothing I *can* do.'

'You're asking too much.'

'We have to be in this together, on equal terms, or not at all.'

'But you don't understand the terms.'

'Then help me to.'

'Would it make things easier,' put in Derek, 'if I left?'

'Perhaps,' said Charlotte.

But Griffith shook his head. 'No. If I'm to tell you, I should tell you both.'

'This is a family matter,' said Charlotte. 'Mightn't it be best—'

'No,' Griffith insisted. 'It's been a family matter too long. Let him stay. Maybe it *will* help his brother for him to understand what Tristram and Beatrix did.'

'Very well,' said Charlotte, glancing at Derek.

The imminence of the disclosure hung around them like an electrical charge in the air. They crouched forward in their chairs, as if expecting Griffith to whisper the secret in their ears. But when he spoke, he did so in an unaltered tone. Now he had resolved to tell all, it seemed he had decided to tell it aloud.

SIX

Bujaraloz,
7th September 1937

Dear Sis,

I have reached the front. I've been judged worthy to share the hazards and privations of active military service in the wind-blasted heat-blistered battleground of Aragon. There's almost a snatch of poetry in that, don't you think?

But not enough. Not enough by far. It was ever thus, of course. The thought. The image. And now the act. But never the true and sparkling exactitude of the right and perfect word. Unless it's a requiem. Maybe that at least I can hope to compose – or perhaps to inspire.

I must choose my words carefully. It's late to learn such a lesson, don't you think? But there it is. I can't, for obvious reasons, say much of what we're doing here or of how successful our efforts may be. What I can say is that it's grim and mad and maybe even pointless. But it's also glorious and wonderful and worthier than anything I've ever done before.

The battalion's been substantially reinforced with Spaniards, yet its British identity remains. At its core are not the officers with their Ruritanian pretensions, their public-school accents and Communist credentials dazzlingly intact. Oh no. They're so much candy-floss. What holds this battalion together – what binds its wounds and stiffens its sinews – are the rough tough crude complaining working class. The Glaswegians and the Geordies, the Scousers and the Swansea boys who left the dole queues to come here and fight for freedom.

It's strange and bewildering, sometimes almost embarrassing, to find out what putting principles into practice really means. Not pontification or pamphleteering. Not versifying, either. Nothing so easy or comfortable as any of that. It means marching when you're thirsty, humping loads when you're hungry, fighting when all you want to do is sleep. It means finding out what you're really made of. And not being ashamed by the answer.

There's a sergeant in my company called Frank Griffith. Hard as granite. Bright as a diamond. Sure of himself. Unsure of what we're doing here. Sick of it, in fact. But he'll never show it. No fool. No hero. But the best and only kind you want beside you at times like these. He won't cut. He won't run. He won't ever let you down.

Do you know what book – what slim little intellectual volume – he carries in his pack? The other fellows told me and I've seen it for myself since, though he doesn't know I have. *The Brow of the Hill.* Yes, that's right. The rotten Brow of the fraudulent Hill. Doesn't it make you want to laugh? Or weep?

I'm glad he hasn't faced me with it. I'm glad he hasn't requested an autograph or told me 'False Gods' is his favourite poem of the century. Because I don't know what I'd say if he did, I really don't.

The old lie is redundant here, you see, just like every other preconception. It won't serve. It's not enough. It's less than men like Frank Griffith deserve. I'd gag on the words. I'd choke on the lie I've spent ten years perfecting. I simply couldn't do it.

Pray he doesn't speak, Sis. Pray for my sake and for yours. Because, if he does, I'll have to tell him the truth. I'll have to tell him who really wrote the poems, every one, every verse. My dear unworldly neglected sister, who wants neither credit nor fame. Not me. Not the bronzed and burnished simulacrum of a poet they call Tristram Abberley. But you. The overlooked twenty-four carat reality of rhyme and reason.

Don't worry too much. It'll probably never happen. He won't speak and neither will I. Our secret's safe. I'll go on pretending to be what you can never be and what I can't help being thought: a soldier *and* a poet.

I'll write again as soon as I can.

Much love,

Tristram.

SEVEN

'WELL?' FRANK GRIFFITH LOOKED at each of them in turn, a measure of defiance restored to his gaze. 'Don't you have anything to say? You wanted to know Tristram's secret. Now you do.'

Derek frowned. 'He wasn't really a poet at all?'

Charlotte heard the remark clearly enough, but it seemed to echo, as if reaching her along a speaking-tube from a distant room. At every turn, it seemed, her hopes were to be dashed, her assumptions overturned. Emerson McKitrick was not to be trusted. Ursula was not to be relied upon. And everything Beatrix had ever said about her late and lionized brother was to be disbelieved. 'Beatrix wrote the poems?' she murmured. 'All of them?'

'Every one,' Frank replied, his voice grim and insistent, as if he had decided to spare her no single fragment of the truth now she had demanded to be told it. 'Tristram's mind was alive with ideas and images, but he lacked the facility to translate them into poetic form. Beatrix, on the other hand, was uninspired but technically brilliant. Together, they made a poet. Apart, they were merely a dreamer and his down-to-earth sister.'

'When did you find out?'

'When I reached Tarragona in March of 'thirty-eight and found him dying. He told me then. It was his deathbed confession. He didn't want a priest to absolve him. He wanted me — one of his readers.'

'And did you absolve him?'

'As far as I could. I was shocked, of course, but I didn't feel betrayed. I'd grown to know and like him for the man he was rather than the poet he wasn't. The poems were just words, whereas he was flesh and blood. The fact he hadn't written them couldn't blot out our friendship or diminish the memory of him I was determined to hold. Tristram Abberley was a good man. Even then, I understood that was more important than being a good poet.'

'But why? Why did they do it?'

'It started as a joke, while Tristram was at Oxford. They submitted "Blindfold" for inclusion in the anthology Auden edited as an experiment, to see whether it would be praised or derided. Beatrix had deliberately guyed the style of Auden's circle and had predicted the poem would be well received by them so long as they thought it was the work of one of their own kind. Well, she was right. It attracted more favourable attention than either of them had anticipated. The title was part of the joke. "*Bind the cloth tightly, lest you see too brightly.*" "*Who faces the men? Who holds the pen?*" There were hints and double meanings in virtually every line, but nobody noticed them, or understood them if they did. The experiment was a complete success.'

'Which they decided to repeat?'

'No. It was meant to end there, as a joke they could relish and share. And so it would have, but for the rift between them and their father. When they were turned out of the family home without a penny in the winter of 'thirty-two, Beatrix thought poetry was worth trying as a way of keeping the wolf from the door. Tristram's reputation at Oxford was all they had to capitalize on, so they put together *The Brow of the Hill* under his name. From then on, it was too late to turn back. Nobody wanted to hear that Beatrix wrote the poems when Tristram fitted the bill so much better. And he enjoyed the attention he received, whereas Beatrix wanted none of it. She wrote the second collection under protest. They were no longer short of money. It was only Tristram's standing in the literary world which required him to go on producing poetry. Reluctantly, Beatrix obliged.'

'Did my mother know?'

'Not while Tristram was alive. And he asked me not to tell her after he was dead. In the end, it was Beatrix who broke the news, years later, at the time of *Spanish Lines*.'

Charlotte's reactions were lagging behind her understanding. Suddenly, she realized the publication of Tristram's posthumous collection must have rested not on one lie, but on several. 'There were no poems sent back to my mother from Spain, were there?'

'No. Of course not.'

'Then . . .'

'Money's important. Only those who have never been without it will tell you otherwise. Well, in post-war Britain it was in short supply. Your father's company was floundering and Tristram's poetry was bringing in virtually nothing by then. Beatrix conceived the idea of *Spanish Lines* as a way of helping her relatives. And me. It wasn't as good as the earlier stuff. Beatrix recognized that. Without her brother's inspiration, what she produced was mechanical, somehow heartless. It's a pity he couldn't have known that. Known, I mean, that he really was a poet, or at least part of one. But *Spanish Lines* achieved its purpose. It revived Tristram's reputation just when it seemed to be in irreversible decline. The earlier collections were reprinted. People started talking about him again, reading his work, making a cult of the poet who had died in Spain. With the proceeds, Ladram Aviation was put back on its feet, at least for a while. And Beatrix bought Hendre Gorfelen for me. So, you see, I'm party to the conspiracy.'

The anxious family conferences Uncle Jack had reported made sense now. As did the delay in publishing *Spanish Lines*. Charlotte thought of her mother's explanation that she had found it too painful at first to consider publication and flinched with the shock of realizing she had lied. There had been nothing to publish – until Beatrix had written it. How far did the lies run, she wondered? How many had been told her in the course of her life? 'Who knew, Frank? You, Beatrix and my mother, obviously. But who else?'

'Your father. Nobody else. Not then.'

'But since?'

'I don't know. None of us had anything to gain from sharing the secret with an outsider. Your father and mother didn't even know I was in on it. As far as they were concerned, it was between them and Beatrix.'

Charlotte nodded, wrestling within herself to assemble and identify the consequences of what Frank had said. They would all have kept the secret. That was clear. Which meant Beatrix would never have told Emerson McKitrick about the letters. So, who had told him? Her mother? It hardly seemed likely, but who else was there? When she looked up, she found Frank's eyes trained upon her, guessing it seemed the direction of her thoughts.

'McKitrick was lying. I knew that as soon as I heard his story. Beatrix wouldn't even have given him the train times to London. He was put up to it, by somebody who knew the letters existed but not where they were, who needed to find them but who couldn't afford to let others know why.'

'Who also broke into Jackdaw Cottage,' put in Derek, 'and murdered Beatrix in search of the letters?'

'I think so,' said Frank.

Charlotte glanced first at Derek, then at Frank. Was it possible, she wondered, that they had already reached the conclusion she was approaching now with reluctance and distaste? The person they were referring to could only have learned about the letters from Ronnie or Mary Ladram. And he could only have recruited Emerson McKitrick to do his dirty work if he had visited the United States between the time of Beatrix's death and Emerson's arrival in England. 'You mean Maurice, don't you?' she asked hesitantly.

'Well,' said Frank, 'he is the only candidate, isn't he? Your mother might have felt he was entitled to know the truth about his father.'

'Yes, but—' Charlotte's instinct was to defend Maurice, but she needed time to consider whether her instinct was correct. Was Maurice capable of such acts? If he was, what was his motive? If he had none, who else did? If Maurice was ruled out, who was ruled in? No sooner had she formed the questions in her mind than they dissolved into one determined assertion. 'I refuse to believe my brother may be a murderer.'

'Half-brother,' Derek corrected her.

She turned and glared at him. 'What difference does that make?'

'Perhaps you don't know him as well as you think.'

'As well as you know *your* brother, you mean?'

'Yes, I suppose you could—'

'Maurice is a more honourable man than your brother, Mr Fairfax. Take my word for it. I've known him all my life. He's kind, intelligent, hard-working and thoroughly admirable.'

'Charlotte,' said Frank, 'all I'm trying to—'

'What possible reason could he have for doing what you've suggested? Why should he want to expose his father as a fraud? Why should he be prepared to murder his aunt in order to discredit the whole family? It's preposterous, absurd, unthinkable.'

Charlotte blushed at the vehemence of her outburst and Derek and Frank seemed at first too taken aback by it to speak. Those few occupants of the ward capable of doing so looked across at her and stared. Then Frank said calmly: 'I know. It's all the things you say. But Beatrix *was* murdered. And I *am* lying here with a gashed head. And the letters *are* missing. Those events aren't imaginary. They won't go away. How do you explain them?'

'I can't.'

'No. And neither can I. But maybe Maurice can.'

EIGHT

AS SOON AS SHE had reached Ockham House, Charlotte telephoned Ladram Avionics. To her immense relief, Maurice's secretary had not yet left for the weekend.

'What can I do for you, Miss Ladram?'

'It's about Maurice's current visit to the United States.'

'Oh, yes?'

'When's he due back?'

'Wednesday.'

'In the morning?'

'His flight's due into Heathrow at . . . let me see . . . nine-thirty. I believe he's coming straight on here.'

'Thank you.' So, only four days separated her from the reassurance she was sure Maurice would give her. How she felt for him at the moment. Betrayed by Ursula. Traduced by Frank Griffith. And unaware of it all, unable to defend himself in any way. 'I am correct in thinking, aren't I,' she continued, 'that he flew to New York yesterday?'

'Of course. Didn't you know?'

'It's a question of timing. Somebody . . . somebody we both know . . . thought they caught sight of him . . . in London . . . last night.'

'Quite impossible, Miss Ladram. Mr Abberley flew out on Concorde yesterday morning at ten-thirty. I booked the seat myself.'

'A mistake, then, obviously.' A wave of relief swept over Charlotte. The idea that Maurice had stolen the letters from Hendre Gorfelen had always been far-fetched. Now it was also a practical impossibility. 'Thank you for the information. Goodbye.'

She put the telephone down, walked into the lounge and poured herself a large gin and tonic, then added more gin. The first gulp took some of the pain away, the second some sharpness of memory. Emerson's flowers still stood in brilliant blossom in several vases round the room, but, if she tried hard enough, she could blot out most of the words he had used and virtually all of the sounds she had heard. But not everything. Even if she emptied the bottle, the burning sense of her own gullibility would remain, the horrid squirming truth of his last gibe. *Shall I tell you what really disgusts you, Charlie?*

'No,' she mumbled into her glass. 'Please don't.'

The doorbell rang, magnified by the silence of the house, startling Charlotte so that she spilled some of her drink on the sleeve of her blouse and had to bite back a sudden inclination to cry. She put the glass down and hurried into the hall, hoping, whoever her visitor was, to be alone again soon.

It was Derek Fairfax. He was smiling uncertainly. 'Miss Ladram,' he began, 'I'm sorry to . . . sorry if this is . . .'

'What do you want?'

'Could I come in?'

'Why?'

'I have something to say . . . to ask . . . It could be very important.'

A weariness with argument of all kinds overcame Charlotte. 'All right,' she said, opening the door wide. 'Come in.'

She led the way back into the lounge and turned to look at him, determined not to offer him a drink or a seat, or any other excuse to linger.

'Well?'

'I'm sorry if what I said . . . at the hospital . . . offended you.'

164

'How could I not be offended by an accusation of murder against my own brother?' She paused. '*Half*-brother, as you pointed out.'

'I only meant—'

'As it happens, I've just confirmed he was already in New York when Frank was attacked. So, you'll have to look elsewhere for a suspect, won't you?'

'Not necessarily.'

'What do you mean?'

'A possible explanation for all this came to me after you'd left. You won't like it, but I think you ought to hear it.'

'What explanation?'

'How much in royalties does Tristram Abberley's estate earn per year?'

'I beg your pardon?'

'Tristram's poetry. What are the royalties worth?'

Charlotte stared at him for a moment, trying to reconcile his presumptuousness with his timidity, then said: 'What possible business is that of yours?'

'Fifty thousand? Sixty? More?'

'I repeat: what has that to do with you?'

'You don't deny it's a considerable sum?'

'No.'

'Or that your half-brother receives the bulk of it?'

'Of course he does. He's Tristram's son.' The death of Charlotte's mother, followed by that of Beatrix, meant in fact that all royalties now went to Maurice. But Charlotte did not propose to tell Derek Fairfax so until she knew where his questions were leading. 'What of it?'

'Those royalties will run out soon, won't they? Copyright in Tristram Abberley's work expires at the end of next year. There'll be an extension for the posthumously published poems, of course, but your brother will have to do without what the rest earn straightaway.'

'So?'

'So a large and regular source of income will dry up.'

'Maurice is a wealthy man in his own right. Ladram Avionics is a highly successful company. He'll scarcely notice the loss.'

'My experience as an accountant, Miss Ladram, tells me that nobody could fail to notice such a loss. It also tells me that people's finances aren't always as secure as they lead others to believe. Perhaps he needs the money more than you think.'

'I doubt it,' Charlotte snapped. 'But even if he does, there's nothing he can—'

'That's the point!' Fairfax was suddenly animated, gleeful almost at the chance to unveil his theory. 'There *is* something he can do. Don't you see? The letters prove Beatrix wrote – or at the very least co-wrote – all of Tristram's poems. If they were made public, the literary world would have to acknowledge her role in their composition. As would the legal world.'

'The *legal* world?'

'I used to handle the tax affairs of a playwright who collaborated on some of his works with another playwright. As a result, I had to familiarize myself with the copyright laws, particularly those relating to cases of co-authorship.'

'I don't understand what you're getting at.'

'Copyright, Miss Ladram! A lucrative commodity where the poems of Tristram Abberley are concerned. And copyright expires fifty years after the death of the author. If there are two or more co-authors, it expires fifty years after the death of whichever one survives the longest. If Beatrix Abberley is recognized as the author or co-author of her brother's poems, copyright in the work will be extended until fifty years after *her* death. Fifty years from *now*, in other words. Either way, your half-brother benefits. The royalties continue to flow for the rest of his life, to him and to him only. He's the sole surviving heir of both Tristram *and* Beatrix, isn't he?'

'Yes,' Charlotte replied with bleak neutrality. 'He is.'

'If he knew from your mother that Beatrix wrote the poems, if he came to know she possessed the letters proving her responsibility for them, if he realized the advantage of making the fact public, if Beatrix refused to co-operate—'

'But he was in New York last night. And he probably has an equally good alibi for the night of Beatrix's death.'

'Does Brian Spicer have an alibi?'

'Who?'

'Spicer. Your brother's former chauffeur.'

'What about him? He was sacked, months ago, for drunkenness.'

'But he was seen in Rye on the twenty-fifth of May. What was he doing there?'

'How should I know?'

'Preparing to break into Jackdaw Cottage, do you think? What better way to suggest he had no connection with your brother than for him to be sacked? But was he sacked – or simply given a better paid job with the same employer?'

'That's ridiculous.'

'It was your brother who told me Frank Griffith had the letters. By visiting Hendre Gorfelen and demanding to see them, I covered the tracks of whoever was planning to steal them. And I provoked Frank into fetching them from their hiding-place, which the thief was waiting patiently for him to do. Spicer again, do you think?'

'No.' Charlotte turned away and stared through the window, concentrating on the trimmed and orderly section of the garden she could see beyond. To believe what Fairfax had suggested was unthinkable, but to dismiss it was impossible. She needed time and silence and solitude. Above all, she needed Maurice to lead her by the hand back to calm and sane normality. 'My brother is incapable of doing such things. Or of paying others to do them. He's not short of money. Even if he were, he wouldn't have Beatrix killed to . . . simply to . . .'

'Remember what Frank Griffith said. Those events aren't imaginary and they can't be wished away.'

At that she rounded on him, a stray thought renewing her confidence. 'If you're right, Mr Fairfax, we'll soon know, won't we? Maurice has only to make the letters public to prove your point.'

'But he could wait more than a year before doing so. If necessary, he could even wait until copyright had lapsed. He can choose his moment. He can say he found the letters, stumbled across them by chance, received them anonymously through the post. He can explain himself in any way he pleases. Whatever I or Frank Griffith think – whatever you think – we won't be able to prove anything. And my brother will stay in prison.'

'You believe Maurice fabricated the case against him?'

'I believe he may have done. The royalties are substantial, aren't they? Was fifty thousand a year so very far out? If not, over ten years, that's half a million. Invested at a modest rate of interest, it would—'

'I don't want to know!' She almost shouted the words and then, as soon as they were out, realized how horribly true they were. She did not want to know. But she would have to. 'Did you tell Frank Griffith about this?'

'No. I thought I should speak to you first.'

'Thank you for that at least. Please don't tell him. Not yet. Not until I've seen Maurice and satisfied myself that you're wrong.'

'He's hardly likely to admit any of it.'

'No. But I shall know if he's lying.'

'And if he is?'

'Then my closest relative – in many ways my closest friend – is a thief and a murderer.'

Fairfax stepped closer. 'Miss Ladram, I . . . I'm . . .'

'Please don't say you're sorry.'

'But I am. To cause you this distress, to level accusations at those you love . . .'

'Never mind.' Stubbornly, Charlotte smiled. 'You must do what you can to help your brother. And so must I.' She could maintain this façade of self-control only a little longer, she knew. She had to be rid of this man with his mild questioning eyes, his hesitant surmising that was worse than the calling of names and slinging of mud, his unconscious displays of a nature similar to her own. 'Maurice flies back from New York on Wednesday. I shall meet him off the 'plane and lay everything you've said before him. When I've heard his response, I shall tell you what my conclusions are. After that, you must act as you see fit. But, until then, will you promise to do and say nothing about any of this? There's no reason why you should agree, but, as a personal favour . . .'

'I agree.' He solemnly extended his hand. 'You have my word, Miss Ladram.'

It was strange, Charlotte thought as she put out her hand and let him shake it, that she should seek or accept a promise from anybody about anything after all she had recently endured. But seek one she had. And accept it she did.

NINE

Albacete,
30th October 1937

Dear Sis,

The Aragon offensive is over and I've survived my first taste of action. With some distinction, I'm assured, though believe me I've no wish to crow. I enjoy a big advantage over most of my comrades. This was my first, not umpteenth, experience of military defeat.

And I haven't yet come to share their no doubt justifiably cynical view of the cabals and commissariats that govern our fate.

So, as we rest here and try to recuperate, there's time to reflect on the consolations of a soldier's life, whether he's on the winning or the losing side, the right or the wrong. The greatest of all is the peerless brand of friendship bred by danger and adversity. I spent the best part of a day trapped in no man's land with two men who I'd never have met but for each of us being caught up in this chaotic affair and, absurd as it may sound, I'm glad I volunteered for that reason alone.

You may meet Frank Griffith one day and I'm sure you'll like him if you do. He'll never be invited to a Bloomsbury cocktail party – unless it's one I throw in his honour – but you could trust him with your life and not be disappointed. There's not much higher praise than that, is there?

Vicente Ortiz is an anarchist, by party and inclination. But he recognizes his party's faults. He knows – and he's told me – the mistakes their leaders made and how they undermined their position in the Republican movement. He also knows his ideology makes him a marked man, at best an embarrassment, at worst a target. But he doesn't seem to begrudge the fact. It's all one to him. Fighting the Fascists is what he regards as important, not evening the ideological score. If only more Republicans thought the same! Remember what happened to the POUM?

But you don't want me to lead you into the tangled forest of Republican factions. Perhaps you knew the fervour we sensed in Madrid six years ago would lead to this. Perhaps you even told me so. It wouldn't have been like me to listen, would it?

With autumn well entrenched, my thoughts turn to Mary and the boy. How is the little chap? He must be seven months old now and growing fast. I worry about him more than I worry about his mother. I feel nervous about what sort of a man he'll grow to be, about how my example will influence him. It's not much of one, after all, is it? Not what you'd want anybody to model their life on. What do you think he'll say about me when I'm dead and gone? Will he thank me or curse me, respect my memory or revile it? If only we knew, eh, Sis? If only we had the chance to alter the effect we have on the future and the people who inhabit it. Well, on reflection, perhaps it's best that we don't. We've plenty to put right in the here and now. Why waste energy on the yet to be?

Don't worry about me. I don't feel half as gloomy as this letter sounds. And I'll write again as soon as I can.

Much love,

Tristram.

TEN

'IT'S ASTONISHING, CHARLIE. QUITE astonishing. I really don't know what to say.' Maurice frowned and shook his head and sipped distractedly at his coffee. And Charlotte watched him.

They were in the air-conditioned lounge of one of the low-rise hotels on the northern perimeter of Heathrow Airport, seated in huge and squeaky leather armchairs, flanked by glossy-leafed pot-plants, walled in smoked glass, bathed in muzak. A more disorienting venue for their discussion Charlotte could not have imagined, but, having surprised Maurice by meeting him off his flight from New York, she had been in no position to object when he had offered to postpone his return to Ladram Avionics on her account.

'The idea that Beatrix wrote my father's poems . . . Well, I'd have said it was about the craziest suggestion I've ever heard. Still would, if it comes to it. But if the letters leave no room for doubt . . .'

Derek Fairfax had kept his promise and Frank Griffith had gone home to Wales following his release from hospital. Charlotte was therefore confident Maurice had received no warning of what she had to tell him. She had spent four days preparing herself for their encounter, scouring her memory for hints of the truth Beatrix might have let slip, probing for flaws the logic that focused suspicion on Maurice. She had studied his face with the clarity of a searchlight, weighed his words with the zeal of an inquisitor. And still she was not sure. Was his dismay artificial? Was he a good enough actor to deceive her without even the opportunity to practise his lines? Or was he as taken aback as he appeared to be?

'I can't come to terms with it, Charlie. I can't think through all the implications. I suppose Griffith's explanation makes sense, but are you sure he's to be believed?'

'I believe him.'

'Then that's good enough for me.' He let out a slow and thoughtful breath. 'The question is: why would anybody want to steal such letters? What would they have to gain by it?'

'I don't know. But I know what Derek Fairfax would say.'

'Quite.' Maurice placed his hand over hers. 'It was good of you to put the lid on that particular notion. I don't need to tell you, of course, that it's completely without foundation.'

'Of course.'

His hand withdrew. 'I can see why concern for his brother might make Fairfax want to believe it. After all, he doesn't know me. He doesn't know *us*. It's the way an accountant might reason. It adds up, even though it's wrong in every respect. I haven't seen Spicer since the day I sacked him. I don't know anything about the letters. And the loss of the royalties won't dent my finances in any way.'

The effort of concentration – of analysing every nuance of Maurice's reactions while suppressing the desire to confide in him – was beginning to tell on Charlotte. She thought of all the generous acts he had performed, the stray kindnesses and magnanimous gestures. She thought of the many occasions he had comforted and consoled her, of the love he had always shown her. To harbour a secret doubt about him, to put it to the test while declaring her loyalty, was in itself an act of treachery.

'But none of that's really the point, is it? If I were reduced to my last penny, I still wouldn't be able to do what Fairfax is suggesting. It's a matter of breeding, isn't it, Charlie? A matter of right and wrong. Conspiring to murder Beatrix? Can you imagine how many principles and instincts would have to be conquered in order even to consider the possibility? I can't. I can't begin to imagine.'

'Because you never did consider it?'

'Exactly. All I did was make the mistake of telling Fairfax about Frank Griffith. And why? Because I thought he was entitled to know. I wanted to give him a helping hand, for God's sake. And what's my reward? To be accused of murdering Beatrix for the sake of some paltry royalties I didn't even know might be due to her.' He was becoming angry, as was understandable. Astonishment was giving place to indignation. 'My God, Fairfax has a nerve to try this on. Does he really expect to help his brother wriggle free by smearing me in this way?'

'I think he may believe it, Maurice. As you said yourself, he doesn't know you. And there's so much . . . apparent corroboration.'

He frowned. 'Such as?'

'You prompted his visit to Hendre Gorfelen.'

'I've just explained that. I was trying to help him.'

'And it was you Emerson McKitrick contacted.'

'What of it?'

'Well, he must have been lying, mustn't he? About the letters, I mean. In view of what we now know they contain, it's inconceivable Beatrix would have mentioned them to him.'

'So it is.' Maurice looked at her sharply. 'I hadn't thought of that. Have you challenged him on the point?'

'No. I didn't want to do anything without consulting you first.' Charlotte struggled to erase any hint from her expression that there might be other reasons why she should have wished to avoid Emerson McKitrick.

'Good girl.' Maurice grasped her hand and squeezed it. 'He has some explaining to do. I'll see him straightaway.'

'You think he holds the key to all this?'

'He may do. If there is a key. If it isn't just a huge coincidence.'

'How can it be?'

'Easily.' He stared at her. 'Isn't it obvious? McKitrick may have been trying his luck. Talking vaguely about old letters to see what he could uncover for his blasted new edition of Tristram's biography. By chance, there actually *were* some letters. At least, so Griffith claims. Until I see and read them, I won't really believe they exist.'

'You're suggesting McKitrick stole the letters?'

'Or Griffith dreamed the whole incident. Either way, it probably has nothing to do with Beatrix's death. She died because a petty villain broke into her house, put up to it by Colin Fairfax-Vane.'

Maurice was retreating before Charlotte's eyes, recoiling from the consequences of accepting any part of Derek Fairfax's theory. This was natural, but it was also consistent with another interpretation of his behaviour. He had played for time when taken unawares. Now he had devised a strategy and meant to pursue it.

'If Griffith is correct – and it's a big if – McKitrick's the obvious candidate for having stolen the letters.' Did he have an alibi for Thursday night? Charlotte wondered. Was it one that would cause Maurice more pain than any of Fairfax's accusations? 'And since what they contain – what they *supposedly* contain – turns his account of Tristram's career on its head, he's probably already destroyed them.'

'I don't think so.'

'No? Well, we'll see.' For the first time, Maurice smiled. His confidence was returning as Charlotte watched, bringing warmth to his gaze and fluency to his thoughts. 'Leave this to me, old girl. I mean to put a few hares back in their traps.'

'You really think you can?'

'Oh, yes.' Maurice was back to his self-assured best, neither as arrogant as Emerson McKitrick nor as hesitant as Derek Fairfax. This was what Charlotte had hoped he would be from the first. This was what she had been sure would rid her mind of doubt. How strange, then, that now it came to the point the doubt remained, as stubborn as it was insistent, greater indeed than it had been before. 'You've done well, Charlie. And I'm grateful. But now I think I'd better take over. Don't you?'

ELEVEN

DEREK'S SECOND BOUT OF absenteeism had been greeted by David Fithyan with a silence more ominous than any censorious interview. Derek had therefore beavered his way through the first three days of the following week, endeavouring never to be seen to be other than industriously engaged. He was well aware Charlotte Ladram was to meet her half-brother on Wednesday morning, but it was not until the early evening that he felt able to leave Fithyan & Co. with a clear conscience and proceed to Ockham House, high and cool in its leafy setting above the town.

When he drove up the drive, he saw Charlotte at once, seated on a wicker chair in the corner of the lawn where the setting sun still lingered. She was wearing a cream pinafore dress with a navy blue cardigan slung round her shoulders and a wide-brimmed straw hat that made her look younger and more carefree than he knew she was. In his rumpled office suit, he felt miserably shabby, unequal to whatever the occasion represented. But there was a second empty chair beside Charlotte's and she seemed to be smiling as he approached. He was expected and, if not welcome, could at least be sure that on this occasion he would not be turned away.

'Miss Ladram . . . I . . .'

'You're later than I thought you'd be, Mr Fairfax.'

'I'm sorry. It's been . . . difficult.'

'Please sit down. Can I offer you a drink, perhaps?'

She was being too polite, too altogether reasonable, for his peace of mind. There was an awkwardness to her expression at odds with the relaxation of her tone. What it meant he could not discern. 'No. Nothing to drink, thank you.' He sat down. 'You . . . er . . . saw your brother?' He nerved himself to use the word without prefix, wondering whether she would notice or take it amiss if she did.

'Yes. I saw him.'

'When we spoke last Friday . . .' But last Friday seemed an age ago. As did the truce they had come close to declaring. He had been certain then that she meant to be honest, with him and with herself. Now he was not so sure. 'When we spoke, you undertook to put all the points I made—'

'I did.'

They stared at each other in silence for a moment. Then Derek said: 'What conclusion did you reach . . . might I ask?'

'Maurice is innocent of any wrong-doing.' But her gaze had faltered. She looked down and away, squinting into the sunlight. 'I'm sure of it, Mr Fairfax. Absolutely sure. He's as unable to account for events as I am.'

'I find that hard to believe.'

A compression of her lips was the only sign of irritation. 'I promised to inform you of my conclusions and that's what I've done.'

'But the circumstances, Miss Ladram. The circumstances are just too—'

'Coincidence! Nothing more. I know you want to believe otherwise, but you're wrong.' Her outward show of calmness was what gave the game away, Derek realized. If she really trusted Maurice, she would defend him with spirit and vigour, not a cool veneer of reason. 'I'm sorry, truly sorry, but there's—'

'Hi, Charlie!' The voice, raised and drawled, reached them across the lawn. Derek looked round and saw a tall broadly built man striding towards them. Dark hair and a trimmed beard framed a handsome smiling face. He wore a loose fawn suit and open-necked shirt and was aiming his left hand at Charlotte in the likeness of a gun, thumb raised, index finger pointing. 'Didn't think I'd catch up with you, did you?'

'Emerson!' Charlotte's exclamation and the American accent confirmed to Derek that this was Emerson McKitrick. As he towered above them, he gave every impression of being more than slightly drunk.

'Who's your friend?'

'Derek Fairfax.'

'Oho! Buddying up with the enemy now, are we? Leastways, Maurice's enemy.'

'I don't know what you mean. We're simply—'

'Save the denials for big brother, Charlie. I don't need them.'

'What are you doing here, Emerson?' Charlotte's voice cracked as she spoke.

'Had the bum's rush from Swans' Meadow. Thought I'd spend a couple of nights here before flying back to Boston. I'm staying at the Spa Hotel. Why don't you join me for dinner?'

'I hardly think so.'

'Your loss, sweetheart.'

'I'm not your sweetheart.'

'Wanted to be though, eh? Wanted to be another of my many conquests. I could have had you the first night we met.'

Charlotte's flinch of shame at the words drove Derek from his chair. 'That's enough!'

'Enough?' bellowed McKitrick. 'I haven't even started yet. Why don't you crawl back to your counting-house, Fairfax? Leave Charlie and me to bill and coo at each other like the pair of love-birds we aren't.' He was not only drunk, but angry, though whether with Charlotte or Derek or somebody else altogether was far from clear.

'I don't want you to leave,' said Charlotte, looking up at Derek in direct appeal.

'Don't be too sure,' said McKitrick. 'You mightn't want him to hear what I have to say. It's time you learned the truth about brother Maurice, you see. And I'll bet you won't want to share it, let alone with your tame accountant.'

'He's not *my* accountant.'

'No? Well, maybe he ought to be. You'll surely need one in this affluent future Maurice has planned for you.'

'What are you talking about?'

'Don't tell me you're not taking a cut. Isn't that how he means to shut you up?'

'A cut of what?'

'The royalties, Charlie. The royalties that won't run out next year. Maurice has told me all about it. He had to, even though he knew it meant I'd realize what he'd been up to right from the start. *He* approached *me*, not the other way round. *He* told *me* about the letters. Beatrix never did. He knew I'd be unable to resist the lure of fresh material on Tristram. That's how he led me on. He said we'd have to keep his role in the whole thing secret to ensure your co-operation, which, as heir to Beatrix's property, we had to have. I was happy to go along with it, of course. I was happy to do just about anything to lay my hands on those letters. For the sake of scholarship, I might add. Not for money.' He grinned. 'Well, not just for money.' At that he paused and leaned against the back of Charlotte's chair for support.

'You're saying Maurice put you up to this?' Charlotte was staring up at him, eyes wide with fear of what he might yet reveal.

'Sure, Charlie. You've got it. He claimed he wanted to make his father's biography as complete and accurate as possible. I never swallowed that, of course. I expected a trade-off when we found the letters. *If* we found them. What I didn't expect was that Maurice was playing a deeper game, for bigger odds than I'd ever imagined. We found the letters for him, you and me. And now he's snatched them from under our noses. I'm not sure how, but I'm damn sure why. So he doesn't have to go short after the expiry of copyright. Because it won't expire, will it? Not now he can prove Beatrix was the real poet. Not now he can show up my study of his father's life as a sham, built on a lie it'll suit him to expose. Do you know what this will do for my reputation, my academic standing? Do you have any idea? I'll be a laughing-stock. Students sniggering in my seminars. Colleagues whispering behind my back. My whole career may go down the tube. And why? To serve the truth or honour the dead? Hell, no. Not for anything as high-minded as that. Just to keep Maurice's royalty account topped up for the rest of his life.' He pushed himself away from the chair, swayed slightly, then clapped a hand to his brow. 'I've been taken for a fairground ride, Charlie. And kicked out of the chair at the top of the ferris wheel. So you'll have to excuse' – he glared at Derek – 'any lack of courtesy.'

Charlotte had screwed her eyes tightly shut as McKitrick spoke. Now she slowly opened them and looked at Derek, her face pale, her lips parted, her knuckles white where she clasped the arms of her chair. Then her gaze shifted past him and she said: 'I had no idea . . . I didn't know . . . anything about this.'

'Then you're a bigger fool than I took you for,' said McKitrick. 'Though not as big a one as I'll look. In time, that is. In Maurice's own sweet time.'

Derek stared at each of them in turn. McKitrick was not lying and Charlotte knew it. And the truth of what he had said dictated another truth, greater and more hideous by far. In Charlotte's expression he could see its realization. In his own mind he could sense it spreading. 'Why did Beatrix go to such lengths to hide the letters?' he asked.

'Because she must have known what Maurice was planning,' said McKitrick. 'Known and refused to go along with it. Maybe she didn't want to sully Tristram's reputation or expose her part in the fraud. Or maybe she just wanted to spite Maurice. Either way, she wouldn't give in. So Maurice decided to . . . over-ride her objections.'

'Murder her, you mean?'

'Reckon so, don't you? He must have thought it was just a question of knocking the old lady on the head and faking a break-in, then blaming it on your brother and pocketing the letters. Only Beatrix had put them out of his reach, so he had to use me to find them. And you, of course, Charlie. You were one of his pawns as well. How does it feel?'

Charlotte did not look at McKitrick as she responded. 'What do you propose to do now?' she murmured.

'There's nothing I *can* do. That's the worst of it. Or the best of it, from Maurice's point of view. My evidence wouldn't stand up in a thesis, let alone a court of law.'

'Then why are you telling me all this?'

'So you'll know, when he unveils the letters a year or so from now, and claims he found them, or was sent them, or was sold them, or whatever damn story he comes up with – so you'll know then, and ever after, what the truth of it is. That Beatrix was beaten to death, and this man's brother was jailed, and I was ruined, just to feather Maurice's nest. And yours, of course. I don't doubt he'll be generous. He can afford to be now, can't he?'

'Please go.' Still she did not so much as glance at either of them. 'Please go now, both of you.'

'It'll be a pleasure.' Unexpectedly, McKitrick stepped forward, raised Charlotte's hand from the arm of the chair, and kissed it. 'So long, *sweetheart*.' With that he turned and strode away across the lawn. Derek heard Charlotte release a deep breath she had been holding and watched her slowly wipe the hand McKitrick had kissed against her dress.

'You want me to leave as well?'

'I would be grateful.' She spoke softly and precisely, stressing each syllable equally.

'Without further discussion?'

'What is there to discuss?'

'You heard what he said. It proves I'm right.'

'Perhaps.'

'How can you doubt it?'

'Maurice is a wealthy man.' She seemed almost to be in a trance, hypnotically convinced that such phrases, if repeated often enough, would hold his guilt at bay. 'He didn't need to do this. Any of it.'

'But he did do it. You know he did.'

At last she looked at him. 'What now, Mr Fairfax? What next?'

'I . . . I shall inform my brother . . . and his solicitor . . . but . . .'

'Yes?'

'Nothing can be proved. McKitrick said so. And he's right.'

'Exactly. Nothing can be proved.' She raised one hand to her forehead. 'Don't you see why that's as awful for me as for you?'

'Frankly, no.'

'Because nothing can be *disproved* either. Nothing, one way or the other, can be known for certain. Your brother's not the only one in prison, Mr Fairfax. From now on, we all are.'

TWELVE

SUMMER RAIN, GENTLE BUT insistent, smeared the world grey and green. Charlotte stood at her bedroom window, watching it fall and wishing it would continue for ever, listening to its peck and patter against the glass, wanting the stain of every sunny day washed from her memory.

Hope Cove, at the dawn of her childhood recollection: the sand between her toes; the tiny crabs scuttling in the rock pools; her mother warmly scented and ever smiling: her father boisterous and laughing; and Maurice in his late teens, self-conscious and wary, uncertain whether he wanted to join the game on the beach or stand apart and scoff. It had been sunny then, the whole fortnight. And already the lie had begun.

Charlotte lowered her chin to meet the soothing coolness of the bathrobe and closed her eyes, prising apart the tangled undergrowth of long-ago incidents in search of the discrepancies she should have noticed, the inconsistencies and contradictions which must have formed the fabric of the lie. But there were none. They had remained loyal to each other. They had let nothing slip, nothing show, nothing reveal the falsehood upon which they were set. *'This is a photograph of Tristram Abberley, Charlie.' 'This is a book of his poems.' 'These are the verses that feed and clothe you, Charlie.' 'These are the secret we will never tell.'*

She turned and walked into the bathroom, where already the water was halfway up the tub. She looked in the mirror and cursed her weakness that showed in the brimming redness of her eyes. She could not free her throat of the constricted urge to sob, to weep and surrender to the bitterness she felt. A night had passed since Emerson McKitrick had forced her to confront the possibility that everything alleged against Maurice might be true, a night since Maurice had telephoned her in a fluent yet flawed attempt to set her mind at rest.

'It's possible you might hear from McKitrick, Charlie. He's in a vindictive mood and I wanted to warn you not to take what he says seriously.'

'What might he say, Maurice?'

'That I told him about the letters. I couldn't have done, of course, because I didn't know they existed. But he'll try anything to wriggle out of admitting how he found out about them.'

'You didn't learn who put him up to it, then?'

'My bet is he put himself up to it. My bet is he stole the letters and destroyed them and is prepared to blacken anybody's name if he thinks it'll help to cover his tracks.'

'Blacken your name, you mean?'

'Exactly. He might even be able to persuade some people to believe his story.'

Maurice had paused, waiting, it seemed, for Charlotte to assure him that she would not place a scrap of faith in anything McKitrick said. She stepped back from the mirror and turned off the taps remembering the momentary silence with which she had tortured him.

'Charlie?'

'I'm still here, Maurice. And don't worry. If Emerson McKitrick contacts me, I shall know how to deal with him.'

'Well, these Americans are great ones for conspiracy theories. They can only thrive if people want to believe them.'

'Quite. I do understand, believe me.'

'That's all I wanted to be sure of.'

'Then I'll say good night. It's late and I'm very tired.'

But she had not been tired. Her mind had teemed with competing thoughts, scrabbling and scrambling towards the truth. Fatigue, which dragged now at her every bone, had seemed then a condition she would never again experience. After bidding Maurice good night, she had scoured the house for records of her family's past: snapshots, postcards, letters, greetings, books, papers, cuttings, jottings; the scraps and remainders left behind and overlooked wherein she had hoped to find, but had not, the answer she was still bound to seek.

Charlotte let her robe fall to the floor and lowered herself into the consoling warmth of the bath, closing her eyes and stretching back as the heat relaxed her muscles and the steam invaded her senses. There was no alternative to the course she had decided upon. They had left her none, with their lifetime of deceptions and evasions. *Her* lifetime, built on *their* lie. Now she had to know. She had to be certain. In her own mind, this one issue demanded to be settled.

An hour later, cleansed and utterly calm, she descended to the hall, checked the time, then picked up the telephone and dialled Swans' Meadow.

''Ello?'

'Aliki, this is Charlie. Is Ursula there?'

'Oh, 'ello Charlie. Yes, Meesus Abberley is 'ere. I put you through.'

A lengthy pause. Charlotte looked at herself in the mirror. Her face was a model of self-possession. So far, so good.

'Hello, Charlie. This is a surprise.' Only the choice of phrase, not its tone, hinted at irony on Ursula's part. 'What can I do for you?'

'You can have lunch with me.'

'*Today?*' Shortage of notice, it seemed, was a greater obstacle than Charlotte having overheard her having sex with Emerson McKitrick. 'I'm afraid I can't. I have too much on.'

'You had nothing on last time I was at Swans' Meadow. Unless you want me to tell Maurice exactly what I witnessed on that occasion, you *will* have lunch with me.'

Several seconds passed before Ursula replied. 'Lunch it is then, Charlie. Such an unexpected pleasure.'

THIRTEEN

CHARLOTTE AND URSULA MET at the Inn on the Lake in Godalming. The venue was ostensibly chosen because of its equidistance between Bourne End and Tunbridge Wells, but neutral ground seemed suitable for non-geographical reasons as well. Not that Ursula's *sang froid* was in other than excellent repair. She contrived to sustain a monologue about the arrangements for Samantha's twentieth birthday party, to be held at Swans' Meadow on the first Saturday in September, until aperitifs had been consumed and they had been shown to their table next to the restaurant's internal fishpond, where the artful cascading of water conferred a heightened degree of privacy.

Regarding her sister-in-law across the virginal tablecloth and winking crystal, Charlotte could not suppress a stab of admiration that disguised, she knew, a pinprick of envy. The highlighted hair; the plain but flattering suit; the discreetly glittering jewellery and extravagantly impractical clutch-bag: all these and the cherry red co-ordination of lipstick and nail-varnish signalled sophisticated sensuality within, though only just, the confines of Home Counties etiquette.

'Enough of small talk,' Ursula disingenuously remarked as she swallowed a heart-shaped slice of avocado. 'You didn't ask me here to learn the price of hiring a marquee.'

'No.'

'Why, then?'

Charlotte took a sip from her glass of wine, reminding herself of the need for poise as well as precision. 'I want to know the exact condition of Maurice's finances.'

Ursula abandoned her fork where it was embedded in the next slice of avocado and stared at Charlotte. 'You want to know *what*?'

'I believe you heard.'

'Of course I heard, Charlie. What I found difficult was to believe my own ears. Maurice's finances? You know as much about them as I do, I should imagine.'

'Hardly.'

'You're a shareholder in Ladram Avionics. Read the annual report and you'll—'

'It's his personal outgoings I'm interested in.'

Ursula's eyebrows shot up. 'Indeed.' She lowered her voice and leaned forward slightly. 'Are you feeling quite yourself, Charlie?'

'I want to know how much he spends and what he spends it on. I want to know whether his present income is more than adequate to sustain his expenditure – or barely so.'

'I see.' She glanced at Charlotte's plate, then at her own, then slid her fork free of the avocado and summoned the waiter. 'I think we've finished this course, thank you.'

The plates were removed, their glasses recharged with chablis. Ursula lit a cigarette and took several draws on it, rolling the smoke around her mouth like wine whilst gazing at Charlotte with a mixture of disdain, surprise and amusement.

'It's hardly necessary for me to point out that my husband's finances are none of your business.'

'It's hardly necessary for me to point out that he might be shocked to learn what occurred in his bedroom last Friday afternoon. And several other afternoons, no doubt.'

'Just Friday, actually.' Ursula smiled. 'Nothing improves with repetition.' The smile vanished. 'Certainly not a threat.'

'I shall tell him if I have to.'

'Yes. I rather think you would.'

'Well then?'

The smile returned. 'What makes you think I possess such information?'

'You're his wife.'

'Ah, yes. His wife. I suppose that might make you think such a thing – you who have never been a wife.'

'Nor are likely to be? Is that going to be your next put-down, Ursula?' Charlotte's face had coloured. Instantly, she regretted rising to the bait. But relief was at hand. Their main courses were arriving and a truce of several minutes was declared whilst vegetables were dispensed and glasses topped up. When the interlude was at an end, Ursula sampled some of her salmon and took a few sips of wine before breaking the silence.

'I think you must take after your father, Charlie. I never met him, of course, but according to Maurice he was wildly impractical and unbelievably naïve about other people's motives. Rather like you.' She consumed a baby potato. 'Head either in the clouds or in the sand.'

'Are you going to tell me what I want to know?'

'I shall tell you what you *need* to know. Which is a lesson I learned when I was very young. Compromise is the key to success in life. Not perhaps the key to happiness, but I've found that to be an over-rated commodity. If you'll take my advice—'

'I didn't come here for advice!'

Ursula stared appraisingly at Charlotte for a moment, then said: 'No. No, of course you didn't.' She smiled. 'You came here because our mutual friend, Emerson McKitrick, has persuaded you that his allegations against my husband might just possibly be true. And because you've calculated that only financial desperation could have driven Maurice to do what Emerson alleges. Well, so be it. I have expensive tastes, as you must be aware. I do not stint myself.' The smile became almost wistful. 'In anything.' Then her concentration seemed to step up a gear. 'But Ladram Avionics is doing well, very well in fact. As its managing director, Maurice enjoys an income quite adequate to keep Sam and me in the manner to which we're accustomed. Tristram's royalties are strictly surplus to his requirements.'

'If that's the case . . .'

'It is.' Her mouth curled in mockery. 'Or would be. If Sam and I were Maurice's only dependants. But we aren't, you see.'

'What do you mean?'

'I've long suspected something of the sort, but only recently have chapter and verse come my way. In an envelope posted in Gloucester on the twenty-third of June, to be precise.'

'The letter from Beatrix?'

'Yes. It didn't contain blank paper.'

'What, then?'

'A report from a private enquiry agency commissioned by Beatrix on exactly the same topic you asked me here to discuss: Maurice's finances. It seems the old bitch—' She broke off with a grin. 'I'm sorry. What I meant to say was that Maurice's dear and charming aunt had been checking up on him. And evidently thought I should know the results. They were, to say the least, illuminating.' She paused. 'Are you sure you want to hear what they were? They don't paint Maurice in a flattering light. And since I know you've always had a high regard for his—'

'Just tell me!'

'Very well. Maurice spends a great deal of time in the United States on business. The company maintains an apartment for him in New York. But he makes little use of it. He already owns another apartment, it seems, on Fifth Avenue, and a weekend retreat in the Hudson Valley.'

'I didn't know—'

'Neither did I. The report told me these things, along with what it costs him to run them. And to run the mistress he shares them with, of course. It appears she has even more expensive tastes than I have. Her name is Natasha van Ryneveld.'

'Van Ryneveld?'

'Yes. Not van Ryan, as Lulu Harrington misremembered it. The report contained little in the way of personal details, for which I was grateful. It was only concerned with how Maurice funds such an extravagant commitment. The answer is by siphoning money from a range of personal investments, which are topped up from the royalty account.'

'You mean—'

'I mean that, when copyright expires on his father's work, Maurice is going to have to make some awkward decisions about what he can and can't afford. He's going to have to economize. But, believe me, I've no intention of doing any such thing myself. So, he'll have to look elsewhere for savings, won't he?'

Charlotte gazed at Ursula in mounting horror. It was inconceivable that the implications of what she had said were lost on her. The report proved Maurice really did have a compelling motive for forestalling the expiry of copyright, a motive, indeed, for murder. But this did not appear to interest Ursula. The security of her dress and lunching-out allowance was evidently much more significant. 'Does . . . Does Maurice realize you know all this?'

'No. Though he may suspect it. I don't think he was ever convinced by the blank paper story.'

'But if he doesn't know . . .'

'Why am I telling you? To prevent you making a fool of yourself, of course. My little fling with Emerson hardly compares with Maurice's standing arrangement in New York, does it?'

'Is that why you did it? For revenge?'

Ursula let out a peal of laughter, then leaned across the table. 'Sex is for pleasure, Charlie, not revenge. Didn't anybody ever explain that to you? Emerson was actually rather good at giving pleasure. Better than I'd expected.' She lowered her voice to a whisper. 'Bigger as well.' Then, grinning mischievously, she swayed back. 'You should have found out while you had the chance. It would have been an education for you.'

Charlotte closed her eyes and told herself that Ursula did not matter. Nor, now, did Emerson McKitrick. All that mattered was whether Maurice had done what she could not help believing he had. She opened her eyes again. Ursula had pushed her plate aside and was lighting another cigarette. 'Would you be prepared to show me the report?'

Ursula shook her head. 'Don't be silly, Charlie. It's *my* insurance policy, not yours. I'll use it if I have to, but otherwise not. That's what I meant by compromise. Maurice may not be a faithful husband, but he's a generous paymaster. As long as he remains generous, I shan't quibble.'

'But don't you see what the report proves? Don't you see why Beatrix commissioned it? She must have feared . . . must have suspected . . .'

'I see nothing. Unless I choose to. I shall tell Maurice we met – and why. But I shan't tell him anything else. If he contacts you – as I suspect your curiosity about his financial circumstances will prompt him to – I advise you to assure him of your absolute confidence in his loyalty and integrity. That way, he won't think you're threatening him.'

'And if I ignore your advice?'

'You'd be very foolish. I have insurance, remember. You don't.'

'Meaning?'

'Meaning it's better to let sleeping dogs lie. And dead aunts.' Suddenly, she extinguished the cigarette and drained her wine-glass. 'Now, why don't you ask for the bill? I have the strangest feeling neither of us wants a dessert.'

FOURTEEN

DEREK FAIRFAX'S LUNCH HAD been a frugal affair: cheese-and-tomato sandwiches followed by an apple, consumed on a bench in Calverley Park. Not that he would have enjoyed anything more lavish. He had too much on his mind to concentrate on what he ate or drank.

The same could not be said of David Fithyan, who returned from his own lunch shortly before three o'clock and clambered from his Jaguar with the clumsiness and flushed countenance of a man to whom food and drink were matters of considerable importance. Watching him from his office window, Derek noted the characteristic scowl of impending liverishness and decided to avoid him for the rest of the day. Unfortunately for him, such a decision was not his to take. Less than ten minutes later, he was summoned to Fithyan's presence.

'I said nothing about your absence last week, Derek, did I?' He spoke in a slurred growl betokening indignation as well as intoxication. 'You'll agree that was generous of me.'

'Er . . . yes. I suppose it was. I—'

'*Exceedingly* generous of me.'

'Well . . .'

'I'm a tolerant man. Always have been. *Too* tolerant, the wife says.'

'Really? Well, I'm not sure—'

'We had to send Rowlandson out to that firm in Sevenoaks to cover for you. He made an utter balls of it.'

'I know. I'm sorry about—'

'But I said nothing. And why? Because I thought we understood each other.'

'We do. I—'

'No we don't !' Fithyan bought the flat of his hand down hard on his blotter. 'But we will before you leave this room.'

'I'm not sure I—'

'I had lunch with Adrian Whitbourne.'

'Oh, yes?'

'Whitbourne & Pithey are one of our biggest clients.'

'I know.'

'Good. I'm glad you know that, Derek. Perhaps you also know who one of their biggest customers is.'

'Sorry?'

'Ladram Avionics. Mean anything to you?'

'Well, of course. I—'

'Shut up! Shut up and listen!' Fithyan's forefinger waggled ominously at Derek. 'Whitbourne as good as told me today that if a certain member of our staff goes on antagonizing and harassing the managing director of Ladram Avionics – as he has been doing – then Whitbourne & Pithey will start looking for a new accountant.'

'Oh.' Derek looked past Fithyan, past indeed the treetops waving beyond the window, and saw his own naïvety staring back. Maurice Abberley was bound to have contacts and bound to use them when challenged. It was as obvious as it should have been predictable. 'I see,' he mumbled.

'If we lost a client as important as that, we'd probably have to review our staffing levels. We wouldn't need so many people, would we?'

'I suppose not.'

'But we aren't going to lose them, are we?'

'I certainly hope not.'

'We aren't going to lose them because the managing director of Ladram Avionics isn't going to have occasion to complain about us to Whitbourne ever again, is he?'

Derek looked at Fithyan and realized the utter hopelessness of appealing to his better nature. The human race was divided in his mind not by race or creed or politics but by whether they mattered or not, whether they wielded power or were wielded by it. On one side of this divide stood Maurice Abberley. On the other stood Derek and his brother. Questions of right and wrong were therefore irrelevant. A man of influence had spoken. And Fithyan had listened.

'Well, is he?'

Derek shook his head. 'No. Absolutely not. If I'd had any idea this would embarrass the company, I'd have—'

'I want this . . . whatever it is . . . dropped. Is that clear?'

'Yes. Completely. And it will be. You have my word.' But, even as he said it, Derek prepared an escape clause for his own reference. A promise given to David Fithyan was as valid as a promise given by him. The great divide might yet intrude.

FIFTEEN

THE MORE DISTANT HER childhood became, the more often Charlotte revisited it in her dreams. She did not do so as the child she had once been, rather as the adult she now was, dwelling within her vastly younger body, limited by what it could do and say, yet aware of all the knowledge and sadness that was to overtake her as the years passed.

Beatrix was dozing by the fire at Jackdaw Cottage, a book cradled in her hands, a shawl about her shoulders, an expression of perfect contentment on her face. And Charlotte was trying to wake her. She had something to tell her, something very important, something terrible but imprecise which Beatrix would want desperately to know, if only she could be woken. But though she shook her vigorously and shouted in her ear, Charlotte's efforts seemed in vain. Beatrix's eyes would not open. Her expression would not alter. And then, as Charlotte persisted, she felt a hand on her own shoulder and a voice clamouring for her attention.

'Charlie! Listen to me, Charlie. Look at me.'

To turn and look was like wrestling free of a choking but welcome embrace. She did not want to, yet she knew she must.

'Charlie!'

At that she turned. And woke. And froze with horror. Maurice was sitting on the side of her bed, a hand resting on her forearm, a smile flickering about his lips.

'It's all right, Charlie. It's only me.' The smile broadened and Charlotte relaxed by the fraction that was sufficient to free her mind and body. It was the morning following her lunch with Ursula. Sunlight was streaming through the gap in the curtains. When she glanced at the alarm clock, she saw it was just after half past seven. And Maurice was there, above and beside her.

'I rang the bell, but you can't have heard. So I used my spare key. Sorry to have surprised you.'

She would have heard. She was sure of it. Pushing herself up on her elbows and shaking her head, she stared at him uncomprehendingly. Why was he here? What did he want?

'I think you must have been dreaming.' He left the bed and sat down in the nearby chair. He was dressed in a lightweight suit and pale tie and looked groomed and placid enough for this visit to be an entirely normal feature of his journey to work. 'I brought you some breakfast, by the way.' He pointed to a tray on the bedside cabinet. 'Orange juice, muesli and black coffee. Is that right?'

'Yes,' she heard herself reply. 'Thank you.'

'This must seem a strange time to call.'

'Well . . .'

'But I have a busy day planned. So, there seemed nothing for it but to leave home early and take you in on the way, so to speak.'

'Take me in? I don't quite—'

'Ursula told me about your lunch yesterday. About your . . . request for information.'

'Oh.' Charlotte reached for the glass of orange juice and swallowed some. 'I see.'

'Do you, Charlie? Do you really? I have the feeling you may not see at all – and that it may be my fault you don't.'

'I'm sorry?'

Maurice stretched out his legs and gazed up towards the ceiling, joining his hands behind his neck to support his head. 'I was fourteen when you were born. It's a big gap in age. It made me see you as more of a child than a brother normally would. Then again, when your father died, you were only twelve, whereas I was all of twenty-six, so I not only *felt* responsible for your welfare, I really *was* responsible. Everything I've done since then has been intended to benefit you as much as my own family. I've never looked upon you as an outsider just because your surname isn't Abberley. You do know that, don't you?'

'I've never doubted it.'

'Good.' He glanced across at her, then back at the ceiling. 'Ladram Aviation was a disaster until I took over. Your father was a lovely man, but he had no grasp of business principles. *My* father's royalties were the only thing keeping *your* father afloat. I don't say that out of resentment. I say it to remind you of the uphill task I had to put the company – and the family – back on its feet. It was when I enquired into our finances and found out how dependent we were on Tristram's royalties that Mother told me the truth about his poems. She had to. Otherwise, I might have questioned why so much royalty income found its way to Beatrix, for her to spend on God knows what.' He chuckled. 'We know now, of course, don't we? A retirement home for Lulu Harrington. A farm for Frank Griffith. And probably a host of other gifts to people we've never heard of. Beatrix was a generous woman, wasn't she? Generous to strangers, anyway.'

'Maurice—'

'Please listen to me, Charlie. I've never said this before and I never want to say it again. A son either idolizes his father or hates him. That's human nature. Well, I idolized Tristram. He was dead, he was a poet, he was a warrior. What more could a son ask? Can you imagine, then, how it felt to be told he was no poet at all? To be told his sister had written every word for him? To be—' He broke off, then resumed in a more measured tone. 'Well, that was a long time ago. I'll spare you the soul-searching I went through, as I spared it you then. I was persuaded the secret had to be kept, but against my better judgement. Once I knew, I wanted us to make a clean breast of it, to face the world with the truth about Tristram Abberley. But Beatrix didn't want that to happen. She was afraid of being branded a fraud and a cheat and maybe she was right to be. At all events, without her co-operation, nothing could be done. I'd have made a fool of myself if I'd announced our secret to the world without a shred of proof and then been contradicted by Beatrix. Not to mention my own mother. How would she have explained the publication of *Spanish Lines* without admitting her part in the deception? No, the reality was that they were right. The secret had to be kept.'

He rose and strolled to the window, whilst Charlotte sipped abstractedly at her coffee and watched him. He was the only one left alive of those he had named. He was free to say whatever he liked about them, to confer upon them the motives and intentions most suitable to his version of events. As he opened the curtains wide and turned back to face her, it was as if he were unveiling a stage-set of his own past, on which the characters would move and speak according to the script he had written for them.

'But Mother and Beatrix are dead now, Charlie. We're free to set the record straight. Don't you think we should? Don't you think the world's entitled to know the truth about Tristram Abberley?'

'Er . . . Yes. I suppose it is.'

'I'd have told you sooner, but, to be honest, I was hoping to avoid having to admit lying to you all these years. That's why I approached Emerson McKitrick. I thought that, if you and he found the letters together, the truth would emerge without my part in it becoming known. It was vain and foolish of me. I see that now. Will you forgive me?'

She replaced the coffee-cup on the tray and summoned a sisterly smile. 'Of course.'

He returned to the chair and lowered himself into it. 'Mother told me about the letters. Beatrix had shown them to her to convince her she really had written the poems. I knew McKitrick would be interested in finding them and I persuaded him not to reveal the source of his information. But I hadn't realized Beatrix would go to such lengths to conceal them. Once you'd established they were hidden at Hendre Gorfelen, McKitrick was bound to try and steal them. I was worried he'd succeed – and destroy them when he found out what a threat they posed to his academic reputation. So, I decided to forestall him. I told Fairfax about the letters, knowing he would alarm Griffith into retrieving them. And I employed . . . well, let's just say I employed somebody . . . to take them off him. I wouldn't call it theft. They belonged to my father. I was simply repossessing them. Naturally, I'm sorry Griffith was injured in the process. That was never my intention.'

'What is your intention – now you have them?'

'Publication. Next year, perhaps. To mark the fiftieth anniversary of my father's death.'

'You know what some people will say, don't you?'

'That money's my real motive? Of course. The petty-minded will always say such things. But you and I know they're wrong. It was naughty of you to ask Ursula rather than me.' He raised his finger in good-humoured reproof. 'But never mind. Perhaps she convinced you where I couldn't. I've reached a position in life where money doesn't matter, as Ursula explained to you.'

Charlotte could not help wondering whether she would have believed Maurice if Ursula really had told her money meant nothing to him. She suspected not. But it scarcely mattered. She knew now she could not believe a single word he said. He changed his account of himself as he would his suit, to match the company and fit the facts. If one seemed inadequate, there was always another, pressed and waiting in the wardrobe. Money *was* his motive. And time *was* running out. Indeed, it would have run out but for Beatrix's death. As the thought struck Charlotte, a shudder ran through her. The hired thief must be Spicer, supposedly sacked more than seven months ago. That meant Maurice had been planning this even then.

And what he had been planning included Beatrix's murder. There was as little doubt of it as there was proof.

'Are you cold, Charlie?'

'No.'

'I thought I saw you shiver.'

'Well . . . a little perhaps.'

'I'd better leave you to dress, then.' He glanced at his watch. 'I must be going, anyway. Duty calls.' He rose, smiling, and stepped towards her. 'Still, I'm glad we've had this little chat.'

'So am I.'

'It clears the air. Ensures we both know where we stand.'

'Yes.'

He was leaning over her now, one hand resting on the headboard, the other hovering above the coverlet. 'He was *my* father, Charlie. Nobody else's. I think I'm the best judge of how he should be remembered. What do you think?'

She looked up into his face, forcing herself to smile, recalling the multitude of times she had trusted him – as she never would again. 'Oh, I think you're right, Maurice. Absolutely right.'

'That's my girl.' He patted her outstretched hand. 'You just leave it to me.' Then, stooping forward, he kissed her lightly on the forehead. 'All to me.' And somehow, with an effort she hardly thought she was capable of, she did not scream or recoil, but continued to smile, willing him to believe he had convinced her. As he had. Only too well.

SIXTEEN

Alfambra,
1st January 1938

Dear Sis,

I couldn't see the New Year in without penning you an overdue line, though, to be honest, being held in reserve while the battle we may join rumbles on to the south doesn't encourage seasonal reflection. Nor, come to that, does this frozen-to-the-bone *pueblo* where we're billeted. When it isn't snowing, there's a marrow-chilling frost and our real preoccupation isn't the state of the war or the prospects of peace, but how to keep warm and dry. My good friends Frank Griffith and Vicente Ortiz appear to be more adept at this than I do, but I'm slowly learning their secrets!

What the British press may have said about the Teruel offensive I don't know, of course, but we reckon the generals hope Republican success there (which seems at present to be coming to pass) will persuade Franco to offer a truce. If so, they're whistling in the wind to my way of thinking, because Franco just isn't the compromising kind. And an icy wind it is too. According to Vicente, who knows the town, Teruel is the coldest place on Earth (by which he really means the Iberian peninsula) and he may well be right. If he is, the good news we're getting from the units engaged there may not outlast the winter. Vicente's also heard that one of the colonels on the Fascist side is a bloodthirsty devil called Delgado, a fact which seems to depress him beyond measure.

We had a visit from three Labour Party bigwigs early last month. No doubt you read about it. Clem Attlee, Ellen Wilkinson and Philip Noel-Baker sat down to dinner with the battalion, condemned non-intervention, ate heartily, sang *The Red Flag* and departed to a chorus of hollow cheers, hollow because most of the chaps here would have been glad to go back with them, rather than face a second winter fighting Fascism. It's my first, of course, so I haven't any of their excuses. Even so, I have to say that my morale was singularly unboosted by the event.

Not that it was in need of boosting. Despite all the privations, I don't want to be anywhere else but here when this war ends. I want to see and hear and feel and understand it happening. I want to be part of it. And so I shall. Which is why, without a single hint of irony, I can wish you the very happiest of New Years.

Much love,
Tristram.

SEVENTEEN

SIX WEEKS AGO, ALL in Charlotte's life had been sane and normal. Beatrix had still been alive, whiling away her octogenarian days in Rye. Maurice had still seemed the model half-brother, affectionate without being overbearing. And Tristram Abberley had still been the poet whom one remembered as a brother and the other as a father.

Even a week ago, Charlotte's vision of her world had been intact. Beatrix was dead and strange discoveries had been made in the wake of her death. But fundamentally nothing had changed. Charlotte had understood the past as readily as the present. Or so she had supposed.

No longer. All now was altered, thrown into a chaos from which it could never be rescued. It was as if a jigsaw-puzzle she had completed years before had been suddenly overturned and, kneeling to re-assemble it, she had realized the pieces were no longer the same, that a new and nightmarish picture had been substituted for the old and reassuring one and that the substitution might have taken place long ago without her even noticing.

For an hour or so after Maurice's departure from Ockham House, she was scarcely able to move, let alone think. Her body and mind were numb with the shock of what he had said, revealing as it did much more than he could ever have intended. She wandered from one room to another, staring about at the brightness of the morning whilst dread and disbelief wrestled queasily within her.

Then, at last, she abandoned the mental struggle and gave way to the desire for physical flight. She left the house and drove west, retracing at first the journey with which she had set the wheels of her present plight in motion. But she did not stop at Cheltenham. Lulu could be left in enviable ignorance. Instead, she pressed on into Wales and so arrived, in the heat of the early afternoon, at Hendre Gorfelen once more.

The yard was still and silent, held in a windless trance. Of dog and chickens there was no sign. The door of the house stood ajar and to Charlotte's knock there was no answer. Some quality of the atmosphere in the passage as she walked in told her that Frank Griffith was not at home. Which might, she reflected, be just as well.

She entered the room to her right: Frank's study. There was a mustier air there than before, disclosing stray signals of dust and neglect. There were no flowers on the mantelpiece and the ashes of a long spent fire lay uncleared in the grate. Stepping towards it, Charlotte noticed a half-empty vodka bottle standing beside one of the armchairs. On the broad arm of the chair was a book. Charlotte had to crook her head to decipher the title on its frayed and discoloured dust-jacket. *The Brow of the Hill* by Tristram Abberley. The 1932 first edition. She might have known.

She picked the book up and opened it at the page marked by a slip of card, guessing before she saw it that the poem she would find there was 'False Gods'. And so it was. Tristram Abberley's finest work. And Frank Griffith's favourite.

> *Hold out your hand and ask for a job.*
> *They'll make you a promise and spare you a sob.*
> *For theirs is the truth that does not pay,*
> *While yours is the dog that has no day.*
> *Heed, if you must, the gods of tin*
> *And let them explain your original sin,*
> *But never—*

In an instant, the focus of Charlotte's gaze switched from the familiar lines of verse to the card held between her fingers. There was a date pencilled in the top left-hand corner: *23 Dec '38*. When she turned the card over, she saw that it was in fact a passport-size photograph of Beatrix, smiling warmly at the camera, young enough in appearance to confirm the recorded date of December 1938, when Frank had stayed with her in Rye – and taken away, it seemed, at least one memento.

Charlotte stared at a Beatrix she could not herself remember – at a confident and self-possessed woman of exactly her own age – for a minute or so, then she slipped the photograph back into its place, closed the book and replaced it on the arm of the chair. There must be no more reading between the lines, no more peeping between the pages. She knew that now. What would Frank Griffith do if she told him all she feared and believed about her brother? It did not bear contemplation. Certainly he would not sit idly by and wait for Tristram's letters to be made public. That was certain. What had she been thinking of? What had she been hoping to provoke?

She moved to the desk, found a sheet of paper and wrote a hasty message on it in capitals.

FRANK,
I CALLED BUT YOU WERE OUT AND I COULD NOT STAY. I WANTED TO TELL YOU THIS. I AM CERTAIN NOW EMERSON McKITRICK STOLE THE LETTERS AFTER ALL AND DESTROYED THEM ONCE HE HAD REALIZED THE MOCKERY THEY WOULD MAKE OF HIS BOOK. SO, THE OUTCOME IS WHAT YOU YOURSELF IN-TENDED. THERE'S SOME COMFORT IN THAT, ISN'T THERE? PHONE ME IF YOU WANT TO TALK. I HOPE THE HEAD IS HEALING WELL.
CHARLOTTE.

She wedged the note under the Tunbridge Ware stationery box in the centre of the desk, where it could not be missed, took a glance around the room to make sure she had disturbed nothing else, then hurried out, praying she could make good her escape before Frank returned, shaking her head at the folly of her visit. And her prayers were answered. He was nowhere to be seen. She climbed into her car and drove back up the track as fast as she dared, looking neither to right nor left, sure of little beyond what Beatrix had seemed silently to tell her from fifty years away. Make an end of meddling. Let the bad become at least no worse. And leave the good, the dead and all the rest in whatever peace they may have found.

EIGHTEEN

ALBION DREDGE LEANED BACK awkwardly in his chair and pushed the window behind him open still further, though the total lack of movement in the air ensured his action would do nothing to lower the temperature in his oven of an office. He had already discarded his jacket and his grimaces as he prised at his shirt collar suggested his tie would have gone the same way had he been alone. As it was, the presence of a client deterred him, though it occurred to Derek that this was just about the only concession he did seem willing to make to him.

'I don't want to be a wet blanket, Mr Fairfax,' Dredge said, abandoning his various efforts at ventilation, 'but I'm obliged to be realistic. The theory you've put forward——'

'It's more than a theory!'

'Quite possibly. But though you may believe it, *I* have to prove it. So, let me just be clear what it is you're saying. One——' He held up a pudgy forefinger. 'The late Miss Abberley wrote her brother's poems for him. Two——' He raised a second finger. 'Her nephew wanted her to make this fact public so copyright in the work would be extended and royalties would continue to be paid to him. Three——' Up went a third finger. 'Miss Abberley refused, so he decided to overcome her objections by murdering her. And four——' His little finger joined its perpendicular fellows. 'He made sure your brother took the blame for her murder by decoying him to Jackdaw Cottage and later planting the stolen items of Tunbridge Ware in his shop.'

'Correct.'

Dredge sighed. 'Well, it's an interesting theory. Very interesting indeed. If true——'

'It's true. I've no doubt of it.'

'I'm sure you haven't, Mr Fairfax, but others less – how can I put this? – less eager to entertain notions of your brother's innocence might regard it as fanciful and entirely unsupported by the available evidence.'

'How can you say that? Frank Griffith will confirm the stolen letters prove Beatrix's authorship of the poems.'

'Mr Griffith sounds an unreliable witness to me, Mr Fairfax. Didn't you say he had a history of mental illness?'

'Yes, but——'

'That plus years of living as a recluse in the wilds of Wales and a recent knock on the head would be used to undermine his evidence, even if it needed undermining, which lack of corroboration suggests it wouldn't. Besides, you've admitted Mr Abberley was in New York at the time of the theft.'

'I never suggested he stole the letters personally. I'm sure he used his former chauffeur, Spicer, to carry out the crimes.'

'For which your evidence is Spicer being seen in a pub in Rye nearly a month before Miss Abberley's murder.'

'Well . . . yes . . .'

Dredge clicked his tongue like a reproving schoolmaster. 'For which there could be any one of a number of simple explanations.'

'He was clearly embarrassed to be seen there.'

'Your witness—' Dredge glanced down at his notes. 'Miss Abberley's housekeeper's husband *thought* Spicer was trying to avoid him. I wouldn't say he was *clearly* anything.'

'What would you say, then?' Derek was beginning to feel angry. After being leaned on by Fithyan, what he needed was encouragement, not Dredge's ponderous brand of nit-picking.

'That your theory is coherent, Mr Fairfax, even attractive. But it lacks substantiation.' Dredge smiled. 'Better for me to point out its deficiencies to you now than for you to harbour false hopes – or raise them in your brother.'

'What can we do to substantiate it?'

'Find Spicer. Establish his whereabouts on the dates in question. And vet his financial circumstances for signs that he has been paid for murdering Miss Abberley, framing your brother and stealing the letters from Mr Griffith.'

'But he could be anywhere.'

'Exactly. We would need to use a specialist in search and surveillance. I can recommend one. I can even engage him on your behalf. But I must warn you his services are expensive and, in this case, might yield nothing at all.'

'What else, then?'

'Nothing.' Dredge spread his hands. 'Nothing, so far as I can see, is to be gained by monitoring Mr Abberley's activities. If you're right, he intends to sit tight until the time is ripe to publicize the letters. If there's a weak link in the chain, it's whoever he used to commit the crimes. If it was Spicer, we have a chance, though a slim one. If not—'

'We have no chance at all. Is that what you're saying?'

'I fear so, Mr Fairfax. Which brings me to your opening question.'

'Should I tell my brother?'

'Exactly.' Dredge leaned back and joined his hands across his ample stomach. 'It's your decision, naturally, but I'd advise you to consider the consequences very carefully. My impression is that he's come to terms with his situation, that he's prepared himself for the worst. If you make him think there's a real prospect of him being acquitted when in reality there isn't . . .'

'I take your point, Mr Dredge. I'll give it some thought. Now, about tracing Spicer—'

'You want me to proceed?'

'Yes. I do.'

'Very well. I'll put the wheels in motion.'

'One other thing.' Derek's self-respect rebelled at the necessity of what he had to say. 'I'd like great care to be taken to avoid Maurice Abberley becoming aware that I've initiated such enquiries.'

'Nobody wants him to become aware of it, Mr Fairfax. Alas, I can't give you an absolute guarantee that he won't.'

'No. Of course not.'

'You have some particular reason for mentioning it?'

'Indirectly, he wields a good deal of influence with my employer.'

'Ah. That kind of reason. I sympathize. In view of the likelihood of a negative outcome to our enquiries, perhaps the risks of putting them in train – the risks to your career, I mean – are simply not worth taking.'

'Perhaps they're not.' Dredge's eyebrows were raised in expectation of his next remark. But Derek had already debated the matter with himself, long and hard. He was not about to knuckle under, however easy it would have been to believe it was the best and wisest course to follow. 'But I mean to see this through to the end. So, such risks as there are, I'm prepared to take.'

NINETEEN

SATURDAY THE FIRST OF August was bright and sunny, with a fresh enough breeze to dispel sloth if not despondency. To Charlotte, who craved a restoration of order and complacency in her life, it seemed important to do the little she could to bring that about in as brisk and business-like a manner as possible. She therefore took exaggerated care with her dress and appearance before leaving the house and stopped in Tunbridge Wells to buy a punctiliously listed assortment of domestic necessities before driving south-east towards Rye and a rather more demanding task she had decided to set herself.

Jackdaw Cottage was, as usual, clean and well-aired. Charlotte walked around it slowly, schooling herself to see it as a piece of property, not a repository of dreams and regrets. She was surprised by how successful she was, by how obedient her emotions were. There had to be a way of coming to terms with the discoveries she had made in the past week and she was determined to find it. So far, the only way she could imagine was to isolate herself from Maurice, from Beatrix's memory and from every tangible reminder of their importance in her world. And so far, it seemed, so good.

From Jackdaw Cottage she went straight to an estate agent in the High Street, where she deposited a key and arranged for the house to be valued and put on the market as soon as possible. Then she called on the Mentiplys and told them what she had done. They were not surprised. Indeed, they had been expecting her to make such an announcement for some time. Charlotte was persuaded to stay for coffee and while Mrs Mentiply was in the kitchen preparing it she asked Mr Mentiply, in as casual a manner as she could contrive, to confirm his sighting of Spicer in Rye on 25 May.

'It was him all right. Not a doubt of it. But how did you know I spotted him? I only told that brother of Fairfax-Vane. The Missus reckoned I shouldn't have. Has he been bothering you?'

'Not exactly.'

'Making trouble? He seemed the type.'

'I suppose you could say so. But don't worry. I can handle the situation.'

Charlotte's choice of phrase lodged in her mind and acquired a guilty resonance as the day progressed. After leaving Rye, she drove to Maidstone and located the street where she had been born and her parents had entered into their secret pact with Beatrix. The houses were more dilapidated than she remembered, the parked cars more numerous but less highly polished. Her birthplace had its sagging curtains drawn in the middle of a hot afternoon, with deafening rock music billowing from the only open window. For this she felt oddly grateful. Nostalgia and noise were mutually exclusive. And she had no use for nostalgia.

She returned to Tunbridge Wells just as the coolness of the evening was beginning to drain some of the heat from the day.

She thought of what she had said to Mr Mentiply, of how true it was and yet how shameful. She thought of how intolerable it would be to continue, week after week, pretending Derek Fairfax and his imprisoned brother did not exist. And at that she surrendered to impulse.

He had written to her from his home address in Speldhurst, a well-to-do commuter village north-west of the town. Charlotte drove directly there and found Farriers, a cul-de-sac of widely spaced bungalows, without difficulty. But at number six there was no answer and she retreated, uncertain whether to be disappointed or not. A few minutes later, passing the pub in the centre of the village for the second time, she glanced into its garden and noticed a solitary figure sitting at one of the trellis tables. It was Derek Fairfax.

Charlotte overshot the entrance to the car park and had to reverse some distance up the lane to reach it. This manoeuvre, of which Fairfax had a clear view, seemed certain to attract his attention, but he failed to look up as she approached his table. He was casually dressed, doodling with a ball-point pen on a paper napkin whilst cradling his beer-glass against his cheek, completely absorbed, so it seemed, in his own thoughts.

'Mr Fairfax?'

He started violently and, as his eyes flashed up to meet hers, she noticed him screw the napkin into a ball and drop it into the ashtray. 'Miss Ladram, I didn't . . . I'm sorry, I never . . .' He frowned. 'Were you looking for me?'

'Yes. I've just called at your house.'

'Really? Why?'

'I'm not completely sure. I . . .'

'Would you like a drink?' He rose, smiling awkwardly.

'Yes. Yes please. A gin and tonic.'

'Sit down. I'll go and get it.' He drained his glass and set off with it across the garden. Charlotte sat down and watched him until he had vanished into the shadowy interior of the pub. Then, licking her lips nervously, she plucked the screwed up napkin from the ashtray and flattened it out on the table. A diagram confronted her, comprising names both familiar and unfamiliar, juxtaposed according to principles she could not immediately grasp.

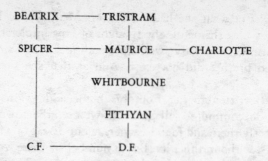

```
BEATRIX ———— TRISTRAM
   |              |
SPICER ———— MAURICE ———— CHARLOTTE
              |
          WHITBOURNE
              |
           FITHYAN
              |
C.F. ———————— D.F.
```

She realized D.F. and C.F. must represent Derek and Colin Fairfax and knew Fithyan & Co. was the accountancy firm Derek worked for, but who Whitbourne might be she could not conjecture. As for her own position, marginal to the rest, no more, in one sense, than an adjunct to Maurice, she could not decide whether to feel relieved or insulted. Nor could she risk prolonged scrutiny of the diagram, for already Fairfax had reappeared in the pub doorway. She compressed the napkin in her hand and replaced it in the ashtray, then looked up to meet his gaze. She wanted to smile, to assure him that his preoccupations were hers as well. But, in the event, she merely thanked him for her drink in a cautious murmur.

'So, why did you want to see me?' He took a gulp at his beer as he sat down.

'To . . . To ask if you'd done what you said you would.'

'Tell my brother and his solicitor that I believe *your* brother was responsible for Beatrix Abberley's death, you mean?'

'Well . . . Yes.'

'I told his solicitor. You'll be glad to know he was unimpressed.' He swallowed some more beer and Charlotte became aware of a vein of sarcasm in his remarks which alcohol could easily turn to bitterness.

'What about your brother?'

'I visited him today in Lewes Prison. In fact, I've just returned from there. The trip left me feeling in need of a drink. Of several drinks, come to that.'

'It's a depressing place, I imagine.'

'Yes. It is. But it was worse today than usual.'

'Why?'

'Because I lied to him.'

'You did what?'

'I lied. He asked if I'd found anything out. And I said I hadn't.'

'Why did you do that?'

'Why do you think?' He set his glass down and leaned forward across the table. 'Because there's no evidence, Miss Ladram. Not a shred. I know what your brother's done. And so do you. But I can't prove it. I can't even suggest it without . . .'

'Without what?'

'Never mind.' He waved away a gnat and took another gulp of beer. This glass, too, would soon be empty. 'Your brother's in the clear. And so are you. What more do you need to know?'

'Why do you say I'm in the clear?'

'Because, without evidence of his guilt, you can pretend he's innocent, can't you? And benefit from his crime.'

'Benefit? In what way?'

'I assume some element of the royalties goes to you.'

'You assume wrong.' Charlotte felt herself flush. 'My mother bequeathed all her royalty income to Maurice. As did Beatrix.'

'Wonderful.' He smiled humourlessly. 'That salves your conscience very neatly, doesn't it?'

'It doesn't need salving.' But Charlotte knew otherwise. Fairfax was right. Indirectly, she was bound to benefit in some way. Perhaps she already had, for Maurice had never pressed her, as he reasonably might, either to sell Ockham House or to buy him out of his share of it. The sale of Jackdaw Cottage might solve that problem, of course, but it would not be Charlotte's to sell if Beatrix were still alive. 'What do you want me to do, Mr Fairfax? As you say, there's no evidence to support your theory.'

'What if there were?'

'That would be—' She broke off, reminding herself that Fairfax did not know – and must not know – why Maurice needed the royalties to continue. 'But there isn't,' she said with stubborn finality. 'And there can't be, because Maurice didn't do what you seem to think he did.'

'You have to say that, of course. But you don't believe it, do you?' His eyes were fixed on her in open challenge.

'I most certainly do.' She glanced away, knowing what he would conclude from her inability to face him. 'I think Emerson McKitrick stole the letters from Frank Griffith and destroyed them in order to protect his account of Tristram Abberley's life. I've told Frank so. And now I'm telling you.'

'How did Frank react?'

'I didn't—' She forced herself to look back at him. 'I haven't spoken to him. I left a note at Hendre Gorfelen when I drove there yesterday. He wasn't in.'

'Couldn't you have waited?'

'I suppose so. But it's a long—'

'You didn't want to wait, did you? You were glad he wasn't there.' He quaffed some more beer. 'Perhaps you should have left me a note as well. It's so much easier on paper, isn't it? So much more . . . convenient.'

The truth of his words and the falseness of her own struck home at Charlotte. If she remained, she would either compound the lie she had told or confess to it and all she could be certain of was that she must do neither. 'There's nothing more to be said, is there?' She stood up. 'I think I'd better leave.'

'So do I.' Fairfax drained his glass and rose to confront her across the table, his glare crumpling suddenly into something forlorn and appealing. 'I'm sorry if I've offended you. I realize you're in an invidious position. But it's a great deal better than my brother's position, isn't it?'

'Yes. And—' The look that passed between them in that instant carried with it a disturbing quality of self-recognition, as if each saw clearly their own frailties reflected in the other. 'I'm sorry too. But sorrow doesn't help, does it?'

'Not a scrap.'

'Goodbye, Mr Fairfax.' She was tempted to offer him her hand, then decided that any suggestion of agreement between them – of unity of purpose – was best suppressed.

'Goodbye, Miss Ladram.'

She turned and walked quickly away across the garden. When she reached her car and glanced back, she saw he was already heading towards the doorway of the pub, head bowed, empty glass suspended in his hand. They would not meet again. If they did so by chance, they would pretend not to know each other. This was the end both of them had feared from the moment Frank Griffith had agreed to share his secret. This was knowing the truth and knowing it could not be changed.

TWENTY

Tarragona,
20th February 1938

Dear Sis,

I don't know what reports have reached you, but I hope this letter will reassure you that your little brother's still in the land of the living, though not exactly up and about. I am, in fact, recovering well from a bullet-wound in the left thigh despite – rather than because of – the rough-and-ready techniques of the doctors who tend us in this large and cheerless hospital.

How did it happen? Well, to be honest, I'm not sure. My company was involved in a fairly desperate action to prevent the Canadian Battalion being cut off in the hills outside Teruel. In the course of it, we were exposed to rifle fire from a superior position and I was hit. All very random, you see. Nothing personal or even vaguely vicious about it. Just a misfortune of war.

And it may not have been such a misfortune. A friendly orderly brings me English papers when he can, so I know you'll be well aware how badly – and predictably – wrong the Teruel operation went. Rumour has it that the final battle for the city has already begun and, frankly, there can only be one result. So you'll understand that I'm more worried about my friends and comrades still stuck there than about my own condition, which seems to be a great deal better than I've any right to expect.

Frank Griffith and Vicente Ortiz both knew the generals were putting our heads in a noose at Teruel and, in many ways, I wish it could have been they who slipped out of it with nothing worse than a flesh-wound rather than I who was always thirstier than them for action. How they've fared since I was evacuated I dread to contemplate. I can't help wondering whether I'll see either of them again. If not, it won't be the end of the matter, because— But let that pass. Suffice to say my thirst for action has been well and truly slaked. Whatever happens after this, I aim to call it a day as far as the International Brigade's concerned. What follows I don't know. When I volunteered last year, I wasn't looking far ahead and I still can't. But it seems I'll be back in England before many months are out, with a limp to add to that albatross of a poetical reputation, facing the future with far from starry eyes.

I don't know what sort of an impression my letters have given you of the seven months I've spent in Spain. Inaccurate and patchy, I dare say, as gauche and ill-formed as those sketches of poems you used to shape so adeptly into the real thing. When we can sit down together and talk it all through, you'll have the true picture, of course. Then I'll be able to tell you everything, including things which can't be entrusted to the mail. And then you'll understand, I promise. Then you'll see it through my eyes.

Life's pretty uneventful here, as I'm sure you can imagine. For once, it's all going on somewhere else. And for once, I'm grateful. But, as soon as there *is* something to report, I'll be in touch. Or maybe I'll see you first in person. Who knows? The future's a slippery commodity. You think you've grasped it, then it's escaped you. Perhaps we'd better just await what it brings.

Much love,

Tristram.

INTERLUDE

It is a late August day in the year 1928. Beatrix Abberley is reclining on a cushioned wicker sofa in the conservatory of her father's house, Indsleigh Hall in Staffordshire. She is a twenty-six-year-old spinster of plain but uncompromising looks, whose hair-style — centre-parted and coiled over the ears — and dress — square-necked, short-sleeved and ankle-length — are a few crucial years behind the fashions. Yet it is obvious from the jut of her chin and the intensity of her gaze that she is a woman of vigour and intelligence. Indeed, she has frequently expressed her impatience with the ways of the world and the place allotted to her in it.

Beatrix believes — and few could deny — that her abilities are wasted in the roles she has dutifully if reluctantly filled since her mother's death twelve years ago, those of housekeeper to her father and governess to her young brother, Tristram. She yearns to cut a figure on some wider stage, but knows the opportunity to do so — if it ever existed — is already past. Politics or literature would, she is certain, have proved more receptive to her talents than domestic economics and the limited society of rural Staffordshire. But both realms are closed to her and are likely to remain so.

To pile frustration upon unfulfilment, her hopes of finding consolation in her brother's career are beginning to fade. Tristram has enjoyed all the social and educational advantages she has been denied. Since his boyhood, she has encouraged him to develop as independent and perceptive a mind as she herself possesses, to examine the world critically and impose himself upon it. But now, during the interval between his second and third years at Oxford, it is no longer possible for her to believe she has succeeded. For Tristram, though a quick and ready thinker, is cursed by indolence and superficiality, two traits which Oxford, or, more particularly, the company he has kept there, have only exacerbated. His eagerness to impress has become a willingness to please. His opinions have become prey to his audience.

A case in point is the document, folded in three, with which Beatrix is fanning herself at this humid and uncertain mid-point of the afternoon. Tristram has drifted into a circle of poets and poseurs during the Trinity term just passed. More poseurs, in Beatrix's judgement, than poets, if the selection of their work Tristram has shown her is a fair one. The poor boy has fancied he might emulate them, has put diffident pen to speculative paper during the dog-days of an idle summer and has now sought his sister's dispassionate assessment of what he has produced. He will shortly return from the croquet lawn, where she can hear him running a few aimless hoops, to receive it. And she does not know what she will say. The truth will offend him, but blandiloquence is against her nature. Therefore the truth it will have to be. Unless—

She unfolds the sheet of paper and casts her eye once more over the lines of verse. Gauche and ill-formed though they unquestionably are, they are not altogether without promise. Tristram has the ability to snatch a fitting image from the air, though a regrettable tendency to drain it of poetry while setting it down on the page. And the piece lacks purpose as well as elegance. Its starting-point, a nameless man facing execution in a nameless country, is strong, but its development is weak. The last verse needs rewriting in its entirety and the rest require substantial revision. Subject to all of that, it might be quite a neat and pithy dart at political complacency. Indeed, had the idea been hers, she could, she suspects, have made something of it.

Beatrix leans her head back on the cushions for a moment. She frowns in concentration, opens her mouth slightly and runs her tongue along her front teeth. Then she reaches across to a low table beside the sofa and picks up the pencil with which she earlier completed the *Daily Telegraph* crossword. She re-reads Tristram's poem once more, rocking the pencil between index finger and thumb as she does so and reciting the words beneath her breath. Then she smiles faintly, raises the pencil and strikes out the title. 'The Firing Squad' is altogether too specific. Something more metaphorical is called for. In bold capitals, she writes the title she would have chosen. 'Blindfold'. Then she pauses. Why not go further? Why not rewrite the entire poem? It would not be difficult, now Tristram has done the groundwork. He may even enjoy the joke, since egotism is not one of his faults. Yes, why not indeed? It is no great matter, after all, merely a brief light-hearted indulgence. In such a spirit, Beatrix sets to work.

The same day, transplanted by almost sixty years. Far from Stafford-shire, in an air-conditioned bedroom high above New York's Fifth Avenue, Beatrix Abberley's nephew, Maurice, wakes from a post-coital doze to the cooling caress of silk sheets and a glimpse of his own face reflected in one of the many mirrors his mistress has installed to ensure her beauty need never be overlooked.

He is alone, though he does not expect to remain so for long. He can hear a faint hissing from the direction of the bathroom that tells him Natasha is taking a shower and will soon return, refreshed and receptive to whatever he may have in mind. Glancing down at the floor, he notices one of her black stockings, lying where it must have fallen after he peeled it from her leg and tossed it aside. He smiles, in anticipation as well as recollection. A second bite at the cherry — so to speak — may be even more enjoyable than the first — and certainly more leisurely. After an absence of several weeks — much of it spent enduring Ursula's sarcastic smirks and ambiguous asides — he was no sooner inside the apartment this afternoon than he was urging Natasha towards the bedroom and the frantic coupling from which he is only now recovering. They have expended a good deal of breath since his arrival, but none of it on what could be called a conversation.

As a result, Natasha has yet to hear Maurice's confident assertion that all obstacles to the success of his plans have been removed. Stretching deliciously beneath the sheets, he reminds himself of what he has achieved. Fairfax-Vane has been framed and his brother silenced. Spicer has been paid off and McKitrick sent packing. Charlotte has been deceived and Ursula appeased. While Beatrix, reaching out from beyond the grave to defy him with her posthumous ploys, has been defeated. She was better prepared than he expected, more devious than he ever anticipated. Yet still she was no match for him. It was a relishable contest, but really the old girl should have known better than to embark upon it. She should have accepted the terms he offered her last Christmas and been grateful.

At moments of self-satisfaction such as this, Maurice is able to acknowledge that greed was not the only reason why he was determined to outwit his aunt. Certainly the royalties will help him to maintain Natasha in the luxury she demands, but there was always more to it than that. It was a question of pride, a simple matter of not being prepared to take no for an answer. Beatrix had no right to refuse him, especially not when her reasons for doing so amounted to nothing but selfishness and spite. In the circumstances, he cannot help wishing she knew how futile her resistance has proved to be.

In an act similar to one he has performed frequently over recent weeks, Maurice extends his arm to his jacket where it is draped over the back of a chair and lifts his wallet from the inside pocket. Holding the wallet in front of him, he slides a tightly folded sheet of paper from one of the interior compartments. It is a banker's receipt for a sealed packet consigned to safe deposit during Maurice's last visit to New York. The time to collect has not yet come and will not come for many months. Until it does, this thin *pro forma* document must serve as the only token of his victory. But it is sufficient, for patience has always held his greed in check. Besides, less flimsy consolations are on hand. Indeed, if the suspension of hissing in the bathroom is any guide, they will shortly be *in* hand. Maurice grins at himself in the mirror, slips the receipt back into his wallet and stretches out to replace it in his jacket.

At the same moment, on the other side of the Atlantic, in his office at Fithyan & Co.'s premises in Tunbridge Wells, Derek Fairfax is also inspecting a document, though with exactly the opposite emotion. It is a copy, sent to him by Albion Dredge, of a private detective's report on the whereabouts and activities of Brian Andrew Spicer, chauffeur, until the end of last year, to Maurice Abberley. And it does not make rewarding reading.

> Spicer gave a week's notice to his landlady in Marlow on Christmas Eve and moved out before it expired. He did not leave a forwarding address. He said he was going to join a former fellow Royal Marine in a limousine hire business in Manchester. This seems to have been a lie. There is no indication that he has worked as a chauffeur since then. None of his known friends have heard from him. He has, to all intents and purposes, disappeared.

Derek sighs and turns back to Dredge's covering letter. Brief and neutrally phrased though it is, the solicitor's opinion is clear enough.

> The question arises as to whether you wish these enquiries to continue in view of the lack of progress to date and the costs incurred (see interim account attached).

Derek lets letter, report and interim account flutter to rest on his blotter, then leans back in his chair, removes his glasses and slides one hand down over his face. This, he supposes, is where his efforts on his brother's behalf stumble to their overdue and unavailing conclusion. This is where he decides that enough is enough. He has done all Colin could reasonably have expected of him and now is the time to call a halt. Replacing his glasses, he seizes a sheet of scrap paper and begins to draft a reply.

Dear Mr Dredge,
Thank you for your letter of 26th August. I have considered the position very carefully and have concluded—

He breaks off and glances across at the window, where sunlight is streaming through the grimy pane. If there were anything he could usefully do for Colin, he would do it. Of that he is certain. But Colin is not. And now he never will be. Of that too Derek is certain. He looks down at the sheet of paper and raises his pen.

I have considered the position very carefully and have concluded that no purpose would be served by taking this matter any further. I should therefore be grateful if . . .

Even as Derek Fairfax writes what he would much rather not, a door opens a mile away for the first time in a fortnight and Charlotte Ladram makes a reluctant homecoming from a less than successful holiday. She is tired, hot and burdened with luggage, but none of these conditions is what prompts her to lean heavily against the wall in the entrance porch of Ockham House, to close her eyes and to sigh despondently.

An old schoolfriend, Sally Childs, now Sally Boxall, had often asked Charlotte to visit her and her husband, a high-powered form of Eurocrat, at their home near Brussels. Charlotte had taken up the invitation on this occasion because it offered her a bolt-hole when she was badly in need of one. She had hoped two weeks of sightseeing and girl-talk in a country of which she knew nothing would drive thoughts of Beatrix and Maurice and Derek Fairfax from her mind. But her hopes were not fulfilled. Nor, she now realizes, were they ever likely to be. Sally's endless monologues on Belgian chocolate, her husband's career and the marriages and motherhoods of a dozen half-remembered old girls had succeeded only in casting Charlotte's preoccupations into stark relief.

Stooping to gather up an accumulation of mail from the mat, she presses on into the hall, encountering at once that smell unique to every building which is neither aroma nor odour and which only several days of emptiness can reveal. Its effect is to remind Charlotte of returning to the house as a child after family holidays of seemingly unalloyed happiness. Resenting the effect as much as the memory, she deposits the mail on the telephone table and begins to sort through it in search of some, indeed any, distraction.

But the distraction she comes upon is, in many ways, worse than what drove her to seek it. A letter, posted three days ago, addressed to her in Ursula's unmistakable hand. Normally a punctilious wielder of the paper-knife, she resorts on this occasion to her thumb, tearing the envelope nearly in half as she pulls out the contents.

It is an expensively printed invitation to Samantha's twentieth birthday party, to be held at Swans' Meadow on Saturday week. Until now, Charlotte has succeeded in forgetting the event. Until now, she has assumed that many weeks, if not months, will pass before she is obliged to meet Maurice face to face and to pretend all is well between them. But not so. A confrontation is close at hand. And there is Ursula's scrawled note in the corner of the invitation to prove it. *Charlie – Hope you can make it – Love, U.*

The instigator of Charlotte's distress is presently inspecting herself in a fitting-room mirror towards the rear of an exclusive boutique in Beauchamp Place, Knightsbridge. Several dresses lie over a chair-back, but the clinging petrol-blue concoction in which she is precariously clad is, her expression implies, the one she will take. It is both dramatic and flattering and should attract a good deal of attention from the handsome young men who bulk so large on her daughter's guest-list. Yes, she is going to enjoy this party. Of that there can be no question.

As Ursula steps out of the chosen dress, she pauses to inspect the price-tag and smiles approvingly. Had it been too cheap, she would have been tempted to discard it, however ideal it seemed. But it is far from cheap, even by her standards. And that, she concludes, is as it should be. If Maurice is prepared to go to such lengths to safeguard his royalty income as it seems he has, the least she can do is to ensure his efforts are not wasted.

What else, then, may be required to complete her outfit? She considers the point as she takes the skirt she came in from its hanger. A pair of those extremely brief ivory silk knickers that caught her eye earlier, perhaps, with matching suspender belt and strapless bra? If so, the sheerest of stockings will also be required. Why bother when the evening may be warm enough to go bare-legged? Because, of course, there just is no knowing what opportunities may arise. Beatrix's thoughtfulness in bringing Maurice's New York arrangements to her attention has given Ursula a delectable sense of irresponsibility, a licence, as it were, to exploit the unpredictable. Accordingly, the fifth of September, and its every possibility, cannot come soon enough for her liking. It is as much as she can do not to lick her lips at the prospect.

As Ursula ponders the lubricious potential of silk lingerie, her daughter Samantha takes the momentous decision to turn over on her sun-bed in the garden at Swans' Meadow. She does so in a practised movement that ensures her dark glasses and Walkman remain undisturbed. Then she reaches behind her back to unfasten the strap of her bikini top.

As she does so, she looks up, taking in the vista of weeping willows and placid river, with the roofs of Cookham beyond. There are some children on the opposite bank, feeding the ducks, and also a solitary dark-haired young man in jeans and a white shirt. He is holding what looks like a pair of binoculars in his right hand and is gazing vacantly in her direction.

Samantha stares at the man for several seconds, wondering if he could be the muscular foreigner who stopped her in Station Road yesterday and asked her for directions to Cookham Dean. His accent and olive skin suggested he was from a Mediterranean country – Italy perhaps, or Spain. Yes, she concludes, it could indeed be him. Presumably, he is spending a holiday in the district. Has he, she wonders, been training his binoculars on her? If so, she hopes he approves of what he has seen. Not that it matters. The chances of meeting him again are remote. She lowers her head on to her arms and surrenders herself to the music pounding in her ears.

Half an hour has passed since Beatrix Abberley began amending her brother's poem. She is still engaged upon the task when the conservatory door opens and Tristram Abberley walks in, smiling blandly.

He is a slim good-looking man of twenty-one, clad in baggy cream flannels, a white shirt and a striped cravat. His hair is boyishly unruly, but already he has the raised eyebrows and cocked chin of the aspiring aesthete, though whether his manner declares or disguises his personality it is impossible to tell.

'Well, Sis,' he remarks, 'what's the verdict?'

'You tell me,' Beatrix replies, handing him the sheet of paper on which she has been working.

Tristram subsides languidly into a chair and scrutinizes the document, his eyebrows descending and bunching into a frown as he does so. 'You . . . You've changed it.'

'Improved it, I hope.'

'But . . . But it was . . .' His words trail into silence. A minute or so passes, then he looks up and says: 'I call this the bally limit.'

'Why?'

'Because you *have* improved it. Incomparably. It . . . Well, it's . . . It's very good, isn't it?'

'I'm glad you think so.'

'It makes my effort look quite pitiful.'

'Not really. The idea is all yours. Without it, I'd have had nothing to improve.'

'Maybe not, but . . . What do I say to the chaps now? "I'm a duffer, but I have a sister who can knock spots off the lot of you"?'

'I don't think that would go down at all well, Tristram. You're what they think a poet should be. I'm not.'

'You won't let me show them this?'

'Oh, you're welcome to. As long as you take the credit. Or the blame, of course.'

'But it's not mine.'

'What does that matter? They need never know.'

'Never know?' Tristram contorts his face in mock outrage. 'I'm surprised at you, Sis. Your suggestion is positively dishonest.'

Beatrix smiles. 'Well, I shan't force you to take it up. If it offends your artistic integrity, feel free to—'

'I never said that. No, no.' Tristram rubs his chin reflectively. 'After all, what harm can possibly come of a little collusion between brother and sister?'

'None whatsoever.'

'You're sure?'

'Absolutely.'

Tristram grins. 'Then . . . Why don't we see what happens?'

And Beatrix grins back at him. 'Why not indeed?'

PART THREE

ONE

SIX WEEKS HAD PASSED since Charlotte's last visit to Swans' Meadow. The simple act of starting out on the route from Tunbridge Wells to Bourne End was nevertheless sufficient to call to her mind every detail of what she had seen and heard that afternoon. She could only hope – with little confidence – that the riotous atmosphere of Samantha's twentieth birthday party would help her to suppress the memory.

The weather was warm and sunny, with the merest hint of a breeze. Charlotte found herself resenting even this element of her relatives' good fortune. For others the clouds might gather and the rains fall, but never for Maurice and those around him. For them high summer was a permanent condition. Whereas for her— She gripped the steering-wheel tighter and managed to block out the thought. Anger was useless, she knew, unless it led to a solution. And to her predicament there was no solution.

She had timed her arrival for half an hour after the party was due to commence, calculating that this would find the host and hostess busy with other guests, leaving her free to mingle and, with any luck, to slip away early. She had deliberately chosen an outfit likely to reinforce the general perception of her as Samantha's frumpish maiden aunt – floral-patterned dress and plain cardigan. She did not want to be liked or admired. She especially did not want to enjoy herself.

So absorbed was she in the effort of preparing herself mentally for what lay ahead that she did not glance upstream as she drove across Cookham Bridge and wonder why there were no party-goers gathered round a marquee on the lawn of Swans' Meadow, why indeed there was no marquee pitched on the lawn at all. The silence and emptiness of the scene did not become apparent to her until she turned into the drive of the house and realized there were no other cars parked there, no gaily clad groups tripping towards the garden, no jazz band to summon them nor hired flunkeys to greet them, no pop of champagne corks nor buzz of conversation, no bunting, no balloons, no merriment of any kind.

When she had stopped the car and climbed out, she wondered for a moment whether she had come on the wrong day or at the wrong time, though she was sure she had not. She took the invitation out of her handbag and confirmed as much. *Mr and Mrs Maurice Abberley request the pleasure of your company at a party in celebration of their daughter's twentieth birthday, to be held at Swans' Meadow, Riversdale, Bourne End, Buckinghamshire at three o'clock on the afternoon of Saturday 5th September. RSVP.* And here she was, at Swans' Meadow, on the day in question. And, when she glanced at her watch, she saw that the time was thirty-two minutes past three. But of a party there was no sign.

Suspecting some bizarre practical joke, Charlotte marched up to the front door and rang the bell. There was no response. She rang again and was about to ring for a third time when the door was pulled abruptly open.

'Charlie!' It was Ursula, dressed in slacks and a loose cotton top. She was wearing neither jewellery nor make-up. Her hair was tousled and looked in need of brushing. And she had been crying. Her eyes were red and puffy and the remnant of a tear was still moistening her left cheek. She was so unlike the groomed and unemotional woman Charlotte knew that, for a second, she thought she might actually be somebody else.

'Ursula . . . What . . . What's happening?'

'I wish I knew.' Ursula dabbed at her cheek with the back of her hand. 'Why are you here?'

'For the party.'

'Oh, Christ! Didn't we . . . Hell, I forgot the family. If you can call it a family.'

'What's going on?'

'There's no party, Charlie. You may as well go home. You'll be better off there, believe—' She broke off and turned away, her face gripped by a sob.

'What's the matter?' Charlotte stepped forward, uncertain whether to offer comfort where it had never previously been needed. She ended by placing one hand tentatively on Ursula's shoulder.

'The matter?' Ursula retreated into the hall, distancing herself from the gesture, imposing a fraction of her normal self-control. 'The matter is Maurice. What a bloody fool I was to trust him even in this.'

'In what? I don't understand.'

'No. You don't, do you? Well, perhaps you should. He's your brother. And do you know what kind of a brother you've got, Charlie? I mean, really know?' She stumbled away towards the lounge, neither forbidding nor encouraging Charlotte to follow. But follow she did.

Once there, Ursula poured more gin than tonic into a tumbler and drank at least a quarter of it in one gulp. Then she snatched a cigarette from a box, her hand shaking so much she laughed at the difficulty she had in lighting it. Charlotte stared at her in utter amazement, for she had never seen – nor dreamt of seeing – her sister-in-law in such a condition.

'I have to tell somebody,' she said, drawing deeply on the cigarette. 'Who better than you? Perhaps not letting you know the party was off was a Freudian slip. Perhaps I wanted—' She whirled away towards the window and stared out at the garden. 'Christ, what a bloody mess!'

'Why was the party cancelled, Ursula?'

'Because Sam isn't here.'

'Where is she?'

'I don't know. Nobody knows. Except—'

'Except who?'

'She's been kidnapped.'

'What?'

'Kidnapped. Abducted. Carried off. Call it what you bloody like. Taken by some devils Maurice has managed to call up with his too-clever-by-half pat little schemes. It's his fault, all of it. Unless it's mine, for letting him—' She swung round and stared at Charlotte, who could see her jaw muscles straining with the effort of ensuring she did not cry. 'Sit down, Charlie. Sit down and I'll tell you in joined-up sentences what your brother has managed to inflict on us.'

Charlotte lowered herself into the nearest chair and watched Ursula lean slowly back against the window-sill, one hand grasping the edge tightly while the other held her cigarette.

'Sam went missing on Tuesday. I was in Maidenhead and Aliki was out shopping. She left a note, saying she'd be away until Friday, but not why or where she was going. She'd taken some clothes, though scarcely enough, even for three days. I phoned all her friends, but none of them knew anything. Maurice suggested some mystery boyfriend and I thought . . . Well, maybe so. What else was I to think? I was worried, of course, but I assumed she'd explain herself when she came back. It was only three days. Young girls like to rebel a little. So, don't fight it. That's what Maurice said. That's what I said as well. Don't fight. Just wait. And everything will be all right. But it isn't, is it? It's not all right. It's all wrong. And Maurice— Sorry. You want the facts, in their proper order. Well, on Thursday afternoon, Maurice was phoned at the office by a man with a foreign accent who said he wanted to talk to him about Sam. You can hear their conversation if you like. Maurice has a gadget to record any telephone calls he wants to. He has one fitted here as well as at the office, so he need never be in doubt about agreements he reaches or deals he makes. I'll play you the tape.'

Ursula crossed to the hi-fi cabinet, removed a small cassette from one of the units and slipped another one in, then pressed a button.

'He switched on after they'd started talking, but you'll soon catch the drift.'

There was a crackle, then Maurice's voice in mid-sentence: '— *this is all about.*'

'*It is about your daughter, Mr Abberley.*' The other man was certainly foreign, but he spoke excellent English, in a tone devoid of all expression. '*I represent those who are holding her.*'

'*Holding her? What do you mean? She's—*'

'*Our captive, Mr Abberley.*'

'*I don't believe you.*'

'*Then believe your own ears. Listen to this.*'

The quality of the recording declined suddenly, but not enough for Charlotte to doubt it was Samantha's voice she heard next. '*Mum and Dad, it's me, Sam. I'm all right. I don't know where I am or who these people are, but they haven't harmed me. They just . . . won't let me go.*' She sounded frightened but not hysterical and somehow much younger than usual. '*Do as they say and they'll release me. I don't know what they want, but give it to them, Dad, please. I just—*'

The man's voice cut in. '*Do you believe me now, Mr Abberley?*'

'*Yes.*'

'*Good.*'

'*What do you want?*'

'*Ah, you are going to be sensible. That is better still.*'

'*How much do you want?*'

'Not money. We know you have a lot. But we do not want any of it.'

'What, then?'

'The papers you stole from Frank Griffith, Mr Abberley. They are what we want.'

'What?'

'You heard. The papers you stole from Frank Griffith.'

'You mean . . . my father's letters . . . to my aunt?'

'Everything he sent to her. Everything you have. All the papers. Every one.'

'You can't be serious.'

'But we are. Extremely.'

'There's been some . . . mistake. I don't have . . . I've never had . . .'

'Do not deny stealing them, Mr Abberley. We know you have them. If you refuse to give them up, your daughter will be killed.'

'Good God.'

'Do we understand each other, Mr Abberley?'

Maurice did not answer.

'Mr Abberley?'

Yes. All right. I understand.'

'We think you are storing the papers in New York. Is that correct?'

'How did you— Yes. It's correct.'

'Then this is what you will do. Fly to New York tomorrow morning. Collect the papers. Return on the Pam Am flight scheduled to reach Heathrow at seven fifty on Saturday morning. Go to the chemist's shop in Terminal 4 called Waltham Pharmacy at nine o'clock. Stand by the external display of sunglasses. A man will approach you. He will hand you an envelope containing a photograph of your daughter, which will prove she is alive and well.'

'How? How will it prove that?'

But Maurice's interruption was ignored. 'In return, you will hand him the papers, packed in a plain buff envelope. You will then leave. Your daughter will be released within twenty-four hours.'

'What if the flight's delayed?'

'We shall know if that is the case and we shall expect you to be late for our appointment. But no other excuse will be accepted.'

'How can I be sure you'll release Sam?'

Once again the interruption was ignored. 'If you go to the police, she will be killed. Is that clear?'

'Wait a minute. I must have—'

'Is that clear?'

'Yes. Of course it's clear.'

223

'That was my reaction. As I put the 'phone down, I said to myself: Maurice couldn't have done this. Not to Sam. Not to me. He just couldn't. Nobody could. Not with their daughter's life at stake. But I had to be sure, didn't I? You do see that, don't you?'

'Yes,' said Charlotte cautiously.

'Then come with me.'

Ursula led the way into the hall and marched up the stairs, with Charlotte following. They went straight into the master bedroom, where a leather briefcase stood open on the floor. Around it were scattered papers, pens and folders.

'That's the case Maurice took with him to New York,' said Ursula. 'I searched it, just to be sure.'

'What did you find?'

'Look in the inside zip pocket.'

Charlotte knelt beside the case. Along one side of the interior ran a zip-fastened pocket. She opened it, slipped her hand inside and pulled out an old frayed envelope. It was addressed, in a faltering hand, to *Miss Beatrix Abberley, Jackdaw Cottage, Watchbell Street, Rye, East Sussex, Inglaterra*. And the barely legible postmark removed the last shred of doubt about who had sent it. *Tarragona, República Española, 17 Mar 38*.

'It's the last letter Tristram sent to Beatrix,' said Ursula. 'Maurice must have hoped the kidnappers would think the sequence had ended one earlier. That way he could have his cake and eat it too. Sam free. And one letter still left to prove Beatrix wrote the poems. The bloody fool!'

'How could they know there was another?'

'How could they know any of it? But they do. Every single thing. Every move we make. It's useless to try and deceive them. But Maurice had to, didn't he? He just couldn't help himself.'

'I'm sorry, Ursula. I really am.'

'Don't be. It's Maurice who should apologize. To all of us. And I mean to make sure he does. But first he's going to have to stop lying. Once and for all.'

'May I read the letter?'

'Be my guest. Be Maurice's. After all, it's only thanks to him you have the chance.'

TWO

Sis,

I'm too weak to write much, so this has to be brief. I've been going downhill for several days now. Blood poisoning seems the problem. Not surprising, really. The Spaniards are stronger on honour than hygiene. Where there's life, etc., so don't despair yet, unless— Well, you know. What I want to say is this. I'm sending you a document I've been keeping for a friend. I promised him I'd pass it on to his relatives if I could find them, anyway keep it safe in case he managed to get out too. He thought I'd soon be on my way back to England, you see. So did I. Now I'm not so sure. And I must do my best to keep my word while I still have the strength. From what I hear, he's probably already dead. Maybe you can find out. I don't know. Anyway, I'm sending you my translation of the document as well. So decide what's best when you've read it. I know I can trust you to do that. I always could. The poems were your only real misjudgement, I reckon. We should never have let the world think I wrote them. Not when every word was yours. You should have had the credit. Maybe you will now. Claim it with my blessing, Sis. It all seems pointless now. Such a foolish conceit, in both senses, eh? If this is my last word on the subject, I'm sorry it has to be so close to bathos, but that's how I feel. Maybe hubris is nearer the mark. I don't know. And I'm too tired to write any more.

All my love,

Tristram.

THREE

'FOR YOUR DAUGHTER'S SAKE, *Mrs Abberley, make sure your husband does as he is told this time. It is your last chance. No more tricks. Good afternoon.*'

As the recording ended, Maurice rose, walked slowly across to the hi-fi and switched it off. Charlotte saw him glance out through the window and clench his teeth before turning back to face Ursula. He had bought some time for himself by refusing to answer any questions till he had heard the tape. But now time had run out.

'There's no way they could have known there was another letter.' The denial was as stubborn as it was futile. 'If I'd thought there was—'

'You think too much, Maurice, that's your trouble!' Ursula's interruption was almost a scream. 'You can't stop twisting and scheming and now Sam's life is in danger because of it.'

'No, no. It won't come to that.'

'It already has! Do you think these people are playing a bloody parlour game?'

'Of course not. But I couldn't let them have the last letter. You must see—'

'I *see*, all right. I see even our daughter is expendable to you when it comes to safeguarding those bloody royalties.'

'It's nothing to do with the royalties.' Maurice looked hurt at the very suggestion and suddenly Charlotte felt she was seeing beyond what had once been opaque but was now transparent into the cogs and coils of her brother's mind. She realized that the mechanics of his deceitful nature would function whatever he truly felt, that the conveyor-belt of lies would continue to be fed even when the demand for them had ceased to exist. 'I was just playing safe,' he protested. 'The letter mentions a document Tristram was sending to Beatrix, a document I don't have. I was afraid the kidnappers would think I was holding it back. So, it seemed wiser—'

'Bullshit!' shouted Ursula 'I know why you kept that letter and you know I know.'

'Well, if you're not going to listen to reason . . .'

'You listen, Maurice!' Ursula strode to within a foot of her husband and stared straight at him. Charlotte could see her hand shaking where it held the cigarette, this time with rage rather than fear. 'I don't care who these people are or why they want the letters, but when they phone tomorrow you're going to agree to whatever they demand. Is that clearly understood?'

'What else would I do?'

'I don't know. I can't imagine. But then I can't imagine why you took such a risk with Sam's life in the first place.'

'I've just explained.'

'Let me explain something! If, thanks to you, my daughter comes to any harm, I'll make sure the world knows every detail of how and why she came to be in danger.'

'What do you mean?'

'What do you think I mean? I've closed my eyes to your activities long enough. Well, they're open now. And what they see I'll tell, unless Sam's back here soon, safe and sound.' With that, Ursula turned on her heel and marched out of the room, throwing the parting remark, 'I need some air!' behind her as she went.

Maurice stared after her for a moment. Then, when the back door slammed, he looked down at Charlotte. There was a fleeting nakedness to the silence hanging between them, an admission of all her worst suspicions and beliefs, a hint that Maurice might now be prepared to confess. Then he drew back. 'I'm afraid Ursula's rather upset,' he said, attempting a smile. 'It's understandable, of course, but it means she's not being very rational.'

'You can hardly expect her to be.'

'Exactly. Which means I have to be rational on her behalf. I can't afford to give way to my emotions. You do see that, don't you?'

'I . . . suppose so. But—'

'Who are they, Charlie? That's what I have to ask myself. Who are they and what do they want?'

'They want the letters. All of them.'

'But why? If I understood their motive, I could try to . . . to negotiate . . . to reach some kind of . . . compromise.'

'Why not just give them what they want?'

'Because I'm not sure what that is.' He grabbed the letter from the bureau. 'Just this scrap of paper in exchange for Sam's life? It doesn't make sense.'

He was vulnerable now, Charlotte sensed, more vulnerable than he was ever likely to be again. If there was a time to gain his confidence, this was it. 'Why *did* you keep it, Maurice?'

He was tempted, she could see, tempted in his weakness and despair to lay his sins before her, to release the secrets bottled within him. But his nature was stronger than his conscience, his instinct more powerful than his reason. He replaced the letter on the bureau. 'Who knew about them, Charlie?' he said, staring down at it. 'Who knew I had them? You, Frank Griffith and Emerson McKitrick. Plus Fairfax, of course. But he hasn't the nerve for this kind of thing. Nor has McKitrick. Besides, neither of them could have known how many there were.'

'You're not suggesting Frank Griffith kidnapped Sam?'

'No. I'm not. I've had him . . . checked, so to speak. He's at Hendre Gorfelen – alone.'

'How do you know?'

'Never you mind.' Resilience was the key to Maurice's existence, Charlotte realized. He could be knocked back on his heels, but never for long. He could be defeated, but never demoralized. 'I'm sorry you should have become involved in this, Charlie. It would have been better if you hadn't.'

'I didn't choose to be.'

'No. That's true, of course.'

'What do you intend to do?'

'What Ursula wants. Wait for them to call again. When they do, agree to their terms.'

'And abide by them?'

But Maurice ignored the question. 'Until then, I'd be grateful if you stayed here. Ursula would benefit from your company.' It would also mean, as Charlotte knew, that awareness of what was happening would remain under one roof, that her judgement of what should and should not be done could be neutralized along with Ursula's. 'Will you do that for me, Charlie?'

Even now she felt sorry for him, unable to fix at the front of her mind the full extent of what she believed he had done. It was absurd, but still she could not quite suppress the sisterly instinct to help him. 'Yes, Maurice. I'll stay.'

FOUR

IT SEEMED TO CHARLOTTE as if she did not sleep at all that night, though her subsequent recollections of dreaming about telephones and disembodied voices suggested otherwise. At all events, she was awake with the first streaky light of dawn. And the faint sound of movement from below told her she was not the only one.

By the time she reached the hall, it was clear the sound was coming from the study. As she moved in that direction, she glanced into the kitchen and caught sight of the clock. It was a quarter to six and seemed even earlier because it was Sunday. The world held its breath.

Maurice was sitting sideways behind his desk, feet up on the radiator beneath the window, one hand flexing his lower lip while the other trailed across the blotter. He was fully dressed, his shirt creased enough to imply he had not been to bed at all. In front of him on the desk lay what looked improbably like a holiday brochure.

'Maurice?'

He started and swung round, blanched visibly, then recovered himself. 'It's you, Charlie,' he said, passing a hand across his forehead.

'I'm sorry. Did I startle you?'

'No. That is . . . The dressing-gown made me think . . . just for a moment . . .'

'Ursula lent it to me.'

'It's an old one of Sam's.'

'Oh, God. I am sorry. If I'd known—'

'Never mind. Trouble sleeping?'

'Yes. You too?'

'I haven't tried. I've been thinking.'

'About the kidnappers?'

'You heard the tapes. do you think the man who rang is Spanish? The fellow I met at Heathrow never spoke. He just handed me the photograph of Sam, then took the letters and walked away. He was young. Mid-twenties, I should say. And tough. Dark-haired, with sallow skin.'

'Perhaps they are Spaniards, then. Foreign, certainly.'

'But Spain's the point, isn't it? Something's snaked its way out

231

of their Civil War – from fifty years ago – to wrap itself round our throats.'

'Surely not.'

'I picked this up from a travel agent in Marlow yesterday afternoon.' He held up the brochure. 'It lists car ferry sailings from Plymouth to Santander, on the north coast of Spain – the only direct link. There are two a week, on Mondays and Wednesdays. The crossing takes twenty-four hours.'

'What of it?'

'I've been working it out, Charlie. Why did they wait two days before making contact? Sam vanished on Tuesday. They didn't phone until Thursday afternoon. Well, suppose they took her to Spain. Drove her there, I mean, trussed up in the boot of a car. Either aboard the ferry from Plymouth to Santander or across the Channel and down through France. They'd have had to wait until she was in Spain before showing their hand. That would explain why they used the *International Herald Tribune* in the photograph. A Spanish paper would have given the game away and an English one would have been out of date. It would also explain the delay in releasing her after handing over the letters.'

'Wouldn't the car have been searched?'

'Mine never has been at a Channel port. And I don't suppose they're very strict at the Franco-Spanish border.'

'Then yes, I suppose it is possible. But—'

'And another thing. Have you ever heard Uncle Jack refer to a Spaniard calling at Jackdaw Cottage while we were staying there in the summer of 1939?'

Charlotte had. Indeed, Jack's account had floated into and out of her mind several times in the course of the night. *'Not exactly the Spaniard who blighted my life, but he looked like he'd blighted a good few others.'* There was no reason to connect this distant visitation with what had now occurred, yet Charlotte could not suppress the suspicion that such a connection existed. And evidently Maurice felt the same. 'Uncle Jack told me about him only recently,' she said. 'Surely you don't—'

'He'd known Tristram. And he had business with Mother and Beatrix. What business, eh? Who was he? What did he want?'

'We'll never know, Maurice. It's nearly fifty years ago. He's probably dead by now.'

'Maybe. Maybe not.' His eyes drifted out of focus. 'In the letter,

Tristram said "I'm sending you a document I've been keeping for a friend". Did he mean he was enclosing it? Or sending it separately? Or intending to send it later?'

'We'll never know that either.'

'But what if it's the document they're after, Charlie? Not the letters at all.'

'Then they'd have said so, surely?'

Maurice looked directly at her. 'If there *is* a connection, I'm dealing with—' Then he broke off and his gaze slipped down to the car ferry brochure. Across its glossy cover, his right hand was stretched wide, the fingers straining towards some unattainable circumference. 'Never mind,' he murmured. 'I've no choice but to go through with it. Speculation's pointless.'

'Would you like a cup of coffee? I thought I'd make some.'

'Yes.' Maurice sighed. 'Let's drink some coffee and wait in the time-honoured fashion.'

Charlotte was glad of the excuse to leave him and busy herself in the kitchen. Samantha's abduction in itself had left her curiously unmoved and she could not understand why. Perhaps if she had been seized by orthodox kidnappers, demanding millions of pounds in ransom, it would have been different. Or perhaps, as Charlotte was reluctant to admit to herself, some part of her secretly approved of this blow at the heart of Maurice's greed and Ursula's complacency.

Besides, too much had been laid bare in the wake of Samantha's disappearance to be forgotten however soon she reappeared. For six weeks, Charlotte had sustained the pretence that her suspicions about Maurice could somehow be stifled. But he had himself confirmed them now, too blatantly for her to ignore them any longer. When and if Samantha was restored to her father, he would have to face another kind of reckoning. Whether he realized that Charlotte did not know. But she knew. And the knowledge drained her of desire for an end to their ordeal. For it would merely herald the beginning of another.

'Remember the last time we waited together like this, Charlie?' The sizzling of the water in the kettle had masked the sound of Maurice's footsteps and Charlotte's heart lurched at the realization that he was standing next to her, so close she could imagine he had read her thoughts.

'The . . . The last time?'

'When Mother was dying, I mean.'

'Oh . . . Of course. Yes.' It was less than a year ago, though it seemed far longer, that they had kept each other company at Ockham House during the long bleak hours it had taken Mary Ladram to die. He was the Maurice Charlotte had always known then, the Maurice she had loved as a brother and trusted as a friend. And he still was. The only difference was that she understood him now. But to understand Maurice Abberley was also to fear and to loathe him. For the moment, Charlotte could do neither. But already she sensed that in the end she would. 'A lot's happened since then,' she ventured. 'Hasn't it?'

'Do you really think so?'

The kettle began to boil. She stretched across to switch it off, grateful for the distraction. 'I'm not sure what I think,' she said. She spooned coffee into their cups and reached out for the kettle. 'I just—' But Maurice was there before her. She jumped back in surprise as she felt his fingers beneath hers, twined around the handle.

'Sorry.' He smiled reassuringly at her. 'This uncertainty is hard on the nerves, isn't it?'

'Yes. It is.'

'But it won't last much longer. After Sam's been released, life will revert to normal.'

'Will it?'

'Oh, yes.' He filled the cups, then returned the kettle to the hob. 'I'll make sure of that.'

'How?'

'The same way I always have.' He looked straight into her eyes, insisting by the force of his gaze that he could somehow persuade her to forget everything she had learned about him since Beatrix's death. 'Trust me, Charlie. That's all you have to do.'

FIVE

'BOURNE END 88285.'

'Mr Abberley?'

'Speaking.'

'Good afternoon, Mr Abberley. I represent those who are holding—'

'I know who you are, dammit.'

'Good. Then you will also know how stupid it was of you to attempt to deceive us.'

'*I never—*' Maurice broke off, then resumed in a calmer tone. '*I'm sorry. I shouldn't have done it. And I won't again.*'

'*No. You will not. Because this time we will take measures to protect ourselves against your duplicity.*'

'*What do you mean?*'

'*This is what you will do. Refer to Ordnance Survey Landranger Map 174. Drive to the parking area and viewpoint shown on the western side of Walbury Hill, grid reference 370 east, 620 north. Arrive at midnight tonight. Come alone. And bring everything else you stole from Frank Griffith.*'

'*There's a problem. I—*'

'*The only problem is that we will kill your daughter if you do not do exactly as you are told.*'

'*And I will. It's just—*'

'*Do you understand your instructions?*'

'*Yes, but—*'

'*Then there is no more to be said. Good afternoon, Mr Abberley.*'

The tape clicked off and Charlotte looked across at Maurice, who had the relevant map spread open on his lap. Ursula was standing behind his chair. 'Have you found it?' she asked.

'Yes. A few miles south-west of Newbury. About thirty miles from here.'

'When will you leave?'

'It's less than a hour's drive. But let's say ten-thirty to be on the safe side'.

'Let's say ten o'clock. I don't want there to be any question of you being late. And check the car this afternoon. Tyres, petrol, oil, everything. This has to go without a hitch.'

'It will. Don't worry.'

'It's not too late to inform the police,' put in Charlotte, pausing to study the other two's reactions and finding them to be exactly what she had expected. Ursula wanted her daughter free at any price and did not mind what risks Maurice had to run to bring that about. While Maurice had his own reasons for resisting police involvement in the affair. 'I'm not saying you *should* inform them. I'm just—'

'Sam's my daughter, not yours,' snapped Ursula. 'I've no intention of allowing PC Plod to wreck our chances of getting her back. All they want is this bloody letter and we're going to give it to them. Is that clearly understood?'

'Yes. Of course.'

'Good.'

With a parting glare, Ursula stalked from the room, leaving Maurice to fold the map shut and smile across at Charlotte. '"*My* daughter". Did you notice that, Charlie? Not *ours*.'

'She's upset.'

'Aren't we all? But I'm the one who'll be waiting at Walbury Hill tonight, with nothing but my father's last letter to his sister to buy Sam's freedom with.'

'Which is why I mentioned the police. You said yourself the kidnappers might—'

'No! I have to handle this alone. There's no other way. Holding the letter back was a mistake. Now I have to make amends.'

'But Maurice—'

'Don't say any more, Charlie.' He held up his hand to silence her. 'Not till Sam's back with us, safe and sound. Then you can say whatever you like.'

The afternoon and evening seemed to pass with agonizing slowness, yet, when the time came for Maurice's departure, it felt to Charlotte as if it had crept up and taken them by surprise. Little more had been said since the telephone call. They had each kept their own counsel. What Ursula and Maurice were really thinking Charlotte could not tell. For her own part, she was filled with neither hope nor dread, rather a fatalistic inability to foresee the future. What would be would be. Samantha might be back home by the early hours of Monday morning. Or they might hear she had walked into a police station somewhere later in the day. Or she might call them from a telephone box on a lonely road. Or—

She watched from the unlit half-landing window as Maurice climbed into the Mercedes, its rear lights blurred and twin exhausts clouding in the misty air. The night was overcast and moonless. Up on the downs it would be dark as a velvet bag. She saw him take the envelope from his pocket and show Ursula the letter inside. There was no farewell kiss, merely a nod of mutual understanding. Though she knew he did not deserve it, Charlotte could not suppress a stab of sympathy for him. It seemed to her that, despite all he had done, Ursula might have spared him a word or gesture of encouragement. But she did not. As he started the car and moved away, she turned and walked back into the house. Charlotte heard the front door close and realized she alone was watching as the white halo of the headlamps traced his progress along the drive. The brake lights flared suddenly red as he reached the end. Then he turned into Riversdale and vanished beyond the trees.

SIX

THEY HAD NOT EXPECTED him back before one o'clock. It was not until two o'clock therefore that they became anxious enough to call him on his car telephone – only to find it had been switched off. By three both felt certain something was wrong and a nervous debate began about what they should do. Charlotte suggested contacting the police, but Ursula would not hear of it. Her own preference was for retracing Maurice's route at first light in case he had suffered a breakdown or been involved in an accident. Reluctantly, Charlotte agreed, even though she was sure he would already have been in touch with them in such an event. Whether Ursula shared her growing sense of foreboding she did not know. Nor did she care to ask.

They set off at half past five in Charlotte's car. The morning was grey and cool, the roads virtually empty. Charlotte could have wished they were busier. The noise and bustle of workbound humanity would have made their journey seem more normal. Their destination lay patiently in wait on the grey crest of the downs, while below, across the broad green Kennet valley, they approached along winding lanes through slumbering villages. Then the habitations fell away behind them as their ascent began between thorn-spattered banks and hangers of oak. And suddenly, true to the route Ursula had picked out on the map, they reached the crest and saw Maurice's car, parked at the far end of the lay-by where he had been told to wait, maroon and solitary against the pale expanse of chalk-smeared turf.

Charlotte pulled off the road and stopped. The Mercedes was thirty yards or so ahead of them, facing out across the valley, with the summit of Walbury Hill behind. And there was a man in the driving seat, leaning back against the head-rest, making no move to acknowledge their presence. Yet who could he be but Maurice? Glancing round at Ursula, Charlotte realized she too had seen the figure.

'Is it Maurice?' she whispered.

'It must be,' Ursula replied.

'Then why hasn't he seen us?'

'Perhaps he's asleep. Sound the horn.'

Charlotte obeyed, but the only reaction came from a sheep beyond the nearby fence, who looked up in surprise. The occupant of the Mercedes did not stir. Ursula leant across and pushed the horn herself three more times, but still there was no response.

'Something's wrong.'

'Shall we go and see?'

'No.'

'What?' Charlotte looked at Ursula and saw a frozen expression of horror on her face. 'What's the matter?'

'You go, Charlie. Please. I don't think I can . . . Please go and see if he's all right.'

The imploring note in her voice left Charlotte no choice. 'Very well,' she said. Then, hurrying lest her nerves fail her too, she unbuckled her seat-belt and climbed out.

The world beyond the confines of the car was silent but no longer still. A breeze ruffled her hair and set hanks of wool waving on the fence-wire. The faded heads in a patch of thistle between her and the Mercedes seemed to beckon. And she followed, up the flint-strewn slope, across the swell of the down that seemed, at this altitude and hour, like the curve of the Earth beneath her feet.

She did not look back at Ursula or down into the valley, but trained her eyes forward, fixing them on the interior of the Mercedes and the dark shape of its occupant as, with every step, clarity threatened to break upon her vision.

It *was* Maurice. She recognized his check trousers and bottle-green sweater. But she could not make out his face, obscured from her by shadow and the oblique angle at which he had set his seat.

She began to divert from the path, tracing a semi-circular route round the bonnet of the car. As she did so, the windscreen reflected the cloudy sky back at her as a white sheet. Only when she was on the other side of the car could she gain a clear view of Maurice and only then by closing to within a few yards.

Suddenly the shadows resolved themselves and the reflections fell away. Suddenly the truth was before her, hideous and unambiguous. Maurice was dead, his throat slit wide in a collar of congealed blood. He was held in a reclining position by his seat-belt, with his head bent back and his mouth open, his eyes staring up at the roof of the car, his right arm hanging straight down, his left snagged on the gear-stick. All this Charlotte saw in a single glance.

Another showed her the dark stains down his chest and across the dashboard and windscreen. While a third, as she stepped closer, revealed that his mouth, though open, was not empty. Some object was lodged between his teeth, forcing them apart.

She leaned for support against the wing of the car, breathless and trembling, wondering if she would scream or vomit. She must prevent Ursula seeing this, at all events prepare her for the reality of it. She must remain in control of herself and her actions. She must not disintegrate.

There was a conscious effort involved in raising her eyes to look once more. She reminded herself that nothing must be touched or disturbed. Yet surely she could render her brother one service to which the dead are always entitled. His sightless eyes should be closed. And she should close them now, before Ursula ran to join her or her hands shook too much to obey her. She opened the door, looking away as she did so and listening for a second to the song of a skylark on the wind. Then, taking a gulp of air, she leaned into the car and pressed his eyelids shut with the forefinger and thumb of her right hand, shuddering as the icy coldness of his flesh communicated itself to her. And then, with his face no more than a foot from her own, she saw what was wedged in his mouth. It was a roll of freshly minted banknotes.

SEVEN

FOR THE REST OF that day, Charlotte felt she was at one remove from reality, viewing events through an invisible screen equipped to filter out the extremes of sensation. The grief and horror she would have expected to experience were somehow blunted and held at bay, though whether permanently or not she had no way of knowing. She began to suspect her mind had no room for such emotions while there were more urgent issues to be addressed and wondered if, when she was alone and at rest, they would suddenly overwhelm her. If, that is, she ever was alone and at rest again.

The nearest she came to solitude was the interval that elapsed after she had forced herself to dial 999 on Maurice's car telephone. Standing on the ridge above the Kennet valley with their backs turned against the spectacle of what they had found, she and Ursula said little as the early morning slowly advanced. Indeed, only when the first wail of an approaching siren drifted up from below did Ursula remark: 'I suppose we'll have to tell them everything.'

'I think we'd better, don't you?' Charlotte replied.

'I don't know what I think. Except that I hope to God they let Sam go.'

Charlotte said nothing, though she thought even then it was a frail hope. Maurice had not given the kidnappers what they wanted. No other interpretation of what had happened seemed sustainable. As to the kidnappers' next step, she was confused but pessimistic. If they were prepared to murder once, they would certainly be prepared to murder again. But she did not propose to point this out to Ursula. If she believed in the possibility of Samantha's early release, so much the better.

The police, when they arrived, were models of efficiency and solicitude. Charlotte and Ursula were whisked away to Newbury Police Station, where a pixie-faced detective constable, Valerie Finch, took their preliminary statements. Ursula was anxious to stress that her daughter's safety was now her only concern and became impatient with the methodical nature of their questioning, but Charlotte knew it could not be otherwise. Then the officer in charge of the case, Detective Chief Inspector Golding, returned from the scene and persuaded them to repeat everything for his benefit. Though eager to express his sympathy, he had a sceptical air guaranteed to rile Ursula, in whom anger turned rapidly to hysteria. At this, Golding decided they should be driven back to Swans' Meadow, accompanied by Finch and a lugubrious detective sergeant called Barrett. There, he assured them, they would be kept fully informed of developments.

Ursula seemed somewhat calmer once she was home, not least because she was within earshot of the telephone, which she continued to think might ring at any moment, bringing news of Samantha. Finch encouraged her to talk about Sam, which she did to nervous excess, while Barrett made innumerable cups of tea and coffee. Eventually, in the middle of the afternoon, Golding arrived with his superior, Detective Superintendent Miller, and a squad of technicians, who began making intricate modifications to the telephone in order to monitor incoming calls. Barrett supervised this operation, while Miller and Golding, with Finch sitting in, questioned Ursula and Charlotte in the lounge.

Miller's involvement seemed to mark a change of gear in the police's approach to the case. He was a large rumpled red-faced man in his late forties, with huge hands and a fog-horn voice, disinclined to waste time on niceties. He had clearly emerged from a rougher mould than the well-mannered and smooth-tongued Golding. On several occasions Charlotte detected a *frisson* of mutual resentment between the two, though for the most part they functioned adequately as a partnership.

'Why didn't you contact us as soon as you knew your daughter had been kidnapped?' was Miller's unceremonious introduction of a point Charlotte had been expecting to hear raised all day.

'Because my husband was confident he could deal with the matter on his own,' Ursula replied. 'He insisted we should keep it secret.'

'Delay greatly complicates the gathering of evidence,' said Golding. 'Your neighbours may have seen something the day your daughter was seized. But they've already had the best part of a week in which to forget.'

'I'm sure we all appreciate it was a terrible mistake,' said Charlotte. 'My brother believed he was acting in Sam's best interests. So did we.'

'Of course,' murmured Golding.

'What I want to know,' said Ursula, 'is what you're going to do now.'

Miller's face darkened for a moment. Then he said: 'Your husband's murder will be reported, but there'll be a media black-out where the kidnap's concerned. After that it's a question of waiting for them to contact you again. When and if they do—'

'But if they don't?'

Miller said nothing. His expression implied that the problem, if it eventuated, was not of his making. Golding spoke for him. 'If the kidnappers don't have what they want, Mrs Abberley, they'll be in touch. They're bound to be.'

'You're sure money wasn't demanded?' asked Miller.

'If only it had been,' said Ursula. 'At least there'd have been no doubt about our ability to pay. Whereas supplying what *they* wanted . . .'

'A set of correspondence between the poet Tristram Abberley and his sister,' said Golding hesitantly. 'I do have that right, don't I?'

'Yes. You do.'

'Chief Inspector Golding reckons himself something of an expert on poetry,' said Miller, with the hint of a sneer. 'The only rhyme I know is crime and time.'

'Tristram Abberley was a distinguised poet,' said Golding, refusing, it seemed, to be provoked. 'But I don't entirely understand why this correspondence should have been so . . . valuable.' He leafed through his notes. 'Are you seriously saying it proves his sister was responsible for his work?'

'We are,' said Charlotte.

'Incredible.'

'Also irrelevant,' said Miller. 'I'm sure you ladies don't expect us to believe *that's* what lies behind all this.'

'No,' said Charlotte. 'The letter Maurice took with him last night referred to another document which he didn't have. He was afraid – and I think now he was right to be – that it was what they were really after.'

'Not money?'

'I've told you, Superintendent,' snapped Ursula. 'Money wasn't the issue.'

'Then how do you explain the wad of twenty quid notes stuff—' Miller paused for a moment and softened his tone. 'We found five thousand pounds on your husband's body, Mrs Abberley. What are we to make of it?'

'I think Maurice hoped to buy them off if the letter didn't satisfy them,' said Charlotte. She glanced at Ursula, who nodded in reluctant agreement. 'I'm afraid it's just the kind of reasoning he would apply. Clearly, if money had been the kidnappers' motive . . .'

'They wouldn't have left it behind in such a contemptuous fashion,' said Golding. 'Quite.'

'All right,' said Miller, with a glare at his colleague. 'For the ladies' benefit, Peter, perhaps you'd like to run over what we've so far established.'

'Certainly, sir.' Golding smiled at Ursula and Charlotte in turn. 'We can't fix a definite time of death until after the *post mortem*, but we're working on the assumption that it was shortly after the time agreed for the rendezvous – midnight. Chalky footprints in the back of the car suggest two men joined Mr Abberley, occupying the rear seats. The quantity of soil deposited suggests they had walked some distance, perhaps from the lay-by on the other side of Walbury Hill. If so, the purpose was presumably to take Mr Abberley by surprise.

The letter he had with him is missing. The money . . . we have already discussed. Our reconstruction of events assumes a conversation between them, culminating in an argument and Mr Abberley's murder. He appears to have been grabbed from behind, then, using a knife, his assailant . . . Well, perhaps I need not continue.'

'Any idea who we're dealing with?' asked Miller.

'Madmen,' was Ursula's bleak reply.

'Maurice thought they were Spaniards,' said Charlotte.

'Because his father was killed in the Spanish Civil War?' enquired Golding.

'Principally, yes. But also because of the delay in making contact. And the use of the *International Herald Tribune* in Sam's photograph.'

'Which we have?' Miller looked across at D.C. Finch.

'Yes, sir.'

Finch handed the photograph to Miller, who did no more than glance at it before passing it on to Golding and muttering: 'Could be anywhere.'

'The man who telephoned certainly spoke with a foreign accent,' Charlotte pointed out.

'Ah yes, the tapes,' said Miller, with a roll of his eyes. 'High time we heard them, I think. Any objections, Mrs Abberley?'

'Of course not.'

Miller nodded to Finch, who rose and moved to the hi-fi cabinet, where the three cassettes stood ready for use. She inserted the first in the machine and pressed the button. For several seconds, Charlotte expected to hear Maurice's recorded voice. Then she realized something was wrong. Finch ejected the cassette, peered at it, replaced it and tried again. But the result was the same: the faint whirring of a blank tape.

'What's going on?' demanded Miller.

'I don't know, sir. These are the tapes Mrs Abberley showed me earlier.'

Ursula tossed her head in irritation and bustled across to join her. Then, as she inspected the cassette, irritation turned to bafflement. 'This *is* the right one,' she insisted.

'Try the others,' suggested Golding.

But even before they had Charlotte knew what they would find. She knew because, albeit too late, she had come to understand her brother. Maurice was as cautious as he was clever. Or had been, she mentally corrected herself. The tapes represented proof of his involvement in the theft of the letters and, by inference, in Beatrix's murder. He had clearly been afraid they might be used against him after Samantha's release. Therefore he had taken what must have seemed an obvious step to protect himself.

'I don't understand,' said Finch, as, with Ursula, Miller and Golding gathered around her, she played each side of each cassette to no avail. 'There's nothing on them.'

'Nothing?' growled Miller.

'Oh, Christ!' Ursula turned away and instantly caught Charlotte's eye. 'He wiped them.'

Charlotte nodded. 'I think he must have.'

Golding stared at Ursula. 'You mean your husband deliberately obliterated these recordings?'

'I'm afraid so, Chief Inspector.'

'Why?'

'Because they proved he'd stolen the letters,' said Charlotte in a dull voice she scarcely recognized as her own. 'They were incriminating evidence.'

'But they were also the only evidence as to the identity of the kidnappers,' protested Golding.

'I know.'

'Let's get this straight,' put in Miller. 'The letters have been surrendered to the kidnappers. The tapes have been wiped. And apart from a next-to-useless photograph all we have—'

'Is Maurice dead,' murmured Ursula. 'And Sam missing.'

EIGHT

THE SHOCK OF MAURICE'S death finally overtook Charlotte when sleep had undermined her defences. Lying in bed at dawn on Tuesday morning at Swans' Meadow, she felt the stirrings of grief more as a physical process than a mental one. Her eyes were tearful, her hands trembly, her palms moist. And the horror of how Maurice had died could not be set aside, even when she was awake. Whenever she was not concentrating on something else, it sprang into the foreground of her thoughts.

Yet beyond this involuntary level, she was aware of an altogether more complex reaction. She felt no desire to avenge her brother's murder. Indeed, some part of her approved of the justice of it. Maurice had murdered Beatrix, albeit not with his own hands. He had brought about her death to satisfy his greed and his pride. He had brushed her aside because he believed his needs and wishes were more important than hers. And now he had been made to pay for what he had done.

But why? There her conjectures reached an abrupt end. Nothing in Tristram's letter could have provoked such a response. Nothing, at all events, that she had noticed. And, since the letters were now gone, it was too late to scan them for clues. She could not even remember exactly how Tristram had phrased his reference to the document he meant to send to Beatrix. No wonder Superintendent Miller had become exasperated. His parting remarks last night had suggested he did not believe anything they had told him. And, in the circumstances, who could blame him?

Not that his scepticism about the letters would last much longer, since Chief Inspector Golding was to travel to Wales today to interview Frank Griffith. Nevertheless, Charlotte could not see how their enquiries were to be taken forward. Ursula was clinging to the belief that Samantha would soon be released. Her daughter's safety was all she cared about. In many ways, she would prefer not to know the identity or motive of her captors. If time began to undermine her confidence in such an outcome, it would be different. But until then . . .

Charlotte climbed out of bed, put on her borrowed dressing-gown, crossed to the window and pulled back the curtains. The night had strewn a carpet of dew-beaded cobwebs across the lawn and mist was rising from the river. Autumn was reclaiming summer and with it the sun-gilded image of Samantha, last and most innocent of all the Abberleys. Would she ever again pad across the grass, barefoot in her bikini? Or stretch her limbs and laugh at the careworn ways of her elders? How long, Charlotte wondered as she bit her lip to hold the tears at bay, would the question remain unanswered?

Derek Fairfax learned of Maurice Abberley's death from a headline in the *Financial Times*: LADRAM SHARES SLIP ON NEWS OF CHAIR-MAN'S MURDER. It was such an utterly unexpected development that his mind could not register any immediate reaction beyond amazement. He bought half a dozen other newspapers and read every word they had printed on the subject, but none added much to his knowledge. *Maurice Abberley, fifty-year-old chairman and managing director of Ladram Avionics, was found murdered in his car in a hilltop lay-by near Newbury, Berkshire, early yesterday morning. Police said his throat had been cut. The discovery was made by his wife and sister.*

Derek debated whether to telephone Charlotte Ladram and offer his condolences, but, in the end, he decided not to. He did not want her to think he was gloating. Later, he began to wonder whether, with her brother dead, she might be prepared to tell the police how he had almost certainly murdered his aunt. If so, it would surely only be after a period of mourning. He would have to let her recover from the shock before contacting her. Even then, she might not respond well to the suggestion. But, for Colin's sake, he would have to put it to her.

In so far as Derek thought at all about who had murdered Maurice Abberley — or why — he supposed a crazed hitch-hiker must have been responsible. The possibility that he had been killed for some reason connected with his father's letters did not occur to Derek. Even for a single moment.

At Swans' Meadow, Charlotte and Ursula had no time to brood. Police officers of various ranks and specialisms came and went all day, checking for forensic evidence relating to the kidnap, intercepting some telephone calls and listening in to others. Friends and business associates of Maurice were in frequent contact. Some were judged trustworthy enough to be told about Samantha's abduction. Others were not. Uncle Jack fell into the latter category, Ursula vehemently rejecting his offer to lend a hand. The police took the immediate neighbours into their confidence out of sheer necessity, hoping one of them might have seen or heard something significant the previous Tuesday; but none had.

Ursula's concern for Samantha's safety seemed to eclipse any grief she felt on Maurice's account. She was happy to let Charlotte deal with the registrar, coroner and undertaker, with whose procedures Charlotte was only too familiar. The pathologist had finished with Maurice's body, which now lay in a chapel of rest in Maidenhead, awaiting a decision on when and where the funeral was to be held. Charlotte felt it was for Ursula to say, but all Ursula could think about was her living daughter, not her dead husband.

In the afternoon, D.C. Finch drove Charlotte to Newbury Police Station to collect her car. Nothing was said, but she had the impression it had been examined almost as closely as Maurice's. Superintendent Miller, it seemed, was leaving no stone – or mat – unturned.

She returned to Bourne End by a circuitous route along minor roads. The winding lanes and grey stillness of early autumn combined to soothe her spirit. But a stray recollection of a golliwog Maurice had given her for her fifth birthday undid the effect in an instant and she reached Swans' Meadow with her eyes red and face blotchy from tears, only to find to her surprise that Ursula was in a similar condition.

'It's having to tell so many lies, Charlie. It's the strain of remembering who knows and who doesn't. Friends of Sam have been on, wanting to speak to her, eager to offer their condolences. And I have to keep saying she's out, busy, emigrated, in the bath, gone to bloody Timbuktu.'

'There's been no news of her release, then?'

'No. And now I'm beginning to wonder if there ever will be.' She poured herself a gin and tonic and took up a position she had frequently occupied since the kidnap – standing by the lounge window, staring out into the garden, glass cupped in her right hand and cradled against her breast like a child, cigarette held aloft in her left hand, mouth half-open, eyes fixed intently on some distant and perhaps invisible object. 'Everyone's been so bloody kind. I think that just makes it worse. So understanding, so very *solicitous.*'

'They're only trying to help.'

'Even Spicer rang. Can you imagine? Even he thought he ought to—'

'*Spicer?*'

'Our boozy ex-chauffeur. Surely you remember?'

'He phoned? Today?'

'Yes.'

'What did he want?'

'To express his sympathy, I suppose, which I could have done without. It was difficult to get rid of him, actually. He was full of the usual questions. How? When? Why? Anybody would have thought—'

'Where did he phone from?'

'A call-box somewhere. Or a pay-phone in a pub. I don't know. Does it matter?'

'It may do. You see, I—'

'Wait!' At the first note of the doorbell's chime, Ursula swung round and signalled Charlotte to be silent. 'This may be news of Sam. I'll go.' She almost broke into a run to reach the hall.

Charlotte heard her wrench the front door open and exclaim: 'Chief Inspector Golding! Is it about Sam?'

'I'm afraid not, Mrs Abberley. Can I come in?'

Ursula's reply was not audible. A few moments later, she reappeared in the lounge, with Golding behind her.

'Ah, Miss Ladram,' he said, smiling at Charlotte. 'I'm glad you're here as well.'

'I thought you were in Wales, Chief Inspector.'

'I've just got back. In fact, I came straight here.'

'Frank Griffith told you all about the letters?'

'Not exactly. That's why I've called. There's a substantial discrepancy between your account and his.'

'*Discrepancy?*' Ursula rounded on him. 'What bloody discrepancy?'

'Perhaps it would be more accurate to call it a total contradiction.'

'For God's sake say what you mean,' she snapped.

'Very well. Mr Griffith is a prickly character, as I'm sure you're aware. Unforthcoming, to put it mildly. But he was emphatic on one point. He knows nothing about any letters from Tristram Abberley to his sister.'

'You're joking.'

'No.'

Charlotte stared at Golding, hoping she had somehow misunderstood. '*Knows nothing?* He said that?'

'He denies ever reading or possessing such letters. Hence he also denies they were stolen from him. By Mr Abberley or anybody else.'

'But we saw them,' shouted Ursula, stubbing out her cigarette so violently the ashtray vibrated beneath it. 'At least we saw *one* of them.'

'So you said.' There was a flatness in Golding's voice, a deliberate suppression of meaning.

Charlotte looked straight at him. 'Don't you believe us, Chief Inspector?'

'It's certainly hard to imagine why you should invent such an elaborate story.'

'We didn't invent it.'

He smiled faintly. 'Well, that remains to be seen, doesn't it? As a detective, I have to keep an open mind. I have to consider every possibility.'

'Including the possibility that we're lying?'

'Exactly so, Miss Ladram. *Including the possibility that you're lying.*'

NINE

THE FIRST TELEPHONE CALL Derek Fairfax received after reaching the office on Wednesday proved what he had begun to suspect: that the death of Maurice Abberley amounted to rather more than the newspapers had revealed.

'Fairfax.'

'Good morning, Mr Fairfax. My name's Golding. Detective Chief Inspector Golding of Thames Valley CID.'

'Thames Valley?'

'I'm investigating the murder of Mr Maurice Abberley. Perhaps you've read about it.'

'Er . . . Yes, I have.'

'Your name's been given by the murdered man's sister, Miss Charlotte Ladram, as somebody able to corroborate certain aspects of the evidence she's laid before us.'

'Really? What evidence?'

'I'd like to talk to you about it. Would that be possible?'

'Well . . . Yes, of course. But—'

'Could I call on you later? This afternoon perhaps?'

'You mean . . . here?'

'If it's not inconvenient.'

'No, no. I'm sure—.'

'Shall we say two-thirty?'

'Well . . . all right.'

'Until two-thirty, then. Goodbye, Mr Fairfax.'

Derek put the telephone down slowly, frowning as he did so. If he had not been so taken aback, he might have suggested a different venue. But it was too late now. What form of corroboration did Golding have in mind? he wondered. Why had Charlotte Ladram decided to involve him when she had previously been so eager to exclude him? Impulsively he grabbed the telephone directory, looked up her number and dialled it. But there was no answer.

He tried again ten minutes later, then at half hourly intervals throughout the morning. But the result was always the same. Charlotte Ladram was not at home.

Charlotte was in fact driving west along the M4 to South Wales, intent upon extracting from Frank Griffith some explanation of why he had misled Chief Inspector Golding. By noon she was on the Brecon by-pass and, less than an hour later, was steering gingerly between the ruts on the rough and winding track to Hendre Gorfelen.

It was as she was approaching the last crest before the house came into sight that she suddenly had to stamp on the brakes as a Land Rover came pitching round the hillside. The two vehicles came to a halt virtually bumper to bumper, with no room to pass each other between the dry stone walls. And there, staring back at Charlotte from the cab of the Land Rover, unsmiling and motionless, was Frank Griffith.

Charlotte switched off the ignition and climbed out. The Land Rover engine rumbled on as she walked round to the driver's door and waited for him to look at her. Eventually, just when she thought he never would, he turned it off.

'Frank?'

He continued to stare straight ahead.

'You must have been expecting me.'

Still there was no response.

'Why did you lie to the police?'

Now, at last, he did acknowledge her presence, with a faint nod and a stubborn extension of his lower lip. 'I did what you wanted me to do,' he said.

'What I *wanted* you to do?'

'Forget the whole thing. Leave well alone. Stop causing trouble to you and your family.'

'I never said that.'

'You meant it, though.' He glared round at her. 'Why else would you have left me that note? You didn't believe McKitrick had stolen the letters, did you? It was a lie. So, before you start demanding to know why *I* lied, perhaps you'd like to tell me why *you* lied.'

'All right.' She hung her head. 'There seemed to be no way of proving what Maurice had done. Nor of preventing him from publishing the letters. So I thought . . . I thought it would be for the best to . . . to . . .'

'Fob me off?'

'Yes.' She forced herself to meet his gaze, to admit the truth of his accusations as openly as she could. 'But everything's changed now, don't you see?'

'No. I don't.'

'Didn't Golding tell you about my niece?'

'Yes. He told me.'

'She's in danger, Frank. Grave danger. Aren't you willing to do anything to help her?'

'There's nothing I can do.'

'You can convince the police the letters really exist. That they're what this is all about.'

'But they're not. They have nothing to do with it.'

'They must have. Nothing else makes any sense. In his last letter, Tristram referred to a document he was sending – or intending to send – to Beatrix. And the kidnappers demanded everything Maurice stole from you. They must have meant that to include the document, but Maurice didn't have it.'

'Because I didn't have it. Beatrix sent me the letters and that's all. She never mentioned receiving anything else from Tristram, with or after his last communication.'

'Don't you have any idea what it might be?'

'None. Besides, it makes more sense to me to believe your brother was the victim of one of the many enemies I'm sure he made in the course of his life. As for your niece . . .'

'Yes, Frank? What about Sam? She's just twenty years old. Younger than you were when you volunteered for Spain. Younger than Beatrix was when she wrote Tristram's first poem for him.'

His expression remained as unyielding as ever. 'I can't help her.'

'Won't you even try?'

'Beatrix asked me to keep her secret. Your brother's death means I can. It's a second chance I don't deserve. But it's one I don't intend to waste.'

'What about Sam?'

'I'm washing my hands of your family.' He stared out intently through the windscreen. 'I'm forgetting everything I've ever known about them. I'm doing what I should have done from the start.'

'Which is?'

'Thinking of myself.' He turned and looked straight at her 'Now, why don't you reverse to the bridge? You can turn round there. Then we can both go our separate ways.'

TEN

Derek's previous experience of dealing with the police amounted to clarifying some technical points for the Fraud Squad when a client of Fithyan & Co was arrested for tax evasion. On that occasion he had been treated with a degree of courtesy nor far short of deference and he had subconsciously expected the same of his interview with Chief Inspector Golding. But his expectations were not to be fulfilled.

Golding was a lean and outwardly languid man of about Derek's own age, smartly dressed in a dark suit, striped shirt and mono-grammed tie. This and his expression of heavy-lidded scepticism gave him more the appearance of an Old Etonian stockbroker than a police-man. It enabled him to ask the bluntest of questions in the politest of tones and to disguise his opinion behind the blandest of smiles. When he invited Derek to confirm the existence of Tristram Abberley's letters to his sister, it was impossible to guess at the purpose of his enquiry. And when Derek emphasized, as he was determined to, that the contents of the letters supported his brother's protests of his innocence, Golding heard him out with patient inscrutability.

It was, indeed, only when their conversation seemed to be moving towards a close, with Derek none the wiser about why it had taken place, that Golding began to apply a steely edge to his questions.

'Why do you suppose Mr Griffith might deny possessing the letters, Mr Fairfax?'

'I don't suppose he would.'

'But he has. There's my problem. He denies it point-blank. And you've never seen any of them, have you?'

'No, but—'

'So, strictly speaking, you can't corroborate Miss Ladram's account, can you?'

'I most certainly can. She—'

'Why do you think Mr Abberley was murdered?'

'I don't know.'

'For the letters?'

'I wouldn't have thought so. But then, as you've pointed out, I don't know what they contain.'

'Something worth kidnapping Mr Abberley's daughter for, apparently.'

'I beg your pardon?'

'Mr Abberley's daughter has been abducted and is still missing. The letters were demanded as ransom. All of this was prior to our involvement, of course.' Derek felt taken aback, as he knew he was meant to be, by this sudden revelation. 'For the present, I must ask you to say nothing to anybody about this aspect of the case.'

'Of course . . . Of course not.'

'The kidnappers' motive is a complete mystery to us. Money is the norm where abduction is concerned. Generally lots of it. A fifty-year-old cache of letters hardly seems to fit the bill, does it? If you'll pardon the pun.'

'I suppose not.'

'Could these letters be worth anything?'

'No. I don't see—' Derek struggled to order his thoughts. 'Only to Maurice Abberley.'

'Because they would unlock fifty years' worth of royalties on Tristram Abberley's poems?'

'Yes.'

Golding fell silent for a moment, tugging reflectively on the lobe of his left ear. Then he said: 'If the letters can't be recovered, your brother's defence collapses even before it's been assembled, doesn't it?'

'Yes.' This conclusion had not occurred to Derek, but it was true nonetheless. He felt helpless, overwhelmed by a tidal rush of events he could not hope to understand.

'And if they are found, it's too late for Maurice Abberley to benefit from their publication, isn't it? The royalties would go to his widow and daughter?'

'I suppose so.'

'Or just his widow, if his daughter isn't released alive.' Golding's voice sank to a murmur, as if he were talking to himself rather than Derek. 'There's something here nobody's seeing. A pattern to the missing letters and wiped tapes, the denials, the contradictions, the downright—'

'Wiped tapes?'

Golding stared at Derek in surprise. 'What?'

'You mentioned some tapes.'

'Did I? Extraordinary. Well, never mind.' He smiled. 'I'd better not hold you up any longer. One last thing.'

'Yes?'

'Where were you last Sunday night?'

'At home.'

'Alone?'

'Yes.'

'There's nobody who could confirm that?'

'No. Why do you ask?'

'Because you blame – or blamed – Maurice Abberley for your brother's arrest. You've admitted as much. In other words, you've admitted to having a motive for his murder.'

'I've done no such thing.'

'You have, actually.' Golding grinned at him. 'I was just trying to rule you out from the start. It's a pity I can't.' His grin broadened. 'Isn't it?'

After Golding's departure, Derek made several further attempts to contact Charlotte by telephone. When it became obvious she was not at home, he decided – against his better judgement – to try Swans' Meadow, directory enquiries furnishing the number. This time there was an answer, but it was the one he had dreaded.

'Hello?' He recognized the voice instantly as Ursula Abberley's, but knew it would be best to pretend he had not.

'Could I speak to Charlotte Ladram, please?'

'Who's calling?'

'Er . . . Derek Fairfax.'

'*Derek Fairfax?* This is Ursula Abberley speaking, Mr Fairfax. Charlotte's not here. Even if she were, I can't think she'd want to talk to you.'

'I'm sorry to disturb you . . . at this sad time, Mrs Abberley . . . but it's very . . .'

'If you were really sorry to disturb me, you wouldn't have, would you?'

'Well, I—'

'Goodbye, Mr Fairfax. Please *don't* call again.'

When Charlotte reached Swans' Meadow late that afternoon, tired and dispirited after her journey to Wales, she found Ursula in a further stage of her adjustment to Maurice's death and Samantha's disappearance. It was one of wistful regret rather than fretful anxiety and had taken her to her daughter's bedroom, where she was sorting through the show-jumping rosettes Samantha had accumulated during her hippomanic early teens.

'There's no news, Charlie,' she mournfully announced. 'No word. No sign. Nothing.'

'I wish I could tell you I'd expected there to be.'

'Why are they keeping her? We gave them everything they wanted.'

'Everything we had of what they wanted, you mean. And they don't know that. They must think we're holding out on them. That's why they killed Maurice.'

'But who are they? And if they want more − of whatever it is − why don't they tell us?'

'I don't know. Perhaps they're waiting for the police to lose interest.'

'Then they may have to wait a long time. D.C. Finch was here again today, enquiring after my health, checking on my movements, watching, prying, probing.'

'It's her job.'

'And doesn't she just love it? Spying on me is so much pleasanter than directing the bloody traffic.' Ursula's mood was changing again, reverting to anger and impatience. She rose from the bed where she had spread out the rosettes, strode to the window and stared down into the garden. 'They listen to every telephone call, you know, in *and* out. They're all recorded, logged and traced.'

'In case one of them's from the kidnappers.'

'Or *to* the kidnappers. They think we know more than we're telling, Charlie. How can we convince them we don't?'

'We can't. Frank Griffith has made them wonder if the letters really exist. And there's nothing I can do to make him say otherwise.'

'Then we're hoist with our own petard. If the police think we made them up, they'll think the same about the tapes, maybe about the kidnap itself.'

'Surely not.'

'It's how their minds work.'

'But they know Sam's missing. As soon as the kidnappers make contact—'

'Exactly!' Ursula turned to look at her. '*As soon as they make contact.*

But what if they don't? What if we never hear from them again? What then, Charlie? What will the police think then?'

ELEVEN

TENSION EASES WITH THE passage of time, no matter how unbearable it seems at the outset. The human condition adapts in spite of itself, turning abnormality into a form of routine. So it was that by Thursday morning Charlotte could detect within herself an ebbing of urgency, a slide towards fatalism, a creeping acceptance that Samantha's absence might be as permanent as Maurice's.

Some similar process in Ursula presumably explained her willingness for the first time to discuss arrangements for the funeral, which they agreed should be held as soon as possible. Charlotte was in fact on the point of telephoning the undertaker to put matters in hand when she was intercepted by an incoming call.

'Hello?'

'Who's speaking, please?' The voice was low and huskily feminine.

'Charlotte Ladram. Who—'

'This is Natasha van Ryneveld. I know who you are, Charlotte. Do you know who I am?'

'Yes.'

'I thought you might, though Maurice chose to believe otherwise. I learned of his death when I tried to telephone him at Ladram Avionics. It was a shock. I would have liked to have been told less . . . abruptly. But perhaps you think I had no right to be.'

'Perhaps I do.'

'How is Ursula?'

'She's . . . bearing up.'

'May I speak to her?'

'I'm not sure.' In fact the doorbell had just rung and Ursula had gone to answer it. Charlotte was relieved to be able to say honestly, 'Actually, I'm afraid you can't.'

'What happened, Charlie? May I call you Charlie? Maurice always did. How did he come to be murdered? What were the circumstances?'

'I can't discuss them.'

'Why not?'

'It's . . . complicated.' Charlotte heard Superintendent Miller's gruff tones in the hall. 'I must go now. I'll tell Ursula you called.'

'But—'

Charlotte put the receiver down and felt positively grateful for the lack of opportunity to consider her reaction to the conversation. As she looked up, Ursula returned to the room, with Superintendent Miller, Chief Inspector Golding and D.C. Finch behind her. The three police officers were grim-faced and intent. They acknowledged Charlotte with peremptory nods.

'We've just held a case conference, Mrs Abberley,' Miller began. 'And we've decided on a change of approach.'

'We're hampered by a total lack of evidence,' said Golding. 'The only way we can set about obtaining some is to raise the public profile of the case, which is so far limited to the bald facts of your husband's murder.'

'Accordingly,' said Miller, 'I propose to hold a press conference this afternoon at which I'll reveal we're dealing with a kidnap as well as a murder.'

'You *propose*,' said Ursula. 'Are you asking for my agreement?'

Golding smiled at her. 'Naturally, we hope you'll see the wisdom of taking such a step. Indeed, we hope you'll be willing to attend the press conference and answer questions.'

'But it'll go ahead anyway,' growled Miller. 'I don't need your consent.'

'Won't publicity frighten off the kidnappers?' asked Charlotte.

'The embargo hasn't flushed them out, has it?' Golding countered. 'We need a public response. Sightings. Suggestions. Tip-offs. We need information.'

'Shouldn't you wait a little longer?'

'Nine days is long enough,' put in Miller.

'People forget quickly, Miss Ladram,' said Golding. 'We can't afford to delay.'

'Very well,' said Ursula. 'Hold your press conference.'

'And you'll attend?' asked Golding.

'Yes.'

Charlotte was watching the two policemen as Ursula replied. She saw them glance at each other and exchange a conspiratorial arching of the eyebrows, compounded in Miller's case by the faintest of nods. Ursula's participation would evidently strengthen their chances of success. But what success represented to them she was no longer sure she knew.

Derek started watching the six o'clock news on television that evening in a distracted mood, only for his attention to be seized by mention of the name *Abberley* during the preamble to film of a press conference held earlier in the day at Newbury Police Station.

The reporter referred to sensational developments in the Abberley murder case. Then attention switched to a Superintendent Miller of pugnacious appearance, who described in clipped and guarded police-speak how twenty-year-old Samantha Abberley had been abducted nine days previously. Anybody who had seen or heard anything suspicious in the neighbourhood of her home on Tuesday 1st September was urged to contact Thames Valley CID. A photograph of the missing girl was displayed, looking wholly unlike Derek's single memory of her. Then, with Chief Inspector Golding visible in the background, Ursula Abberley made a personal plea for her daughter's release.

Her performance – particularly in response to questions – was not what Derek was used to when viewing such events. There was none of the customary tearfulness, no hint of hand-wringing despair. Instead, she spoke calmly and rationally, more like a mediator than a mother. All the words were in place – '*I would not wish this on my worst enemy*'; '*Sam's safety is my only concern*'; '*I appeal to the public to help in any way they can*'; '*I beg those who are holding her to let her go*' – but the heart seemed strangely absent.

Something else was also absent. Derek waited for Superintendent Miller to mention Tristram Abberley's letters but he never did. What the kidnappers wanted was not specified. What the police expected them to do was not hinted at. And by the end Derek was more confused than ever.

Charlotte and Ursula watched the broadcast together at Swans' Meadow, Ursula nursing a gin and tonic as she did so. When it was over, she walked across to the television, switched it off, turned to look at Charlotte and said: 'They made me sound like an unfeeling bitch.'

'Nobody will have thought that.'

'Oh, yes they will. You're expected to behave as if you're in a soap opera these days. Floods of tears. Torrents of emotion. Self-control counts against you.'

'Perhaps you shouldn't have taken part.'

'How could I have refused? Imagine the capital Miller and Golding would have made out of it if I had.'

'They're trying to help, Ursula.'

'Are they? I don't think so. I think they're trying to do exactly the opposite.'

'Oh, come on.' Charlotte summoned a smile. 'It's their duty to find Sam – and to protect her.'

'No it isn't. It's their duty to find somebody they can convict of Maurice's murder.'

'Isn't that the same thing?'

'They don't think it is. Come into the garden with me.'

'Why?'

'Come outside and I'll explain.'

With a shrug of her shoulders, Charlotte rose and accompanied Ursula out through the kitchen and into the garden, where a calm and picturesque evening was spreading long shadows and rectangles of gold across the lawn.

'See the man feeding the ducks on the other side of the river?' Ursula pointed towards the Cookham bank, where an unremarkable middle-aged man in a brown anorak was tossing crumbs to a quacking and splashing circle of waterfowl. 'Recognize him?'

'No.'

'He's a policeman.'

'How can you possibly know?'

'Because I never saw him before Monday and I haven't stopped seeing him since. Him and a couple of others out of the same mould. They're not looking for Sam, Charlie. They're looking for Maurice's murderers. And they think they've found them. Here. In this house.'

'That's ridiculous.'

'Yes. But they don't realize it is. And there's nothing we can do to make them. So, while they watch us watching them . . .' Her voice trailed into silence. Her chin drooped. The tears she should have shed movingly on television but had not were there now, clear to see, brimming in her eyes, absurdly beautiful in the slanting sunlight. 'While they play their bloody silly games and force us to do the same . . .' She swallowed hard and looked straight at Charlotte. 'Sam's chances of coming out of this alive diminish all the time.' Then she raised her head and shouted loud enough to make the man on the other side of the river glance towards them, '*With every day they waste,*' before adding in a murmer: 'The thread Sam's life hangs by grows thinner and thinner.'

TWELVE

ON FRIDAY, CHARLOTTE WENT home. She justified her departure on the grounds that, with arrangements for Maurice's funeral on Monday now in place, there was nothing to detain her at Swans' Meadow. Ursula did not attempt to persuade her to stay, for which she was grateful. If pressed, she might have revealed just how eager she was to be gone. Although she had expressed doubts about Ursula's interpretation of the police's conduct, it had rung truer to her than she had cared to admit. What worried her most of all was that she might be held in equal suspicion. By returning to Ockham House, she could distance herself from events and reclaim a reassuring degree of privacy.

She could not escape altogether, of course, as a clutch of telephone calls swiftly demonstrated. Several acquaintances and former workmates had seen the television broadcast and wanted to offer their sympathy and advice, which was generally as well-intentioned as it was useless. Uncle Jack called to complain of being kept in the dark just when his expertise in such matters – of which Charlotte was unaware – might be most valuable. And Lulu Harrington rang to express her dismay at what had occurred, enabling Charlotte to confirm something Ursula had already deduced.

'The person in New York you sent a letter to on Beatrix's behalf – could her name have been van Ryneveld rather than van Ryan?'

'Why, yes, it certainly could have been. What makes you think so?'

'She's been in touch. But Madame V from Paris hasn't. I don't suppose you've remembered her name?'

'I fear not. I've racked my brains, but at my age there are precious few left to rack. I still can't call more than the initial letter to mind.'

'You'll let me know if you do?'

'Most certainly.'

After Lulu had rung off, Charlotte thought about the four letters

Beatrix had left with her and reflected that the contents of two were still a complete mystery. Maurice must have known what was in the one to his mistress. At least, he must have known what she said was in it. But she was presumably as capable of lying as Ursula. Yet the tone of her telephone call to Swans' Meadow had implied she knew nothing of Samantha's abduction – or of what her kidnappers had demanded in return for her release. If so—

The jangle of the telephone, by which Charlotte was still standing, fractured her thoughts. She grabbed at it in irritable haste.

'Yes?'

'Er . . . Miss Ladram?'

'*Yes.*'

'This is Derek Fairfax.' Guilt washed over Charlotte at his words. She had given his name to Golding on Tuesday but had made no effort to contact him since to explain the situation. 'I've been ringing you for days. The police have been to see me.'

'Yes. They would have been. I'm sorry. That was my fault.'

'Since then I've seen the broadcast about your niece. Nothing was said about ransom on the television, but the officer who interviewed me, Chief Inspector Golding, said Tristram Abberley's letters were demanded. Is that true?'

'Yes.'

'But I don't understand. Who . . . Who could possibly—'

'None of us understands, Mr Fairfax. If only we did.'

'And Frank Griffith has denied the letters ever existed?'

'Yes. But we can't discuss this now.' Yet Charlotte did feel the need to discuss it. And she suddenly realized that Derek Fairfax was one of the few people who would view matters in the same light as her. 'Perhaps we could meet.'

'Certainly. I'd like to.'

'Can you come to lunch tomorrow?'

'Yes.'

'All right, then. Let's say midday, shall we?'

'Fine, I'll see you then.'

'Yes. Goodbye, Mr Fairfax.'

Charlotte put the receiver down and pondered the mystery of why she had issued such an invitation. It would be folly to raise his hopes just when the loss of the letters had effectively dashed them. Yet she badly needed an ally, a friend who would listen and advise. Why look for one in Derek Fairfax? Because, she supposed, there was nowhere else to look. He was her last resort now as well as his brother's.

She wandered into the kitchen and began assembling a shopping list. Cooking lunch for a guest might at least take her mind off the intractable problem of Samantha for a while. When the telephone rang yet again, she was inclined not to answer it. But, when it showed no sign of stopping, she relented.

'Hello?'

'Miss Ladram?'

'Yes.' The caller's voice was familiar to her, clipped and formal with the hint of an accent. She realized who it was a fraction of a second before he spoke again.

'I represent those who are holding your niece, Miss Ladram.'

'What?'

'You heard. And I rather think you understood. Police surveillance has prevented us contacting your sister-in-law. We have therefore turned to you.'

'Who do you represent?'

'It is better you should not know.'

'Why did you kill Maurice?'

'Because he did not deliver all the papers. And because he had the effrontery to offer money instead.'

'He gave you everything he had.'

'There is more. And we want it.'

'We don't have it.'

'Then find it. We know Beatrix Abberley had what we require. Therefore it must lie within your power to locate and surrender it.'

'Tell me what we're looking for.'

'A document sent by Tristram Abberley to his sister in March 1938, written in the Catalan language.'

'What sort of document?'

'I have said enough. We are patient, but not infinitely so. We will keep your niece alive for one month from today. You have until October eleven to procure the document. When you do, place an advertisement in the personal column of the *International Herald Tribune* to read as follows. *Pen pals can be reunited. Orwell will pay.*' He paused for a moment. 'You have that?'

Charlotte read back her own scrawled note from the jotter beside the telephone. 'Pen pals can be reunited. Orwell will pay.'

'Correct. If such a message appears on or before October eleven, we will contact you.'

'You must give me more information.' Charlotte knew she should glean as much as she possibly could, but her brain seemed sluggish and uninventive. 'We're prepared to do anything to get Sam back.'

'All you have to do is meet our requirements, fully and promptly. Do not tell the police we have made contact. If they seem to be drawing close to us, we shall kill your niece without hesitation.'

'How . . . How is Sam?'

'She is alive.'

'Can I speak to her?'

'Enough of speaking. You agree to our terms?'

'Of course. But—'

'Then our business is concluded. Good afternoon, Miss Ladram.'

THIRTEEN

DEREK'S FIRST SURPRISE WHEN he arrived at Ockham House shortly before noon on Saturday was the cancellation of lunch. Charlotte Ladram was more obviously nervous than he had known her to be on any previous occasion and professed herself reluctant to remain indoors, let alone cook a meal. She suggested a walk in the open air and he readily agreed. Her willingness to talk verged on a compelling need and after all his previous attempts to gain her confidence, which had made little headway, he knew he must not let such an opportunity pass him by.

They drove towards Ashdown Forest, and even before they had found a suitable place to stop, Charlotte had begun to recount the events of the past week in such detail that it was obvious she was holding nothing back. She slipped, without appearing to notice it, into addressing Derek by his first name and, after some initial awkwardness, he reciprocated. Her brother's death seemed to have removed a barrier between them. It was no longer necessary to pretend they knew less or more than they did. Their obligation to be honest with each other outweighed for the first time whatever they owed to anyone else.

They parked near Camp Hill and walked out aimlessly across the heath amidst the estranged fathers flying kites with their sons and the headscarfed ladies exercising their labradors. Everyday preoccupations had never seemed more remote, the present never more real, than now.

'I suppose you think I should tell the police,' said Charlotte, after describing the telephone call with which her niece's kidnappers had broken their silence.

'Are you afraid they won't believe you?'

'I wouldn't blame them if they didn't. They've seen and heard nothing to convince them. For all they know, Sam's abduction may be a figment of our imaginations.'

'But she *is* missing.'

'Or hiding. How are they to know which?'

'If you don't tell the police, what will you do?'

'Try to find the document the kidnappers want. Offer it to them in exchange for Sam's release.'

'But where is there left to look? You've combed through Beatrix's possessions time after time. And I can't believe Frank would be holding anything back if he thought it could save a young girl's life.'

'Neither can I. Which leaves the two other recipients of letters from Beatrix.'

'One of whom is still unidentified.'

'Yes. But one isn't. Natasha van Ryneveld.'

'Maurice's mistress? Why would Beatrix have sent a document entrusted to her by her brother fifty years ago to her nephew's mistress?'

'I can't give you a reason. But she sent her something. That we do know.'

'Surely Maurice would have known what it was – and handed it over to the kidnappers accordingly.'

'Not necessarily. Natasha may have lied to him about what her letter contained – as Ursula did. After all, Beatrix wouldn't have sent her anything unless she had good reason to think it would be kept from Maurice. And I'm pretty sure Natasha knew nothing about the kidnap. Maurice probably didn't want to risk her objecting to the surrender of Tristram's letters. So, if what she received from Beatrix is what the kidnappers want, she's not to know, is she?'

'It still doesn't seem very likely.'

'I agree. But isn't it worth a try?'

'I suppose so. What will you do? Visit her in New York?'

'Well, I doubt she'll come here. There are some awkward questions she may not want to answer.'

'About what?'

'About your brother, Derek. Who rang him in May to make the appointment for him to visit Jackdaw Cottage? Not Beatrix, obviously. But it *was* a woman, wasn't it?'

'Natasha van Ryneveld?'

'Who else?'

They reached Airman's Grave and paused together beside its perimeter wall, gazing in at the poignant tribute to one victim of a long-ago conflict, though not as long-ago, it occurred to Derek, as the conflict which had recently extended its crabbed old hand to touch their lives. 'Chief Inspector Golding pointed out to me . . .' he hesitantly began.

'Pointed out what?'

'That Colin's defence, such as it is, collapses completely without Tristram's letters.' He looked round to her and tried to smile. 'Sorry,' he murmured.

'Don't apologize. It's I who should apologize to you – and your brother – for what Maurice did.'

'But as Colin is to me, so Maurice was to you. We can't choose our brothers. Or cease to care about them.'

'You reminded me once that Maurice is only – was only – my half-brother.'

'Perhaps that's what I was apologizing for.' Before caution could restrain the impulse, he placed his hand over hers where she was resting it on the low wall in front of them. She made no move to shake it off. 'You do have my sympathy, you know. My sincere sympathy.'

She glanced at him. A smile flickered across her lips. 'Thank you,' she said softly.

Derek removed his hand, glad he had been allowed to decide when he should do so. 'Do you think this is really about the Spanish Civil War?' he enquired.

'The document dates from then and is written in Spanish – or Catalan. What else are we to think?'

'Nothing. Which is what worries me.'

'In what way?'

'If it – whatever it is – matters enough, fifty years later, for people to kill and kidnap for . . .'

'Yes?'

'Then you need to be careful. Very careful.'

'Being careful won't help Sam.'

'Perhaps not. But I don't know Sam, I only know you. I'm only worried about you.'

'Don't be.'

'If there's anything I can do . . . to help . . .'

'There's nothing.' She shook her head. 'If Natasha will talk to anybody, it's me.'

'What about Ursula?'

'There'd be too much tension between them. Besides, the police are keeping a close watch on her. I shall tell her what I propose to do, of course. If she insists on informing the police, so be it. But she won't. Take my word for it. She'll agree it's best for me to go – alone.'

Charlotte turned away and started back up the slope towards the road. As Derek caught her up, a possibility came into his mind to which he gave immediate voice. 'Is Natasha the only person you plan to visit in the States?'

Charlotte frowned. 'Who else would I visit?'

'I don't know. It's just . . .' He gritted his teeth, determined to put their new-found trust to the test. 'I've been thinking. Why didn't the kidnappers try to obtain the document earlier? Why wait fifty years?'

'Because they didn't know where it was.'

'But now they do. Or they think they do. Something – or someone – drew their attention to Tristram's letters. Who? Only a few people knew about them You. Me. Maurice. Ursula. Frank Griffith. And Emerson McKitrick.'

Charlotte did not reply at once. They walked on in silence for a minute or so, then she said: 'If you genuinely want to help me, Derek, don't ask about Emerson McKitrick.'

'All right. I won't. But he is another reason why you should be careful.'

'Then I promise I will be.' She stopped and looked at him. 'Satisfied?' There was no sarcasm in the remark. Her expression hovered, as Derek suspected his own did, on the brink of admitting what neither of them could quite believe.

'Not really, Charlotte, no,' he said with a smile.

She smiled back. 'Everybody calls me Charlie.'

'Could I be an exception?'

'You could be, yes.'

'Then I rather think I'd like to be.'

*　　　*　　　*

Halfway back to Tunbridge Wells, Charlotte said suddenly: 'I'd like to visit a bookshop.' Seeing Derek's puzzled look, she added: 'You mentioned the Spanish Civil War and I've been thinking about the message the kidnappers told me to use to contact them.'

'Pen pals can be reunited. Orwell will pay.'

'It has to be George Orwell, doesn't it? Didn't he fight in Spain?'

'He may have done.'

'Then he's bound to have written about it. Park at the railway station and we'll try in Hatchard's.'

Half an hour later, they were scanning the autobiography shelves in Hatchard's. Orwell was represented by *Down and Out in Paris and London* and one other volume whose title seized their immediate attention: *Homage to Catalonia*. Charlotte lifted it from the row and together they read the note on the back. *This is Orwell's famous account of his experience as a militiaman in the Spanish Civil War. In it he brings to bear . . .*

'Orwell will pay homage to Catalonia,' said Derek under his breath. 'That must be what it means.'

Charlotte nodded, turned to the front of the book and pointed to the year of first publication.

'1938. The year Tristram died.'

'And the year he entrusted a document written in Catalan to Beatrix. Maurice was right.'

Charlotte marched to the counter and paid for the book. Derek waited until they were standing outside, with Saturday afternoon shoppers bustling past them, before asking: 'What was Maurice right about?'

'"Something's snaked its way out of the Spanish Civil War – from fifty years ago – to wrap itself round our throats." Those were his very words. I pooh-poohed them at the time. And less than twenty-four hours later he was dead.' She turned to look at Derek. 'He could feel it, you see. And now I think I can too.'

FOURTEEN

MAURICE'S FUNERAL WAS IN many respects indistinguishable from Beatrix's. Both were well-attended and efficiently staged. Both progressed smoothly from sun-lanced church to manicured crematorium. And both seemed to be over before they had begun. Yet there were also significant differences. Most of those who had come to Beatrix's had done so out of love, whereas duty clearly impelled the score of senior staff from Ladram Avionics who turned out to bid Maurice a corporate farewell. The same could be said of Miller, Golding and D.C. Finch, who contrived to look more like miscellaneous employees of the undertaker than police officers, let alone friends of the deceased. And there was not even a pretence of mourning among the reporters and photographers who clogged Cookham churchyard and followed the cortège to Slough Crematorium and back.

Nor did a spirit of affectionate remembrance obtain among the few whom Ursula felt obliged to entertain afterwards at Swans' Meadow. Aliki had returned from Cyprus in time to cater for the event, but nobody displayed much appetite for the food she had prepared and most departed as soon as decency permitted. The only exception to this rule was Uncle Jack, who clearly had his sights set on several more whiskies when Charlotte insisted, at Ursula's request, on driving him to the station and seeing him aboard the London train.

When she returned to Swans' Meadow, she found Ursula had embarked on a cold-blooded drinking bout and was reluctant to accompany her into the garden, the one venue where Charlotte felt she could safely disclose what had happened. But accompany her she eventually did. And sobriety was instantly restored when she heard Charlotte's news.

'You know what this means, don't you?' she responded, a sudden access of hope lighting up her face. 'It means Sam still has a chance.'

'Only if we can find the document,' Charlotte cautioned. 'That's why I think it would be worth going to New York.'

'Thank God you're prepared to, Charlie. I'd never be able to without the police getting wind of it. And they mustn't, they absolutely mustn't.'

'I agree.'

'When will you go?'

'As soon as you can supply me with Natasha's address and telephone number.'

'You propose to forewarn her?'

'I can't risk her being away. And I don't think she'll refuse to see me, do you?'

'I really couldn't—' Ursula pursed her lips and suppressed her evident irritation. 'No, I don't suppose she will.'

'Is the . . . er . . . the report Beatrix commissioned here?'

'Yes. You may as well take it away with you. After all, I don't need to insure myself against Maurice's treachery any more, do I?' Ursula flicked a fragment of cigarette ash off the sleeve of her black dress and added, almost as an afterthought, 'Poor Maurice,' before turning and walking away towards the house.

As Charlotte started after her, it crossed her mind that this throw-away remark was the kindest thing Ursula had found to say about the man she had been married to for more than twenty years since the day they had found him dead. She had succeeded in damning him with the faintest of eulogies.

Charlotte did not read the report until she was back at Ockham House. She wondered how Beatrix had reacted to its revelation of the double life Maurice was leading. Had it been the final confirmation of her suspicions? On finishing it, had she realized for the first time that he meant to kill her? If so, she had prepared for the event more thoroughly than he could ever have imagined. And she had needed to, for she had known – as Maurice had not – that there was more at stake than Tristram's royalties, far more.

Poor Maurice, as his widow had truly said. He had expected everybody to abide by the rules he had applied to his own life. He had expected weakness to yield to strength. He had expected money to answer every need. No doubt, even at the end, as he saw the blade of the knife flash in the moonlight, he had assumed his killers would rob his corpse. But they had not. Instead, they had fed it with the only food he knew.

Charlotte wept then, more freely than at any time since his death. She wept for them all – Tristram, Beatrix, Maurice and Samantha. And lastly she wept for herself. Then she dried her tears and read aloud the epigraph Orwell had chosen for *Homage to Catalonia* to make sure her voice would not betray her.

'"Answer not a fool according to his folly, lest thou be like unto him. Answer a fool according to his folly, lest he be wise in his own conceit."' She was reminded of a remark in Tristram's last letter to Beatrix – *Such a foolish conceit, in both senses, eh?*' – and she wondered if she was about to succumb to a similar temptation. To start what she could not finish. To initiate more than she knew. 'No matter,' she said to herself as she walked into the hall. 'It must be done.' She picked up the telephone and dialled the number recorded in the report for Maurice's Fifth Avenue apartment.

'Yes?' The voice came distantly, accompanied by an echo that seemed to rob it of identity.

'Natasha van Ryneveld?'

'Who is this?'

'Charlotte Ladram.'

'Why, Charlie, you take me by surprise.' The accent was superficially American, but beneath there seemed to lie some other tongue, threatening to emerge at the end of every sentence. 'I hadn't . . . Why have you called?'

'Maurice was cremated today.'

'Ah. Was he? I thought it would be about now. If only . . . But still you don't say why you've called.'

'I think we should meet.'

There was a lengthy pause before Natasha replied. 'For what purpose?'

'You asked about the circumstances of Maurice's death.'

'And you want to tell me about them?'

'Yes.'

'You will come here?'

'Yes.'

'Just to satisfy the curiosity of your brother's mistress? I don't think so, Charlie, do you?'

'When you hear what I have to say, you'll understand. And I hope you'll want to help.'

'Help with what?'

'We must meet if I'm to explain.'

Natasha sighed audibly and said nothing for so long Charlotte thought she had walked away from the telephone. But she had not. And when she spoke it was so suddenly and decisively that

Charlotte felt her heart pound at her words. 'Come then, Charlie. Perhaps, after all, it's time we met.'

FIFTEEN

CHARLOTTE HAD NEVER CROSSED the Atlantic before. It seemed so quick and easy when the time came that she wondered why she had waited so long. But as the taxi bore her in from JFK Airport along featureless expressways beneath a gun-metal sky, her wonderment fell away. This was an alien landscape, man-made in its totality according to a scale she could not comprehend. When the taxi emerged from a tunnel beneath the East River amidst Manhattan's towering walls of glass, she suddenly felt unequal to the task she had set herself. She was too small, too weak, too long sheltered from the harshnesses of the world.

But inadequate and ill-prepared though she felt, she knew she could not turn back now. Already they were on Fifth Avenue, with the open expanse of Central Park on one side and a phalanx of elegant apartment blocks on the other. The taxi drew to a halt where a purple awning reached out to the edge of the pavement. She checked the number on the polished brass wall-plaque and knew she had arrived. As she climbed out and approached, the door was opened from within. A uniformed doorman smiled in welcome and confirmed Miss van Ryneveld was expecting her. And so she entered one more hidden compartment of her brother's life.

Natasha was waiting at the door of the apartment when Charlotte emerged from the elevator. She was a dark-haired woman of medium height with a faintly Asiatic cast to her brow and complexion. She held her head proudly and, even before she moved, conveyed a feline quality of grace and languor. She was wearing a loosely belted grey dress and black high-heeled shoes with very little jewellery or adornment save a jet pendant at her throat. Charlotte was immediately disconcerted by this hint of mourning and was grateful when Natasha smiled and stepped back, inviting her to enter.

'Come in, Charlie. You're exactly on time. Just as I'd expect of Maurice's sister.'

'Half-sister, actually.'

'Of course.' The smile acquired a glacial edge. 'Such a fine but vital distinction.'

She led the way down a short and curving hall into the lounge – a rugged expanse of blue and gold that seemed to glow in the light admitted by three high windows. Couches and armchairs as big as beds were surrounded by Graeco-Roman statuary and Oriental urns. Vases sprouted flowers on every surface, their blooms multiplied by huge gilt-framed mirrors. And when Charlotte glanced up, she was astonished to see that the ceiling had been painted as one vast rolling cloudscape. Beneath it, across the ornately worked rugs Maurice had undoubtedly paid for, Natasha strode purposefully ahead. She was of about Ursula's age and height, Charlotte estimated, but narrower in the waist and somewhat heavier around the hips and bosom. She moved in a way that seemed to emphasize the body beneath the clothes, to hint at the purposes to which it might be put. There was no mystery about what Maurice had seen in her. It declared itself at every step.

'Would you care for tea, Charlie?'

'Er . . . Yes please.'

Natasha rang a small bell and, almost instantly, a maid entered through another door. They exchanged a few words in what sounded like Spanish. Then the maid retreated.

'Won't you sit down?'

'Thank you.'

Charlotte chose one of the least ostentatious chairs, only to find, when she rested her hand on the rounded end of the arm, that it had been carved in the likeness of a naked woman bending forwards, between whose ample gilded buttocks one of her fingers was dangling. She pulled it abruptly away and felt herself blush.

'One of Maurice's favourites,' said Natasha with a smile. 'I can see you don't approve.'

'I'm not . . . It's not for me to approve or disapprove.'

'It's kind of you to say so. But I'm sure I know what you really think.'

'I didn't come here to discuss the past, Natasha. I didn't come to argue about what you meant to Maurice.'

'Good. Because I meant a good deal, as a matter of fact. More than just what money could buy.'

'Quite possibly. But Maurice is dead now. All that's ended.'

'Yes. And you promised to tell me why and how it ended. Well, I should like to know, Charlie.' She fondled the jet pendant. 'Even a mistress has a right to understand her grief.'

The maid reappeared, carrying a tea-tray. Silence was observed as she moved a table to stand between Charlotte and the chair Natasha had sat in, then arranged the china and poured the first cups. During this interlude, Charlotte reminded herself of the different bluffs and deceptions each was practising. Would Natasha admit she had known of Maurice's plan from the outset? Or would she pretend she had never known anything about the letters? How many lies should Charlotte let go unchallenged? How much should she reveal, how little assume?

As if determined to seize the initiative, Natasha said as soon as the maid had gone: 'I was shocked to hear of Sam's abduction. Ursula must be beside herself with worry.'

'Yes. She is.'

'Maurice told me nothing of it, you know. Not a word.'

'Really?'

'Well, he hardly had a chance, did he?'

'He came to New York on the fourth. Didn't he see you then?'

'No. I last saw him in August. I had no idea he'd been since.' But she should have been more surprised than she sounded. She returned Charlotte's gaze and sipped her tea, apparently content to let the pretence go undisguised.

'He gave up the letters, Natasha. All of them. They were the ransom – or part of it.'

'What letters?' The arch of her eyebrows declared the pretence was to be total.

'Tristram's correspondence with Beatrix. The correspondence proving Beatrix wrote his poems.'

'You have me at a disadvantage, Charlie. I know nothing of any of this.'

'I'm not here to accuse you, Natasha. I suspect we're both well aware who telephoned Colin Fairfax-Vane in May, claiming to be Beatrix. But, since proving that person's identity is impossible—'

'All of this is way over my head.'

'Maybe. Maybe not. Either way, I hope you'll do what you can to help us rescue my niece.'

'Your half-niece, you mean.' Natasha smiled. 'I fail to see what help I can offer.'

'Then let me explain.' As Charlotte did so, she felt increasingly impatient with the veiled sarcasm to which she had been subjected. Natasha gazed at her with an expression in which caution and disdain were perfectly balanced. It was impossible to tell if the plight of a girl she had never met made any impact on her at all. Even if it did, Charlotte sensed her response would be determined by a fine judgement of how her own interests might best be protected.

When Charlotte had finished, emphasizing how vital it was to find the document the kidnappers wanted, Natasha poured them both more tea before she made any remark. When she spoke, it was in a guarded tone. '*If* Maurice did these . . . these terrible things `. . .` it was without my knowledge. He mentioned no letters to me. Nor any accompanying document. He left nothing here.'

'The terrible things you refer to were intended to ensure you could continue to live here – in the style you obviously do.'

'I own this apartment outright. A gift from Maurice, it's true, but not one I'm in any danger of forfeiting.'

'He spent a great deal on you, I imagine. He meant to go on doing so.'

'No doubt he did. I'm sorry he won't. Sorry for him and for me.'

'But at least you're alive.'

'Yes. I am.' A distant look came into her eyes. 'I never expected Maurice to die in such a way. Sacrificing himself for his daughter . . .' She shook her head in puzzlement.

'Won't you help me prevent it being a pointless sacrifice?'

'If only I could.'

'He must have stored things here. Clothes. Books. Papers. Possessions of one kind or another.'

'Clothes only. And not many of those. You're welcome to search them, of course.'

'I'd be grateful.'

'Come this way, then.' They rose and Natasha led Charlotte out into a short passage. At the end, through an open doorway, she glimpsed a bedroom, richly hung in peach-toned fabrics, expanded by yet more mirrors in one of which she could see the reflection of a large oil painting. The subject was a nude, reclining suggestively across a bed. The picture was of such clarity that it might even have been a photograph. As to the identity of the nude, Charlotte was just too far away to be absolutely certain. Natasha moved ahead, closed the door and turned back, smiling faintly. 'Maurice used this.' She slid open a fitted wardrobe to their left to reveal a few suits and pairs of trousers hanging from a rail. 'They're all he kept here.'

As Charlotte checked the pockets, she knew she would find nothing. What she could not decide was whether there had ever been anything to find. She had pleaded for help as eloquently as she could. She had refrained from criticizing Natasha, far less condemning her. Yet her restraint had failed to achieve its purpose, perhaps because Natasha was genuinely unable to assist, perhaps because she was too frightened to do so. They returned to the lounge, but, this time, Charlotte made no move to sit down.

'I'm sorry if you've had a wasted journey, Charlie.'

'Is there nothing you can tell me?'

'Only that you could try the company apartment on Park Avenue. Maurice might have stored some papers there.'

'I'm going there when I leave here. In fact, I intend to spend the night there.'

'Before flying back to England?'

'Not necessarily.'

'I shouldn't have thought you'd have any reason to stay longer.'

Suddenly, Charlotte's patience snapped. 'You know what this is all about, Natasha. Why pretend otherwise? Maurice took you into his confidence from the start.'

'How can you be so sure?'

'Beatrix is dead. Maurice is too. For God's sake give it up. There's an innocent man in prison and an innocent girl missing from home. Don't they mean anything to you?'

'I've never met them.'

'What did Beatrix send you?'

'I beg your pardon?'

'She sent you a posthumous letter. What was in it?'

'You mean the bundle of blank paper? Maurice surmised it was from his aunt. It made no sense to me.'

'Blank paper?'

'Yes. Weird, don't you think? Quite incredible, really.' Natasha grinned, admitting by her expression that she knew what Charlotte would conclude from this recycling of Ursula's lie.

'You stole Ursula's husband. Won't you raise a hand to prevent her losing her daughter as well?'

'I stole nothing from Ursula, certainly not Maurice. *He* found *me*, not the other way around. And what he found was a woman who understood him a great deal better than his wife ever did.'

'Perhaps so. But—'

'If you think Maurice ever loved Ursula, you're wrong. He never loved anybody except himself. Oh, and maybe you, Charlie. Maybe he loved you. I always reckoned so, anyway.'

'What Maurice did – what you helped him do – was wrong. By helping me, you'd undo a little of that wrong.'

'But I can't help you, Charlie. I can't and that's the truth.'

'Beatrix was a fine woman. She shouldn't have died as she did. Fairfax-Vane is just a glib-tongued antique dealer. He doesn't deserve to be facing a long prison sentence. And Sam is a lively girl on the brink of adulthood. She's entitled to find out what it means, don't you think? Rather than dying for a reason she doesn't comprehend.'

'I don't comprehend the reason either.'

'I'm not saying you do. But if you'd stop lying, for one second, we might—'

'That's enough!' The real Natasha had found both her voice and her face. She was angry, trembling with rage – and maybe with guilt as well. 'You've no right to come here – to my home – and call me a liar.'

'I believe I have. I believe it's my duty. As I believe it's your duty to tell me whatever you know.'

'Get out! Get out this minute!' She marched into the hall and flung the front door open. 'I should never have agreed to meet you. I shan't make the same mistake again.'

It was futile to linger or protest. Charlotte could see from Natasha's expression that losing her temper had been counter-productive. She walked slowly towards the door, struggling to regain her composure.

As they came alongside each other, Natasha said: 'I once asked Maurice why he thought so highly of you, Charlie. Do you know what he said? "Because she's retained a naïve faith in human nature." Not much of a compliment, is it? But he meant it. And he did his best to keep your faith intact. Now he's gone, I think it's time you admitted how false it always was.'

'Was it?'

'Oh, yes. You see, you're the liar, Charlie, not me. You keep insisting on what you know is impossible. You keep pretending something can be done. To rescue Sam. To free Fairfax-Vane. To redeem Maurice's memory. But it can't. Nothing can be done. About any of it.'

'Are you sure?'

'As sure as I am that you'll leave New York as you arrived – empty-handed.'

SIXTEEN

THE APARTMENT MAINTAINED BY Ladram Avionics on Park Avenue was small but comfortably fitted out in contemporary style. It was neither homely nor luxurious and Charlotte doubted if Maurice had done more than visit to check the mail in recent months. Nevertheless, she set about searching it in a methodical fashion, discovering in the process just what she had expected: nothing. She did find an Italian restaurant a couple of blocks away to dine in, however, and there made a point of drinking enough chianti to ensure a good night's sleep, which her plans for the following day suggested she would need. For she was not yet willing to admit defeat and retreat to England. There was one stratagem left to try first.

She slept longer than she had intended and woke to the glare of full morning and the bleat of the telephone. As she grabbed for the handset, she guessed it must be Ursula and wondered if there was news of Samantha. But she had guessed wrong.

'Charlie? This is Natasha. I'm glad I caught you.'

'Why?'

'Because I've been thinking over what you said and . . . Can we meet before you leave New York?'

'Is there any point?'

'Very much so.'

'Then, yes, we can meet.'

'Do you know the Frick Collection?'

'I've heard of it, certainly.'

'It's on Fifth Avenue, at East Seventieth. Walking distance from where you are. I'll meet you there in one hour.'

Only when she arrived did Charlotte realize that the Frick Collection was housed in nineteen separate rooms on the ground floor of the late collector's mansion. Since Natasha had not specified which room they were to meet in, there was nothing for it but to progress through each, ignoring the paintings and studying only the other visitors.

She was halfway round and beginning to fret when she entered the Fragonard Room and was briefly transported to a French *salon* of the eighteenth century. Fragonard's series of paintings, *The Progress of Love*, was displayed on the walls. Beneath one of them – in which a maiden seated by a statue was glancing about in fear of discovery as her lover scaled the garden wall to press his suit – stood Natasha, apparently lost in thought. She was wearing a short lilac dress and a pale cashmere jacket, beneath which the jet pendant glimmered in inky symbolism. Charlotte had to touch her elbow to gain her attention.

'Why, Charlie!' She smiled. 'On time again, no doubt. Though for quite another kind of meeting than this.' She nodded towards the anxious lovers.

'What do you want, Natasha?'

'I come here often. To this room, I mean, not the others. The French understand love. Better than the Americans, anyway, and for certain better than the British.'

'I don't have very long. Could we—'

'You have long enough to lose yourself in Fragonard's world, Charlie. We all have. Cherubs and doves frolicking in perpetual summer. Temptation. Pursuit. Consummation. Nostalgia. Regret. Abandonment. They're all here in these canvasses.'

'Quite possibly. But—'

'Look around for one moment. Please.'

Irritably, Charlotte looked. On every wall, Natasha's point was made. The man offering what the maiden affected not to want. The man winning her over with gifts and endearments. Then the maiden alone, with only her melancholy for company. But it was a point entirely lost on Charlotte. 'If you have something to tell me, Natasha, I'd be grateful if—'

'I am telling you. This is part of it. There are letters even here.' She pointed to one of the paintings on the south wall, in which the maiden sat on a plinth beneath bowering trees, reading a billet-doux whilst its author wrapped his arms around her waist and rested his head against her neck. 'Is he really there? I sometimes wonder. Or is she imagining him as she reads? Is he already somewhere else, betraying her love, preparing to desert her? Hers is every woman's fallacy and every woman's fate. She'd do better to throw the letter away unread, wouldn't she?'

'Perhaps.'

'As Beatrix should have done with Tristram's letters from Spain.'

'But she didn't.'

'No. And now others must suffer for it.' She looked intently at Charlotte. 'I don't intend to be one of them.'

'Why *did* you ask to meet me, then?'

'To give you something. To act more charitably than I customarily do. Come with me and I'll explain.'

Natasha led the way through several more rooms until they emerged into a pillared roof-lit court at the centre of the mansion, where a fountain played amidst tropical plants. They sat on a marble bench near the fountain, into whose plashing water Natasha stared as she spoke.

'I was Maurice's mistress for twelve years. He treated me well. As I'm sure you're aware, he was a generous man. He made it clear he could never acknowledge my existence to his family and I didn't expect him to. I was his secret. Or one of them. He had many, of course. Many more than either you or I will ever know about. But I found out his real secret a long time ago. I found out what made him tick.'

'What was it?'

'Secrecy itself. The greatest pleasure I gave him was the fact that nobody knew about me. It was the biggest thrill for him in everything we did together.'

'But Beatrix found out about you.'

'Yes. She did.' Natasha sighed. 'I'm not going to admit anything, Charlie. I'm not going to incriminate myself. What Maurice did he did. You'll never force me to say I was a party to it.'

'I'm not trying to.'

'Good. Then don't challenge what I'm about to tell you. Any of it.'

'All right. I won't.'

'Let's walk.' Natasha rose abruptly and began a slow circuit of the court, with Charlotte beside her. 'If Maurice had possessed what the kidnappers want, he'd have given it up. I'm absolutely certain of that. He left nothing of the kind with me and never made any reference to such a document. You drew a blank at the Park Avenue apartment, I assume?'

'Yes.'

'There you are, then. No, I fear I can't help you in this search.' She glanced round at Charlotte. 'Honestly. You can believe what I say.'

'In that case—'

'What do I have for you? Firstly, my apologies for becoming angry yesterday. We shouldn't have met at the apartment. There were too many reminders of Maurice. Here I can remain calm. Secondly, to tell you what Beatrix really sent me. Not blank paper, obviously. But a tape, on which she recorded a conversation she had with Maurice a few weeks before her death. Their last face-to-face conversation, as a matter of fact. In it, she confronted him with evidence she'd unearthed of a conspiracy against her and accused him of being behind it. Maurice didn't know their discussion was recorded, of course. And I never told him. I taunted him with the same lie Ursula used. He didn't know which of us to believe or disbelieve. Now, I suppose I regret holding out on him. But perhaps it's as well I did. He'd have destroyed the tape for sure.'

'Why *did* you hold out on him?'

'Because the tape was evidence I could use against him. If I needed to. Or wanted to. And mistresses always anticipate desertion. Unlike Fragonard's star-struck damsels, we keep one eye permanently trained on the future. Beatrix must have known that. She was a clever old— Well, let's just say she was cleverer than Maurice thought, though not as clever as she needed to be. Or maybe her friends weren't. If they'd done exactly what she asked, she'd have outmanoeuvred Maurice completely, as she assumed she would. That's why she sent me the tape. Because, without the royalties, he'd have abandoned me. But, with the tape, I'd have been able to extract a pretty pension from him, as Beatrix calculated. It would have been a double twist of the knife. Neat, don't you think?'

'Yes. But Beatrix was. Very neat.'

'With the private detective's report on Maurice's finances *and* the tape, you should be able to clear Fairfax-Vane. I'm afraid he's the only one of your innocents I can help. But the tape's no use to me now, so he might as well benefit from it.' She took a miniature cassette from her pocket and slipped it into Charlotte's hand. 'Maybe this will help me jump the queue in Purgatory.'

'I'll make sure it reaches his solicitor. This is . . . very good of you.'

'It's not such a big deal. There isn't the ghost of a case against me in anything you have. I'm not stupid. But I'm not vindictive either.' They paused by the bench they had left earlier, with one revolution of the court complete. Natasha licked her lips, uncertain, it seemed, how to conclude their encounter. 'Where will you go from here, Charlie?'

'Boston.'

'Ah. To see Emerson McKitrick, I suppose.'

'Yes.'

'It'll be a wasted journey.'

'Perhaps.'

'But you'll go anyway?'

'Yes.'

'Be careful.'

'People keep telling me that.'

'Because it's good advice. On the tape, Beatrix says something I didn't pay much attention to when I first heard it. She tried to warn Maurice he was playing with fire. But he wouldn't listen. He didn't take her seriously. Neither did I. But I do now. And so should you.'

'I'm bound to do what I can to help Sam.'

Natasha gazed at Charlotte and shook her head. 'Maurice always said you had his share of virtue as well as your own. I wish you luck.'

'Thank you.'

'For myself—' She glanced wistfully into the fountain. 'I think I'll take another look at the Fragonards before I go. He died in poverty, like most artists. I don't plan to. But I'm no artist. Be sure you don't become one, Charlie – like Maurice's father. It doesn't pay in the long run. As Maurice found out. Just too late.' She smiled, patted Charlotte's arm and walked slowly away, the clip of her heels on the marble floor lingering even after she had turned a corner and vanished from sight.

SEVENTEEN

BEATRIX: Come into the lounge and make yourself comfortable, Maurice. Did you have a good journey?

MAURICE: So-so. Too many Sunday drivers for my liking.

BEATRIX: Of course, it's Sunday. Do you know, I'd quite forgotten. One tends to at my age.

MAURICE: Really? You hide it well, Aunt, I must say.

BEATRIX: Now you're flattering me. But it's true. My memory's failing. Names. Faces. Dates. They're all going. For instance, is it the thirtieth of May today or the thirty-first?

MAURICE: The thirty-first, as I suspect you know. You're going to Cheltenham tomorrow. I'm sure you haven't forgotten that.

BEATRIX: No, no. It's why I wanted you to come this afternoon. So we could meet before I went away.

MAURICE: To discuss something important, you said.

BEATRIX: Quite so. Oh! There's the kettle boiling. Would you mind filling the pot, Maurice? There's tea already in it. Then you can bring the tray in.

MAURICE: Leave it to me.

BEATRIX: Don't forget the biscuit-barrel. I have some of those fruit Shrewsburys you like.

MAURICE: (*from a distance*): I hope you didn't buy them just for me. There was no need.

BEATRIX: But I wanted to. And I always make a point of doing as I please. It's one of the few privileges of old age.

MAURICE: Are you trying to tell me something, Aunt?

BEATRIX: Put the tray down here. Let me clear these magazines.

MAURICE: When you phoned, I thought you might have changed your mind.

BEATRIX: About what?

MAURICE: You know full well.

BEATRIX: Do I? As I explained, I'm growing more and more forgetful. I wouldn't want us to find ourselves talking at cross-purposes. Why don't you remind me?

MAURICE: You don't need reminding.

BEATRIX: Humour me, Maurice.

MAURICE: (*sighing*): I thought you might have changed your mind about publishing the letters.

BEATRIX: Tristram's letters, you mean? The ones he sent to me from Spain? The ones proving I wrote his poems for him?

MAURICE: Yes, Aunt. *Those* letters.

BEATRIX: Well, I wouldn't want there to be any misunderstanding.

MAURICE: There isn't. Have you?

BEATRIX: Have I what?

MAURICE: Changed your mind!

BEATRIX: Pour me some tea, would you? I don't want mine to stew
. . . Thank you.

MAURICE: Well?

BEATRIX: It's perfect. Just as I like it.

MAURICE: For God's sake!

BEATRIX: Drink your tea, Maurice. And help yourself to a fruit
Shrewsbury. Then listen to me. It's important you shouldn't
interrupt me.

MAURICE: *Interrupt?*

BEATRIX: Quite so. I'm not a quivering junior at Ladram Avionics,
you know. So, do I have your attention?

MAURICE: Undividedly.

BEATRIX: Excellent. It's nearly six months since you broached your
scheme to me. During those months you've frequently
explained how we would both benefit from informing the
literary world of the trick Tristram and I played on it. And
I've frequently explained how fame and wealth mean very
little at my age. Less, indeed, than my late brother's good
name, which I consider to be more important than any
financial inconvenience you may be caused by the expiry
of copyright. It's not that I begrudge you your father's
royalties. Far from it. It's simply that I'm not prepared to
see him branded a fraud and a charlatan merely in order
to prolong your receipt of them.

MAURICE: You haven't changed your mind, then?

BEATRIX: I did ask you not to interrupt, didn't I?

MAURICE: (*sighing*): Sorry.

BEATRIX: To proceed. About ten days ago, an antique dealer called
Fairfax-Vane came to see me, claiming to have an appointment to value my Tunbridge Ware. He has a shop
in Tunbridge Wells. You may remember him. Ah, yes, I
see you do. In connection with some furniture poor Mary
was ill-advised enough to sell him last year. Well, I'd made
no appointment with him, of course. I assumed he was
chancing his arm. So, I sent him away with a flea in his
ear. Then, last Monday, who should I see skulking – yes,
I think skulking is the word – around Church Square but
your former chauffeur, the bibulous Mr Spicer. He beat a
hasty retreat when he spotted me approaching, but it was
not hasty enough. You look surprised, as well you might,

though more by his incompetence than his presence in
Rye. That, I feel sure, is scarcely news to you.

MAURICE: I don't know what you mean.

BEATRIX: Please be quiet, Maurice, and attend to what I'm saying. Mr
Spicer was not in Rye for the purpose of a seaside holiday. I
think we may take it as certain he had business here. Business which necessitated some preliminary reconnaissance.
So I concluded, anyway. It was a conclusion reinforced by
a subsequent telephone conversation with Mr Fairfax-Vane,
who convinced me an appointment had indeed been made
for him to come here – by a woman clearly younger than
me, who spoke with a faintly American accent. And the
appointment, I realized, was timed to ensure Mrs Mentiply
would be here with me. As a witness, so to speak. I began
to see a pattern to these puzzling events, a distinct and
disturbing trend. Perhaps I might not have done but for
information which has recently come my way concerning
your financial circumstances. However, since—

MAURICE: My *what*?

BEATRIX: Your financial circumstances. And kindly do not bellow.
It really should not strike you as odd that I have been
enquiring into your affairs – if I may so phrase it. Your
persistence – nay, your vehemence – on the subject of
Tristram's letters suggested your need of the royalties was
greater than you were prepared to admit. When I hired a
private detective to test this hypothesis—

MAURICE: A *private detective*?

BEATRIX: There's no need to repeat everything I say. I feel sure you
can hear and understand me. The report I commissioned on
you makes for interesting reading. Particularly in respect
of the mistress you maintain in New York. No doubt her
charms are as considerable as they are expensive.

MAURICE: Good God, this is—

BEATRIX: What you have driven me to. It is useless to beetle your
brow in what you clearly believe to be a threatening fashion.
I am only ensuring we both know where we stand. I have
developed a theory to explain recent incidents in the light
of what I have learned about you. Would you like to hear
it? . . . I shall take your glowering silence to indicate
you would. If Mr Spicer's dismissal for drunkenness last

Christmas was a charade; if he is still in fact in your employment though not as a chauffeur; if your American mistress telephoned Mr Fairfax-Vane and lured him here; if I should happen to fall victim to a break-in apparently arranged by Mr Fairfax-Vane in order to lay his hands on my Tunbridge Ware but actually carried out by Mr Spicer in order to bring about my death; if my demise should leave you in possession of your father's letters and free to publish them . . . Well, if I am right in all this – and I rather think I am – then you have decided to override my objections to publication in the most effective and heartless manner possible, haven't you?

MAURICE: Of course I haven't. This is all – every word of it – the most preposterous nonsense.

BEATRIX: Is it? Is it really?

MAURICE: Yes. And if the only reason you asked me here was to inflict this on—

BEATRIX: But it wasn't. Not quite the only reason, anyway.

MAURICE: Why else, then?

BEATRIX: To ask for time to reconsider my position. I want to think the whole thing through, very carefully, while I'm in Cheltenham. To weigh my principles against the risks I appear to be running.

MAURICE: You're running no risks!

BEATRIX: You should be pleased I think otherwise. It means you may get your way without having to resort to desperate remedies.

MAURICE: Well, if you're having a change of heart . . .

BEATRIX: Don't count on it. I'll telephone you when I return from Cheltenham with my final decision. There's a great deal to take into account. More than you realize. Far more. If your father's reputation were the beginning and the end of the matter, I might have been less intransigent all along. But it isn't, believe me. There are other dimensions to this. Other repercussions. You would do well to beware them.

MAURICE: How can I beware what I know nothing about?

BEATRIX: You can't, so long as you remain as pig-headed as you have been all your life.

MAURICE: Now look here—

BEATRIX: Out of interest, could you tell me what this is really all about? There has to be more to it than money. What is it? Simply your inability to accept that your wishes do not always take precedence over other people's?

MAURICE: Oh, for God's sake—

BEATRIX: What? Leaving so soon?

MAURICE: I'm glad you're having second thoughts, Aunt, whatever the reason. I'll look forward to hearing from you after your holiday, hopefully with good news. But, meanwhile, I've no intention of swallowing any more of your insults.

BEATRIX: As you please. I believe we've both said what needed to be said. I believe we understand each other now.

MAURICE: Perhaps we do.

BEATRIX: Don't forget what I told you. there's more at stake here than you can possibly imagine.

MAURICE: That's eyewash and you know it.

BEATRIX: I know you think it is. But you're wrong. Not that I expect you to heed my warning. I'd be surprised if you did.

MAURICE: And surprises aren't good for delicate old ladies, are they?

BEATRIX: They're not as bad as nocturnal intruders.

MAURICE: No. But you can take precautions against *them*, can't you?

BEATRIX: By agreeing to your terms, you mean?

MAURICE: By being sensible.

BEATRIX: I shall certainly endeavour to be that.

MAURICE: Good.

BEATRIX: Can you see yourself out?

MAURICE: Yes. Of course.

BEATRIX: Goodbye, then.

MAURICE: (*from a distance*): Thanks for the tea. I'll speak to you soon. Have a nice *thoughtful* time in Cheltenham, Aunt.

BEATRIX: I'll be sure to.

MAURICE: (*from a distance*): 'Bye.

BEATRIX: (*in an undertone*): Goodbye, Maurice. Thank you so much for your co-operation. It's been invaluable.

EIGHTEEN

CHARLOTTE HAD BOUGHT A pocket cassette player before leaving New York and listened to the tape of Beatrix's conversation with Maurice over and over again during the five-hour rail journey to Boston. At times she could imagine she was in an adjoining room at Jackdaw Cottage, eavesdropping on what they said. At others the realization that both of them were now dead rendered their words distant and ethereal. But the meaning of those words never altered. Beatrix had set a trap for Maurice and he had walked straight into it. Nobody who heard the tape could doubt his guilt. He had even specified the date of his unwitting confessional. Natasha was right. It would almost certainly be enough to acquit Colin Fairfax. He at least would go free.

But Samantha's freedom still seemed a long way off. *'There's more at stake here than you can possibly imagine,'* Beatrix had said. And subsequent events had shown just how much more. But what was it? What had she held for so many years in trust and secrecy? What had rendered her and Tristram's literary fraud trivial by comparison? Charlotte longed to be able to ask her, to turn to her and have every question instantly answered, every problem magically solved. But she was no longer there. Only her voice lingered in Charlotte's ear. And what it said could never be altered. It could be heard at the press of a button. But it would always be the same.

Charlotte booked into a hotel in the centre of Boston and hunted down the telephone directory in her room as soon as the porter had left. Emerson McKitrick's address was clearly shown, at a place called South Lincoln. Tomorrow, she would have to find him, there or wherever he was hiding. Tomorrow, she would have to forget the humiliation she had suffered at his hands and plead for his help in what threatened to be a hopeless task.

When tomorrow came, Charlotte faced it with as much resolution and efficiency as she could muster. She bought a map, hired a car and drove nervously to Cambridge, where the opening week of Harvard's autumn semester was in frantic progress. At length, she located the literature department and, entering, asked the first student she came upon where she might find Dr McKitrick.

'Not here, ma'am. He works at home most Fridays. Do you want the address?'

'No thank you,' Charlotte replied. 'That won't be necessary.' She was, in fact, relieved to learn he was not there. Confronted in his domestic environment, he would find it more difficult to fob her off.

An hour later, she had reached Drumlin Hill, South Lincoln, a lushly wooded cul-de-sac of executive residences beyond Boston's western suburbs. McKitrick's house lounged on a maple-strewn ridge, sleek and contemporary, with a gable end sporting one huge circular window that stared down at her like an unblinking eye.

The door was answered by a slim blonde-haired woman of about her own age dressed in jeans, trainers and a candy-stripe shirt several sizes too big for her. Bending one knee to restrain an enthusiastic red setter, she unzipped a dazzling smile. 'Hi! What can I do for you?'

'Good morning,' Charlotte ventured. 'I'm looking for Emerson McKitrick.'

'He's not here right now.'

'Will he be back soon?'

'Any minute, I guess. What . . . Is he expecting you?'

'No.'

'You're English, aren't you?'

'Yes. I'm sorry. My name's Charlotte Ladram.'

'Ladram? Don't I know . . . Hey, Ladram Avionics, right? The corporation Maurice Abberley ran.'

'Maurice Abberley is – was – my brother.'

'Your *brother*? You'd better come in.' She opened the door wide and held back the dog, whose tail was beating wildly on the wall behind it. 'It's OK. He just gets over-excited. Come on in.'

Charlotte stepped into the hall and grinned down at the dog. 'Hello, boy.'

'Go on through. I'll get rid of this brute.' The woman led him away, leaving Charlotte to wander into a long pine-panelled room with a huge stone fireplace at the far end and a picture window to her right commanding a view of the terraced front garden and the curving drive up which she had walked. The seating was low and yielding, the decoration largely subordinate to a vast abstract oil painting on the longest wall. Charlotte was gazing at its aimless explosion of colour when her hostess returned, still smiling broadly, and extended a hand in formal greeting.

'Sorry about the dog. I'm Holly McKitrick, by the way.' It was probably Charlotte's frown of puzzlement that prompted her to add: 'Emerson's wife.'

'Oh. I see.' As soon as the handshake was complete, Charlotte turned away, eager to look elsewhere for the instant it took her to absorb the simple fact of his marriage. He had lied about this as about much else and she knew she should feel neither hurt nor surprised. But in reality she felt both. 'You have . . . er . . . a lovely house,' she said, glancing back at Holly McKitrick to find her blue eyes trained studiously upon her.

'Glad you like it.'

'I expect you're . . . er . . . wondering what brings me here.'

'Well, we heard about your brother's death through Emerson's British publisher. It sounded awful. And his daughter's been kidnapped, hasn't she? She's your niece, right?'

'Yes.'

'If you've come all this way at such a time . . .'

'It's because Emerson may be able to help us secure Sam's release.'

'You made his acquaintance when he was over in July researching Tristram Abberley?'

'Yes. I did.'

'Well, I'm sure he'd want to help any way he can, but I don't rightly see—'

'We have to try everything.'

'Yeh. Of course.' She smiled. 'Would you like some coffee while you wait?'

'Er . . . Thank you.'

'It won't take a second.'

Left alone, Charlotte walked slowly down the length of the room, debating with herself how much or how little Holly McKitrick might know. By the time she reached the fireplace, she was also beginning to wonder whether Maurice had known McKitrick was married. If so— But speculation was cut off when, turning round to retrace her steps, she caught sight of a red sports car winding up the drive. She moved to the window and watched it pull up. Emerson McKitrick climbed out, dressed casually in jeans and a tennis shirt. He looked relaxed and carefree, singing under his breath as he lifted a bulging paper sack from the back seat, then started towards the house. But something made him glance up at the lounge window as he approached. And the sight of Charlotte, staring down at him, stopped him in his tracks.

What followed was for Charlotte a demeaning and ultimately frustrating experience. She had planned to appeal to Emerson's better nature, or, if this failed, to argue that he owed her whatever assistance he could give in return for his earlier deceit of her. But Holly's presence ensured she could no neither. Instead, she was obliged to subscribe to Emerson's misleading account of their acquaintance. This he unveiled with grinning blatancy whilst clasping his wife ostentatiously round the waist. In defying Charlotte to contradict him, he was on safe ground, for she knew – as she felt sure he did – which of them Holly would believe.

The worst of it was that Charlotte had intended to emphasize how she had come in search of information, not confrontation. But the lies Emerson had told sprang up as a barrier between them, insurmountable because they could not be acknowledged. When she explained what the kidnappers were after and asked if he had any idea where or what the document might be, his reply was predictably negative. Heard in the context of his and Holly's gushing sympathy, it sounded very like the truth. But Charlotte would have needed to be alone with him, decks cleared of their differences, for certainty on the point. And that he seemed determined to avoid.

'I can't help you, Charlie. I've never heard of any of this before. A document written in Catalan and entrusted to Tristram by a friend. Which friend? About what? And why, all these years later, would it suddenly matter so much?'

'I don't know. But the kidnappers know about the letters. So, they must have learnt about them from somebody. You're one of the few who was aware of their existence. If you mentioned them to a colleague or—'

'But I didn't. Holly here's the only living soul I told. The letters knocked a hole in my book about Tristram. Why should I publicize them?'

'Charlie's not saying you did, honey,' his wife put in. She smiled across at Charlotte. 'You're just checking every possibility, aren't you?'

'Yes. It's . . . er . . . not been made public, but the kidnappers have set a deadline of October the eleventh for handing over the document.'

Emerson's eyebrows twitched up. 'Failing which?'

'They say they'll kill Sam.'

'Oh, God,' murmured Holly.

'So you see—'

'That's tough,' said Emerson. 'She's a good kid. It'd be a tragedy if . . .' He shook his head. 'If there was any way I could help, believe me, I would.'

'But there isn't?'

'No.' He met Charlotte's gaze for a moment and it seemed to her that in this at least he was sincere. 'No way in the world.'

When she left, Emerson volunteered to escort her to her car at the bottom of the drive. Charlotte realized he was still stage-managing their encounter, moving Holly into and out of the wings as and when it suited him. Now, when there was a strict limit to how long he would have to talk to her, it was convenient – perhaps even imperative – to do so unimpeded by a third party.

No sooner had they set off than he said, in a tone completely different from the one he had used in Holly's presence: 'You shouldn't have come here, Charlie, you really shouldn't. You could have phoned. There was no need for this.'

'I wanted to see you face to face.'

'Well, now you have. What have you gained from it?'

'Nothing. Unless you count nailing another of your lies.'

'Pretending I was unattached was Maurice's idea. He reckoned it would make you more . . . susceptible.'

'It's easy to say that now he's dead, isn't it? Easy to blame him for everything.'

'Yuh. It is. But it also happens to be true. He *is* to blame – for starting whatever the hell it is Sam's kidnappers mean to finish.'

'And you really have no idea what that might be?'

'Not a clue. My researches into Tristram's time in Spain were geared to the effect it had on his poetry. They never touched on anything even remotely like this. And I'm glad they didn't, if what happened to Maurice is any guide. One word of advice—' They reached the foot of the drive and paused. 'All I *do* know about the Spanish Civil War is it left a lot of scars that never healed. Feuds. Vendettas. Debts of honour. And some of blood. If Maurice succeeded in calling one of those in . . .'

'Yes?'

'Then the only smart thing to do is to stay out of it. Right out.'

NINETEEN

CHARLOTTE HAD TELEPHONED DEREK from Boston late on Friday night to ask if he could meet her off the plane at Heathrow on Saturday morning. Naturally, he had agreed. Only later had it occurred to him to wonder whether he should feel alarmed by Charlotte's anxious tone or flattered that she felt she could turn to him for advice. There was something about the mystery she seemed determined to solve which both excited and enthralled him. Until, that is, he remembered what had happened to Maurice Abberley. Then the profit-and-loss column of his mind blared out its warning. And sometimes he was inclined to listen.

Not, however, when Charlotte sat opposite him in an eerily empty airport café and described her experiences in the United States while gazing at him with an expression implying what he most wanted to believe: that she trusted him unreservedly. It was a miracle, given how often her trust had been betrayed of late. But it was a miracle, he well knew, born of desperation.

'I wanted to speak to you before I saw Ursula,' she concluded, 'because she might object to my giving you the private detective's report on Maurice's finances.'

'You're giving it to me?'

'Yes. And the tape I obtained from Natasha.'

'But . . . why?'

'Because they should persuade the police of your brother's innocence. Or at least make them doubt his guilt.'

'Yes. They should. But it's *your* brother's reputation that will pay the price.'

'It can't be helped. Maurice brought it on himself.' Her mouth set in a stubborn line. Her decision represented the final abandonment of a lifetime's loyalty and could not have been easy to take. For though it was true Maurice had brought it upon himself, he had also brought it upon her. And she did not deserve to suffer because of it.

'I'm grateful. I'm sure Colin will be too. But what about Ursula? She won't thank you for blackening her late husband's name.'

'Then she must curse me. I want to put an end to every consequence of Maurice's scheme. And this is one end I have the power to bring about.' She reached into her holdall, pulled out a large buff envelope and slid it across the table. 'The report.' Then she unzipped her handbag, took out the cassette and placed it on top of the envelope. 'And the tape. They're yours. On one condition.'

'Which is?'

'Don't use them until Sam's been released or . . . Well, another few weeks in prison won't make much difference to your brother, but it might to my niece. I don't want to encourage the police to ask any more questions. And I don't want to have to lie to them. The kidnappers have given us until October the eleventh to deliver the document and I haven't despaired of finding it before then. But if the police learn I've been to America, they'll ask why. And if I refuse to tell them, they'll become suspicious.'

'Then don't worry. I'll keep these safe. But I won't breathe a word about them until after October the eleventh.'

Charlotte's expression grew suddenly sombre. 'I've just thought. It's three weeks tomorrow. I wonder what those three weeks will bring.'

'Your niece's safe return home.'

'Really? At the moment, I don't see how.'

'While you were away, I remembered something which might just help.' The flash of hope in her eyes made him wish he could report a more substantial discovery than the meagre piece of intelligence he had to contribute. 'The document's written in Catalan, right? Presumably, therefore, *by* a Catalan. The capital of Catalonia is Barcelona. Tristram's last letter to Beatrix implied the document had been given to him by a friend. What friends did he have in Spain apart from other International Brigaders? Like Frank Griffith and—'

'Vicente Ortiz!'

'Yes. Ortiz. According to Frank, he was a native of Barcelona.'

Charlotte leant back in her chair. 'You're right. It must be Ortiz who wrote it.'

'That's what I thought. I'm not sure it takes us very far, of course. Ortiz is long dead.'

'Not necessarily.'

'But Frank said—'

'He didn't see him killed!' She was so eager to embrace the chance of Ortiz being alive – of him holding the key to Samantha's freedom – that she shouted the words, rousing the waitress from a slumped reverie by the till. She blushed and lowered her voice. 'Frank must be told,' she whispered. 'This alters everything.'

'He may not agree. And even if he does—'

'Could you come with me to see him? Tomorrow, perhaps?'

Uncertain whether to admit his pleasure at being asked to assist, he said merely, 'If you'd like me to.'

'I would. Very much.'

'Then certainly I'll come.'

She looked doubtful for a moment. 'You don't have to.'

'I know.'

'If you're only agreeing because of the tape and the report, then I'd rather you refused. I didn't expect anything in return for them.'

'I know that too. But I'd still like to come with you.' Recognizing much of his own diffidence in this display of it on Charlotte's part, he added: 'I'd be honoured to.'

'Thanks.' She smiled warily. 'Right now, I think I need . . .'

'A helping hand?'

'Yes.'

'Then look no further.' He reached out to touch her fingers where they rested on the table. 'You've found one.'

TWENTY

'You did what?'

The violence of Ursula's reaction convinced Charlotte she had been wise to meet Derek Fairfax before going to Swans' Meadow. There would have been no possibility of winning her consent to handing him the tape, let alone the private detective's report. It might have been different had Charlotte been able to claim any success for her American trip. As it was, she could not. The hopes Ursula had nourished in her absence had been dashed. All of which would have been bad enough without Charlotte's final revelation.

'You gave them to *Fairfax*?'

'He has a right to them, Ursula. His brother is completely innocent.'

'So's Sam, in case you've forgotten.'

'I haven't. But this has nothing to—'

'How do you think she'll feel when she knows you helped brand her father a murderer?'

'Badly. As I did when I found out what he'd done.'

'But the report was *mine*. Beatrix sent it to me, not you!'

'And you were prepared to let Fairfax-Vane go to prison despite having the means to prevent it. That *might* have been forgivable while Maurice was alive. But not now.'

'This has nothing to do with Maurice.' Ursula's voice dropped. Her eyes narrowed. 'Or some washed-up antique dealer. You've done this to hurt *me*, haven't you?'

'Of course I haven't.'

'Yes you have. This is your way of getting back at me for Emerson.'

'Don't be ridiculous. I'm simply trying to repair some of the damage caused by Maurice's greed.'

'And I suppose you know nothing about greed. Or envy. Or lust. They're total strangers to you, aren't they, Charlie? They've never crossed your virtuous path through life.' She stepped closer. 'What a nauseating little Miss Perfect you are.'

'Insulting me isn't going to help Sam.'

'No. But nor is letting *your* conscience govern *my* life. I trusted you with that report – and with the information it contained. If I'd known what you intended to do with it, I'd never have told you it existed.'

'Then I'm glad you didn't know.'

A stinging blow from the back of Ursula's hand caught Charlotte round the mouth before she was aware of it being aimed. She rocked back on her heels and clutched at the bureau for support. 'What . . . What are you doing?' She cried.

'Get out of this house, Charlie! Get out of my bloody sight!'

'But . . . We need . . . We need to talk.'

'I don't need to talk to you. That's the very last thing I need to do. Now, for Christ's sake, get out!'

'What about Sam?'

'Let me worry about her!'

'But there's so much—'

'I'll handle this on my own, as I should have done all along, without any interference from your bloody conscience!' They stared at each other for a moment, then Ursula added, emphasizing every word: '*Please leave my home. Now!*'

Charlotte could find no answer. There suddenly seemed to be

nothing between them except the hatred flaring in Ursula's eyes. The pact they had silently concluded after Maurice's death stood exposed as a sham. Their alliance was at an end. If, indeed, it had ever begun. Without another word, Charlotte turned and hurried from the room.

She drove across the bridge into Cookham, scarcely able to see for tears of shock and anger. There she stopped in a car park to dry her eyes and dab the blood from the tear at the corner of her mouth. She guessed Ursula's diamond-encrusted eternity ring had inflicted the damage and recalled being shown it for the first time nearly ten years ago. '*Look what Maurice has given me,*' Ursula had cooed, displaying her ring finger for Charlotte's admiration. '*He's such a darling, isn't he?*' Everything about those distant days had been false and fraudulent – every gift, every smile, every declaration of love and loyalty. Yet at times such as this Charlotte wished she could still believe all the lies she had been told. They were so much more comfortable than the truth she was left with in place of them. And had now to face. Alone.

TWENTY-ONE

DEREK COLLECTED CHARLOTTE FROM Ockham House early on Sunday morning. He had looked forward to the long drive to Wales as an opportunity to push out the boundaries of their friendship, to gauge whether it might flourish in more normal circumstances than those in which it had begun. But the opportunity proved to be illusory. Charlotte seemed too distracted to give him much attention. Every word had to be prised from her, every smile coaxed. In the end, he fell victim to her gloom and lapsed into silence.

On nearing Hendre Gorfelen, however, Charlotte was suddenly transformed into the alert and confident young woman Derek thought he knew. She even apologized for having been poor company on the journey. 'I've a lot on my mind. Too much, I sometimes feel, for it to hold.' Derek assured her he understood. And so he did. But still it was clear that, amidst her preoccupations, there was scarcely room to think of him as anything more than a temporary ally. Hardly a friend at all.

The dog was in the yard and barked a desultory warning of their arrival, but made no attempt to stop them approaching the house. The door was open and orchestral music could be heard from a radio somewhere within. Charlotte knocked, then shouted: 'Frank!' The radio was switched off, but there was no other response. The sound had come from the kitchen and Charlotte led the way through to where Frank Griffith sat smoking over the remains of a bread and cheese lunch. He stared at them without speaking, conveying his meaning by the blank coldness of his gaze.

'The document the kidnappers want was written by Vicente Ortiz,' said Charlotte in a rush. 'We've come for your help.' Frank's eyebrows bunched into a frown at the mention of Ortiz's name, but still he did not speak.

'It's true,' said Derek. 'They've specified a document written in Catalan by a friend of Tristram Abberley. Who can it be but Ortiz?'

'Vicente's dead,' Frank responded at last. 'Let him rest in peace.'

'He may not be dead,' put in Charlotte, drawing from Frank a withering glare.

'If you're trying to link poor Vicente with your niece's abduction . . .'

'Nobody's trying to do that,' said Derek. 'But we have to do everything we can to find whatever it was he gave to Tristram before October the eleventh.'

'The date they say they'll kill Sam,' explained Charlotte, 'unless the document is delivered to them.'

'*Kill* her? For something Vicente *may* have written nearly fifty years ago?'

'Those are their terms.'

'They make no sense.'

'We know,' said Derek. 'But they're the terms they've set.'

Frank stared at him. 'What's *your* interest in this?'

'I'm just trying to help. Won't you do the same?'

'*Please*, Frank,' said Charlotte.

Frank looked at each of them in turn, then sighed. 'I can't. You come here talking to me about Vicente Ortiz, about a document he may or may not have given to Tristram and which Tristram may or may not have sent to Beatrix. It's meaningless and long ago and far away and—' He tapped his pipe out aggressively in a saucer. 'They're all dead, for God's sake, every last one. What can it matter now? Who can it matter to?'

297

'Didn't Vicente ever say anything to you?' asked Derek. 'Or Tristram? Or Beatrix? Didn't one of them imply or suggest something – however vague – that might explain this?'

Frank thought for a moment, then said: 'No. If they shared a secret, they kept it from me. Perhaps deliberately. Perhaps—'

'A Spaniard visited Beatrix in Rye during the summer of 1939,' interrupted Charlotte. 'Uncle Jack told me about him. He was looking for something. He must have been. Could it have been the document?'

'Describe him,' said Frank.

'Cold and forbidding, according to Uncle Jack. Tall and thin with a hooked nose. And a touch of the Nazi about him.'

'A Fascist by the sound of it,' murmured Frank. 'Not Vicente, for certain. Your Uncle Jack would have been all over him.'

'Do you recognize the description?' asked Derek.

'No,' Frank replied. 'But why should I? He could have been anybody. Or nobody. It's as if . . .' His words petered out. He leant back in his chair and thrust the unlit pipe into his mouth, holding the stem in that strange but characteristic grip between the first and second fingers of his left hand.

Charlotte glanced quizzically at Derek, who shrugged back at her. Then she said promptingly, 'Frank?'

He raised his right hand to silence her and continued to stare at the tabletop before him, head cocked to one side. Fully two minutes must have passed before he plucked the pipe from his mouth and said: 'I don't know what the document contains. Something important, obviously. Something dangerous. Vicente might have entrusted it to Tristram because he was being evacuated from Teruel and was expected to go back to England. And Tristram might have sent it to Beatrix when he realized he was dying. None of them told me about it. None of them breathed a word. Even Tristram. I suppose he thought it was safe with Beatrix. As presumably it was. Until Maurice hatched his benighted scheme. So, what did she do with it? Send it to me? No. Send it to Maurice's wife? I hardly think so.'

'She didn't send it to Natasha von Ryneveld either,' put in Charlotte. 'She's who Lulu misremembered as van Ryan. A mistress Maurice maintained in New York. I've spoken to her – and seen the contents of Beatrix's letter to her. It isn't what we need.'

'Then it must be Madame V in Paris, mustn't it?'

'Yes. But who is she, Frank?'

'I don't know. I've no way of knowing. Or of finding out.'

'Nor have we. It's why we came.'

'Then you've had a wasted journey, haven't you?' A crushed grimace of defeat crossed Charlotte's face at his words. Derek saw it and saw also Frank's reluctant flinch of sympathy. The old man rose, walked to the back door, pushed it open and inhaled a lungful of air. Then, without turning round, he said: 'I'm sorry I lied to the police. I suppose I shouldn't have. But I'd had a bellyful of your family and I just wanted to stay out of the whole rotten business. And to keep my promise to Beatrix. Not that she would want me to keep it now it's gone this far. She'd want me to help your niece, not a doubt of it. The trouble is I can't. None of us can. Your only hope is to find Madame V – and pray the letter Beatrix sent her contains what the kidnappers want.'

'But if it doesn't?' asked Charlotte in a flat and weary tone. 'Or if we can't find her?'

Frank did not answer, other than to shake his head and sigh. Nor did Derek. There was, in all truth, no answer to give except what they were not yet quite despondent enough to admit: that Samantha was beyond their help.

They returned to Tunbridge Wells via Cheltenham, where Lulu Harrington gave them tea and her fulsome apologies for being unable to remember the full name and address on Beatrix's fourth letter. Something neither short nor long, beginning with V. Somewhere in or near Paris, though how near could be at the mercy of French postal zoning. There was even the possibility that it was Mademoiselle V rather than Madame. As to the addressee being a woman, she was adamant. Or was she? The more they pressed her, the more confused she became. They left with their path ahead no clearer. Indeed, the path ahead could scarcely be said to exist. In every direction lay dead ends. Even the route they had followed to this point seemed now to have closed behind them.

TWENTY-TWO

CHARLOTTE PASSED A GLUM and largely sleepless Sunday night, unable to restrain her mind from rummaging again and again through the clues that always led, however often they were re-examined, to the most hopeless of conclusions. Monday dawned still and misty, with a promise of autumn sunshine. Gazing out at the grey sky turning slowly blue, or glancing aimlessly through the newspaper's parade of politics, fashion, commerce and sport, Charlotte felt a numb remoteness from the wider world. It would whirl on regardless to October the eleventh and beyond. And at some point in those looming weeks space would be found to report what had become of Samantha Abberley, only daughter of the recently deceased chairman and managing director of Ladram Avionics. MIRACULOUS RESCUE. UNEXPLAINED RELEASE. STILL MISSING. FOUND DEAD. Charlotte could almost suspect the headline had already been selected, the outcome already determined. It was as if only she was not yet to be told which it was to be.

When the doorbell rang shortly before ten o'clock, she assumed it was the postman and answered it ill-prepared for the face that greeted her. It belonged to Chief Inspector Golding. And he was not smiling.

'Could we have a word, Miss Ladram?'

'Certainly. Come in.'

They went into the lounge. An offer of coffee – even of a seat – was declined.

'What can I do for you, Chief Inspector?'

'I'll come straight to the point, Miss. Your sister-in-law, Mrs Abberley, has informed us of your recent contact with her daughter's kidnappers.'

Charlotte was aware of Golding's eyes watching her closely to gauge her reaction. She could not suppress a reddening of the face, though it was occasioned more by anger than discomfort. However anxious Ursula might be, there could be no excuse for this. If she had insisted on telling the police, Charlotte would not have objected. But to do so in this way was to make her appear the villain of the piece. As was perhaps the purpose.

'I take it you don't deny speaking to them?'

'No. I don't.'

'Or trying to persuade Mrs Abberley to keep it to yourselves?'

'We agreed . . . for the present . . . in view of the doubts you'd expressed . . .'

'The doubts *I'd* expressed?' Golding treated her to a scornful look. 'Have you any idea how irresponsible you've been, Miss Ladram? Mrs Abberley is under a great deal of stress. By taking advantage of her vulnerable condition—'

'I didn't take advantage of her. And I didn't persuade her to do anything against her will. Irresponsible or not, it was a joint decision.'

'That's not Mrs Abberley's version of events.'

'I'm sure it isn't.'

He frowned at her. 'Have you and she . . . fallen out?'

'You could say so, yes.'

'About what, might I ask?'

'You may already know.'

'Ah! You mean the private detective's report and the tape recording which Mrs Abberley said you passed on to Mr Fairfax?'

'Yes.'

'I see.' He deliberated for a moment, then said: 'Whoever persuaded who, the fact is you both behaved very foolishly.'

'Perhaps we did, but—'

'Not to mention criminally. You could be charged with obstructing the police in the execution of their duty.'

Charlotte made to reply, but suddenly felt exasperated and wearied by the hoops she had been obliged to jump through. With a tired little toss of the head, she turned away and sat down in an armchair, motioning for Golding to do the same. After some hesitation, he did so.

'Well,' he said, more moderately than before, 'there won't be any charges of course. But it's as well Mrs Abberley made a clean breast of it when she did, especially since the tape recording confirms – so she tells me – the existence of the letters which . . . which has been called into question in certain quarters.'

'Yes. It does.'

'I must ask for your assurance that there will be no repetition of this kind of conduct.'

'You have it.'

'And your co-operation in the monitoring of all future calls to this number.'

'You have that as well.'

'Finally, I shall require the immediate surrender of the report and the tape.'

'Mr Fairfax has them.'

'Yes. But I thought you might like to explain to him why he must give them up. Rather than let me do it.'

'Thank you. I would.'

'Very well. If you and Mr Fairfax come to my office at' – he glanced at his watch – 'four o'clock this afternoon, bringing those items with you, we will regard the subject of your withholding them until now as closed. Is that agreed?'

'Yes. It's agreed.'

'I can only express the hope that you've not endangered your niece's life by such behaviour.'

'So can I.'

'I shall of course require a full statement from you concerning your contact with the kidnappers.'

'I'll make one out this afternoon.'

'Good. Well . . .'

'Is there something else?'

'No. Nothing else' He rose. 'Until four o'clock then.'

'Yes, Chief Inspector. I'll be there.'

'I'll see myself out, Miss.'

Charlotte waited until she heard the front door close behind him. Then she hurried into the hall and picked up the telephone, intent upon speaking to Ursula and demanding an explanation. But even as she framed the words in her mind, confidence deserted her. What was the point of further recrimination when Ursula's motive was plain to see? The tape – and her disclosure of its existence – would gain her Golding's confidence. It would focus his attention where it should be focused: on finding Samantha. To that extent, what she had done was understandable. Letting Charlotte take the blame was merely a side-effect, almost an after-thought, though one she might well have relished. Why give her the satisfaction of knowing her ploy had succeeded? Why give her anything at all?

Charlotte pressed the receiver down, then dialled the number of Fithyan & Co.

TWENTY-THREE

AN EARLY LUNCH AND A failure to return to the office afterwards was not how Derek would have wished to start the week at Fithyan & Co. Once he had heard of Charlotte's predicament, however – explained to him in a quiet corner of the Beau Nash Tavern, Mount Ephraim – he realized there was nothing else for it. Reluctant as he was to part with evidence that went a long way to exonerating Colin, he knew surrendering it voluntarily was vastly preferable to having it seized. Accordingly, he drove Charlotte to his house straight from the Beau Nash. There they collected the report and the tape recording – and Derek paused long enough to telephone Carol with a flimsy excuse for his absence. Then they headed for Newbury.

Their reception at the police station was a bewildering mix of the gruff and the polite. Golding asked to speak to Charlotte alone and Derek was left on an uncomfortable chair in a busy corridor studying a LOCK IT OR LOSE IT poster for more than an hour before being summoned to join them.

Golding's office was grey and cheerless, with the disorientating feature of being substantially higher than it was wide. The only source of colour was a multi-hued venetian blind, in front of which Golding sat at his desk, with a female officer beside him. On the other side of the desk sat Charlotte. Beside her was an empty chair towards which Golding flapped his hand.

'Take a seat, Mr Fairfax.'

'Er . . . Thanks.' Derek looked at Charlotte as he sat down, but all she could manage was the faintest of smiles.

'Sorry to have kept you waiting so long, sir. There's been a great deal to discuss. As I'm sure you can imagine. But I think I have the whole picture now. Wouldn't you agree, Miss Ladram?'

'I've certainly told you everything I know, Chief Inspector.'

'Quite so. Better late than never.' Golding grinned sarcastically.

'I've listened to the tape recording and I've perused the report. As I assume you've also done, Mr Fairfax?'

'Yes.'

'I'm not investigating the murder of Miss Beatrix Abberley, but I shall certainly pass on my tentative conclusions to the Sussex Police. They may well feel the case against your brother is substantially weakened by what's come to light. This fellow . . .' He sifted through some notes. 'Spicer. The late Mr Abberley's former chauffeur.'

'He phoned Ursula the day Maurice's murder was reported in the press,' said Charlotte, glancing at Derek. 'I'd forgotten about it till now.'

'Which means we can find out where he called from,' said Golding. 'Mrs Abberley's phone was being monitored by then. All calls were automatically traced.'

'I see.'

'I have one of my men working on it. We should have the result soon.'

'Er . . . Good. I . . . I'm grateful.'

'I think you can rely on my colleagues in Sussex dealing with the case energetically. It promises to be rather more straightforward' – he grinned – 'than my own enquiries.'

'How will those be . . . taken forward?'

'I can't be specific at the moment, sir. No doubt we shall consult the Spanish police, since it seems clear matters Spanish lie at the root of this. We may also ask the French police for help in tracing Madame V. But it's a tall order. There's not much time left and a great deal we still don't know.'

'I've already apologized for withholding the information, Chief Inspector,' said Charlotte edgily. 'Several times.'

'So you have, Miss. Nevertheless—' He was interrupted by a knock at the door. A middle-aged man eased his way into the room. 'Yes, Barrett?'

'We've traced the call, sir. He rang just before midday on Tuesday the eighth. Identified himself as Spicer. Which is how Mrs Abberley addressed him. He was calling from a pay-phone in a pub at Burnham-on-Crouch in Essex. The Welcome Sailor.'

'The Welcome Sailor,' mused Golding. 'And the missing chauffeur. Thank you, Barrett.' The door closed again. 'Well, Mr Fairfax, as you can see, we've already made more progress than you managed on your own.'

'Yes. So it seems. I—'

'Mr Fairfax only did what I asked him to do,' put in Charlotte. 'He didn't persuade me any more than I persuaded Ursula.'

'Maybe so.' The sarcasm drained from Golding's face and was replaced by a steely earnestness. 'But I want to make it clear to both of you – as I shall to Mrs Abberley – that any further information you come across touching on this case should be communicated to us immediately. We shan't be so tolerant if this happens again. There must be no more going it alone.'

'I'm sure—' Derek began, only to be cut short by Charlotte.

'There won't be, Chief Inspector.'

'Good, because—' Golding broke off, then made a vague temporizing gesture with his hand and said: 'Well, perhaps the point is made.' He sighed. 'You can go now, Mr Fairfax. I just need Miss Ladram to sign her statement.'

'Oh, right. I . . .' Derek rose, looked uncertainly at Charlotte, then turned to confront Golding's slack-jawed stare. 'Well, thank you, Chief Inspector.'

'Don't mention it. Only doing my job.' His stare hardened. '*My* job. Not yours.'

Derek waited for Charlotte in the car park. When she emerged, looking tired and exasperated, he made various consoling remarks, most of which she seemed not to hear. She had lapsed into gloomy self-absorption, perhaps in reaction to Golding's interrogatory methods. Whatever the cause, it placed her beyond Derek's reach. He could only wait patiently for her to draw closer once more.

'Do you want to go home, Charlotte?'

'Not yet. Unless you're keen to get back.'

'No.'

'Then could we drive to Walbury Hill? It's only a few miles away.'

'Where your brother was . . . Where you found him?'

'Yes.'

'Are you sure you want to go *there*?'

'I'm sure.'

It was a cool and breezy evening of clear air and limitless horizons. There were only a few other cars in the lay-by at Walbury Hill and their occupants had scattered far and wide. Of the scene Charlotte and Ursula had confronted two weeks before there was neither sign nor trace. Charlotte stood on the spot where Maurice's car had stood that morning and gazed to the north, her coat buttoned to the collar, scarf wound around her neck. She looked cold and Derek wanted to put his arm round her, to give her some measure of warmth and comfort. But he only shifted his feet uneasily beside her and broke the silence with a banal remark.

'Golding seems a good man. I'm sure he'll do his best.'

'There's nothing he can do.' Charlotte did not phrase her response as a rebuke, but it had much the same effect.

'They are the experts.'

'Not in what's befallen Sam. They'll question Frank again and maybe Lulu. They'll consult the Spanish police. And time will slip by. And come October the eleventh, they won't know any more than we know now.'

'You mustn't give up hope.'

'Why not?' She turned to look at him. 'I've been thinking about Sam in the same way as Maurice and Beatrix recently. No longer here. Nor ever likely to return.'

'But Sam isn't dead.'

'Not yet. That's what makes it worse. I can't help it, Derek. If nothing can be done to save her, I almost wish she was already dead.' Her chin drooped. 'There, I've said it. I've said what I should never even have thought.'

'It's understandable.'

'No. It isn't. Nothing has been since . . .' She swung round, confronting the patch of chalk and turf where the Mercedes had been. 'Since Maurice heard them coming for him that night.'

'I'm sorry, Charlotte.' Tentatively, Derek touched her elbow. 'Really, I'm so very sorry.'

She pulled away. 'It's September the twenty-first today,' she declared. 'Three weeks from now, it will be all over. Maurice's folly will have run its course.' Her tone altered as she glanced at Derek. 'I'd like to walk to the top. It's only a little way up the track. Will you wait for me in the car?'

She did not want his company. She had no use for it. That was clear. He murmured his agreement and watched her walk across to the bridlepath and start up it towards the dome-shaped summit. Did it end here? he wondered. Was this a more than merely temporary parting of the ways? The wind was tugging at her hair, the setting sun turning it to false and fleeting gold. His brother was to be given a second chance. But for her brother there could be no reprieve. On this hilltop, she walked in his shadow. And in the shadow of events yet to be. Which Derek could neither alter nor prevent.

PART FOUR

ONE

EVERY MORNING WAS THE same. Samantha woke and for a split second imagined she was still at home, still free to stretch and rise and walk and wash, still at liberty to heed her instincts and indulge her whims. Then reality closed its cold hand around her and she remembered her captivity as one seemless procession of days that had begun just like this.

The air was chill. She could see her own breath as she exhaled. Each day the sun rose later and weaker and with it her strength too seemed to ebb. Along with hope in a future not bound by the rough blankets rubbing at her chin, the cobwebbed ceiling above her head, the tiny window, the table in the corner, the hard wooden chair, the threadbare rug, the wax-choked candlestick, the bucket, the crucifix, the chain trailing from the bed-post to her wrist beneath the covers. As she stirred, so its heavy links sounded their familiar reminder.

What was the date? Wednesday the thirtieth of September or Thursday the first of October? She had felt so confident at the outset in her ability to keep track of time, but now it was beginning to desert her. She could ask Felipe, but he would probably only shrug and pretend he did not know. As for Miguel, he would treat her to a long stare with those soulful eyes and mutter something she did not understand.

Not that it really mattered. Whatever the precise date, she knew she had been here for the best part of a month, confined in this tumbledown shepherd's dwelling among the mountains. Which mountains was another question, but they were not so very far from the coast, to judge by how long it had taken to drive here from whatever port they had arrived in. Northern Spain, then, which the steadily falling temperature tended to confirm. Spain for certain. That much Miguel had volunteered to her at an early stage.

'You are in España, señorita.'

'Where? Where in Spain?'

'You will stay here — with us — until we have what we want.'

'What is it you want?'

He had not replied, then or later. Was it money? If so, surely her father would have paid long since. Or her mother would have forced him to. Either way, ransom would have been no problem. Yet a problem there undoubtedly was. For the first few days, they had been calm and relaxed. Then something changed. A man she had never seen before or since came at night. He was thin and softly spoken and smoked an expensive cigar. He had asked how she was. He had smiled. He had been a model of courtesy. Yet he had argued with Miguel. In Spanish, of course. She had not understood a word. Except her own name. *Abberley.* Repeated over and over again.

'What did he say?'

'He said you will stay here.'

'How long?'

No answer. No answer to that or any other question. She stayed and they waited. Every day the same. Or almost. Occasionally a third man, José, would take Felipe's place for forty-eight hours. But Felipe would always return. She became more anxious than usual in his absence. José stared at her with greedy eyes and touched her and muttered suggestions of which no translation was necessary. Miguel often went away for hours on end, but never when José was there. Perhaps he too felt anxious about what might happen if he did.

After the coming of the man in the night, Miguel had grown glum and thoughtful. He too stared at her a lot, but in pity, it seemed, not lust. As for Felipe, perhaps his ignorance was not feigned. They played chess and draughts and she helped him improve his English. He was cheerful and good-natured. But even he was being worn down by the uneventful march of days.

'What do you mean to do with me?'

'Do not worry. It will be OK.'

'Has my father paid the ransom?'

'I know nothing about ransom. I know nothing about anything.'

'Why won't you let me go?'

'We play chess again, yes?'

'I don't want to play bloody chess!'

'But you will, yes? Just for me.'

She raised her hands behind her, grasped the brass rails of the bed-head, and squeezed them tightly, wondering how long it would be before Felipe came in with her breakfast. He and Miguel were up. She could hear them yawning and coughing as they moved around. How she hated the weary familiarity of those sounds. If only she had realized in time what was happening. Her only chance to escape had been at the beginning, when Miguel had loomed above her as she lay in the garden. She could have screamed or run. He had a gun, of course, but now she thought he would not have used it. Maybe not, at all events. She could have refused to write that note to her parents or walk obediently to the car and climb into the boot. She could have . . . But she had been so frightened, so shocked, so bewildered by the sudden invasion of her life. And she had wanted so badly to stay alive.

Fear had been at its pitch during the first few hours and days. It was the fear of death and all the ways in which it might arrive: shooting, strangulation, suffocation. At night, she still dreamt of the endless drugged hours she had spent jolting and rolling in the darkness of the car-boot, the hours of motion on land and sea of which she had only been dimly aware. All they had led to was the squalor and isolation of this room they kept her in, and the one beyond, and the yard outside they sometimes let her walk in, and the empty hillside, and the whitewashed wall of the barn against which she had stood to be photographed, clutching the *International Herald Tribune* for 4 September.

Even 4 September seemed an age ago now, part of a deluded past when she had believed her abduction was a simple crime committed for gain, when she had thought her release was imminent, her restoration to the pampered life she had led merely a matter of time and money. She knew better now. Or worse.

'*When are you going to let me go, Miguel?*'

'*When we are told to.*'

'*Have you spoken to my father?*'

'*You ask too many questions, señorita.*'

'*He'd pay you well to release me.*'

'*It is too late for that.*'

'*What do you mean?*'

'*I mean . . . We wait as long as we have to.*'

'*But how long?*'

Always the same circular conversation, leading, through every variation, back to where she had started and seemed likely to remain. She sat up in bed, rubbed the sleep from her eyes and blew irritably at a hanging strand of her hair. It was filthy, she knew, and quite possibly lousy. As were her clothes. As was her whole body. When she thought of the baths she had wallowed in at home, the scented soaps and thick towels, the perfumes and the lotions, she wanted to cry. At least here there was no mirror to show her what she looked like. Though the lack of one gave her little comfort as she glanced at her arms and noticed the fresh red flea-bites of the night. Why was she still here? Why had her father not yet bought or won her freedom?

'What are you waiting for?' she murmured, imagining his face set in a stubborn frown. 'Get me out of this. Please. For God's sake. I don't think I can stand much more. What are you waiting for, Dad? What is it?'

Abruptly, the door opened and Felipe advanced into the room, carrying a tray. He smiled at her and said, '*Buenos días, señorita,*' as blithely as if he were bringing breakfast to her room in a Costa del Sol hotel. He set the tray down on the table and she identified the predictable ingredients: coffee in a bowl and a hunk of bread smeared with honey.

'Is there any news, Felipe?'

'Bilbao won last night.'

'What?'

'*El fútbol.*' He grinned.

'About me!'

'Ah!' He scratched his stubbly chin. '*Lo siento.* There is no news about you.'

'How much longer is it going to be?'

'I do not know.'

'You must have some idea.' Ignoring her, he turned away. 'What's the date today, Felipe? The thirtieth of September or the first of October?' He looked at her and shrugged. 'Why won't you tell me? It's not much to ask.'

'*La fecha*? I do not know.'

'It's one or the other, isn't it? Which?' There was a hint of weakness in his expression. She decided to persist. 'Please, Felipe. Just the date.'

He moved to the bedside and leant over her. She caught a gust of cigarettes and stale garlic on his breath. 'You will say nothing to Miguel?' he whispered.

'Nothing. You have my word.'

He deliberated a moment longer, then said: '*Es el primero de octubre.*'

TWO

'I'M AFRAID CHIEF INSPECTOR Golding's out, Miss Ladram,' came D.C. Finch's voice down the telephone. 'Can I help?'

'I'm simply calling to see if there have been any developments.'

'None, I'm afraid. Hasn't Mrs Abberley been keeping you up to date?'

'I haven't liked to trouble her.'

'Ah. I see. Well, there's been no response so far to the appeal in the French press for Madame V to come forward. And nothing's come to light in Spain either. So . . .'

'We're none the wiser.'

'I wouldn't say that. Urgent enquiries are continuing. No effort's being spared.'

'I'm sure. But it's a month today since my niece was kidnapped, isn't it?'

'Er . . . Yes. Yes, it is.'

'And still nothing.'

'Would you like Chief Inspector Golding to call you when he returns?'

'No, thank you. I have to go out myself. I'll 'phone him. Later.'

They were doing their best, Charlotte knew. But their best was pitifully inadequate. As soon as she had put the telephone down, she headed for the door. A journey to Rye lay ahead of her. She had not visited Jackdaw Cottage since putting it on the market two months ago. But the estate agent had now found a buyer, one who was eager to move in as soon as possible. The emptying of the house could therefore no longer be postponed and Charlotte had decided to put matters in hand without further ado. Part of her was glad to have a practical task to address. It was a distraction her mind badly needed.

At Lewes Prison, Colin Fairfax was grinning broadly at his brother across a bare table in the visiting room, which was otherwise deserted.

'Word's got round,' he announced. 'I can do virtually whatever I like here now. They know I'm not staying long.'

'According to Dredge,' Derek replied, 'things certainly look promising.'

'Promising? I should say so. Spicer's been arrested, hasn't he? It's only a matter of time now before they find some forensic evidence linking him to the scene of the crime.'

'Is that what Dredge told you?'

'They know he did it, Derek. Where did he get the money to set himself up with a yacht in Burnham-on-bloody-Crouch if it wasn't a pay-off from Maurice Abberley for services rendered?'

'You don't have to convince me.'

'No. But I do have to thank you. Dredge tried to hog the credit, but it's clear to me where it really belongs. With you. You've done more to help me that I ever deserved. And to think I doubted your commitment! You've come up trumps, Derek. I'd be proud of you if I weren't so grateful.'

'There's no need to thank me.'

'But there is. It's why I was so glad you could come today.'

'I was on my way to an auditing job in Newhaven. It was no problem to stop off.'

'Tough job, is it?'

'Not particularly.'

'Then why are you looking so glum? To judge by your face, you'd have thought I'd just been sentenced to hang, not thrown a lifeline.'

'Because . . . Well, it was Charlotte Ladram who supplied the tape recording and the private detective's report. Without them, the police would never have started looking for Spicer.'

'And it's good to know one member of that family has a conscience. But so what?'

'*So what?*' Derek bridled. 'She's lost her brother as well as her aunt, Colin. And her niece has been kidnapped. None of this was her fault.'

'Nor mine.' Colin sat back in his chair and cocked his head. 'You haven't taken a shine to the girl, have you?'

'Of course not. I'd just like to be able to repay her generosity.'

'By riding out on a white charger and rescuing her niece?'

Derek stared hard at his brother. 'Imprisonment hasn't blunted your sarcasm, I see.'

Colin raised his hands in mock surrender. 'Sorry. I don't mean to pry. If you and she . . . Well, what *can* you do to help?'

'Nothing.'

'Hence the gloomy physog?'

'I suppose so. Besides . . .' Derek leant forward and lowered his voice. 'It hasn't been made public, but the kidnappers have said they'll kill the girl if they don't have what they want by the eleventh of October.'

Colin whistled. 'And today's the first.'

'Exactly. Time's running out. All too quickly.'

THREE

CHARLOTTE HAD JUST BEGUN to take stock of what needed to be removed from Jackdaw Cottage when Mrs Mentiply arrived, intent on discharging her housekeeping duties to the bitter end. Well-intentioned though the dear soul undoubtedly was, Charlotte had hoped to avoid her, since they had not met since Maurice's death and Mrs Mentiply could be relied upon to be as curious as she was sympathetic. In the end, it seemed easier to surrender to her eagerness for information, to let her make coffee for both of them, then answer her innumerable questions as best she could.

'Mr Mentiply and I were terribly shocked to hear about your brother, my dear. And your niece as well, of course. How is Mrs Abberley bearing up under such an awful strain?'

'Remarkably well in the circumstances.'

'Is there still no news of the girl?'

'None, I'm afraid.'

'Perhaps it's a blessing dear old Miss Abberley isn't alive to witness such sad times for her family.'

'Perhaps it is.'

'Whether she'd approve of the people who'll be living here I don't know. Have you met them?'

'No. But the estate agent said—'

'Stuck-up lot. None of Miss Abberley's refinement. I shouldn't care to work for them even if they asked me.'

'Well, that's for you to decide, of course. But they made a good offer. I couldn't—'

'Oh, I didn't mean you should have turned them down. Not on my account. You have more than enough to worry about without pandering to my likes and dislikes.'

'It *is* a worrying time.'

'Of course it is. And if there's anything I can do – or Mr Mentiply – anything at all, you've only to say the word.'

'It's kind of you, but—'

'Haven't the police any clues as to what's become of the poor girl?'

'Precious few.'

'Or why she was kidnapped?'

'They're trying to find a recipient of a letter Beatrix sent. A woman in France whose surname begins with V. They think she may know something.'

Mrs Mentiply clicked her tongue. 'Sounds like looking for a needle in a haystack.'

'It is, rather.'

'I mean, whereabouts in France?'

'Oh, in or near Paris. It doesn't narrow the field very much, does it? If Beatrix had ever mentioned knowing somebody in Paris, it might be different, but she never did. I don't suppose she ever said anything to you about Madame V?'

'No. I'm afraid she didn't. V, you say?'

'Beginning with V.'

'In Paris?'

'Yes.'

Mrs Mentiply shook her head dolefully. 'It means nothing to me.' Then she summoned a smile. 'Would you like another cup of coffee?'

'No, thank you.'

'I'm sorry I didn't bring any biscuits. If I'd known you were coming . . .'

'It really doesn't matter.'

'Only it's always nice to have a biscuit with coffee, isn't it, or a choc—' Mrs Mentiply broke off. Her face slowly compressed into a frown.

'What's wrong?'

'Or a chocolate,' she said slowly.

'Are you all right, Mrs Mentiply?'

'What?' She looked across at Charlotte, then down at her empty coffee-cup. 'Why, I've just had the strangest thought.'

'About what?'

'Miss Abberley used to give me these chocolates, you see, Christmas and Easter, regular as clockwork. "You have them," she'd say. "They're from a friend. I haven't the heart to tell her I don't like them." Well, as you know, she didn't have a sweet tooth, not her, but I— They were sent to her twice a year for as long as I can remember. A gift from a friend.'

'I don't quite—'

'They were French chocolates, Miss Ladram. From a shop in Paris. And the name of the shop began with a V. I'm sure it did.'

Charlotte felt the sudden acceleration of her thoughts almost as a physical sensation. She sat forward and clasped Mrs Mentiply by the wrist. 'What was the name?'

'Vac . . . Val . . . Vass . . . Something like that.'

'You must remember. For God's sake!'

'I don't think I can.'

Charlotte clamped her eyes shut for an instant to stave off frustration. 'Please try,' she said as she re-opened them. 'It's absolutely—' Then she stopped. Mrs Mentiply was smiling.

'There's no need for me to remember. They came in smart green tins with a label inside the lid showing the name and address of the shop.'

'Quite possibly. But—'

'They were too good to throw away when the chocolates had been eaten!' Mrs Mentiply's smile broadened.

'You mean . . .'

'I've got several at home. I use them to store all sorts of bibs and bobs in. And I'm sure the labels are still on them.'

Mr Mentiply had already departed for his lunchtime imbibition at the Greyhound Inn when they reached the bungalow. Without pausing even to take her coat off, Mrs Mentiply bustled into the sitting room, yanked down the flap of the bureau and pulled out a round tin about six inches in diameter. It was dark green, edged in gold. In her eagerness to remove the lid, she spilt most of the contents – pens, pencils, rubbers and paper-clips – on to the floor. But she paid them no heed as she held out the lid for Charlotte to see. On the inside, as promised, was a label, printed black on gold, scratched and ink-stained but clearly legible.

CONFISERIE VASSOIR
17 RUE DE TIVOLI
75008 PARIS

Visiting Colin had left Derek more uncertain than ever how to bridge the gap ten days of contrasting fortune had opened between him and Charlotte Ladram. He wanted to give her help and support, but in practical terms there was none he could offer. Nor could he avoid reminding Charlotte of the hopeful turn Colin's case had taken – a turn to which she had made a significant contribution – while her niece's plight seemed only to worsen by the day.

Yet he was also reluctant to let events stifle their friendship before it had properly begun. It was the sort of mistake he had made too often in the past and accounted for him standing on the brink of a lonely middle age. Driving back from Newhaven to Tunbridge Wells that afternoon, he had only to think of the empty house and the solitary evening awaiting him at Farriers to rebel against caution and risk a diversion to Ockham House.

But his small rebellion did not bring him even a modest reward. Charlotte was out. Where she might be he could not imagine and the gap between them seemed perceptibly to widen as he sat waiting in his car for a doleful hour of encroaching twilight. When he eventually gave up and drove away, he was weighed down by a leaden conviction that he would never return.

FOUR

CHARLOTTE'S RESPONSE TO HER discovery had been so instinctive, and the action it had prompted her to take so urgent, that it was not until late afternoon, aboard a train drawing ever closer to Paris, that she began to consider the difficulties and possible consequences of the task she had set herself. She had, after all, promised Chief Inspector Golding she would pass any information she obtained on to him immediately. In the event, however, she had not even thought of doing so. Instead, she had sworn Mrs

Mentiply to secrecy, driven back to Tunbridge Wells to collect her passport, then raced to Dover just in time to catch an early afternoon hovercraft to Boulogne.

She had justified her behaviour to herself on the basis that the police would have been much slower and more painstaking. Their heavy-handed approach might also have deterred Madame Vassoir – if there was such a person – from co-operating, whereas Charlotte was uniquely well placed as Beatrix's niece and Samantha's aunt to appeal to her on behalf of the whole family. But there was, as she had realized, another less worthy motive driving her on. She wanted to find the solution to the mystery on her own and to flourish it beneath the noses of those who had doubted her ability – or her right – to do so. She wanted to finish what Maurice had begun.

Wanting and achieving, however, were not the same. She had looked no further till now than finding Confiserie Vassoir, trusting to luck and French shopping hours that it would still be open when she arrived. The train reached Paris at half past six. A drizzly dusk was settling on the city and the imminence of nightfall had an instantly errosive effect on her confidence. But she succeeded in holding it at bay. From the Gare du Nord she took a taxi, stating her destination as *'Dix-sept, Rue du Tivoli'*. Fortunately, it was not far. She was set down in a quiet side-street near the Madeleine. Most of the shops seemed already to be closed and her heart sank as she identified the unlit frontage of number seventeen. All she could do was stare glumly at the sign hanging inside the door – CONFISERIE VASSOIR: *Ouvert* 9.30–18.30 *Mardi à Samedi* – then glance at her watch, which confirmed she was fifteen minutes too late.

Suddenly, there was the hint of a reprieve. It took the form of a blaze of light at the back of the shop. A stocky male figure entered from a room at the rear and began looking for something beneath the counter. Charlotte rapped on the window with her knuckles. He looked up, made a shooing gesture with his hand, then returned to his search. She rapped again and shouted *'Monsieur Vassoir!'*, praying he was indeed Monsieur Vassoir and could hear her. But, having found what he evidently wanted, he only frowned and waved her away once more. *'Monsieur Vassoir!'* she bellowed, striking the glass so hard she thought it might break. *'S'il vous plaît! Très important!'* He stared, then, with an enormous shrug of reluctance, he walked to the door, unbolted it and edged it open.

'*Nous sommes fermés, madame!*' He was a short balding man of late middle age, with a bristling black moustache and a gruff voice. He was clearly annoyed.

'*Monsieur Vassoir?*'

'*Oui, mais—*'

'I hope you speak English. I'm looking for Madame Vassoir. Your wife, perhaps? It's vital I find her. A matter of life and death.' His frown deepened. 'My name's Charlotte Ladram. I—'

'My wife does not know you,' he retorted.

'No. But I think she knows – knew – my aunt.'

'Please go away.' He made to close the door. Desperately, Charlotte thrust her shoulder into the gap.

'Beatrix Abberley!' she shouted. 'My aunt was Beatrix Abberley.'

He pulled back and squinted at her, pushing out his lower lip in a gesture combining pugnacity and deliberation.

'She sent a letter to a Frenchwoman in June. Arranged to have it sent, I should say, immediately after her death. The Frenchwoman's name began with V. If your wife was the recipient, then I must speak to her. There was an appeal in the papers here, I know, for Madame V to come forward. But they won't have explained why it's so urgent. My niece has been kidnapped and the letter may hold the key to her freedom. To her very life!'

'What makes you think my wife is this . . . Madame V?'

'She sent Beatrix chocolates every Christmas and Easter. She was a friend. Beatrix said so. The label on one of the tins is what brought me here.'

He hesitated a moment longer, then grunted and opened the door sufficiently for Charlotte to enter. As he closed it behind her, the lingering aroma of rich chocolate emerged from the gloom around them. The counters and display cabinets were empty, save for a few of the distinctive green and gold *Confiserie Vassoir* tins.

'What has the letter – if there is a letter – to do with your niece's . . . *enlèvement?*'

'It's the letter her kidnappers want.'

'They have said so?'

'Not exactly. But when I spoke to them—'

'You have spoken to them?'

'Yes.'

'What do you know about them?'

'Nothing – except that they're Spanish.'

322

'*Espagnol?*'

'Yes. Definitely.'

'*Espagnol,*' he repeated in a disbelieving murmur. 'Wait here, *madame*. I will telephone my wife.' He hurried into the back room. Charlotte heard him dial, then, a moment later, announce himself. '*Ma chérie? C'est moi. Oui. Au magasin. Écoute bien.*' His speech accelerated beyond Charlotte's comprehension, though she caught her own name – and Beatrix's – on several occasions. Vassoir said less – and listened more – as the call proceeded. It drew to a close with expressions such as '*Oui, oui*' and '*Immédiatement*'. Then he put the telephone down and rejoined her in the shop, frowning solemnly. 'My wife wants me to take you to her, *madame*. She is at our home in Suresnes. It is not far. Will you let me drive you there?'

'She is the Madame V Beatrix wrote to?'

'*Oui.*'

'Then, yes, please take me to her. Straightaway.'

'My car is parked at the back. Come this way.'

'One thing, *monsieur*. When I mentioned Spain, it seemed to make a big difference. Why?'

'Because my wife is Spanish.'

'I see.' Guesswork prompted her to add: 'What was her maiden name?'

'*Pardon?*'

'Her surname – before you married.'

'*Ah, je comprends.*' For the first time, he smiled. 'Ortiz. Isabel Ortiz.'

'And Vicente Ortiz was . . .'

'Her father.'

FIVE

THE VASSOIRS LIVED ON two floors of a gaunt town house west of the Seine. Charlotte was aware of high ceilings and dark passages, large rooms decorated with a restraint bordering on austerity, but only dimly so. Somehow the surroundings seemed blurred by her thirst for knowledge. The answer was close now and the minutes remaining before it was revealed to her were harder to bear than the days and weeks that had gone before.

Isabel Vassoir was a slim elegantly dressed woman in her late fifties with grey hair tied in a bun, immaculately poised between delicacy and frailty. She greeted Charlotte in a drawing room strewn with plants and pictures where an impassive bloodhound dozed before a blazing fire. Marriage to a Frenchman seemed to have erased her Spanish origins completely. There was no breath of the south in her mannered metallic voice. She spoke much better English than her husband and looked at Charlotte with a farther seeing eye. Henri Vassoir left them alone together and Charlotte felt increasingly uncomfortable as she explained how and why she had found her way to Paris. When she concluded by asking if Madame Vassoir still had the letter from Beatrix and if its contents could have provoked Samantha's abduction, her hostess poured them both a glass of sherry before replying.

'Yes, Charlotte, the letter – and what came with it – answers all your questions. As what you have told me answers mine. I read the appeal in the newspapers for Madame V to come forward, but they said nothing about abduction or ransom. Even so, you will wonder, why did I not respond? Well, when you have read what Beatrix sent to me, you will understand. I disclose it now only to help you save your niece. Otherwise, I would refuse. Otherwise, it would be safer to keep it hidden.'

'Why?'

'First, I must tell you how I came to know Beatrix. She was a good and generous person. She was kind to me and to Henri and to my mother. Too kind, it seems, even to tell us she did not like chocolate.'

'I don't recall her ever referring to you.'

'You would not. She kept her friendship with us secret. Why? Because, she said, her family would not approve. Well, it may have been true, but, since receiving her letter, I know there was another reason. But I must begin at the beginning. I was born in Barcelona in 1929. My father, Vicente Ortiz, was a lorry driver and mechanic. I hardly remember him and what I tell you about him was mostly told to me by my mother. She died eight years ago, here, in this house. According to her, he was too clever for his own good. A kindly uncle with no children of his own had paid for him to be educated, but education only made him discontented with his lot in life. He worked for a furniture manufacturer and was an active member of CNT, the anarchist trades union. When the military rising began in July 1936, he joined the CNT militia and went away to fight. From then on we saw little of him.

'You must understand I left Spain before my tenth birthday and have never been back since. It is almost as much a foreign country to me as it is to you. I have studied its history because it is the land of my birth and I feel I know it well, but only as a student, not as a patriot, not even as an exile. It was different for my mother. She regarded herself as a Catalan first and last. She remained loyal all her life to the things Franco swept away. She cheered the day he died. She would have danced on his grave if she could. The Civil War never ended for her. It went on burning inside her head. For me it is just a childhood memory of noise and confusion.

'We lived with my mother's parents in the Gracia district of the city. My mother worked as a seamstress at the Fabra and Coats factory. My grandmother took in laundry and looked after me and my grandfather. He walked with a stick, trailing one leg. It had been damaged in an accident at the locomotive works where he had been employed in his youth. We were poor, but happy, at least as far as I was concerned. After the rising, the workers took control in Barcelona. The revolution had come. Or so it seemed. Certainly my family believed it. Until the following spring anyway, when it began to disintegrate in squabbling and fighting between factions. Stalinists and Trotskyites and Anarchists all putting their feuds first and the fight against Fascism second. Food started to run short around the same time. Franco's noose began to tighten round Catalonia's neck. A cold winter and blanket bombing finished the job.

'That is how my mother said it was and the history books tell the same story. When the army rose, the working classes of Barcelona united to defend themselves – and to change society. But they succeeded in neither. Germany and Italy were funding and equipping the Nationalists. To combat them, the Republican government had to seek help from Russia. And Russia's price was the suppression of revolutionary socialism. The Anarchists were one of the groups they moved against. So, my father ended by fighting for a different cause from the one he had volunteered to defend.

'I knew nothing of any of this. My recollections of Barcelona are a jumble of hooting cars and waving flags, whining bombs and derelict buildings, food queues and rats and ragged clothes and my hands going blue with the cold of the last winter we spent there. My father came to see us just before Christmas. By then he had been transferred to the remnants of the British Battalion of the International Brigade. I cried all night when he went back to the army. And so did my mother. We never saw him again. News came in March that he had been captured and probably killed during the retreat from Teruel. It was the sort of news a lot of wives and daughters were receiving. The whole Republic was in retreat. And it was not only at the front that people were dying. The Italians began bombing Barcelona in February of 1938. I remember the sheer terror of those raids, of seeing dead bodies lying on the pavement, of witnessing what no nine-year-old girl should ever have to. It was the beginning of the end. But the end was a long time coming. And, meanwhile, a strange thing happened. My mother received a letter. From a woman in England she had never heard of.'

'From Beatrix?'

'Yes. From Beatrix. It arrived about two months after the news about my father, although it was only much later that I was told what was in it. Beatrix wrote to say her brother had served with my father and in his last letter to her before dying had asked her to find out whether his old comrade was still alive.'

'Which is exactly what Tristram *did* ask her to do – in the only one of his letters to Beatrix I've read, sent from Tarragona in mid-March 1938.' Charlotte frowned. 'But hold on. How did Beatrix know your address?'

'She said Tristram had told her.'

'No, no,' Charlotte objected. 'He didn't. It wasn't mentioned in his letter.'

'It was in the document accompanying the letter. As you will see.' Isabel Vassoir smiled. 'Let me finish my story. Then you will understand how all the pieces fit together. My mother wrote back to Beatrix, telling her my father was almost certainly dead. She expected to hear no more. But Beatrix wrote again, offering her sympathy – and her help, if we needed it. Well, we certainly needed it. Catalonia was cut off from the rest of the Republic by then and slowly being strangled to death. But what could an Englishwoman we had never met do for us? My mother did not reply. She told me later she could not see the point of such correspondence. And I suspect also she did not want to be reminded of my father. So, she let the matter drop.

'In the autumn, my grandfather died, worn out by the struggle for survival. Then, just after Christmas, the Nationalists launched their final offensive against Catalonia. By the middle of January,

1939, they were within reach of Barcelona. The bombing intensified and panic began to spread. Anybody linked with the Republican cause would be in peril of their life under the Fascists. Franco's ruthlessness was legendary. So, the only thought was how to escape. As the widow of a known Anarchist, my mother had to get away. France had opened its border to refugees and people began streaming north towards it. We joined them, my mother, my grandmother and I, pushing our few belongings in a hand-cart. The journey must have been a torment for them, though for me it was a merciful chaos of trudging along muddy roads, of running for shelter from German fighter planes, of waking in the cart caked with snow while my mother and grandmother strained at the shafts.

'When we reached France, we were put in a crowded camp with no shelter. It was, in fact, the clearing centre at Le Boulou, but nobody had any idea then where we were or where we were going. After a few days, we were taken to a camp for women and children north of Perpignan, where there was food and shelter, although not enough of either. My grandmother fell ill and there were times when my mother said we should have stayed in Barcelona. She could see no end to the squalor and harshness of life in the camp. Then, in her desperation, she remembered Beatrix's offer. She wrote a letter to her, asking her to help us in any way she could. She persuaded a Red Cross representative to send it on. She did not know if it would reach Beatrix, of course, nor whether she would respond even if it did.'

'But it did reach her?'

'Yes. And she responded, though too late to save my grandmother, who died just before Easter. A few weeks later, Beatrix arrived at the camp and took us away.'

'Just like that?'

'For my mother it was a prayer answered, for me like dreaming of paradise and waking to find I was there already. A tall and smartly dressed Englishwoman took my hand and put me in a chauffeur-driven car and, suddenly, after three months of confinement behind barbed-wire fences, we were driving away, through the barrier and down the lanes thick and bright with the leaves and flowers of spring. I cried and laughed and stared and could not believe it was happening. But it was.'

Into Charlotte's mind came what Uncle Jack had said concerning Beatrix's whereabouts in the spring of 1939. *'She'd been to the French Riviera – or it could have been the Swiss Alps – or it could have been both*

– for a good couple of months.' She knew now it had been neither. Isabel Vassoir was right. All the pieces were beginning to fit together.

'How Beatrix arranged our release I do not know. But I imagine the authorities were grateful to anybody who was prepared to take a couple of refugees off their hands and assume responsibility for them. And that is what she did. She rented an apartment for us in Perpignan and bought us food and clothes. She stayed with us for a month while we regained our strength, doing all the cooking and washing until my mother was fit enough to take over. She was our saviour. She was my fairy godmother. She paid for my mother to take French lessons and helped her find work as a seamstress with various drapers in the city. She put us back on our feet and made it possible for us to live again. We owed her everything. It was one of the reasons why I was anxious to learn English at school: so that I could tell her in her own language how grateful I would always be.'

Another beneficiary of Beatrix's generosity had emerged from her hidden past and sat now smiling faintly at Charlotte across a French drawing room. Beatrix had rescued Vicente Ortiz's only surviving relatives from the aftermath of a war. She had done what nobody could have expected her to do. And she had done it in secret. 'Did she tell you about Frank Griffith?' Charlotte asked after a moment's thought. 'Did she tell you how your father sacrificed himself to save Frank?'

'Yes. And she also told us she did not know where Frank was. She said she had lost touch with him. So, even if my mother wanted to contact him, there was no—'

'But that wasn't true!'

'Exactly. Beatrix helped us, but she also lied to us. Or perhaps I should say she did not trust us with everything she knew. But, then, who did she trust with *everything*?'

'Nobody,' Charlotte replied. 'But . . . Why? Why all the secrecy?'

'When you read what she sent me, Charlotte, you will understand. She gave no hint of its existence during my mother's life. She remained our friend and advisor. She sent money to pay for my education. When I married Henri, she was generous to him too, putting up some of the capital he needed to open a *confiserie* in Perpignan. And she helped again later when we moved to Paris. So, you see, we owed her far more than an occasional box of chocolates could repay. But they were all she would accept.'

'What did she send you?' Charlotte heard the note of impatience in her voice, but was helpless to restrain it.

'A document my father had given to her brother. In the accompanying letter, Beatrix said it would be sent to me by a friend in the event of her death. She also implored me not to contact her family. She said she had held the document back for so long because she was afraid it would re-open old wounds for my mother and because she felt sure it was better for us not to know what it contained.'

'And what did it contain?'

'See for yourself. The original is in Catalan, but Tristram translated it into English. I will fetch both versions now and let you read the translation. It is time, I think. High time.'

Madame Vassoir rose and walked quietly from the room, patting Charlotte on the shoulder as she passed. The door clicked shut behind her and Charlotte listened intently to the ticking of the clock and the rhythmic snoring of the bloodhound. It would not be long now. A fragment of the damp Paris night – a portion of heavy-curtained solitude – stood alone between her and the truth. When the door re-opened, Beatrix's last secret would be hers.

SIX

I AM VICENTE TIMOTEO Ortiz, a native of Catalonia. Once I would have said I was also a proponent of the ideals of anarcho-syndicalism. But I am no longer sure enough of anything to embrace a political philosophy when the threat of death is close at hand. I am writing this at a small farm near Alfambra, about twenty kilometres north of Teruel, the capital of Lower Aragon. I am billeted here with the other members of a platoon of the British Battalion of the Fifteenth International Brigade. It is early January, 1938, and we expect to be called up any day to participate in the battle for Teruel which is going on to the south of us. I have a presentiment that it will be the last battle of this war for me, the last of too many. Teruel is a cold sad place. To attempt its capture in the middle of winter is madness. But perhaps its capture is not the objective. Some say the government hopes, by attacking it, to force Franco into an armistice. If so, it hopes in vain. Franco will accept nothing but surrender. And then he will execute those who have surrendered.

I have wondered for more than a year whether to tell this story.

I have hesitated and delayed, always with good reason. Two weeks ago, when my wife lay in my arms for what may have been the last time, I nearly told her. But I held back. And now I am glad I did. She should be spared the danger of knowing what I know. So should any Spaniard. It is why I am writing this now. Because only a foreigner can decide rationally what to do with such information. And among the foreigners whose ranks I now fight in there is at least one I think I can trust to do that.

All my life I have known no quarter would be given by those who seek to suppress the working class of this country. I became an anarchist because I believed only violence would enable us to throw off our shackles. I was born in Barcelona in 1905 and grew to manhood under the governership of General Martinez Anido, who would pay a bounty to any *pistolero* who killed an anarchist but would arrest any anarchist who defended himself and then have him shot while trying to escape. I remember the fate of Salvador Segui and the midnight knock of the Somaten. I remember the machine-gunning of strikers in the Calle de Mercaders and the burning alive of the besieged anarchists in Casas Viejas. And I remember also Bueneventura Durruti and Francisco Ascaso. I salute their memory. I applaud their deeds. I mourn for no archbishop. I yearn for no king. Yet the black-and-red flag will not be my shroud. At the end I will call for no priest of this country's church. But neither will I cry *¡Viva la Anarquía!*', for I would choke on the words.

It is less than two years since I heard the factory hooters sound across Barcelona on a Sunday morning and knew the military rising had begun, but 19 July 1936 seems now like a date from pre-history. For I believed then. I was a man whose faith was still alive. I swapped my CNT card for a rifle and joined the assault in the Plaça de Catalunya. I was one of those who danced and sang in the streets when the military surrendered. And I was a member of the Durruti column when it marched out to capture Saragossa and spread the revolution throughout Aragon. But Saragossa was never to fall. Nor was the revolution to take root. Ahead lay only death and disillusionment.

I see now there was only one hope for us in this war. It was at the very beginning, when we should have attacked society, not Franco's army. We should have altered Spain out of his reach. We should have swept away the Church and every other prop of feudalism. We should have imposed the revolution as we went. Instead, we tried to fight a military campaign on Franco's terms. We dug in and organized. We flouted our own principles because we thought victory was worth any number of compromises. But we were wrong. We could only have won by refusing to compromise. We could only have achieved what we wanted by insisting upon it from the outset.

The acceptance of Russian aid was the key to our defeat. It seems perverse to say so, does it not? Hitler and Mussolini were equipping Franco with men, guns and planes. Was it not therefore logical to seek help from Stalin when nobody else would come to our aid? My answer is no. It only *seemed* logical. For Stalin is as big an enemy of the working class as Franco. I see that now, as do others. Too late, of course. Always too late.

I have another more personal reason for cursing the day Russia intervened in Spain. It became known in early October, 1936, that Stalin had agreed to send arms to the Republic. Enough tanks, armoured cars, artillery, fighter planes and bombers, together with the personnel to use them, for us to overwhelm Franco. Or so we hoped. I was as grateful as everybody else. I will not pretend I saw then what it would lead to. The arms were to arrive at Cartagena on the Murcian coast and the Russians were to set up bases in the vicinity. A great deal of unloading and transporting was bound to be involved. As an experienced driver and mechanic, I was asked to join the Republican reception force in Cartagena. I went gladly. I went not knowing what would happen to me there.

We were kept busy at Cartagena, I and my friend from Barcelona who had come with me, Pedro Molano. After the equipment had arrived, we and the other driving crews would ferry it out by lorry to the Russian bases at Archena and Alcantarilla. The only interruption to the routine was when we helped move a trainload of boxed cargo from the railyard to a large well-guarded cave just outside the city. We were not told what the cargo was. There was an air of secrecy about its arrival and its ultimate destination. One suggestion was that it contained the art treasures of the Prado, sent from Madrid for safe-keeping. I did not believe it. But I would not have believed the truth either.

Pedro and I were billeted with a butcher's family in Cartagena. We drank at a nearby bar most evenings and exchanged the rumours we had heard about how the war was going. One night we fell in with an Andulusian anarchist called Jaime Bilotra. He was a big bluff amiable fellow who saw things just as we did – or claimed to. What he was doing in Cartagena he did not say, until we had met him several times and counted him as a friend. Then he asked us to take a walk with him down by the docks, so he could talk without being overheard. We went. There seemed no harm in it.

Bilotra told us he was working undercover for the FAI, the militant federation of anarchist groups. An informant in the Finance Ministry in Madrid, Luis Cardozo, had warned the FAI of a plan to ship the entire national gold reserve to Russia to prevent the Fascists laying hands on it in the event of them capturing the city and to cover the cost of present and future arms supplies. This was the secret cargo we had handled. Cardozo was among the civil servants who had accompanied it to Cartagena in order to supervise its shipment to Russia, which was now imminent.

We were horrified. We had assumed Stalin had offered to help the Republic for ideological reasons, but it appeared he was no different from any other arms dealer. He was worse in some ways, since, as Bilotra pointed out, once the gold was in his hands, he would be able to dictate policy to the Republican government. And he was no friend of anarchism. That was certain. Already, in the militarization of the CNT militias, his brand of communism was beginning to make itself felt. Eventually, anarchism would be crushed. That too was certain.

What could we do? Nothing, it seemed to us. But Bilotra had a scheme. True, if the government insisted on such folly, we were helpless to prevent it. Yet we could divert a small proportion of the gold – which would still constitute a considerable treasury – and send it to Barcelona, for the FAI to spend on independently equipping the militias. Pedro and I would drive one of the lorries when the gold was moved from its present location to the docks for loading. Cardozo could simply omit our lorry-loads from the official count. We would then be free to deliver them to a large lock-up garage Bilotra had rented for the purpose. They could be moved later to a safer place before being transported to Barcelona. The question was: would we do it? Without us, Bilotra was powerless to prevent the surrender of Spain's most valuable asset: something approaching two billion pesetas in gold bullion. With us, some of it might be saved to take the anarchist struggle forward. He needed our reply within twenty-four hours. We could not seek the approval or opinion of anybody else without imperilling both Bilotra and Cardozo. He was trusting us to do what we knew was right. He was placing the future of anarchism in our hands.

We agreed. It sounds absurdly naïve as I write these words, but neither Pedro nor I doubted Bilotra's honesty. In those early months of the war, there was an innocence in the hearts of those who fought for the revolution that made one forget greed and corruption. Moreover, what he had said made sense. We could not turn our backs on such an opportunity to aid our cause. And secrecy clearly was imperative. So, without hesitation, we agreed to play our part.

The following night, Bilotra brought Cardozo to meet us. He was a nervous young man, a civil servant to his fingertips. But he professed to be as sincere an anarchist as us and he was prepared to take just as many risks. We visited the lock-up garage and discussed what we would do in more detail. Cardozo said the gold was to be moved in the course of three successive nights prior to shipment on 25 October. We would probably make three or four trips per night, but he suggested we should risk diverting no more than one lorry-load each night. Bilotra pressed for more, but Cardozo insisted this was as much as he could safely lose on paper. So, it was agreed.

The scheme worked perfectly. With Cartagena blacked out in case of bombing, there was nobody to see us divert to the lock-up with one lorry-load per night. It was much closer to the storage cave than the docks and we spent the time saved on the journey unloading the boxes with Bilotra's assistance. In the end, about 150 boxes were crammed into the garage.

The Russian steamers sailed for Odessa on Sunday 25 October. Pedro and I watched them go, two of very few people in Cartagena who knew what they contained. The despatch of the gold to Russia seemed to us then – and still seems to me now – like criminal lunacy. But the common citizenry of Spain is accustomed to such conduct on the part of its governments. It is one of the reasons why we have torn each other apart in a civil war. And it is one of the reasons why we will lose whatever the outcome.

The lorry crews were given forty-eight hours' leave at the conclusion of the operation, leaving Pedro and me free to assist Bilotra in the next stage of his plan. He had hired a heavy lorry from a nearby quarry, large enough to hold half the cache of boxes, and had located a suitable hiding-place in the mountains about fifty kilometres north-west of Cartagena. It was, in fact, a long abandoned copper mine, accessible from a rough but passable track. We transported half the gold there the night following the departure of the Russian steamers and half the next night. The loading and unloading was back-breaking work but, between us, we managed it. Bilotra navigated during the journeys.

In the dark, Pedro and I had only the vaguest idea of where we were. On the second night, Bilotra brought some dynamite along, which he used to set off a small explosion, caving in the entrance to the mine. It would ensure, he said, that the gold would be safe until we arranged its collection.

Halfway back to Cartagena, in the early hours of Tuesday 27 October, Bilotra asked us to stop the lorry and pull off the road. We were in the middle of nowhere. I assumed he wanted to relieve himself and complied without really thinking. Then he pulled a gun on us and told us to climb out. His demeanour had changed completely. It was obvious he had deceived us all along. And it was equally obvious, when he led us away from the lorry, that he meant to kill us. We demanded to know why, but he did not reply. Then, as if he wanted to goad us before the end, he said: 'The gold will go to Franco.'

Anger at the thought of that drove out our fear. We made a rush at him. He fired and Pedro fell. But, before he could fire again, I wrenched the gun from his grasp. Pedro was dead and I would have killed Bilotra instantly if it had not been for the realization that only he knew where the gold was. In his pocket, he had a map he had drawn, showing its exact location. I made him hand it over. Then he said something which amazed and appalled me. 'I lied about Franco. Cardozo thinks the gold is destined for the Fascists, but it isn't. They know nothing about it. Nobody does, except the Nationalist officer Cardozo is in contact with, Colonel Delgado. He sent me here to procure what I could for our *personal* use, after the war is over. But I'm not unreasonable. You could share in the wealth too, Vicente. We've hidden something like thirty million pesetas in gold bullion in that mine. Only you and I know where it is. I'm due to meet Cardozo at nine o'clock tomorrow night. Why don't we put a bullet through his head and hope one of your lot puts one through Delgado's before this madness is over? Then you and I can live like kings. We can win while everybody else loses. What do you say, Vicente?'

What did I say? Nothing. There *was* nothing to say, when my friend lay dead beside me and our foolish attempt to aid the anarchist cause amounted only to blood and betrayal and bribery. I shot Bilotra where he stood. I put a bullet through *his* head. And then I tried to think. If I went to the authorities, it would turn out badly for me. The FAI knew nothing about it and would probably disown me, while the government would want to prevent the Russians learning they had been tricked out of some of the gold.

I would be an embarrassment to everybody. And from there it is a short step to being denounced as a traitor and dealt with accordingly. No, it was vital my part in the affair should not become known. Indeed, it was vital the affair itself should not become known.

I took the map and the gun and I walked away, leaving Pedro and Bilotra dead beside the lorry. There was nothing I could do for Pedro without risking discovery. And there was nothing I wanted to do for Bilotra.

I reached Cartagena around dawn. When I reported for duty that morning at the end of forty-eight hours' leave, I told my superiors Pedro was missing. They were not greatly interested, expecting he would show up before the day was out. Otherwise, he would be posted as a deserter. How long it would be before the lorry was found and the bodies beside it identified – if they *were* identified – I did not know. But I had to see Cardozo before that happened. Bilotra had said he was to meet him at nine p.m. and I guessed they had agreed to use the same rendezvous as before. I was right. Cardozo was waiting there when I arrived.

When I told him what had happened, he refused to believe me. I could understand why. The turn of events was as disastrous for him as it was for me. I had to threaten to shoot him before he agreed to tell me the truth. He was a Carlist sympathizer of traditional views who hated everything the Republic stood for. He had been passing information to his contact in Burgos, Colonel Marcelino Delgado, since the outbreak of the Civil War. Delgado had instructed him to help Bilotra in any way he could. This he had done. Bilotra had suggested they pose as anarchists in order to persuade Pedro and me to come in with them. Cardozo admitted playing his part in duping us, but he was incredulous at the thought that he too had been duped. He simply could not bring himself to believe it.

I should have shot him there and then. The secret would have been safe and so would I. But I was no longer angry. I did not despise him as I had despised Bilotra. In a strange way, I felt sorry for him. He believed in his version of Spain as much as I believed in mine. He had acted according to his principles just as I had. And even now he could not accept that we had both been deceived, that our faith in the opposing ideals we stood for had been betrayed.

I hesitated. I lowered the gun. He saw then he had a chance and he took it. He ran and I let him go. Fool that I was, I let him live. I regretted it almost instantly. I still regret it now, though sometimes I am glad I did not add his murder to Bilotra's execution.

Next morning, I was questioned about Pedro's disappearance. When I asked why they were suddenly so interested, they said there had been a coincidental disappearance of a civil servant who was visiting the area with a delegation from the Ministry of Finance. It was Cardozo. He had decided to flee. But where to? Burgos was my guess, either to denounce Delgado, or, if he still thought I was lying, to report what had happened to him. Whichever was the case, as the possessor of Bilotra's map and the only living soul who knew where the gold was hidden, I was perilously placed. I could not inform the Republican authorities without being arrested – and probably shot – as a traitor. If I were captured by the Nationalists and my identity became known, the same fate would await me, albeit after the location of the gold had been tortured out of me. I was caught between two grindstones and knew instinctively there was no way to escape.

My predicament became more acute when, a few days later, I heard the government had been re-formed to include anarchist representatives, with Catalonia's own Garcia Oliver as Minister of Justice. It was a total contradiction of everything we anarchists thought we stood for, a fatal dilution of our revolutionary principles. And it blasted any slim chance I had of convincing the FAI I had acted in their best interests. My fate was sealed.

For the moment, however, I could still hope to avoid it. The Nationalists launched their assault on Madrid in early November and I was recalled to the Durruti column, which was standing by in Aragon to help defend the city. Enquiries into the disappearances of a civil servant and an anarchist lorry-driver's mate in Cartagena were soon overtaken by more momentous events. Whether Pedro's body was ever found and given a decent burial I do not know. I hope so. As for Bilotra, I hope the flies consumed what the rats left of him.

Madrid did not fall. I am proud of what we and my fellow anarchists did to save it, even at the cost of our commander's life. But I am not proud of the squabbling feuding chaos into which the anarchist movement descended during the following winter. I am glad Durruti did not live to see that. I only regret now I could not have died with him and been spared the confirmation of all my worst fears.

I have neither the time nor the heart to describe the insidious way in which Russia, working through its puppet, the PSUC, moved to suppress the revolution we thought the events of July 1936 had set in motion. The most dismal aspect of the affair was the failure of the

CNT to ally itself with the only independent communist group, the POUM. Instead, they were at loggerheads with them throughout the spring of 1937. Even when both groups took to the streets of Barcelona in early May, the CNT still held itself aloof. United and concerted action was the only way to preserve the revolution. But of that the CNT was incapable. I was stationed with what was left of the Durruti column at Barbastro. Many of us favoured marching into Barcelona and confronting the forces of reaction. But Garcia Oliver forbade it and Ricardo Sanz, our commanding officer, complied. We stayed where we were. The POUM was crushed. And later, in Stalin's good time, the CNT was neutralized.

The failure of anarchism as an instrument of revolution was the end for me. I went to Sanz and told him I could no longer fight under its banner. He offered me a transfer to the International Brigades, where reinforcements were badly needed. I accepted. And so, since June 1937, I have served not with my fellow Catalans but with foreigners who volunteered to defend Spanish socialism without knowing what a sham and a fraud it has become. I have made some good friends among these British lovers of liberty. I propose to entrust this account to one of them when I judge the moment is right. He is Tristram Abberley, the poet, and I hope he will be able to use his public reputation to ensure the truth about what happened in Cartagena in October 1936 becomes widely known.

I do not expect to find out whether he succeeds. I do not expect, indeed, to survive the battle for Teruel. I have been lucky too long. Now I sense my luck has run out. Perhaps I should say I know it has. I have heard about Colonel Marcelino Delgado on several occasions in this war. He is reputed to be a brutal and merciless opponent. He is among the commanders of the Nationalist forces engaged at Teruel. I have avoided him till now. But no longer. At Teruel, our paths are destined to cross.

Cardozo must have gone to him, not Franco. If Franco had learned of the gold shipment to Russia, he would have denounced it to the world. But no word of it has been heard. And Delgado is still serving in his army, not rotting in a traitor's grave. Therefore he must have secured Cardozo's silence, probably by killing him. And therefore he must know that only by finding me can he hope to keep his secret safe *and* lay hands on the gold that would make him one of the richest men in Spain.

Bilotra's map rests, as it has since I took it from him, in a waxed wallet in my pack. I will enclose it with this account when I give it to Tristram. It will be the final proof that what I have written is true in every particular.

My chances of escaping alive from the wreckage of the Republic are slim. In many ways, I do not want to. It would be better to die in combat, at Teruel or elsewhere, than face the retribution Franco will visit on those Spaniards who dared to resist him. Should I fall into Delgado's hands – or the hands of anybody else who knows about the gold and means to wrench the secret of its whereabouts from me – I will not give it up. I will hold my tongue to the end. It will be my victory to die knowing that Tristram will broadcast the truth to the world.

When he does so, I will almost certainly be dead. To anybody who reads this I would address only one plea. My wife Justina knows nothing of what I have written here. She and my darling daughter Isabel are innocent of any blame that attaches to me. They live with Justina's parents, Alberto and Rosa Polanco, at 78 Passatge de Salbatore in the Gracia district of Barcelona. Do not let them suffer on my account. Give them as much help as it is in your heart to give. Do so for their sake, not mine. I will be dead. When this war is over, only the living will matter. And the truth, of course. The truth always matters. Which is why I have written as I have.

SEVEN

CHARLOTTE LAID THE PAGES to one side and looked across at Isabel Vassoir, who nodded faintly, as if to confirm what she had not yet said. 'This is why Sam's been kidnapped, isn't it? For the gold only your father knew how to locate.'

'I greatly fear it is, Charlotte.'

'Which means this man . . . Delgado . . . must be responsible.'

'It would appear so, yes.'

'He wants the map.'

'Yes. As my father said, it is the final proof that what he wrote was true.'

'You have it?'

'If only it were so simple,' Madame Vasoir murmured, shaking her head.

'Surely you won't hold it back when it can secure my niece's freedom?'

'It is not mine to hold back.'

'What do you mean?'

She unfolded some sheets of paper which she had been clasping in her hand as Charlotte read. 'This is the letter from Beatrix which accompanied my father's statement,' she said. 'It will explain my difficulty better than I can myself.' Charlotte took the letter from her and recognized Beatrix's handwriting at once. 'It's undated, as you can see,' continued Madame Vassoir. 'But, according to the envelope, it was posted in Gloucester on the twenty-third of June.'

> Jackdaw Cottage,
> Watchbell Street,
> Rye,
> East Sussex,
> England

My dearest Isabel,

I have arranged for this letter to be sent to you in the event of my death, which I believe may well be imminent.

You have been good enough to respect my wish that our friendship should not become known to my family and I would ask you on your honour not to contact them even when I am dead. A situation has arisen which compels me to do something I should perhaps have done a long time ago, namely to surrender to you a document entrusted by your father to my brother in Spain in 1938. When you have read it, you may appreciate why I have withheld it from you all these years. If not, I beg your forgiveness. I have done what I thought was best.

My brother sent the document to me with the last letter he wrote prior to his death in Tarragona in March 1938. The Civil War was still in progress when I received it and I had no way of knowing whether your father was alive or dead. That is why I first wrote to your mother in Barcelona. Given the turbulent condition of Spain at the time, I deemed it prudent to say nothing to her of the document or what it contained. By offering to help her in any way I could, I hoped to honour whatever promises my brother may have made to your father, promises which his untimely death prevented him from carrying out himself.

339

By the time your mother's letter reached me from the refugee camp in France nearly a year later, I had made Frank Griffith's acquaintance and learned how your father had given himself up to save Frank during the retreat from Teruel. The bravery of his conduct seems still greater when one knows what he had to fear from Colonel Delgado. You are entitled to feel very proud of him.

I did not tell Frank about the document, then or later. Nor did I tell your mother. Why? Because, it seemed to me, they both needed to put their experiences in Spain behind them. If they had discovered what your father's fate almost certainly was, they would have wanted to avenge him, to track down Delgado, to expose the scandal of the stolen gold. They would not have succeeded, of course. Franco's iron rule would have seen to that. But they might well have wasted their lives in the attempt. And I was not prepared to be responsible for them doing so.

I have learned, in the course of a long life, that good done stealthily is more durable than charity performed conspicuously. I am regarded by most of those who think they know me – including my family – as a hard-bitten and somewhat reclusive individual. The reality is quite otherwise. I have a small circle of close friends – of whom you are one – whose lives I believe I can justifiably claim to have enriched over the years. One of the things I have helped all of them to do is to throw off the shackles of the past, to enjoy the present by contemplating only the future. In the process, I have collected their discarded histories and served, as it were, as their dispassionate caretaker. But even caretakers must step aside in the end. Now it is time for my collection to be dismantled and for some of its contents to be returned to their rightful owners.

Perhaps I should have told your mother the truth. Not in 1939, of course. I mean later, when she would have been able to view it in a calm and considered light. But equivocation is a vice to which I am no more immune than the next person. The longer I delayed, the harder, I knew, it would be to explain why I had delayed at all. And she seemed so happy, so proud of the career you and Henri were making for yourselves. There was Frank to think of as well. Even now, I am not sure how he will react to such revelations. Is Colonel Delgado dead? I do not know. But I greatly fear Frank might deem it his duty to find out.

Delay, moreover, is a pernicious habit. It tightens its hold as one grows older. No doubt I would have continued to succumb to it, but for certain unforeseen consequences of my own past which are now making themselves felt and which mean this document can no longer be safely left in my possession. The time has come to pass it into your hands.

I have satisfied my curiosity by checking the details of your father's account as best I can. They are entirely consistent with such records as survive. The usual estimate of the quantity of gold shipped to Russia in October 1936 is 1.6 billion pesetas, mostly in coin – Louis d'or, sovereigns, dollars and gold pesetas. Bilotra's exaggeration of the total is perhaps not surprising, but the correct figure remains a staggering one. The total number of boxes involved was approximately 8,000, although there were discrepancies between the Spanish and Russian counts. Stalin never gave any of it back, of course, so such discrepancies, if Franco ever studied them, must have seemed attributable to Russian duplicity. You and I know there may be another reason.

This is where I must utter a word of warning and explain a precaution I feel obliged to take. The stolen gold has never been missed. It is therefore akin to used banknotes in that it represents untraceable wealth. And wealth, in this case, on a colossal scale. So far as I am able to compute, 150 boxes represent between seven and eight tons of gold. At today's prices, this quantity of gold coin would be worth something like forty million pounds. Can we believe such a cache still lies hidden in the mountains north-west of Cartagena? It seems we must. But do we need to? I am not so sure.

Your father said Bilotra's map was the final proof of his words. He was right. It is the only key that can open a door I have held shut for nearly fifty years. I hesitate to let it go. It is right you should read your father's story in his own words. But I am reluctant to accompany it with what may be a danger as well as a curse. Is Delgado still alive? Or Cardozo? If either of them is, they might kill to lay their hands on this old and crinkled sheet of paper. It is a risk I cannot afford to take. It is a burden I will not let you bear. I cannot keep it, but I cannot give it up. Therefore I will destroy the map. Have your father's fine and splendid words to cherish for ever, Isabel. Leave me to seal his secret. I remain your ever loving friend,

Beatrix.

'She destroyed the map?' asked Charlotte incredulously, as she handed back the letter.

Isabel Vassoir's gaze met hers. 'So we must assume. Beatrix said she intended to, did she not? And she always meant what she said.'

'But . . . without it . . .'

'You cannot give the kidnappers everything they want. Exactly.'

'They'll never believe it. They'll think we're trying to trick them.'

'They may do, yes.' Madame Vassoir looked down at Beatrix's letter. 'I am sorry, Charlotte. When I first read this, and recovered from the shock, I was glad Beatrix had destroyed the map. It removed temptation from my path – the temptation to expose an old scandal, I mean, not to chase after buried treasure. It meant I did not have to decide what to do. It told me as much as I wanted to know – and no more. It was both fitting and final.' She sighed. 'But now . . .'

'The map was the key to Sam's freedom as well as your father's past,' murmured Charlotte. 'And Beatrix threw it away.'

EIGHT

'WHAT ARE YOU GOING to do, Charlotte?'

It was the following morning in Suresnes. Charlotte had stayed overnight with the Vassoirs and now, as she prepared to leave, Madame Vassoir put to her a question she had already put to herself many times – without finding an answer.

'It is your decision, of course. You must take my father's statement, both the original and the translation. Take Beatrix's letter as well. Use them with my blessing to free your niece. I only hope they will be sufficient. But, without the map, I am not sure they will be.'

'Neither am I,' Charlotte replied. 'You asked what I'm going to do and the truth is I don't know. If I had the map, I'd be tempted to contact the kidnappers without informing the police. It would be the best way to achieve Sam's safe release. But I don't have it and I can't get it.'

'Then you will go to the police?'

'In the hope that the Spanish authorities can trace Delgado – or Cardozo – before the expiry of the deadline?' Charlotte nodded. 'It seems the best thing to do.'

'But you have doubts. I can see them in your face.'

'Yes. I have doubts.' Charlotte rose and walked to the window. Outside, a grey morning of infinite stillness seemed to be waiting for her decision. Nothing moved, save a pigeon stirring faintly on its perch beneath the mansarded roof of the house opposite. She knew she should set off at once if she was to be back in England by mid-afternoon. But uncertainty dragged at her heels as it dragged at her thoughts. There had to be a way to disentangle Samantha – and everybody else – from the trailing tentacles of fifty years ago. But, if there was, she could not see it.

'I wish I could advise you,' said Madame Vassoir, joining her by the window. 'But I cannot. I do not know enough to judge what it is best to do.' She sighed. 'If only there was somebody who did.'

'Yes,' said Charlotte. 'If only.'

Six hours later, Charlotte was driving west out of Dover, a large buff envelope containing Vicente Ortiz's statement and Beatrix's letter resting on the passenger seat beside her. She was driving fast through the irksomely thick traffic of a Friday afternoon, as if some destination were urgently fixed in her mind, as if doubt had long since given place to haste. But it was not so. Newbury, to tell Chief Inspector Golding everything she knew; or Bourne End, to let Ursula decide what should be done; or Tunbridge Wells, to brood a little longer upon her dilemma: even she could not guess which, in the end, she would choose.

When Derek Fairfax arrived home late that afternoon, tired and depressed, he had no intention of lingering. Indeed, he would have driven straight to the George and Dragon but for a suspicion that he might drink so much when he arrived that it would be prudent to dispose of his car first. To his astonishment, given how few visitors he generally received, there was a vehicle parked in front of his garage at Farriers. To his even greater astonishment, it was Charlotte Ladram's Peugeot.

She was waiting for him, sitting in the car with the window wound down and chamber music playing on the radio. She looked even wearier than he felt, hair awry and eyes heavily shadowed. She did not smile as he approached, merely looked up and met his gaze with a strange expression of frankness and despondency.

'Charlotte! I never . . . What is it?'

'Can we talk, Derek? I need your advice.'

An hour later, they set off together for Wales. Charlotte's argument was that Frank Griffith was uniquely well qualified to decide what to do. He had fought in Spain and come to understand the country and its people. He had known Vicente Ortiz and heard him speak of Colonel Delgado. He had been Tristram's friend — and Beatrix's as well. In that sense, he had a right to decide.

Derek had not opposed the argument, even though he did not subscribe to it. He sensed Charlotte needed some final word with Frank before she could surrender what she had discovered to those whose responsibility it was to rescue her niece. By the same time tomorrow, he imagined they would have placed the whole problem in the hands of the police. He would be glad when they had, though he was glad also of this unexpected chance to salvage their friendship. That, so far as he was concerned, was the only benefit their journey to Wales was likely to bring, the only new beginning it was likely to represent.

NINE

THE FIRE WAS BURNING low at Hendre Gorfelen, but Frank Griffith seemed not to notice. Charlotte studied his lined and narrow face as he read, the hollowness of his eye sockets and the prominence of his cheek bones exaggerated by the flickering shadows of the fading flames. Beside her, exhausted by the long drive from Kent, Derek sat asleep in his chair, his chin sunk upon his chest. But Charlotte felt as if she would never sleep again. Her anticipation of Frank's response to his dead friend's tale kept her senses alert, her thoughts at a jangling pitch. To her it was a fragment of a past she could not hope to understand. But to this old man it was a whisper from yesterday. The gnarled fingers clutching the pages had once squeezed the trigger of a rifle trained on the enemy at Teruel. The eyes peering at the posthumous words had once gazed at their author as he walked to his death in the hills of Aragon. But only now had they touched the truth and glimpsed its meaning.

Charlotte looked up at the clock and was surprised to see midnight had come and gone, though she could not recall hearing it strike. It was Saturday the third of October and already, she knew, she should have acted decisively upon her discovery. But instead . . . She looked back at Frank and started with surprise, for he was gazing across at her, the pages folded in his hands. He had finished.

'Why did you bring this to me?' he asked, in a voice scarcely raised above a murmur.

'Because Vicente was your friend. He died for you. You had a right to—'

'A right?' His face creased as if in pain. He closed his eyes for several seconds, then said: 'Beatrix knew me too well. Perhaps she knew all of us too well. Her decision was the correct one. It would have been better for Vicente's story to remain untold. But for your brother . . .'

'It would have done. I realize that. Maurice was a fool. He had no idea what he was meddling in. But none of us did, did we? Except Beatrix.'

'Except Beatrix,' Frank echoed, sliding her letter to Isabel Vassoir from beneath the other sheets of paper and glancing down at it. 'I loved her, you know.'

'Yes. I think I do know.'

'But she didn't love me. Cared for me, of course, liked me, helped me. But her affections were too . . . too universal . . . for what I wanted. Besides, love implies trust. And she had too many secrets to keep. Too many by far.'

'Frank, about my niece—'

'You believe this is why she was kidnapped?' He tapped the pages with his forefinger.

'Don't you?'

He thought for a moment, frowning in concentration, then replied. 'Yes. It has to be.'

'Delgado?'

'Maybe. If he's still alive. Or somebody who inherited his knowledge. Or came by it. Clearly, they only found out recently that Beatrix had been keeping what they wanted all these years. Maurice must have attracted their attention in some way. Otherwise—'

'Does it matter how they found out? The point is they did.'

'It may matter. It may not.' He stared at her. 'What are you going to do, Charlotte?' It was the same question Isabel Vassoir had asked – in exactly the same words.

'I'm hoping you'll tell me.'

'Me?'

'You were there, in Spain. You knew Vicente. You heard him talk

345

about Delgado. You've a better idea than I have how such people think.'

'Have I?' He grimaced and reached down for his glass where it stood on the floor beside his chair. But it was empty. With a grunt, he levered himself upright and crossed to the desk, where the vodka bottle was waiting.

'Don't you think you've drunk enough?' said Charlotte, instantly regretting her presumptuousness.

'I know I haven't,' he growled, pouring himself a substantial measure. 'I can still remember, you see. The smile on Vicente's face. The fatalistic shrug of his shoulders as he left the barn and scrambled down the slope to surrender. And a question Tristram asked me in Tarragona as he lay dying. "Was the patrol that picked up Vicente one of Delgado's, Frank?" I didn't know, of course. And I couldn't see why it mattered.' He swallowed some vodka. 'Until now.' Then he turned to face her. 'If I *had* known – if Vicente had trusted me instead of Tristram – would I still have let him give himself up?'

'I . . . I can't say.'

'No. And neither can I.' He returned to his chair and lowered himself wearily into it. 'I'm no use to you, Charlotte. I wasn't any use to Vicente either. Don't ask me what to do.' Wounded pride and a troubled conscience were curdling inside him, sucking him down towards introspection and despair. Suddenly, Charlotte realized she had to shock him free of self-pity.

'I am asking you! I'm asking you because there's nobody else. Help me, Frank, for God's sake!'

Derek woke with a sudden jolt and looked round at her. 'What . . . I'm sorry, I must have . . .'

'You've been asleep,' said Frank. 'But not as long as I have.'

'You . . . You've read it all?'

'Yes.'

'What . . . What do you think?'

It was at Charlotte that Frank stared as he replied. 'I think you have three choices. And they may all be wrong. The most obvious is probably the wisest. Go to the police. Tell them everything. If Delgado's still alive – or if Cardozo is – the Spanish authorities should be able to find him. But whoever's organized this is no fool. He won't be waiting obediently with the girl trussed up in his drawing room. She'll be well hidden. And his tracks will be well covered. It's more than possible the police may fail to locate him before the eleventh. Or, *if* they succeed, they may simply frighten him into . . . desperate measures.'

'You mean he'll kill Sam?'

'It's a risk. It's bound to be.'

'But the police are experienced in this sort of operation,' put in Derek. 'They know what they're doing.'

Frank's eyes were still fixed on Charlotte. 'What's the second choice?' she asked.

'Place the advertisement in the *International Herald Tribune*. When the kidnappers make contact, explain your problem. Try to persuade them the map is out of their reach – and everybody else's. Appeal to their powers of reason. But remember: you'll only have one chance at most. When the advertisement appears, the police will see it as well as the kidnappers. And they may respond more quickly. The second choice may become the first choice against your will.'

'Then surely the sensible course of action is to make a clean breast of it straightaway,' said Derek. Out of the corner of her eye, Charlotte could see him looking at her, but she did not shift her gaze from Frank.

'What's the third choice?'

'Assume Delgado is responsible. Then find him yourself. Negotiate with him personally. Make him understand that killing the girl will trigger a scandal destroying his reputation. A good fascist cares about honour more than money. Pray Delgado isn't an exception.'

'But we already know he is,' said Derek. 'Otherwise he wouldn't have tried to keep the gold for himself. He'd have donated it to the cause.'

'True,' conceded Frank.

'And we can't be sure he's guilty. The real culprit might be Cardozo. Or somebody else altogether.'

'Also true,' said Frank.

'Besides, we have no idea where Delgado is and no means of locating him. We don't even know if he's still alive.'

'Not true,' said Frank, his stare at Charlotte intensifying. 'I think I can find out if he's alive and, if he is, where he lives.'

'You can?'

'Yes. The question is: do you want me to?'

TEN

AS THEY ENTERED THE outskirts of Swansea, the task of keeping pace with Frank's Land Rover became more complicated and Derek's reservations about their journey more numerous. It seemed clear to him that there was only one thing to do: go to the police, who had the necessary manpower, resources, contacts and experience, whereas Frank Griffith had only fifty-year-old memories and an excess of stubbornness. He had not even consented to explain why they were going to Swansea or why they had to travel in separate vehicles. Charlotte had freely admitted she had no idea. But she had decided to give Frank his head. And where she went Derek was bound to follow – even against his better judgement. Their friendship was something he valued more highly than logic and responsibility. It had survived several crises already and he was determined not to impose what might be one crisis too many. Charlotte trusted Frank. Therefore Derek was obliged – for the moment – to do the same.

Thankfully, they would not have to cling to the old man's coat-tails much longer. Charlotte had promised as much before leaving Hendre Gorfelen that morning. '*I just want to see what he has in mind, Derek. He seems confident he can learn something about Delgado. Isn't it worth finding out what?*'

'*Before going to the police?*'

'*Yes. Of course. Unless . . .*'

'*Unless what?*'

'*I don't know. Let's just give him a chance, shall we?*'

'*Starting in Swansea? What can we learn about a Spanish fascist in Frank Griffith's home town?*'

'*I told you, I don't know. But I'm going anyway. Are you coming with me?*'

'*Yes. Of course I am.*'

And now here they were, heading south through drab suburbs beneath a louring sky. To their right grey swathes of housing climbed the hills, while to their left factories and derelict plots traced the straggling line of the river Tawe. Somewhere in all that seemed so harsh and alien to Derek, Frank Griffith had led the greater part of his life. And to something here he was now returning.

They reached the seafront through the Saturday morning chaos of the city centre, then followed the line of the bay west towards the distant lighthouse on Mumbles Head. Their surroundings altered as they went, easing them into a gentler world of seaside guesthouses and ice-cream parlours, of putting greens and boating lakes. Then Frank turned up a steep and winding road where pine trees and rhododendrons screened the frontages of discreet Victorian villas. And in one of these they found their destination: Owlscroft House Retirement Home.

'We're going to meet a friend of mine,' Frank explained in the car park. 'Lew Wilkins and I started together as fifteen-year-olds at the Dyffryn Tinplate Works in Morriston. Nine years later, we caught the train to London one Saturday afternoon, made our way to the Communist Party recruiting centre in the Mile End Road and enlisted for Spain.'

'Did he know Vicente as well? asked Charlotte.

'No. Nor Tristram. He was wounded at Jarama early in 'thirty-seven and invalided home.'

'Then why—' Derek began. But Frank did not stay to listen. Already he was marching away towards the ivy-hung entrance, leaving Derek and Charlotte to smile at each other and fall in behind him.

Lew Wilkins' room was small but brightly decorated, with a view of the garden and a distant glimpse of the bay between the tree-tops. He was a slightly built wizened old man unable to rise from his armchair to greet them, whose voice seemed to waver in time to the trembling of his hands. But in his eyes there was the same fire that burned in Frank Griffith's, inextinguishable even by age and infirmity.

'What wind's blown you here, Frank?' he asked. 'And who are these good people?'

'Friends of mine, Lew.'

'Friends? Well, things must be looking up for you, then.'

'Not necessarily. Look, I can't stay long.'

Lew chuckled. 'No more than you ever could.'

'I wanted to ask you about Sylvester Kilmainham.'

'Kilmainham? I thought you'd sworn to have nothing to do with him.'

'I've changed my mind.'

'You've never changed your mind in all the years I've known you.

And that must be sixty or more. So, what's it all about?'

'I can't explain. But I need to contact him. Will you help me?'

'He'll want to ask lots of questions. He'll want to rake over ground you told me you'd turned your back on for ever.'

'I know. Even so . . .' They exchanged a long and eloquent stare.

'Please yourself. You always did.' He looked across at Derek. 'See that pot on the bureau, young fellow my lad? Take a look through it. You should find Kilmainham's visiting card somewhere among the betting slips.'

Derek crossed to the bureau, removed the lid from a fat earthenware pot and lifted out the contents one by one. There was the predicted surplus of betting slips, along with several doctor's appointment cards, sundry bills and receipts, some unidentified tablets running loose . . . and the smartly printed visiting card of Sylvester C. Kilmainham, Esq., complete with address and telephone number. 'Here we are,' Derek announced, holding it up.

Frank walked over and plucked the card from his hand. 'Good,' he said, casting his eye across the inscription. 'He lives in London. We can be there this afternoon. Is there a telephone downstairs I can use, Lew?'

'Impatient after playing hard to get all these years, aren't we?' Lew grinned. 'Yes, there's a phone you can use. Ask the redoubtable matron.'

'Who is Mr Kilmainham?' put in Charlotte.

'Don't you know?' asked Lew. 'Hasn't my old comrade told you?'

'No,' said Frank. 'He hasn't. Why don't you save me the trouble, Lew?'

'If you like. Sylvester Kilmainham is an avid researcher of the Spanish Civil War. I've had him here picking my brains more than once. He's compiling his *magnum opus*, you see. Has been for years. A biographical dictionary of the entire conflict. Everybody who fought in Spain, however ingloriously, on whichever side. He claims to have the most comprehensive collection of biographical information in existence, though, being a perfectionist, he can't regard it as complete until every last foot-soldier and camp-follower has been included. Even now, some – like Frank – continue to elude him. It's been as much as I can do on several occasions not to take pity on him and give him Frank's address, but—'

'His collection covers the Spaniards involved?' Charlotte interrupted.

'A good many, certainly.'

'What about officers in the Nationalist army?' asked Derek. 'Colonels, for instance?'

'Bound to be there. Every last one, I should think.'

'That's what I'm hoping,' said Frank. 'Every last one.'

ELEVEN

CHARLOTTE DID NOT KNOW whether to feel glad or sorry that Sylvester Kilmainham had been at home when Frank telephoned him from Owlscroft House. If he had chanced to be out, she could justifiably have gone to the police with what she knew, arguing any further delay would be dangerous. As it was, having come so far with Frank, she had no choice but to go one step further. Their appointment with Kilmainham was at four o'clock. Afterwards, she promised herself, she would follow the course Derek had been urging upon her. Whatever they learned, she would hesitate no longer.

Kilmainham occupied a basement flat in a quiet street somewhere on the indeterminate boundary between Hampstead and Cricklewood. He was a large not to say corpulent man in his mid-forties with a mop of curly hair the colour and texture of wire-wool and a squint which may or may not have been an illusion produced by his thick-lensed glasses. He was wearing a huge loosely knit sweater long and baggy enough to count as a smock, down which something – food or paint – had recently been spilt. The glee with which he greeted Frank was that of a train-spotter catching his first sight of a long sought-after locomotive. It eclipsed Charlotte and Derek completely and left them merely to spectate at the encounter.

'Mr Griffith! What a rare and unexpected pleasure. I'd quite given up hoping to meet you.'

'Lew Wilkins said you were anxious to speak to me.'

'An understatement. You are one of the few British members of the International Brigades to have slipped through my net. As such, you are more welcome than I can say. Come in, come in.'

Charlotte and Derek were spared no more than a nod as he ushered them into a large and ill-aired front room. Floor space was at a premium, thanks to ceiling-high shelving on every wall, a phalanx of whale-grey filing cabinets and a substantial table overflowing with shoe-boxes. Each was crammed with dog-eared index cards, many of which had flimsy notes attached, all set a-quiver by the draught of their entrance. The sides of the boxes sported titles scrawled in the bluntest of felt-tipped pens. They left Charlotte in no doubt that this was their host's legendary Spanish Civil War archive. REPUBLICANS E–G, RUSSIANS M–R, JOURNALISTS D–F, MISCELLANEOUS A–D. And, pulled forward in readiness, BRITONS F–H.

'I'm thinking of computerizing the whole thing,' Kilmainham announced. 'But I started before such technology was available and now . . . Well, I'll have to get around to it sometime before 2011, won't I?' He grinned.

'Why 2011?' asked Charlotte.

'The seventy-fifth anniversary of the outbreak. That's when I hope to publish. I'd aimed originally for the fiftieth, but it proved . . . over-optimistic. Would you care for some tea?'

'I'd like to settle our business first,' said Frank.

'An admirable attitude, my dear sir. Your card's waiting for you.' Kilmainham seized one standing proud of the rest in the BRITONS F–H box, sat down at the table on a stool and brandished a pen. 'Shall we check the little I already have first? Born Swansea, 1912. Is that correct?'

'Not so fast. I want some information from *you* before I donate any.'

Kilmainham frowned. 'Well . . . This is somewhat unusual. I—'

'Everything you have on a couple of Spaniards in exchange for everything you want from me.'

'I see.' The frown transmuted itself into a smile of resignation. 'Well . . . Why not? Who are they?'

'A Republican civil servant called Cardozo and a Nationalist colonel called Delgado.'

'Cardozo and Delgado? They ring no bells, but . . .' He gestured at the shoe-boxes. 'That scarcely signifies. Let's see what we have.' He tapped his teeth with the pen for a moment, then pulled one of the boxes towards him and fingered through the cards, muttering under his breath as he did so. 'Cab . . . Cal . . . Can . . . Cap . . . Car . . . Cardozo. Ah!' he exclaimed. 'This must be him. Luis Antonio

Cardozo, Junior Secretary at the Ministry of Finance, February to October 1936. Not much known about him, I fear.'

'What *is* known?' asked Frank.

'Well . . .' Kilmainham sucked at his teeth. 'Born Madrid, 1910. Son of a civil servant – bureaucracy in the blood, apparently. Educated at the Augustinian College at El Escorial. Took a law degree at the University of Salamanca. Entered the Civil Service, 1932. Then a series of appointments leading to the one you know about at the Ministry of Finance.' He paused, then added: 'Not a happy ending, I fear.'

'What do you mean?'

'Disappeared in Cartagena, 27 October 1936, while assisting the Permanent Secretary, Mendez Aspe, during supervision of the shipment to Russia of the national gold reserve. Thought to have defected to the Nationalists. Subsequently alleged to have been spying for them from the outbreak of the Civil War. If true, they didn't show much gratitude, I'm afraid. He's thought to have been one of six prisoners executed in Burgos, 7 November 1936, on the orders of Colonel M.A. Delgado. Ah! Delgado. Well, there's a coincidence.' He looked up at Frank. 'Or perhaps not, judging by your expression.' Then he grinned. 'The name's asterisked, which means I have an entry on him. Shall I look it up?'

'If you would.'

Kilmainham pulled another box to the fore, riffled through the cards and picked one out. 'Here we are. Marcelino Alfonso Delgado, colonel in the Nationalist Army. I've accumulated a fair amount on him.' He flicked at some sheets of paper clipped to the back of the card. 'Do you want all of it?'

'Yes please.'

'Very well.' He adjusted his glasses and cleared his throat. 'Born Seville, 1899. Son of a dentist – but no vocation for tooth-pulling, it seems. Educated at Toledo Infantry Academy. Went straight into the army from there. Posted to Morocco, 1919. Gained steady promotion to the rank of captain. Wounded during the campaign against the Riffs, October 1925. Right hand amputated. Nasty, eh?' He broke off and looked round, as if expecting a reaction. When there was none, he shrugged his shoulders and resumed. 'Returned to Spain and promoted to major. Posted to Corunna on the staff of the military governor of Galicia. A quiet berth, I suppose, in view of his disability. But it doesn't seem to have hampered his romantic aspirations. Married a Galician heiress, Cristina Vasconcelez, 1927, thereby acquiring a substantial estate, Pazo de Lerezuela, near Santiago de Compostela. One son, Anselmo, born 1930. When the military rising began in July 1936, Delgado sided with the rebels against the governor, Caridad Pita. A wise choice, since the rebels took Galicia with some ease and Caridad Pita was subsequently executed. Delgado was promoted to colonel and appointed to the staff of the Nationalist *junta* in Burgos, where he established an intelligence-gathering outfit. Hence his link with Cardozo, presumably. Said not to have been well thought of by Franco, however.' He clicked his tongue. 'That probably explains his transfer to a field command early in 1937 and lack of subsequent promotion. He didn't make general until long after the Civil War was over and then only just before retirement. Saw action at Jarama, Guadalajara, Teruel and the Ebro. Acquitted himself well, with a reputation for brutality, both against his own men and the enemy. But the Generalissimo still didn't take to him, so it was back to garrison duty in Galicia in 1939. End of story.'

'There's nothing more?'

'Only some notes about his family. Nothing pertaining to the Civil War.'

'Is he still alive?'

'If he weren't, I'd have heard about it. But I haven't, so, yes, he's still with us. Which is more than I can say for his offspring. The son, Anselmo, followed his father into the army and became a major. He was posted to the Basque Country, where he proved a thorn in the flesh of ETA, the Basque separatist group. They removed the thorn in their customary way – a car-bomb detonated while he was driving his wife and children to church one Sunday in November 1972. They were all killed, except his youngest daughter, Yolanda. Delgado's wife died the following year, so I suppose the old man had to raise his granddaughter on his own. All sounds rather pitiful, doesn't it?'

'Yes,' said Charlotte, moved, though she knew she should not be, by the picture Kilmainham had painted. 'It does.'

Frank glanced coldly at her, then said: 'Still alive, after all that brutality. And still living on the estate he inherited from his wife?'

'Presumably,' Kilmainham replied.

'I'll make a note of the address, if I may.'

'Allow me.' Kilmainham jotted the information on to an empty card and handed it to Frank. 'Now, about your entry . . .'

'Could I ask you to look up one other person first?'

'Is that necessary?' interrupted Charlotte, suddenly guessing who the person was. 'Surely we know enough already.' Derek frowned at her, but she ignored him. Frank's intensity was beginning to worry her. The names and dates at Kilmainham's disposal – the catalogued facts spilling from his index so freshly that the events they were based on seemed more real and recent than any number of memories – were feeding a long-starved desire. Not for justice, she greatly feared, but for revenge.

'I think it's necessary,' said Frank.

'But—'

'And if our host doesn't object, why should you?'

Kilmainham squinted at both of them in puzzlement. 'I . . . er . . . I have . . . no objection.'

'Good,' said Frank. 'What do you have on Vicente Ortiz, a Catalan anarchist?'

This time Kilmainham sorted through his shoe-boxes in silence, the pleasure he derived from displaying his wares crushed out of him. Charlotte hoped he would draw a blank but the sheer quantity of accumulated paperwork suggested the opposite. And so it proved. He pulled the card out and read its contents in a sulky monotone.

'Vicente Timoteo Ortiz, Catalan anarchist. Born Barcelona, 1905. Lorry driver and mechanic. Active member of CNT. Member of Durruti column, July 1936 to June 1937. Then transferred to the British Battalion, 15th International Brigade.' He glanced at Frank before continuing. 'Captured during the retreat from Teruel, March 1938. Reported to have died under interrogation at . . . at Montalban, on or about 16 March 1938.'

'Why did you hesitate?' asked Frank.

'No . . . No reason.'

'Can I see the card?'

'Well . . . I hardly . . .' But it was snatched from his grasp before he could frame a protest.

'As I thought. "Reported to have died under interrogation at the field HQ of Colonel M.A. Delgado."' Frank's voice dropped to a murmur. '"At Montalban, on or about . . . the sixteenth of March . . ."' His fingers released the card, which fluttered to rest on the table. '"1938."' Charlotte saw his jaw muscles clench and his eyes narrow. 'End of story.'

'Frank—'

'I can't talk to you now, Mr Kilmainham,' he blurted out. 'I have to go.'

'But . . . You promised . . .'

'Sorry. I've made other promises which take precedence. I live at Hendre Gorfelen, near Llandovery, in Dyfed. Seek me out some time and I'll tell you everything you want to know. If I'm still there to be sought.' He turned towards the door.

'This is outrageous,' cried Kilmainham, jumping up. 'I've been misled. Come back this minute, Mr Griffith. I absolutely insist.' But it was too late. Frank was already hurrying out of the flat.

'Apologize to Mr Kilmainham for me, Derek,' said Charlotte. 'I must go after him.' With that, she ran from the room, just in time to see the front door closing behind Frank. He was at the top of the basement steps and marching towards his Land Rover when she gained the open air. 'Frank! Frank! For God's sake, stop!'

He pulled up and rounded on her as she reached the pavement. 'What is it?'

'We have to talk. We have to decide what to do.'

'Isn't it obvious? I've found out where Delgado is, as I said I would. Now we go after him.'

'We can't. It's too risky. It's a job for the police.'

'I disagree.'

'Sam's my niece, not yours. It's for me to judge what's in her best interests.'

'This isn't about your niece any more.'

'No. It isn't, is it? Not for you. For you it's about vengeance. Which is exactly what Beatrix spent fifty years trying to save you from.'

The mention of Beatrix's name seemed to penetrate his defences. He hesitated for a moment. His expression wavered.

'You've done enough. Leave it to others now. It's all so long ago. And he's suffered as well since then.'

'Suffered?' Frank stared at her and she realized her mistake. By that one remark – that one false comparison – she had made up his mind. 'He hasn't begun to.'

'We must tell the police everything. We must let them handle it from now on. It's the only—'

'Do as you damn well please!' Violence bubbled beneath his voice, just as it simmered behind his eyes. 'I'll go anyway. It's time Delgado answered for his actions, then and now. I mean to make sure he does. And nothing you can say or do will stop me.'

TWELVE

IT TOOK DEREK FULLY ten minutes to pacify Sylvester Kilmainham. In the end, only the surrender of his address and telephone number made an unharassed withdrawal possible. When he reached the street, he was dismayed to find Charlotte waiting beside his car while Frank sat stony-faced in the Land Rover two parking spaces behind.

'What's going on?' he asked.

'Frank's agreed to stay at Ockham House tonight,' Charlotte replied. 'I suggest we start back for Tunbridge Wells right away. Frank will follow.'

'Aren't we going to the police?'

'I'll explain on the way.'

For what Derek promised himself would be the last time, he stifled his objections and climbed into the car. He headed towards the Finchley Road and made sure Frank was keeping up before risking another question. 'Is there some problem?'

'Yes.'

'What is it?'

'Frank's the problem. I don't know what to do about him.'

Derek glanced across at her. 'You're going to have to explain, Charlotte. I don't understand.'

'Yes. Of course. I'm sorry. Frank intends to see Delgado. To go out there and confront him. Ostensibly to demand Sam's release. But I'm not sure that's the real reason.'

'Why, then?'

'To avenge Vicente Ortiz. Didn't you see how he looked when he read the entry on his card?'

'Yes, I did, but surely he wouldn't . . . I mean, it would be madness.'

'Revenge is a form of madness. Beatrix feared Frank might be susceptible to it. And I'm very much afraid she was right.'

'Good God.' Derek looked in the rear-view mirror and saw the Land Rover trailing behind them, with Frank hunched expressionlessly over the wheel. 'Hasn't he considered your niece's safety?'

'He says a direct approach to Delgado is the best way of saving her. It may be true, though I know you disagree. But, even if it is . . .'

'Yes?'

'I'm worried about what will happen when they meet. Delgado has Vicente Ortiz's blood on his hands – and the blood of God knows how many other men Frank fought alongside fifty years ago. Will Frank negotiate calmly for Sam's release? I don't think so. He's never even met her. But he has met some of Delgado's victims. They were his friends. And he'll remember them when he looks their executioner in the face.'

'Then he mustn't be allowed to. He mustn't go at all.'

'How can we stop him?'

Derek drew up behind a queue of cars waiting to turn on to the Finchley Road and once more studied Frank Griffith's sphinx-like demeanour in the mirror. 'Go to the police. Warn them he may impede their investigations.'

'I can't. He intends to set off tomorrow. If I contact the police, he'll simply bring his departure forward. I'm not even sure they'd take such a warning seriously.'

'We'd have to persuade them to. We can't let Frank *and* the police go after Delgado. They'd be bound to get in each other's way. The result could be—'

'Fatal to Sam. Exactly.'

'What are you suggesting, then?'

'That I go with him.'

'You can't mean it.'

'I am. There has to be somebody with him, Derek, somebody to keep him on the rails. I actually think his approach might work. But only if all the bad blood can be stopped from spilling over.'

Derek looked at her 'I won't let you go, Charlotte.' He was surprised by the vehemence with which he had spoken, the certainty he could command on this point if on no other.

'Neither will Frank.' She stared ahead. 'He pointed out something I'd overlooked. Whatever happens, we may need to contact the kidnappers using the procedure they stipulated. If we do, I have to be in a position to take their call.'

'I'm glad he sees reason about something.' Derek edged forward to the junction and waited for a gap in the traffic.

'Unless you agree to take the call,' Charlotte said hesitantly. 'If it became necessary, I mean.' She looked round at him, uncertain, it seemed, whether to make her appeal overt.

'Me?'

'Who else can I ask?'

'But . . . They'd be expecting to talk to you. How would they react to a stranger?'

'I don't know. It's a risk, I agree, but it's one we'd have to take if I'm to accompany Frank.'

'But you're not going to accompany him.' A two-car space appeared in the southbound stream and he pulled into it, glancing up into the mirror to confirm the Land Rover was following. 'Are you?'

'I have to. He's determined to go and I can't stop him. But I can't let him go alone. So, what choice do I have but to go with him?'

'It's out of the question. I couldn't allow you to.'

Charlotte raised one hand to her forehead. 'I'm grateful for all the help you've given me, Derek, really I am. And I appreciate your concern for my welfare. But this is something I have to do. I'm not asking for your permission.'

Derek could not have specified which of several factors prompted him to react as he did. A momentary rebellion against a lifetime of caution? A refusal to be pushed back into the margins of Charlotte's thoughts? A loss of patience with the inexorability of events? Or a surrender to their logic? Whatever the cause, he snapped down the indicator, swerved to the side of the road, pulled up with a jolt and said: 'Damn it all! If the old fool insists on going, *I'll* go with him.'

Charlotte stared at him in amazement. 'No, no. I didn't mean . . . You *can't*.'

'Why not? You have to stay and *he*' – Derek gestured towards the rear – 'has to go. So, like you said, what choice do I have?'

'But . . . Sam's not *your* niece.'

'No. And Vicente Ortiz wasn't my friend. Perhaps that's just as well.'

'But I don't want you to. It's not—'

'My mind's made up!' To Derek's surprise, his decisiveness was acting like an intoxicant, filling his brain with confidence. 'Let's settle it, shall we?' Flinging open the door of the car, he jumped out and marched back towards the Land Rover, ignoring the blaring horns and angry glares of obstructed motorists. Frank frowned at him and opened the window.

'What are you playing at, boy?'

'Your game, Frank. But not according to your rules. Charlotte tells me you're determined to track down Delgado.'

'What's that to do with you?'

'A great deal You see, I'm coming with you.'

'No you're not.' Frank shook his head stubbornly.

But Derek too could be stubborn. 'Set off without me and I'll make sure the police are on your trail before you reach Spain.'

'You wouldn't.'

'Take it from me, I would. We're going to be travelling companions, Frank. And, if it's any consolation, I don't like the idea any more than you do.'

THIRTEEN

EARLY THE FOLLOWING MORNING, with dawn still scarcely discernible beyond the window, Charlotte and Derek said their farewells in the kitchen of Ockham House after a breakfast neither of them had had much stomach for. Both looked as they felt – tired, edgy, uncertain whether what they had agreed to do was for the best, unwilling to express their doubts in case they were too abundantly shared. At any minute, Frank would come in and announce the Land Rover was as ready as it would ever be to commence its thousand-mile journey to Galicia. Very soon, each would have to take their leave of the other. Yet neither could bring themselves to admit the enormity of the moment. Afraid to say too much, they were in danger of saying too little.

'You should have flown,' Charlotte remarked with a nervous smile. 'It's far quicker. And you could have left later.'

'I agree. But Frank refused point blank. He says planes frighten him.'

'I find that hard to believe.'

'So do I, but . . . Well, it seems we have to humour him.'

'I know. I'm sorry.' She felt responsible for the position Derek found himself in, but she could see no way of extricating him from it. She would gladly have gone herself, but circumstances had conspired to prevent her. It was not her fault Derek was to go in her place. Yet she could not help wondering if he thought it was. 'It's still not too late . . . I mean, I'd quite understand if you . . .'

'Pulled out? No, I shan't be doing that.' His gaze conveyed more than his tone. It hinted at the real reason why he was determined to do something he clearly believed was unwise and ill-judged. 'Don't worry, I'll make sure we tread carefully every step of the way.'

'And you'll keep in regular contact?'

'I'll phone at seven o'clock each evening without fail. All you have to do is be waiting at my house when I call.'

'I will be.' It was an essential precaution, since Chief Inspector Golding had virtually admitted they would tap her telephone. 'If you seem to be getting nowhere . . .'

'I won't hesitate to tell you if I think we should inform the police. After all . . .' His words trailed into silence and fused with a self-mocking smile.

'After all, *you* would inform them now?'

'Probably. But I could be wrong. So could Frank. Delgado might not be the guilty party. Despite what Kilmainham said, he might be dead. We could easily be wasting our time.'

'You don't believe that any more than I do.'

'No.' He looked away. 'I suppose I don't.'

'Tell me your plan again.'

'Contact Delgado. Put it to him that he's responsible for Sam's abduction. Offer him the document. Explain why he can't have everything he wants. Threaten him, if necessary, with exposure. Negotiate terms for an exchange: the document for Sam. And maintain a calm and businesslike front. Hope we're right. And pray we're successful.' He grinned ruefully. 'A piece of cake, wouldn't you say?'

'No. I wouldn't.'

'No.' His grin froze. 'Neither would I.'

She stepped towards him. 'Derek, I . . .' Even as she began to speak, she sensed his eagerness to respond, his absurdly repressed desire to please her. Affection for him – for all his characteristics that were so like her own – swept over her. But, before she could yield to them, Frank Griffith entered the room.

'I'm ready.' His announcement was bleak, his glance at them unsympathetic – or, more likely, unaware.

'Let's go, then,' said Derek.

'Before you do—' Charlotte began.

'No more words,' said Frank. 'There have been too many already.' His face was blank and hard, the lines as stark upon it as the crevices in a cliff. 'I'll wait for you outside.' With that he turned and walked out, leaving Charlotte and Derek smiling at each other in bemusement.

'I'd better be off,' said Derek. 'If we're to be at Dover in good time for the ferry—'

It was impossible, in the end, to let him go without some acknowledgement of what she felt. Rushing forward, she kissed him and was glad when he kissed her back and encircled her with his arms. 'Be careful,' she murmured. 'Please be careful.'

'That's what I told you once. Do you remember what you replied?'

'"Being careful won't help Sam"?'

'Exactly. Nevertheless, I will be. Very.'

'There's something else, though. Another reason why you should be. I—'

'Don't say any more.' He pressed his fingers gently against her lips. 'Frank was right. There have been enough words. Many more and I shan't be able to go through with this. But I must. We both know I must. So . . .' He stepped back and released her. 'Goodbye, Charlotte. Don't wish me luck. I'm very much hoping I won't need any.'

Ten minutes later, Charlotte was alone, oppressed as much by doubts about the wisdom of what they had decided to do as by the knowledge that now there was nobody she could confide in. If their plan was to succeed, she would have to keep her own counsel as the days ebbed away towards 11 October and whatever it might bring. She would have to pretend she was as helpless as everybody else to save Samantha, while contending silently with the possibility that she was wasting their only chance of doing so. And there was another secret she had to protect now, one she would have shared with Derek if he had not stopped her, one that preyed guiltily on her mind as the solitary morning slowly passed and drove her ultimately to pick up the telephone and dial a well-remembered number.

'Bourne End 88285.'

'Hello, Ursula.'

'Charlie? Well, this *is* a surprise.' A veil of sarcasm fell across Ursula's voice. 'What do you want?'

'I thought I should . . . Well, I just wanted to know how you were.'

'How do you think?'

'Look, I—'

'Can you tell me this won't be the last week of Sam's life, Charlie?'

'No . . . Of course I can't. I only wish—'

'So do I. But wishes aren't enough, are they? What else do you have to offer?'

'Well . . . Nothing, I suppose.'

'Then leave me alone. It's all I ask.'

'But Ursula, isn't there—' The burr of a dead line interrupted and left her more certain and ashamed than ever that if it came to a choice, as conceivably it might, Derek's safety mattered more to her now than Samantha's. But, by letting him go with Frank, she had ensured that the choice, if it did arise, would not be hers to make.

FOURTEEN

TO DRIVE TO GALICIA in two days would have been an exhausting experience under any circumstances. To do so in a battered Land Rover which transmitted every unevenness in the road as a bone-jangling jolt was, Derek discovered, to turn exhaustion into a form of torture. The effect was heightened by Frank Griffith's uncommunicative nature. Try as Derek might to relieve the boredom of endless rattling kilometres along featureless French autoroutes by starting a conversation, Frank was not to be drawn. He would say no more than he already had about what they would do when they arrived. Aside from navigational necessity, he scarcely seemed willing to speak. His jaw was clenched as firmly as his hands were fixed upon the wheel and his eyes upon the road ahead. Their destination was all that mattered, its attainment all that concerned him. The rest was silence – and a hunched intensity Derek found increasingly disturbing.

Studying his companion in lengthy interludes of idle discomfort between such unconsoling road signs as TOURS 107 – POITIERS 211, Derek began to regret the promise he had made. He knew why he had volunteered to come and he also knew how pitiful the reason was. To impress Charlotte. To convince her of his loyalty. To demonstrate his love without declaring it. But what had any of that to do with a girl he had met only once? Or with an old man he could not trust because he could not fathom? Nothing. Nothing for sure and certain. Yet still he found himself in search of one along with the other. At first the impetuosity of what he had done had excited him. Now, left with too much time for thought and doubt, his self-confidence had all but vanished. From the flat grey horizons on every side, reality was encroaching.

They spent Sunday night at a motel near Bordeaux. From there Derek made his first scheduled telephone call to Charlotte. It was reassuring to speak to her again, to remind himself there really was a sane and vital purpose to what he had embarked upon. But neither could find much to say. Both were waiting upon events. And it was for Derek to set those events in motion.

They set off again early the following morning and crossed the Spanish border well before midday. It was raining now and continued to do so as they drove west along the Cantabrian coast, the sky descending to meet them in black and churning cloudfuls. The sea, when they glimpsed it, was grey and wind-whipped, the countryside a misty switchback of dank green hills. This was not the Spain Derek had sub-consciously expected, not the arid sun-charred land of his Costa Blanca memories. The contrast depressed him still further. He felt cold and tired and faintly ill, hopelessly unfit for whatever lay ahead. Yet one glance at Frank told him it could not be avoided. There was a gleam in the old man's eyes, a flush of colour in his cheeks. He showed no sign of fatigue or irresolution. And Derek knew he would not – until he had done what he meant to do.

Where Galicia began in their westward progress Derek could not have defined. But, as the rain intensified and they turned inland, the landscape and the settlements huddled within its creases acquired for him a sullen and ever less welcoming character. The patchwork fields and mud-choked farmyards, the ancient black-clad women labouring behind lethargic oxen, the stark concrete skeletons of buildings begun but never finished: all these offended his English sense of order and efficiency; and reminded him how far he had strayed from the world he understood. He did not want to be here and would secretly have given a great deal not to be. But here he nonetheless was, tasting the tomb-damp air and peering vainly through the curtain of rain.

They reached Santiago de Compostela in the gloom of late afternoon and approached the centre through narrow crowded streets. The stone buildings rearing on every side looked centuries old to Derek, but the students bustling between them seemed oblivious to the dripping gargoyles and lichen-rimmed archways. To them it was just a picturesque old university city, whereas to him it was a place of menace and uncertainty.

Weary and dispirited as he was, he was glad he had telephoned ahead from Bordeaux to book rooms at the best hotel, physical comfort offering the only kind of security he could hope to find. Frank had viewed this as a needless extravagance, but, since Derek was paying, he had grudgingly consented. The hotel in question, the Reyes Catolicos, was housed in an old pilgrim inn forming one side of the plaza at the heart of the city. Glancing along its gorgeously carved façade, then back to where the cathedral's still more intricately worked and vastly higher west front loomed through the mist, Derek felt awed and intimidated by such *largesse* of antiquity. He was not here to worship at the shrine of St James, nor even to admire the baroque architecture, but, without such a motive, his true purpose seemed foolish and inadequate, a fleeting delusion flying in the face of piety and wisdom.

If such thoughts crossed Frank's mind, he did not show it. No sooner had they stowed the Land Rover and booked in than he was quizzing the concierge in rusty Spanish about the exact location of Pazo de Lerezuela. A map was produced and directions given. The village of Lerezuela lay twenty kilometres south of the city and the pazo *'muy cerca'* – very close by. All too close, Derek could not help reflecting as they trailed behind the porter through moss-damp courtyards and echoing corridors to their adjacent rooms. He needed more time to adjust to his environment, more time to plan and prepare. But even if delay had been possible, Frank would have opposed it.

'Shall we meet for dinner?' Derek lamely enquired as they parted.

'No. I'll have them send me something. I don't want much – except a good night's sleep. We'll leave at nine in the morning.'

'So early?'

'Why wait?'

'No . . . no reason.'

'Then we'll leave at nine.'

With which Frank closed his door, leaving Derek to unpack the little he had brought and wash away some of the grime of the journey before calling Charlotte.

Once again neither of them had much to report. Charlotte had telephoned Fithyan & Co as planned, claiming to be Derek's cousin in Leicester, with whom he had been spending the weekend when struck down by influenza, a fiction which seemed certain to win him a few days' grace. For his part, he could only say they had arrived and would tomorrow seek the meeting with Delgado on which their hopes were pinned. Charlotte wished him luck and urged him as ever to be careful. He rang off in a manner he feared she might think abrupt, but it could not be helped. To say any more would have been to risk revealing just how deeply his misgivings ran.

With the Spanish hour for dining still some way off, he went to the bar and downed several bottles of the local beer without achieving the faintest degree of intoxication. Trepidation and sobriety went hand in hand, he concluded, wandering out into the plaza and surveying the floodlit majesty of the cathedral from the shelter of a colonnade.

'Don't worry,' he told himself. 'Tomorrow we'll learn Delgado's dead. Or senile. Either way, not guilty. Of the kidnapping, that is. But then . . .' He rubbed his eyes and swore under his breath at the folly of what he had done. All this way and all this risk – of embarrassment or dismissal or far far worse. And for what? Charlotte had not said she loved him. She had not even implied it. Yet it was for her sake that he stood alone in this city of rain and darkness. And for her sake he must remain.

FIFTEEN

IT WAS STILL RAINING when they set off the following morning, though somewhat more fitfully than the day before. The clouds rolled in ugly clumps around the hilltops and spilled along the valleys like drifting gunsmoke. South of Santiago, the countryside was a succession of mournful woodland and sponge-wet farmland from which the water drained in bubbling torrents beside and across the road. Far sooner than Derek had expected, they reached a dismal sprawl of dwellings not unlike several others they had passed through but which, a mud-spattered sign proclaimed, was Lerezuela.

Frank pulled up in the centre – a row of shops whose modern concrete structures seemed to have worn less well than the ancient stone cottages of the outskirts – and entered a bar to seek directions. A glimpse of the cavernous interior, where the flickering of a television revealed nothing save one pot-bellied customer propping up the counter, made Derek glad to wait outside, which he did not have to do for long.

'Close by, as the concierge said,' Frank announced on his return. 'First right, second left. No more than a few kilometres.'

'Did you mention Delgado's name?'

'No. But the barman did. With some slant of meaning I couldn't catch. He asked if Delgado was expecting us. When I shook my head, he laughed. Not humorously.'

'What do you make of it?'

'Nothing – yet. Let's go and find out.'

Their route took them out of the village along a narrow but well-maintained road between a conifer plantation on one side and a high stone wall on the other. At intervals, a coat of arms appeared, carved in the face of the wall, depicting a boar and a sea-horse supporting a quartered shield beneath a helm and crest. The Vasconcelez family, whose land Delgado had acquired by marriage, had evidently been of proud lineage.

This became even more apparent when, at a point where the road ahead deteriorated dramatically, a wide courtyard opened to their left, with a manicured lawn and a fountain at its centre. The boundary wall comprised one side of the yard, facing an ornate tree-bowered chapel. The third side was the colonnaded frontage of a large house, stone-built and terracotta-tiled, with tall balconied windows on two floors above the yard and ornately carved figures decorating the arches and balustrades. The central arch was higher than the rest, disclosing a porch and a firmly closed pair of wooden doors. Wealth and seclusion had suddenly revealed themselves where Derek had somehow thought only poverty and privation were to be found. He was, for the moment, taken aback.

Not so Frank, who drove boldly into the yard, pulled up by the chapel and climbed out. He was already marching towards the entrance when Derek caught him up. 'Remember,' he cautioned breathlessly, 'We must take this slowly.'

'We must take it any way we can.'

'But *diplomatically*. It's our best chance.'

Frank cast him a sidelong glance by way of answer and walked on. A sign fixed to the door ahead proclaimed PRIVADO – PROHIBIDO ENTRAR, of which Derek required no translation. But there was a bell-pull beside it and Frank yanked at this without hesitation. No sound penetrated from the other side and Frank had raised his hand to ring again when a judas flap slid back for a second and was followed by the slipping of a bolt. Then a wicket-gate set in the right-hand door opened just wide enough to reveal a bulky figure dressed in jeans and a black polo-necked sweater. He was of medium height but broad-shouldered and muscular, with a blank intimidating face on which a Viva Zapata moustache did its best to conceal a substantial scar. He did not speak, but eyed them with interrogative coldness. There was absolutely no suggestion in his bearing of courtesy or welcome.

'*Buenos dias*,' ventured Frank. '*Señor Delgado, por favor.*'

The man did not reply. Behind him, across a cobbled yard, Derek could see another fountain and beyond that the clipped hedges and shrubs of a formal garden. Then, clanking its chain as it loped into view, there appeared a huge alsation dog. Derek looked away before he caught its eye.

'*Señor Delgado*,' Frank repeated. '*El general.*'

The man's gaze narrowed. Then he said, in scarcely more than a mumble: '*No está.*'

'Not in,' murmured Frank. 'To us, anyway. I'll ask when he's due back. That should reveal something. *Cuando vuelve?*'

The man shrugged.

'*Hoy? Mañana?*'

Another shrug.

'*Habla usted inglés?*'

The man smiled. '*Si*. I speak English. You are . . . *Americanos?*'

'No. But that doesn't matter. We must see Señor Delgado. It's very urgent. *Muy importante.*'

'No, señor.' The smile broadened. 'It is *muy imposible*. Señor Delgado sees nobody.'

'But—'

'Nobody!' He stepped back and was about to close the door when

Frank reached out and held it open. At that the smile gave way to a scowl.

'If we can't see him, can we at least leave a message?'

'No messages!'

'He'll want to receive this one. He'll thank you for passing it on. He'll blame you if you don't.'

The man relaxed fractionally. The pressure on the door faded.

'Well? Will you deliver our message?'

The answer was reluctant but emphatic, accompanied by a contemptuous curl of the lip. '*Si.*'

Derek wondered what Frank would say next, given that they had made no provisions for such a contingency. To his surprise, the old man pulled a sealed envelope from the inside pocket of his jacket. 'For Señor Delgado,' he said, handing it over. 'For him and nobody else. You will make sure he receives it?'

'*Si.*'

'Today?'

'*Si, señor*. Today.'

Frank nodded. '*Gracias.*' This time, he did not intervene as the door closed, merely turned and walked away towards the Land Rover.

'What was in the envelope, Frank?' whispered Derek.

'A letter. Brief and to the point. I wrote it last night. It invites Delgado to contact the sender at the Hotel de los Reyes Catolicos in order to discuss some papers he has, originally the property of Vicente Ortiz.'

'You knew we wouldn't be admitted, didn't you? That we'd have to leave a message?'

'I thought it likely.'

'Why didn't you tell me?'

'Because you'd have said it was too risky, too direct, too *undiplomatic*.'

'So it is.'

'Maybe. But we don't have time for your methods, whatever they are. So we'll have to try mine, won't we?'

'But what kind of response will there be?'

'I don't know.'

They reached the Land Rover and climbed in alongside each other. The windows of the pazo stared down at them unblinkingly. If they were being watched, there was no twitch of curtain or glimpse of face to confirm it. And the absence of this — the disdainful lack of any response — somehow worried Derek more than the bolted gate or its sullen keeper. 'Is there any chance,' he asked, 'that Delgado will recognize your name as an old comrade of Ortiz's?'

'None.'

'How can you be so sure?'

'Easily. You see, I didn't sign the letter in my name. I signed it in yours.'

SIXTEEN

SUNDAY AND MONDAY HAD fused into a test of Charlotte's endurance. Time was running out for Samantha, but all Charlotte could do was wait and hope and say nothing to anybody about what might be happening in Galicia. Her two telephone conversations with Derek had provided scant reassurance. There had been a note of anxiety in his voice that she found it easy to believe might presage some form of panic. As for Frank, she was as uncertain about what he intended to do as Derek was. And, unlike Derek, she was in no position to restrain him.

As her mind filled with dread-laden speculation, so her fear of discovery mounted. She knew this to be groundless, since the precautions they had taken were more than adequate, but she could not help expecting Chief Inspector Golding to arrive at any moment demanding to know what she thought she was playing at. Perhaps the receptionist at Fithyan & Co. had recognized her voice. Perhaps one of Derek's neighbours had seen her coming and going at Farriers. Perhaps, worst of all, their attempt to negotiate with Delgado would prove to be a disastrous mistake.

Shortly before midday on Tuesday, there came a ring at the door which brought all these doubts crowding to the surface. By the time she answered it, she had almost convinced herself it would be Golding, grim-faced and accusing. But it was not. And the relief that it was not delayed by several seconds the onset of astonishment at her visitor's identity.

'Mrs McKitrick!'

'Hi, Charlie. This is a surprise, right?' Holly McKitrick seemed altered by the switch in locale from expansive Massachusetts to introspective Kent. She was wearing a sheepskin coat with the collar turned up and her smile was faint and cautious where before it had been broad and instinctive. For a moment, Charlotte could have believed she was not the same person. A sister, perhaps, or a total stranger bearing a capricious resemblance. Then she realized her own incredulity lay at the root of the sensation. What was this woman doing here? What could she possibly want? 'Can I come in? I don't have long and . . . There's something I have to tell you.'

'All right. Come in.'

Charlotte led the way into the lounge, took her visitor's coat and offered her a chair. She was wearing a smart black suit and pink blouse, but for all the immaculacy of her appearance there were dark shadows beneath her eyes and a tremor to her hands and voice. An offer of coffee was declined. She sat forward in her chair, slightly hunched, revolving her wedding ring on its finger with the thumb and index finger of her other hand.

'What . . . er . . . is this about, Mrs McKitrick?' Charlotte asked after a momentary silence.

'Your niece.'

'Sam?'

'Yuh. You said . . . her kidnappers had set a deadline.'

'Yes. The eleventh.'

'And today's the sixth.' She stared at her feet for several seconds, then said: 'Emerson doesn't know I'm here. I'm spending a week with my sister in Germany. Her husband's stationed with the Air Force there. I flew across this morning. In secret, I suppose you'd say.'

'To see me?'

'Yuh. To see you.'

'About Sam?'

'Listen to me.' She looked up, her face suddenly hard and intent. 'I can't bear to think your niece may die because I haven't told you what I know. It may help. It may not. But in case it does . . .'

'I'm listening.'

'OK.' She stopped flexing at her ring and laid her hands flat in her lap. 'Emerson lied when you came to see us in South Lincoln. Leastways, I think he did. You asked him if he'd told anybody about Tristram Abberley's letters to his sister and he said only me. But I don't think that's true. He went to Spain, you see, between leaving England and returning to Boston over the summer.'

'Spain?'

'Yes. He hasn't admitted it, but I can see something's eating at his conscience, something to do with your niece, I guess, and whatever he did in Spain.'

'How do you know he was there?'

'His American Express card statement for August showed payments to Iberia Airlines and to a hotel and a couple of restaurants in some place called Santiago de Compostela.'

The connection was made, the pattern complete. McKitrick was Delgado's informant. It had to be so. Revenge for Maurice's deceit of him might have been the motive, but more likely it was simply money. Charlotte felt sorry for Holly, sorry and grateful for her attempt to retrieve what Emerson had done. 'What was he doing in Santiago de Compostela, Holly?'

'I can't be sure. But when he was in Spain researching his book on Tristram Abberley – years ago, before I knew him – he met somebody who offered him a stack of money for any letters or papers Tristram might have left behind concerning his time in the International Brigade.' She smiled bitterly. 'He's probably forgotten telling me about it. He was smashed at the time. But I wasn't. And after your visit I remembered what he'd said. Besides, he's just ordered a new car. The latest Pontiac Firebird. And he's talking about a skiing vacation in Colorado this winter when he's ordinarily content with weekends in Vermont. I've asked where the money's to come from, but all I can get out of him is that royalty income's well up. But it isn't. I've checked. So, where *is* it coming from?'

'Somebody who paid him handsomely for identifying my brother as the holder of the letters?'

'That's how I see it.' Holly bit her lip. 'Emerson's selfish, I know. God, do I know. But he isn't malicious. He couldn't have realized these people – whoever they are – would go to such lengths to get what they want.'

Charlotte could not forget what Emerson had done to her, how he had played on her emotions to feed his academic reputation. Whether Holly would be as charitable if she knew everything her husband had done during his summer in England Charlotte doubted. But she would not be the one to inflict such knowledge upon her. 'I suppose not,' she conceded with a consoling smile.

'I only wish I could tell you who Emerson went to see in Spain, but he's never—'

'There's no need.'

'You know?'

'Yes.'

Holly stared at her in amazement. 'So . . . you've found out who's holding your niece?'

Charlotte nodded. 'I've suspected for some time. Now, thanks to you, I know for certain.'

SEVENTEEN

STILL SMARTING FROM FRANK'S use of his name on the letter to Delgado, Derek lay on his bed at the Hotel de los Reyes Catolicos, listening to the drip and splatter of the rain in the courtyard beyond his window. He could not help feeling annoyed that the ploy made so much sense. There was a slim chance Delgado might have heard of Frank, none at all that he might have heard of Derek. Besides, Derek had expounded the case for cool-headed negotiation and the letter had given him the chance to carry it out. What he really resented, of course, was the exposed position it placed him in. He was no longer anonymous, no longer able to claim neutrality whenever it suited him. And he suspected there was more to Frank's reasoning than he had admitted. Why did he suddenly want Derek to take the leading role? Why was he willing to step aside?

Whatever the answer, it was too late to do anything about it. An hour ago the telephone had rung and Derek had found himself talking to a cultivated English-speaking Spaniard called Norberto Galazarga, none other, it transpired, than Delgado's private secretary.

'*I am Señor Delgado's eyes and ears, Mr Fairfax. I act for him in all matters. I am entirely in his confidence.*'

'*Good. Now, has he—*'

'*Señor Delgado has read your letter and has asked me to meet with you in order to discuss your proposal.*'

'*I haven't made a proposal.*'

'*But you will, will you not?*'

'*Perhaps. I—*'

'*Would eleven o'clock tomorrow morning be convenient?*'

'*Well, yes, I suppose—*'

'*I will call upon you at your hotel. I look forward to our discussion.*'

'*Er . . . Well, so do—*'

'*Buenos tardes, Mr Fairfax.*'

And so the die was cast. One intermediary would meet another under conditions of truce. Delicately and with infinite caution, they would edge towards an understanding. Or so Derek hoped. Though how he would phrase his 'proposal' he did not know. To what kind of approach would Delgado – or his syrup-tongued secretary – be most receptive? To what form of logic would they yield?

Such issues might not be so intractable if he knew more about Delgado. His blood-stained past was one thing. But what of his present? What kind of man had fifty years of peace produced? Frank had insisted they return to the bar in Lerezuela after leaving the pazo in search of precisely such information, but the little they had learned from its lugubrious proprietor and the less reticent among his customers had been neither helpful nor encouraging.

Delgado, it seemed, was held more in awe than affection by the locals. *El guante férreo*, he was nicknamed – the iron glove, a twisted reference to his artificial right hand that was also a metaphor for his pitiless nature. Several families had been turned off Vasconcelez land to make way for Delgado's forestry projects, linked as they were to his wood-pulp business in Vigo. He was believed, indeed, to have a metallic finger in every branch of Galician industry, accumulating thereby a considerable fortune to add to what he had acquired by marriage. The pazo was said to be fabulously furnished, a fortress for his long retreat from the world. Since his son and grandson had been killed by ETA terrorists, he had grown ever more reclusive, to the extent that now he was seldom seen, though staff at the pazo said he was still in good health. His affections were reserved for his allegedly beautiful eighteen-year-old granddaughter, Yolanda, to whom no extravagance was denied. She was at a finishing school in Switzerland, where all traces of her Galician roots were being expensively eliminated. As for Delgado's Civil War record, everybody professed an eloquent ignorance. By their reactions, one might have supposed no such war had taken place.

'*What I'd expected,*' Frank had said during the drive back to Santiago. '*Money. Power. But not much love. It's the reward his type normally reap.*'

'If he's so wealthy, why should he care about the gold?'

'Because he's greedy. Because he can't stand to lose what he plotted long and hard to gain.'

'But he's nearly ninety years old, for God's sake. He'll be dead before he can spend it.'

'He doesn't want to spend it. He just wants to have it. I told you – I know his type.'

This Derek did not doubt. It was one of the thoughts that would not leave his head. Frank knew. But he did not. Frank understood. But he would be the one who met Galazarga tomorrow morning and tried to strike a bargain. He took a deep breath and exhaled slowly, studying the mobile pattern the rain made against the shutters, as serpentine and shifting as the problems his mind could neither master nor discard. Everything was so simple and straightforward according to Frank, everything was cut and dried before it was done.

'Make it clear to Delgado's secretary that we have the means to destroy his employer's good name and won't hesitate to do so if the girl is harmed. Then offer him a straight swap under secure conditions: the statement in exchange for the girl.'

'But what about the map?'

'Tell him the truth. Tell him he can have everything we have – but that doesn't include the map.'

'And if he doesn't believe me?'

'Make him believe you.'

'It's easy for you to say. Not so easy to do. We may be barking up the wrong tree, remember. We may be offering Delgado something he badly wants in return for something he doesn't have.'

'No. Delgado has the girl. You can bank on it.'

But Derek was not convinced. It might still be a colossal misunderstanding. When all was said and done, there was no proof, no clinching evidence that Delgado was their man. As he stared up at the canopy of the bed, across which some medieval hunting party frolicked in embroidered abandon, the thought assumed a comforting dimension. So long as he could believe in the possibility of Delgado's innocence, his meeting with Galazarga was not too dreadful a prospect. Any amount of embarrassment was after all preferable to—

The sudden bleeping of the alarm clock cut short his deliberations. It was seven o'clock and time to call Charlotte again. Sitting up, Derek snapped off the alarm, hoisted the telephone into his lap and dialled the number. Charlotte answered at the second ring.

'Derek?'

'Hello, Charlotte.'

'Is everything all right?'

'Yes. We were turned away from the pazo but I've arranged a meeting tomorrow morning with Delgado's private secretary.'

'You're getting close, then.'

'Maybe. But don't forget Delgado may have nothing to do with this.' He paused for Charlotte's reply, but none came. 'Charlotte?'

'I'm still here.'

'Is something wrong?'

'Not exactly. It's just . . . I have some news for you. What it amounts to is proof.'

'Of what?'

'Of Delgado's guilt. There's no longer any doubt about it, Derek. He's the one who's holding Sam.'

EIGHTEEN

Norberto Galazarga was a dapper little man encased in a perfectly cut three-piece suit complete with gold watch-chain and shot-silk lining. There was more hair on his upper lip, in the form of a trimmed jet-black moustache, than on the whole of the rest of his head. His broad and ready smile sent creases rippling up his brow and over his bald crown until they disappeared from view. His eyes sparkled so noticeably Derek suspected he employed special drops to achieve the effect. And he wore enough cologne to seep through even the pungent aroma of the cigar at which he squinted and sniffed and very occasionally puffed. He embodied nearly every quality Derek felt least at ease with: subtlety and inscrutability complicated by foreign blood and a distracting bundle of affectations. He was so obviously Derek's intellectual superior, so clearly prepared for his every remark, that conversation with him began to resemble a form of self-analysis in which he would periodically intervene with the lofty air of a bored psychiatrist.

'Abduction is such a brutal business, Mr Fairfax. So heedless of the family ties it threatens to sunder. Yet I suppose we could also regard it as a specialized form of commerce. Trade by coercion, so to speak.

Naturally, it is easy for me to philosophize about such matters, when I have no personal experience of them. For your friends, the . . . the . . .'

'Abberleys.'

'Quite so. For them, it must be altogether shocking. Too painful for words, I should imagine.' He raised his cup of chocolate as if to drink, then replaced it in the saucer untouched and leant back in his chair, toying with his cigar. 'They have my sympathy, my heartfelt sympathy.'

Derek told himself, not for the first time, to relax, to view this tortuous discussion as a necessary preliminary to the desired objective. Here they sat in the hotel's plushly furnished lounge, reclining in softly cushioned armchairs beneath a huge gilt-framed portrait of some Hapsburg nobleman, talking their way back and forth in feathery undertones over the one subject neither could mention which was also the sole purpose of their meeting.

'I am surprised, I must confess,' Galazarga continued, 'that you could find time to visit Spain on such abstruse business when your friends' problem – their appalling dilemma – is so critically balanced. One might almost think you hoped to assist them by coming here, though how I cannot understand.'

'Perhaps I've not made myself sufficiently clear.'

'Perhaps not.' The words were accompanied by his characteristic smile.

'Then let me try again. Your response to my letter suggests Señor Delgado is very interested in obtaining the document I happen to have in my possession, a document written by Vicente Ortiz, a native of Barcelona, during the Civil War, in which he describes in detail certain events which took place in Cartagena in October 1936.'

'You have aroused Señor Delgado's antiquarian curiosity, certainly.'

'Does he want it – or not?'

'Forgive me, Mr Fairfax, but it is premature to pose such a question. The issue at this stage is what you want in return.'

'Samantha Abberley's release.'

Galazarga frowned. 'Naturally you do. So do I. So, no doubt – if acquainted with the distressing circumstances – would Señor Delgado. But he is no magician. He cannot wave a wand to grant your every wish. Nobody can.'

'Except the people holding her.'

'Except those, yes.' Another move towards the chocolate cup was aborted. 'But how are you to communicate with them?'

Derek studiously erased all expression from his face as he replied. 'I think I may have found a way.'

'Really?'

'Yes. Really.' Their eyes met and it seemed to Derek that, quite deliberately, Galazarga allowed the veil to rise momentarily from his meaning, the screen around his intentions to slide briefly back. What lay behind was hard and cautious and cunning: Delgado's iron hand in his secretary's velvet glove.

'Congratulations are in order, then.' The smile returned and with it the layers of pretence. 'If you are right, you may be able to render the Abberley family an inestimable service.'

'I'm right.'

'Your confidence does you credit. But permit me to utter a word of warning. You are in a foreign land of which you know very little. Of its history, I would suspect, even less. Remember your own countrymen's proverbs: a little knowledge is a dangerous thing, whereas ignorance is bliss.'

'What Ortiz knew was inescapably dangerous. I have his written record of it. And I'm willing to surrender it.' Derek could feel the perspiration forming on his upper lip and forehead, but knew he could not be seen to wipe it away. It was useless to hope his anxiety had escaped Galazarga's notice. The only question was what he would conclude from it. 'But my willingness is strictly conditional. You follow?'

'I believe I do.' The cigar slipped into his mouth, then was withdrawn. 'I think I can safely say Señor Delgado would very much like to agree satisfactory terms for his acquisition of the Ortiz . . . of the curio you describe.'

'Good.' Derek swallowed hard. 'There's just . . . er . . . one thing I have to explain.' Galazarga's eyebrows shot up. 'Originally, a hand-drawn map was enclosed with the document. Unfortunately, it's been destroyed.'

'Destroyed?'

'By a previous . . . holder.'

'The map does not form part of what you are offering?'

'It would, if it still existed. But it doesn't. Nothing's being withheld, you understand. The map is lost. Gone. Not mine to offer. Nor anybody else's either.'

Galazarga clicked his tongue. 'Oh dear. Oh dear me. This is . . . a sad development.'

'It needn't be. What's gone is also safe. And what isn't gone is on offer.'

'Quite possibly. But the map . . .' He drew lengthily on his cigar. 'Incompleteness, however fractional, is anathema to the true collector. It reduces the value of an item dramatically. It may prove . . . fatal . . . to the prospects of a sale. Yes, *fatal* is I think the word.'

'If it did have such an effect, I'd have to look elsewhere for a buyer.'

'Would you?'

'Yes. And I reckon I'd find one, the absence of a map notwithstanding. Don't you?'

'I?' Galazarga coughed. 'I really could not say. Señor Delgado may feel able to proceed despite your proviso. Or he may not. The decision rests with him.'

'When will he take it?'

'After I have apprised him of the relevant facts.' Abruptly, Galazarga leant forward, took a sip of chocolate, then rose, extending his hand in farewell. 'To which task I shall give my immediate attention. Such a pleasure, Mr Fairfax.'

Derek stood up hurriedly, shook Galazarga's hand and found himself returning the infuriating smile. 'When . . . er . . . when will I hear from you?'

'Within twenty-four hours. Without fail.'

'Right. I—'

'*Adiós*.' With the faintest of bows, Galazarga turned and walked swiftly from the room.

After the door had swung shut behind him, Derek subsided back into his chair and began to retrace their conversation in his mind. He was still engaged in this process when, a few minutes later, Frank Griffith appeared in front of him.

'I saw him leave,' the old man said, lowering himself into the seat Galazarga had occupied and staring intently at Derek. 'How did it go?'

'It went.'

'When will we have Delgado's answer?'

'Within twenty-four hours.'

'And what will it be?'

'I don't know.'

'What do you think it will be?'

379

'I don't think.' He looked straight across at Frank. 'You've told me often enough since we left England to wait and see. Well, you should be glad. Now, that's all I'm capable of doing.'

NINETEEN

EIGHT HOURS LATER, DEREK'S vigil in his room – which he dared not leave in case Galazarga tried to contact him – was wearing on his nerves as well as his patience. A one-sided conversation with Frank and a static-ridden call to Charlotte had failed either to calm or to cheer him. Now, as the evening advanced and the chances diminished of Galazarga being in touch before morning, he decided solitude was no longer tolerable. A visit to the bar, though it did not promise unbounded gaiety, at least constituted a change of scene. Without looking in on Frank for fear the old curmudgeon might object, he set off, pausing at reception *en route* to emphasize where he could be found.

Galician beer having proved a disappointment, he opted this time for spirits, of which Spanish measures proved gratifyingly generous. Halfway through his second substantial *cubalibre*, he was beginning to imagine he really was a match for Galazarga and his elusive employer when a strikingly attractive dark-haired girl in a black combination of mini-skirt, polo-necked sweater and bolero jacket sat down at his table.

'Er . . . Hello,' Derek said, with a frown of puzzlement.

'*Buenas tardes*. Mr Fairfax?'

'Er . . . yes.'

Her voice fell to a whisper. 'I am Yolanda Delgado Vasconcelez. I must speak with you. It is very important.'

'What?' Derek could hardly believe his ears, but there was no doubting her seriousness. Nor her sincerity, to judge by the frankness of her gaze. 'But . . . I was told . . .'

'That I was in Switzerland?' She nodded. 'I am supposed to be. I would still be there now if my grandfather had not . . .' She leant closer, her eyes wide and imploring. 'I must not be recognized, Mr Fairfax. If he knew what I was doing, he would be very angry.'

'Your grandfather?'

'Of course. But I cannot let this go on. Surely you see that.'

'I . . . I'm not sure I—'

'I know about your letter. And your meeting with Norberto Galazarga. I know why you are here.'

'You do?'

'Could we go somewhere else?' She glanced round. 'Somewhere more . . . discreet?'

'Well, I—'

'I can help you.' She placed her hand over his where it rested on the table. 'But only if you help me. Will you come with me?'

'Where to?'

'Not far.' She looked over her shoulder again. 'But it has to be now. Will you come?'

'I . . .' What manner of help she was offering him he could not guess. But he knew also he could not turn his back on it. The chance of a swift end to Samantha's ordeal – and to his – was too tempting to resist. 'All right. Let's go.'

She did not accompany him to the bar to pay, but waited by the side-door that led directly out of the hotel. When he followed, she went ahead, a black-clad figure hurrying into the Santiago night. It was dry now, but still misty, the street-lamps and cathedral floodlights blurred and subdued like nurses' lanterns. The city seemed older and more watchful than by day, its senses sharpened by darkness, its purposes concealed.

They headed downhill, away from the plaza, turning right and then left along deserted dimly lit streets. Before they had reached the end of the second of these, Derek began to regret leaving the warmth and security of the hotel. It would be all too easy to become lost in this cobbled maze of ancient by-ways. Sobered by the coolness of the air, he suddenly began to wonder if Yolanda might be leading him into some form of trap. A noise behind them made him swing round abruptly. But there was no trace of anybody in or between the shadows.

'Don't worry,' said Yolanda, looking back at him as if she had read his thoughts. 'It's just down here. A little café I know where we can talk without being overheard.'

Reassured, he followed her into the mouth of an alley to their left. But reassurance lasted no more than an instant. There were no beckoning lights of a café ahead, no lights in fact of any kind. He pulled up and was about to turn back when he was seized around the waist and dragged to one side. He was aware of two large men hauling him into a doorway, of shapes moving vaguely around and behind him, of muffled words in Spanish, of garlic on the breath of his assailants. All this came into his mind a fraction of a second before it was swamped by fear. Then he was slammed against a heavy wooden door, his arms pinned to his sides, a metal knocker grinding against his spine. The blade of a knife flashed in a shaft of light and he saw two faces close to his own, swollen and distorted by the shadows like pumpkin masks at Hallowe'en. And then a drift of cigar-smoke caught in his nostrils. Galazarga was standing a few feet in front of him, an overcoat slung like a cape around his shoulders.

'We will resume our conversation, Mr Fairfax,' he said in a tone of studied normality. 'Without the need to guard our tongues so closely.'

'What . . . What do you want?'

'The map – along with the other papers.'

'I told you: it doesn't exist.'

'We have searched your room. It is not there. I conclude you value it too highly to part with it. So, please be so good as to hand it over.'

'I haven't got it.'

'¡Cachealos!'

Derek was pulled forward. One of the men twisted his left arm behind his back while the other began searching his pockets, handing the contents to Galazarga as he went. There was not much: wallet, passport, diary, pen, comb, keys, a half-finished packet of peppermints and a few crumpled tissues. Yolanda switched on a torch and trained the beam on the bundle of items while Galazarga sifted through them.

'It does not appear to be here, Mr Fairfax.'

'Of course it isn't. It's—'

'You called at the pazo in the company of an elderly man. Does he have it?'

'No. Neither of us does.'

'What is his name, Mr Fairfax? Where is he to be found?'

'I'm not answering any more questions.'

'I rather think you are. Unless you want to end your days as Maurice Abberley did. The same knife that was held at his throat is now at yours.'

Glancing down, Derek saw the glistening blade, clasped in a large hand that rested heavily on his chest. *Don't try their patience a moment longer*, his racing thoughts bellowed inside his head. *Tell them Frank has the map. Tell them where he is. Tell them whatever you have to.* 'Listen, I—'

'That's enough!' It was Frank's voice, stern and unwavering. He was standing at the mouth of the alley, pointing a double-barrelled shotgun straight at Galazarga. 'Release him now or I'll fire.' For a second, nobody moved. Then Frank said: 'I mean what I say, señor. I've killed men before, most of them Spaniards. The thought of it doesn't worry me. In fact, the thought of killing you is quite attractive. Any more delay and I may be unable to resist temptation.'

How Frank came to be where he was – how for that matter he had come by the shotgun – Derek was too amazed to consider. He was only glad – more glad than he could ever have imagined being – to see the old man's implacable stare. If anybody could win this war of nerves, it was Frank. He was outnumbered and could clearly be overpowered. But not before he had fired the gun. Galazarga had to believe he would do so. If he did not believe it, he might judge the risk worth taking. But Frank's expression was unflinching, his grip on the gun unfaltering. And Galazarga was only a few feet from him. If he did fire, he could not miss.

For another second, Galazarga's reaction remained in doubt. Then he parted his hands in a placatory gesture and said: 'You have the advantage, señor.' He turned to his men. '¡Dejálos-ir!' They let go of Derek and stepped clear of him. The knife vanished.

'Give him back his belongings,' said Frank.

With a little shrug of assumed humility, Galazarga stepped towards Derek and dropped the items into his outstretched hands.

'Now, all four of you, move past me into the street. Very slowly.' Frank edged back to make way for them: the two leather-jacketed thugs, scowling ominously; the girl, head bowed; and Galazarga, pouting with irritation. 'Walk away.' He signalled the direction they should take with a nod. It was a continuation of the route Derek and the girl had been following before they turned into the alley. 'Don't run. Don't stop. Don't look round.'

Galazarga muttered something to his men which was evidently sufficient to secure their compliance. As they set off and the girl followed, he glanced back at Derek and inclined his head, as if in formal leave-taking. '*Hasta luego, señores*,' he said, with the faintest of smiles. Then he fell in behind the others.

The sweat was cooling rapidly on Derek's brow. He became aware of it for the first time, aware also of how badly his hands were shaking as he crammed his belongings back into his pockets. He stumbled forward to where Frank was standing. Galazarga and his companions were twenty yards away already, walking hard, obedient to their instructions.

'Thank God you found me,' Derek murmured.

'Thank my opinion of you. I reckoned it was odds on you'd do something stupid. So, when I heard you leave your room, I thought I'd better keep an eye on you. And it's just as well I did. As soon as I saw you leave the bar with the girl, I knew it would end badly.'

Derek was too drained by fear to bridle at his words. Besides, they were all too accurate. 'She claimed to be Delgado's grand-daughter. She claimed to want to help.'

'She was a liar and an impostor. As you should have realized.'

'I know. I'm sorry.'

'Don't be. We haven't time for regrets.'

'Where did you get the gun?'

'I've had it ever since we left Hendre Gorfelen.'

'So that's why we couldn't fly – because you were smuggling a gun into the country.'

Frank looked round at him. 'I thought we might need one. And it seems I was right, doesn't it?'

At any other time, Derek would have been enraged. But not now. Now, Frank's methods were the only ones that seemed to make sense. 'I never thought . . . I never expected . . .'

'But I did. This was always likely to be their answer.'

'They think we have the map.'

'They can't bear to think we don't have it.'

'How do we convince them?'

'We don't try.' He pointed down the street. 'They're almost out of sight. We ought to be on our way. Before they have a chance to double-back.' He bent to retrieve something from the pavement. It was a threadbare old coat, which he draped over the shotgun before clasping it to his side, stock uppermost.

'Aren't you going to unload the thing?'

'Not until we're out of danger. Come on.' Frank set off back the way they had come, walking fast, eyes trained ahead. As Derek caught up, he said: 'Move, boy. We don't have long.'

'For what?'

'Packing our bags, paying the bill, retrieving Vicente's statement from the safe-deposit – and clearing out of Santiago.'

'To go where?'

'It doesn't matter. Somewhere they can't find us.'

'What if they follow us?'

'With any luck they won't know what we're driving. If they do, we'll just have to lose them.'

'But . . . I don't understand . . . What can we accomplish by leaving now?'

'More than we can accomplish by staying. Like Galazarga said, *we* have the advantage. And we mustn't lose it.'

'The advantage? I still don't—'

'We're going to call Delgado's bluff, boy. We're going to see whose nerve is really the stronger. And believe me, I don't intend it to be his.'

TWENTY

'Hello?'

'It's me.'

Charlotte caught her breath, knowing Derek could only be telephoning her at Ockham House if something had gone drastically wrong. It was not yet ten o'clock on Thursday morning. Another nine hours were due to have elapsed before they spoke again. She wanted to ask what had happened, but could contrive no way of doing so without arousing the suspicion of any of Golding's men who might be listening. And the recent increase in whirrs and clicks on the line had convinced her they *were* listening – all the time.

'Don't say anything,' Derek continued. 'Just be where you would be at seven – in half an hour. We'll talk then.'

In his hotel room in Corunna, Derek put the telephone down and looked across at Frank, profiled against the picture-windowed vista of sea and sky. 'So far so good,' he said. 'I wonder how she'll react when I tell her what you have in mind.'

'What *we* have in mind,' growled Frank. 'You agreed it was the only course left open to us.'

385

Derek could not deny he had. But that had been last night, after he had found his room at the Reyes Catolicos ransacked and they had quit the hotel in a panicky scramble; after they had driven fast along winding roads up into the hills north of Santiago and taken to rough forest tracks until they were sure nobody was following; after they had waited and watched for hours in the inky darkness until they were absolutely certain they had made good their escape. At dawn, they had headed for Corunna, the provincial capital, a modern city crouching grey and wind-scoured on the rocky rim of the Atlantic Ocean. Here, a busy urban populace had supplied much-needed camouflage and a couple of rooms in a high-rise hotel overlooking the sea an ideal sanctuary. And here Derek, his nerve and judgement patched together with food and rest and hot running water, had begun to question the strategy to which he had earlier given his unqualified consent.

'Having second thoughts?' asked Frank.

'No. Not exactly. It's just—'

'It's just you can hardly believe now you were in that back-alley, with a knife at your throat. Or that sweet reason isn't going to win Delgado over.'

'I suppose so.'

'Well, you were. And it isn't.'

'Will your way work any better?'

'I'm not sure.' Frank turned and stared out for a moment at the gulls wheeling and screeching over the harbour. Then he said: 'But, if it doesn't, nothing else will.'

Ten minutes after Charlotte had reached Derek's house, the telephone rang and she found herself talking to him again, this time more freely. When she heard what form Delgado's answer had taken, she did not know who to feel more anxious for: Derek, whom she had led into greater danger than either of them had anticipated; or Samantha, whose freedom now seemed more unattainable than ever. Her instinctive reaction was that the time really had to come to tell the police everything they knew. But, to her surprise, Derek did not agree.

'Frank thinks – we both think – there's one other approach worth trying. We reckon it stands an excellent chance of success.'

'What is it?'

'It's why I phoned you this morning rather than this evening. We can't risk any further direct contact with Delgado. But he does take

386

us seriously now. He's bound to. So, if we could negotiate with him indirectly, through an intermediary . . .'

'What intermediary?'

'You, Charlotte. Frank's plan is to place an advert in tomorrow's *International Herald Tribune*, using the wording the kidnappers stipulated, but specifying they should telephone you there – on my number. That should keep you one step ahead of the police. You could call us here to tell us their response.'

'Their response to what?'

'Our terms. Release Samantha immediately or we'll take Vicente Ortiz's statement to the Spanish press.'

'You wouldn't.'

'Delgado must believe we would. You must persuade him.'

'But . . . the risks are . . .'

'Appalling. As they have been all along.'

'You think they're worth taking? I mean *you*, Derek. *You* think this is what we should do?'

There was a lengthy pause, during which she sensed rather than heard him bite back several possible replies. Then he said: 'If we go to the police now and name Delgado, there's insufficient time left for them to make discreet enquiries. They may well end up alerting Delgado to their suspicions long before they're able to establish where Samantha's being held. What happened last night leaves me in little doubt how Delgado would respond in such circumstances.'

She realized then, as she supposed Derek must already have realized, how irrevocable their decision to go it alone had proved. At some stage of which neither had been fully aware, they had passed the point of no return. There was no way back now. There might indeed be no way out at all. But, if there was, Frank's plan offered the only hope of finding it. 'All right,' she said. 'We'll do it.'

Charlotte telephoned the *International Herald Tribune* offices in Paris straightaway. After parting with her credit card number, she obtained a guarantee that all editions of Friday's paper would carry, prominently displayed in the personal column of the classified advertisements: PEN PALS CAN BE REUNITED. ORWELL WILL PAY. CALL 44-892-315509. Then she called Derek again to confirm it would appear.

'Well done, Charlotte. I'll buy a copy here. After our brush with them in Santiago – and our subsequent disappearance – I don't think they'll be able to resist making contact.'

'And when they do?'

'You must convince them we mean what we say. There really is no other way.'

He was right. But Charlotte suspected he would have preferred to be wrong, would infinitely have preferred, like her, to find some safe and secure alternative. When the telephone rang a few moments after she had put it down, she thought for an instant he might have done just that. In her eagerness to believe he had, she grabbed at the receiver and said 'Derek?'

'Tunbridge Wells 315509?' a gruff male voice enquired.

'Er . . . Yes.' Charlotte winced at her own stupidity. She should have claimed he had the wrong number, put the telephone down and refrained from answering when it rang again.

'Can I speak to Mr Derek Fairfax, please?' The gruff voice was vaguely familiar, but Charlotte could not quite place it.

'No . . . I mean, he isn't here.'

'Who *am* I speaking to, may I ask?'

'I . . . I might ask the same of you.'

'Of course. I'm sorry. My name's Albion Dredge. I'm Mr Fairfax's solicitor. Well, his brother's solicitor, to be precise.' Now the vagueness vanished. She had heard this man pleading on Colin Fairfax's behalf in Hastings Magistrates' Court last June, when the desirability of Beatrix's Tunbridge Ware seemed sufficient explanation of her murder. How naïve such an explanation appeared now, how absurdly and attractively naïve. 'I need to speak to Mr Fairfax on a matter of some urgency. When will he be back?'

'Not for some time.'

'Before tomorrow?'

'No.'

'Can you give me a number where I can contact him?'

'No.'

'Oh dear. How inconvenient. Let me see. I take it you are a friend of his, Miss . . .'

'I'm a friend of his, yes.'

'Then you will be aware of his brother's . . . predicament?'

'Yes.'

388

'Is there any way you could pass a message to Mr Fairfax concerning his brother?'

'Well . . . Perhaps.'

'He'll be appearing before Hastings magistrates tomorrow morning, you see. The police have dropped their objections to bail and I shall reapply for it to be granted. When I first applied, Mr Fairfax offered to act as surety.'

Charlotte's heart sank. 'You mean you need him to do so again? You need him to be in court?'

'Not necessarily. If the magistrates read between the lines, they'll realize it's only a matter of time before the charges are dropped altogether. Then they'll be happy to grant bail on the defendant's own recognisance. But I like to play safe, Miss . . . Miss . . .'

'I'll tell Mr Fairfax if I hear from him. But I may not. You think his brother will be released anyway?'

'Probably.'

'That's all right then, isn't it?'

'Er . . . Yes. But—'

'Goodbye, Mr Dredge.'

'If I could just—'

Dredge's words were cut off abruptly as Charlotte put the telephone down. She stared at it for several seconds, wondering if she should call Derek and tell him what had happened. If she did, he might take it into his head to contact Dredge, thus compounding the damage she had already done. Whereas, if she did not, nothing worse than a delay in Colin's release could result. In any other circumstances, she would have been eager to help. But these were not other circumstances. For the moment, there was no help she could safely give. With a sigh, she rose from the chair and made ready to leave.

TWENTY-ONE

'MAY WE COME IN, Miss Ladram?'

It was four o'clock that afternoon and the very last people Charlotte wanted to see were standing on the doorstep of Ockham House: Chief Inspector Golding, eyebrows critically raised as he surveyed her; Detective Constable Finch, elfin and severe; and a third officer whom she recognized, to her surprise, as Chief Inspector Hyslop of the Sussex Police. 'Yes, of course,' she said. 'Has something . . . happened?'

'Nothing to be alarmed about,' said Golding. 'We'll explain inside.'

Dredge had guessed who she was and told the police. They had identified Derek from their recording of his call to her that morning. Somehow, they had deduced what she was planning to do. Or else their visit was a coincidence. With this last thought she fended off her fears as she led the way to the lounge.

'You must be under a lot of strain,' remarked Golding, as he moved towards the window, placing himself between her and the light. 'The eleventh is awfully close.'

'Yes. It is.' She turned towards Hyslop, eager to involve him in the conversation if only to prevent Golding dominating it. 'It's nice to see you again, Chief Inspector. To what . . .'

'I'd have been in touch anyway, miss,' Hyslop replied. 'Peter suggested I accompany him this afternoon.' He smiled towards Golding. 'Minimize the disturbance, so to speak.'

'It's no disturbance. How have your enquiries into my aunt's death gone since you re-opened them?'

'Satisfactorily. Of course, when it all comes out in court, I'm afraid your late brother's reputation is going to suffer considerable damage.'

'It will come to court, then? You've been able to construct a case against Spicer?'

'We've just had positive results in on some carpet fibres and blood stains found in his car. They link him to the scene of the crime and to the deceased. Since he's never claimed an alibi, he really has no defence.'

'Have you charged him?'

390

'We plan to – when we find him.'

'I thought he was under arrest.'

Hyslop grimaced. 'He was. But we had to release him for lack of hard evidence. That was before the tests on his car were completed. Since then . . .'

'He's done a bunk,' put in Golding. 'Probably realized the game was up.'

'Yes,' said Hyslop defensively. 'But we'll catch him. It's only a question of time.'

'As in the matter of your niece's abduction,' said Golding. 'You seem to be coping remarkably well in the circumstances, Miss Ladram.'

'Well . . . There's nothing I can do, is there? There's nothing anybody can do.'

'Our enquiries have hit a brick wall, it's true. That's why we're considering a change of tactics.'

'What sort of change?'

'One in which we need your assistance.'

'How can I help?'

'We have to communicate with the kidnappers, you see. At this late stage, there's really no alternative. What we propose to do is to run the advert in the *International Herald Tribune* they spoke to you about. You remember – "Pen pals can be reunited. Orwell will pay".'

Charlotte's throat tightened. Golding was looking straight at her, but she could see little of his expression because of the glare from the window behind him. Was he testing her nerve? Was he dropping a far from subtle hint? Or was this merely a sensible proposal born of official desperation? There was no way to tell. 'I remember,' she said hoarsely.

'If and when they respond, they'll expect to talk to *you*. At least in the first instance. We can wean them on to a trained negotiator later, of course.'

'But the advert was to be placed if we were prepared to give them what they want. And we don't have it.'

'No.' He paused and for a moment it was possible to believe he had asked a question rather than stated what he took to be a fact. 'Well, the idea is for you to imply we *do* have it. To keep them talking until we can (a) trace the call and (b) persuade them to extend the deadline.'

Charlotte pleaded silently with her voice and eyes not to betray her as she spoke. 'When . . . er . . . do you plan to run the advert?'

'Saturday.'

It was as much as she could do not to sigh with relief. If Golding had chosen Friday, her own placement of the advertisement would have been bound to come to light. Now there was a slim chance it would not – until it had served its purpose.

'By leaving it as late as possible,' Golding continued, 'we hope to make the kidnappers think we're giving in to the deadline.'

'I see.'

'So, will you help us? Without you, I doubt we'll be able to keep them talking long enough to accomplish anything.'

'What does Ursula say?'

'Mrs Abberley? She's happy for us to do anything we think may save her daughter.' His gaze narrowed fractionally. 'I rather expected you to take the same view.'

'Oh, I do. I do.' Her thoughts whirled ahead of her words, shaping and assessing the consequences of Golding's proposal. She was bound, of course, to agree to it. Therefore, the police would soon be in touch with the *International Herald Tribune's* advertising sales office. With luck, nobody there would remember her call – or comment on it if they did. Her advertisement would still appear in the morning. And the kidnappers would see it. But so, sooner or later, would Golding. He would come looking for her. Failing to find her, he would establish whose number had been quoted. The question was whether he would act fast enough to prevent her reaching agreement with the kidnappers on her own account. She did not know the answer. She did not even know whether she would be able to reach such an agreement. But she did know that now, more than ever, she had to try. 'I'll help in any way I can, Chief Inspector. Any way at all.'

TWENTY-TWO

IT WAS A WINDLESS morning in Speldhurst. Charlotte watched dawn break and spread its bleary greyness across the trim-lawned bungalows of Farriers. A couple of Derek's neighbours had already set off for work in their company cars, speeding towards the bright office lights of normality, minds focused on today's meeting and tomorrow's round of golf. Not for them this eerie vigil she was bound to keep, hidden behind the net curtains of Derek's lounge. Not for them the mind-numbing alternatives she knew she would have to face when and if and every time his telephone rang.

She crossed to the bookcase beside the television and cast her eye along the titles in search of one with which she might ease the tension of waiting. Economic theory. Photography. Natural history. Vintage cars. Fine art and poetry to balance the dog-eared yardage of pulp fiction. The mixture reminded her how little she really knew about him, how abnormal the manner was in which their paths had crossed. She wished it could have been otherwise. And then she saw, lying flat on a rank of paperbacks, *Tristram Abberley: A Critical Biography*. She pulled it out and studied the face of its subject on the cover. What would he have done if he had realized the havoc his literary lie would wreak in the lives of his sister and his son and half a dozen others still unborn when he caught his last breath in Tarragona? It was too late to ask him. Just as it was too late to ponder what she would do if she could know for certain what the next few hours would bring.

In Corunna, Derek had had to walk a mile or so into the city centre to find a kiosk selling the *International Herald Tribune*. Now he hurried with it to a bench in the palm-treed park nearby and turned anxiously to the classified advertisements. PEN PALS CAN BE REUNITED, blared the boxed and capitalized words. ORWELL WILL PAY. And there was his own telephone number in England. It could not be missed. It could not be mistaken. It had begun. Rolling the newspaper in his hand, he rose and set off back towards the hotel.

By ten o'clock, Charlotte had been expecting the telephone to ring for the best part of an hour. Nevertheless, when it did so, she started violently before running to answer it.

'44-892-315509,' she said as slowly as she could.

There was no reply. She waited, then began to repeat the number. But, before she had finished, the line went dead. She glared at the instrument as if it were to blame, then slammed it down. She was still glaring at it when it rang again.

'44-892-315509.'

'Miss Ladram?' To judge by Derek's description, the voice was Galazarga's. But she knew better than to ask.

'Yes.'

'I represent those who are holding your niece, Miss Ladram.'

'I know.'

'We saw your advertisement.'

'Good.'

'Why the change of number?'

'Because the police may be listening on mine. This is safer.'

'I am glad to hear it. The subscriber is listed as D.A. Fairfax. We have recently had some contact with Mr Fairfax. I take it he is a friend of yours?'

'Yes.'

'Then I advise you to be more careful in your choice of friends. We have found Mr Fairfax to be an unreliable man to do business with.'

Now, Charlotte knew, was the moment to be firm. Now was the moment to seize the initiative. But she had only to think of Samantha, alone and frightened, to hold back a little longer. 'I am well aware of Mr Fairfax's dealings with you.'

'In that case, you will be *well aware* of his failure to hoodwink us in the matter of the map.'

'We're not trying to hoodwink you. My aunt destroyed the map before handing the document over to us. I wish she hadn't, but I can't change what she did. It's gone. Only Ortiz's statement remains.'

'We don't believe you.'

'Fine. Don't believe us. But believe this.' Deliberately, she hardened her voice. 'We'll hand the document over to the Spanish press unless you release my niece before the expiry of the deadline.'

There was a pause, then Galazarga said: 'You are bluffing, Miss Ladram. And bluffing poorly. You would not take such a risk with your niece's life.'

'You're right. *I* wouldn't. But I no longer have the document. Mr Fairfax has it. He and his companion don't share my scruples.'

'Who *is* his companion?'

The question was a sign of weakness. Charlotte knew she must exploit it. 'A ruthless man. Just like Señor Delgado.'

She had named Delgado for the very first time, but, if Galazarga noticed, he gave no sign of it. 'Where is this . . . ruthless man?' he asked.

'With Mr Fairfax. In hiding. I don't know where. They thought it safer for me not to know. They can contact me, but I can't contact them. They're waiting to see if they have to carry out their threat. So am I.'

'Come, come, Miss Ladram. They will only do what you tell them to do.'

'Not so. Mrs Abberley and I agreed with them before they left for Spain that they would ignore any subsequent change of mind on our part. It was a precaution we felt we had to take, to protect us from our own weakness as the deadline approached. So, you see, nothing I say will stop them going to the press. Only you can do that.'

'By releasing your niece?'

'Exactly.'

There was a delay of several seconds before Galazarga spoke again. When he did so, Charlotte detected a trace of hesitancy in his voice. 'Miss Ladram, this really—'

'What's your answer?'

'I beg your pardon?'

'I have to know what to tell Mr Fairfax. Your answer, Señor Galazarga. I must have it now, please.'

He did not react to her use of his name any more than he had to her use of Delgado's. 'Very well. I will confer . . . with those I represent . . . and deliver their answer to you.'

'When?'

'This morning. By noon at the latest.'

'All right. But—'

'Goodbye, Miss Ladram.'

Derek walked across to the window of his hotel room and stared out at the harbour, where a red-hulled fishing boat had made no discernible progress towards the open sea since he had last observed it.

'We should have heard from her by now,' he said, turning back towards his companion, who sat in the only armchair, smoking his pipe and gazing at nothing.

'We should hear from her,' Frank said slowly, 'when she has something to report.'

'They must have seen the advert hours ago. What are they waiting for?'

'*If* they're waiting, it's to test our nerves. Yours don't seem to be standing up to the test too well.'

'Oh, for God's—'

'Take some advice from me, boy. The advice of somebody who's waited to go into battle often enough to be an expert. Waiting's hard. But sometimes it's a hell of a sight better than knowing.'

'Thanks, Frank.' With an exasperated shake of the head, Derek returned to watching the fishing boat. 'Thanks a lot.'

Noon was still twenty minutes away when the telephone rang again. Charlotte forced herself to wait until it had completed two rings before picking it up.

'44-892-315509.'

'Miss Ladram?'

'Señor Galazarga?'

'My name does not matter, Miss Ladram. What matters is our answer.'

'And what is your answer?'

'We accept your terms.' Charlotte uttered a silent prayer of thanks. Four simple words justified every chance she had taken. But four words, it transpired, were not all Galazarga had to say. 'On certain conditions which must be scrupulously observed. If they are not, the agreement is null and void. And your niece's life is forfeit.'

'What are the conditions?'

'The document must be brought to a location we nominate, where it will be handed over in return for your niece, who must then be delivered to a police station as if she had been set free without explanation. She must know nothing of the reason for her release and those who do know must say nothing, now or in the future.'

The arrangements for exchange were crucial. They might conceal a carefully planned deception. Charlotte knew this only too well. She had to weigh her eagerness to agree against the possibility of further trickery. But she had no sooner began considering the problem than a ring at the doorbell interrupted her. Rising from the chair with the telephone pressed to her ear, she peered out through the net-curtained window. But no car was visible on the drive or in the road. If, as she greatly feared, it was Golding, he had arrived on foot, which scarcely seemed likely. But somebody had, as a second ring of the bell confirmed.

'Well, Miss Ladram? Do you accept our conditions?'

'I must know more about them. Where . . . Where would the exchange take place?'

'We have chosen somewhere offering privacy and security to both parties.'

There was a tapping on the window. When Charlotte looked round, she saw a bulky figure crouching close to the glass, cupping his hands around his eyes in an attempt to penetrate the screen of net.

'Miss Ladram?'

'I . . . I'm sorry. When . . . When do you envisage . . .'

'Nine o'clock tomorrow morning.'

'So . . . So soon?' It was a stupid remark and she instantly regretted it. Looking round again, she was relieved to see that the figure had vanished from the window. She could only hope he had given up and gone away. 'I'm sorry. Tomorrow morning is fine.'

'Good. You accept, then?'

'Perhaps. Tell me the details first.'

'No. I must have your acceptance first. There can be no quibbling about any of our conditions. They are strictly non-negotiable.'

Another tapping, more like a drumming now. And from a different direction. Charlotte looked up. Standing at the uncurtained patio doors on the other side of the house, staring in at her through the dining room and the arch that separated it from the lounge, was Colin Fairfax. She recognized him at once from his court appearance more than three months ago. He was wearing exactly the same clothes – dark blue blazer, fawn trousers, open-necked striped shirt – and much the same expression of baffled disgruntlement. He tapped again as she watched.

'Miss Ladram, do I have your undivided attention? You seem not to be concentrating on the matter in hand.'

'I'm concentrating. Your conditions . . . I accept them.' Speed was vital now. Colin Fairfax was not going to give up. That was obvious. She had to conclude her negotiations with Galazarga before he decided to take drastic action. 'I accept all of them.'

'Good. These, then, are the arrangements. Make a careful note of them, since I shall not repeat myself.'

Charlotte grabbed a pencil and leant forward to reach the pad of paper she had placed by the telephone earlier. 'I'm listening.'

'Mr Fairfax and his companion will drive to Orense, one hundred and eleven kilometres south-east of Santiago de Compostela. From there they will take the N120 road for Ponferrada. After forty-nine kilometres, they will reach the village of Castro Caldelas. There they will turn off to the north on the minor road to Monforte de Lemos, descending by a series of zig-zags into the valley of the river Sil. They will stop on the southern side of the bridge by which the road crosses the river, arriving no later than eight fifty-five tomorrow morning, Saturday October ten. Our representatives will bring your niece to the northern side of the bridge by the same time. At nine o'clock exactly, Mr Fairfax will walk unaccompanied to the centre of the bridge, taking the document with him, but no weapon of any kind, nor anything that could be mistaken for a weapon. One of our representatives will join him on the bridge and will inspect the document. If it is found to be satisfactory, your niece will be allowed to cross the bridge. Mr Fairfax and his companion will then start back with her towards Castro Caldelas, while our representatives depart in the opposite direction. Mr Fairfax and his companion will deliver your niece to a police station of their choice during the morning, but will not accompany her inside. They will tell her to say she was released by her kidnappers without explanation and does not know where or by whom she was held. They will tell her nothing else. Is that clear?'

'Yes. It's clear.' Colin was banging his fist against the patio door now and shouting. Soon, the neighbours would be bound to hear. And she had still to pass Galazarga's conditions on to Derek. She held up her hand to pacify Colin, but it appeared to have no effect. 'Mr Fairfax will abide by these arrangements to the letter. You have . . . You have my guarantee.'

'And you have mine that we will do the same. I trust there will be no . . . mishaps.'

'So do—'

'Goodbye, Miss Ladram.'

Charlotte slammed the telephone down, hurried across the dining room, released the lock on the patio doors and slid one panel open. Her action seemed to confuse Colin, who stepped back uncertainly.

'Mr Fairfax,' Charlotte said as calmly as she could, 'I am here with your brother's knowledge and consent, so there is no need to create a disturbance.'

His eyes narrowed. 'Don't I know you from somewhere?'

'My name is Charlotte Ladram.'

'Bloody hell! You're Maurice Abberley's sister.'

'Yes. And I greatly regret the injustice you've suffered on his account, but—'

'Was it *you* Dredge spoke to on the blower? I thought it must be some . . . Where *is* Derek? And why wasn't he in court this morning?

You were supposed to tell him about it.' Each remark was accompanied by a stab of the forefinger and an ominous lowering of the brow.

'Derek's in Spain.'

'Spain? But . . . According to his office, he's supposed to be down with flu, being nursed by a cousin in Leicester neither of us has. Do you mean to say I might have had to stay in chokey just because he's decided to have an illicit week in the sun?'

'Of course not. He's not on holiday. And you've been released anyway, haven't you?'

'Small thanks to Derek. If he's not on holiday, what *is* he on?'

'He's doing something for me.'

'For *you*?'

'Yes. But I don't have time to explain. When he gets back—'

A ring at the front door-bell stopped her in mid-sentence. She whirled round, hoping against hope . . . But there *was* a car in the drive now and another in the road, its blue light and Thames Valley Constabulary markings clearly visible. They had come, as she had known they would. But they had come too soon.

'Oh, God, it's the police.'

'The police?' There was a second and longer ring at the door. 'What do they want?'

'Me.'

'You? Come off it.'

Time was running out. If she was lucky, she had a few minutes left, a few minutes which she had to put to good use. To call Derek now was impossible, especially with Colin firing questions and accusations at her. But maybe, just maybe, Colin might be her saviour. 'Come inside,' she said, grasping at his forearm. 'Quickly!'

'What the hell's going on?'

'Listen to me. Please.' Charlotte slid the door shut behind him and locked it. 'I did my best to make up for what my brother did to you, didn't I? I handed over the evidence of his guilt to the police. It's because of that evidence you've been released.'

'I suppose so, but—'

'Now I need to ask you a favour in return.'

'A favour?'

There were three sharp rings at the door, followed by several raps of the knocker. Charlotte ran back to the telephone and grabbed the sheet of paper on which she had recorded Galazarga's instructions. Colin walked slowly after her, his face creased by a puzzled frown.

399

'Aren't you going to let them in?'

'Not yet. There's something I have to tell you first. I need your help, Colin. Desperately.'

'*My* help?'

'Yes. And when you understand, I can only pray you'll agree to give it.'

One o'clock was a deadline Derek had imposed on himself an hour earlier to calm his nerves. As it passed, his patience snapped. He picked up the telephone and began dialling, deliberately avoiding Frank's gaze as he did so. There was a delay of several seconds, then the ringing tone, followed almost immediately by an answer.

'Tunbridge Wells 315509.'

It was not Charlotte. It was not even the form of words she had said she would use. It sounded disturbingly like a policewoman.

'Hello?'

He slammed the telephone down and looked across at Frank. 'It wasn't her,' he said numbly. 'Somebody else answered. Somebody who . . . I think it's gone wrong, Frank. I think it's gone disastrously wrong.'

Two o'clock found Charlotte sitting at a metal table in a bare strip-lit interview room at Newbury Police Station. On the other side of the table, Golding leant forward in his chair, scanning her face for some kind of reaction while Superintendent Miller prowled the linoleumed space between them and the door, venting his anger at Charlotte's conduct. Behind him stood a woman police constable, staring expressionlessly at the opposite wall.

'You've thrown away our best chance of saving your niece. You've ensured we can't contact her kidnappers as we'd planned, can't reason with them, can't negotiate at all. Why, Miss Ladram? Why do such a stupid thing?'

'They may still call on Mr Fairfax's number,' Charlotte replied. 'You can negotiate with them then, can't you?'

'But you won't be there to answer.'

'Well, that's because I'm here, isn't it? That's *your* decision.'

'We can't trust you any more, Charlotte,' said Golding. 'Surely you understand that. How can we when you've gone behind our backs like this?'

'I simply didn't see the need to wait until tomorrow.'

'You didn't see the need to let us know what you said to the kidnappers,' shouted Miller. 'That's the truth, isn't it? You wanted to strike a *private* deal with them.'

'Why, Charlotte?' Golding gently enquired. 'What were you trying to hide?'

'Nothing.'

'What made you think you could do better on your own?'

'I just . . . wanted to try.'

'If you *were* on your own, of course. Where's Derek Fairfax?'

'I don't know.'

'His brother said you refused to offer any explanation for his absence – or for your presence in his house.'

'He told you the truth.'

'But you didn't, did you?' bellowed Miller, bringing the flat of his hand down on to the table so suddenly that Charlotte jumped. 'You were there yesterday morning as well. Why?'

'Derek asked me to look in from time to time while he was away.'

'Away where?'

'He didn't say.'

Miller snorted and turned away. But Golding's gaze did not shift from her face. 'Did the kidnappers ring this morning, Charlotte?'

'No.'

'Do you think they'll ring later?'

'I don't know.'

'Or tomorrow?'

'I don't know.'

'What about Samantha? What do you reckon will happen to her now?'

'I *don't* know.'

'In short, you don't know anything?'

'Nothing I haven't already told you.'

'We don't believe you,' growled Miller.

'And until we do,' said Golding, 'you won't be leaving here.'

Frank's argument that they should wait until nightfall before assuming the worst was wearing thin as far as Derek was concerned. His inability to suggest an alternative course of action was in fact the only reason why he had not left the hotel room, which uncertainty and lack of information had turned into a prison he longed to escape. When the telephone rang, he grabbed at it instinctively, wanting nothing so much as to hear Charlotte's voice at the other end. But he did not.

'Hello?'

'Derek?'

For a second, he did not believe his own senses. It sounded like Colin. It undoubtedly *was* Colin But how? Why? 'Colin? Is that really . . . What . . . I mean . . .'

'I was released this morning. Since nobody seemed to know where you were, I called at your house. I met Charlotte Ladram there. She told me how to contact you.'

'Charlotte did? But . . . Where is she?'

'In police custody.'

'Why?'

'You know why, Derek. You know very well why. Drop the pretence. It won't wash. She told me everything. Well, she didn't really have much choice. It was either that or . . .' Colin sighed. 'Against my better judgement, like the soft-hearted fool I am, I agreed to act as her messenger. I'm at the shop now. By some miracle, the phone's not been cut off. But I certainly can't afford too many international calls. So, pin your ears back. I've a lot to tell you.'

TWENTY-THREE

THEY HAD ARRIVED HALF an hour ago. Since then, the morning had strengthened its chill grasp on the valley. But there had been no other change, no breath of wind to blunt the silence, no hint of movement to lessen the isolation. Derek shifted in his seat and gazed around once more, at the sheer slopes on either side and the flat unbroken body of water between, at the ever bluer gulf of sky above their heads and the narrow winding road down which they had come.

They had left Corunna the previous afternoon and covered the 230 kilometres to Castro Caldelas by early evening. There they had spent the night in a miserable room above the village's liveliest bar, before setting off again at dawn, following the prescribed route down into the deeply cut gorge of the Sil river, zig-zagging round the terraced vineyards and rocky outcrops until they had reached the reservoir at the foot of the gorge and the concrete bridge across it which was their destination.

Frank had turned the Land Rover round to face uphill. He had not explained why and Derek had not asked him to, for the possibility that they might need to make a speedy departure required no explanation. Derek was glad, in a way, not to be able to see the bridge from where he sat. He would see it soon enough, when Galazarga and his men arrived and he would have to set out across its slender span to meet them. Or to meet one of them. Whichever one it was.

If Charlotte had asked him outright to do this, he would surely have refused. But she had not asked him. She had promised he would because she could do nothing else. And now he was about to keep her promise for the same reason. How strange it seemed, how foolish – and yet how inescapable.

He was on the point of looking at his watch to see how much longer they would have to wait when Frank laid a restraining hand on his arm. 'They're here,' he murmured.

And so they were. Two vehicles, one a sleek black limousine, the other a small red van, had appeared on the road and were heading down towards the bridge. No other traffic had passed them in either direction. It had to be them.

Derek watched, transfixed, as the two distant objects moved steadily on, obscured briefly by boulders and bushes, but clearly visible more often than not as their descent continued. Then he did look at his watch. The time was eight fifty-three.

Frank opened his door and climbed out. Derek did the same and joined him at the back of the Land Rover. He could not avoid looking at the bridge now, at its stolid grey legs planted in the water above their own reflections, at the blurred line of the railings which he would shortly follow to its centre.

The two vehicles slowed as they reached a flat stretch of road at the water's edge, vanished behind one last outcrop, then reappeared, cruising to a halt ten yards or so short of the bridge. It was eight fifty-five exactly.

'Prompt, aren't they?' said Frank.

'Let's hope they stick as closely to all the arrangements.'

'Nervous?'

'What do you think?'

'I think it's not too late for you to back out. I'd happily go in your place.'

'But they specified me. So, it has to *be* me, doesn't it? If anyone's to break the agreement—'

'Let it be them, eh?'

'Let it be nobody. That's all I ask.'

Doors opened and closed on the other side. A figure recognizable as Norberto Galazarga conferred with the driver of the van, who climbed out, walked to the back of his vehicle and pulled the double doors wide open. A girl scrambled out, dressed in jeans and a baggy sweater. Was it Samantha? Derek had met her only once, in vastly different circumstances. He could not say for sure. But he wanted it to be her. Very much.

'It's nearly nine,' said Frank.

'I'll move when it's *exactly* nine. Not before.'

'All right. But keep calm. And be careful.'

'I will be. Very careful.'

Galazarga walked forward to the limousine and leant in for a word with one of the occupants. Then he stepped back to allow his interlocutor to climb out. He was a tall frail-looking man wrapped in a large overcoat. Derek had just begun to wonder who he might be when Frank said: 'It's nine on the dot.'

Derek started walking. He patted his jacket pocket and heard the rustle of the envelope containing Ortiz's statement. He did not hurry, but still rounded the bend sooner than he had expected and found himself gazing along the length of the bridge, judging with his eye the point at which he would stop. He looked neither to right nor left, ignoring as best he could the watery expanse on either side, the walls of boulder and scrub ahead, the untouchable ceiling of blue above. He measured each pace as he took it, yet with each one the ground seemed to grow less solid, the information feeding his senses less reliable.

Then he saw the other man, entering his field of vision at the opposite end of the bridge. It was the frail figure in the overcoat, his height exaggerated by his emaciated frame. He was silver-haired and stooping, gingerly in his movements and clearly very old. Something about the way he held his right arm established his identity beyond question.

Derek reached the middle, stepped on to the kerb at the side of the road and placed one hand against the railing. The old man came on. His face was hook-nosed and narrow, lined with a mosaic

404

of creases like the dried mud of a drought-stricken river. One corner of his mouth and the corresponding eyelid drooped as if he had suffered a stroke, but his chin jutted stubbornly and his gaze was unwavering. Beneath the overcoat a starched white collar and tightly knotted black tie could be seen. As he walked, the sunlight caught a gold signet-ring on his left hand, standing out even more prominently than his swollen knuckles. His right hand was gloved and rigid, swinging at his side. Derek wondered if Frank had yet realized who he was. He had come a long way to settle a debt with this man. And now he was expected to stand aside and waive the debt, while Derek bargained for the life of a stranger.

'Mr Fairfax?' the old man asked as he stopped a few feet away. His voice was faint and reedy, as lightly accented as Galazarga's, but with none of the insinuating sweetness of tone. His watery eyes roamed across Derek's face, searching for clues, probing for signs of weakness.

'Señor Delgado?'

'Yes.' He moved on to the kerb and laid his right arm along the railing, his gloved hand coming to rest no more than a few inches from Derek's fingers. 'You have brought the document?'

'Of course.' He reached slowly into his pocket and withdrew the envelope. 'It's all here.'

'Except the map.'

'I explained that to Señor Galazarga.'

'Yes. You explained. And so did Miss Ladram. But tell me again. Why did Miss Abberley destroy the map?'

'To seal the secret of the gold for ever. To draw its poison.'

Astonishingly, Delgado smiled. 'What a wise lady she was.'

'You . . . You approve?'

'I admire the reasoning, certainly. I am eighty-eight years old, Mr Fairfax, and materially well provided for. The gold has never meant less to me than now. When I look back at all the things I did to obtain it . . . When I hear how an English spinster finally cheated me of it . . . What am I to do but smile?'

'But . . . if you don't care . . .'

'Why did I have the girl abducted? That was Norberto's idea. He wants the gold for the leisured future it will buy him after I am dead. I see my own desire for it burning in him still. He is my son, but he is not my heir. His mother was . . . a servant.

405

Thus my sin is his disqualification. And thus he sees the gold as the only inheritance he can hope for. Whereas I see it, with the infuriating piety of old age, merely as a curse. And I do not wish to curse him. For his sake, I am glad the gold is lost for ever.'

'Yet you still want Ortiz's statement?'

'Of course. He died taunting me with its existence. He died knowing I would never be able to rest until I had found it and destroyed it. Map or no map, I must have it.'

'Then take it.' Derek held the envelope out and was surprised when Delgado grasped it with his right hand, the fingers closing expertly around one end and flicking up the unsealed flap. He lifted the contents out with his left hand and began leafing through them, scanning the pages as he went.

'Ortiz's writing. Yes, I recognize it, even after all these years. The bold strokes of a Catalan anarchist. The whip-lash serifs of the one victim I have never forgotten.'

'Victim?'

'My victim, Mr Fairfax. One of many. Are you surprised I admit it?'

'I suppose . . . I expected . . .'

'Dissimulation? Denial? What would be the point? Here, on this bridge, seen but not heard, we can say anything we like. You are a stranger to me. We will never meet again. Thus I can confess my sins to you more freely even than to my priest. For I hold the proof now, in Ortiz's own hand and words. I am safe at last. It is all here, as you promised. All that I hoped to gain from Miss Abberley when I visited her in Rye forty-eight years ago. How well I remember that smug little English seaside town where she outmanoeuvred me over the tea cups and damask napkins, where the methods I had perfected of beating and crushing and squeezing the truth from my victims were useless. When, do you suppose, did she realize she could defeat me?'

'I don't think she was trying to defeat you.'

'Perhaps not. But she did. She and Ortiz and Tristram Abberley between them.' Reaching the last sheet, he sighed, shuffled them together and slipped them back into the envelope.

'What will you do with it?'

'Burn it. Make certain the secret cannot outlive me. Ensure Norberto cannot use it to destroy my granddaughter's opinion of me. When I learned of his contact with Tristram Abberley's biographer—'

'It wasn't *you* McKitrick came to see?'

'No, Mr Fairfax. It was Norberto, seeking the means to make himself rich and me worthless in Yolanda's eyes. She knows nothing of any of this. She is the bright jewel of the barren years I have lived since her father . . . was taken from me. Yolanda deplores what I fought for fifty years ago. But she respects me for *having* fought, for having believed. If she discovered I was a traitor even to fascism, if she learned I was a thief in the midst of war . . . I would die twice. Once, as I shortly must, at God's bidding. And once, more agonizingly, in her wide and trusting eyes.'

'All this,' said Derek slowly, 'Samantha's abduction, her father's murder—'

'Of which she is unaware.'

'Not for much longer. She'll know soon enough. But what she won't know is why.'

'But you will know, Mr Fairfax.'

'Yes. To protect *your* reputation.'

'Does it seem worth it?'

'Not remotely.'

'It would not, to you. But you are less than half my age. When you are as old as I am, you will understand that how we are to be remembered is the only thing that really matters.'

'And how are you to be remembered?'

'As a relic of bygone values. As a hard but honourable man. Not as a thief or a murderer. Not as a traitor or a torturer. Not now I have this.' He patted the envelope and smiled faintly. 'You are thinking I was all those things, are you not? And you are right. But now you will never be able to prove it. Nobody will.'

Suddenly angered by his complacency, Derek said: 'So much for your reputation. What about your conscience?'

'I do not have one. I lost it, along with my right hand, in the service of my country. When I sided with the insurrectionists in July 1936, I did so because I thought they would win. Others fought for their beliefs. We all lost. But I only lost a fortune in gold. They lost everything.' His gaze drifted past Derek, towards the Land Rover and the figure standing beside it. 'Who *is* your companion, Mr Fairfax?'

'He served with Ortiz in the International Brigade.'

'Ah. I might have guessed.'

'Ortiz saved his life during the retreat from Teruel by giving himself up. He didn't know until recently what happened to Ortiz. But now he does.'

Delgado's mouth set in a stern line. 'It would have been better for him to go on not knowing. Better by far.'

For a moment, Derek was tempted to ask exactly how Ortiz had died. Delgado knew. He had been responsible. He had given the orders and watched while they were carried out. Perhaps he had even— But no. Derek would not ask. If he did, he might be told. And if he knew, how could he pretend to Frank that he did not? Ignorance was in the end their only salvation.

As if reading his thoughts, Delgado said: 'Tell him this for me, Mr Fairfax. Ortiz died knowing he had lost everything. And yet he knew also he had won. I did not realize it at the time, of course. But, as the years passed, the havoc his secret would wreak in my life, if it were ever known, grew and grew, till it was a stormcloud large and dark enough to blot out all my achievements. That was his victory. He saw it at the end. He knew what it would mean. He understood. And, later, so did I.'

'Is that supposed to . . . to excuse what you did?'

'No. We are not here to offer or grant excuses. We are here to honour a bargain – and to end my conflict with the family of Tristram Abberley. I have what I came for. And you shall have the same.' He turned and waved stiffly with his right hand.

As Derek watched, Galazarga led Samantha clear of the two vehicles, holding her by the elbow. When they reached a bollard at the end of the bridge, he released her and she started forward hesitantly, then began to hurry, walking clumsily, as if short of practice. She looked haggard and distraught, her hair matted and dirty, her clothes creased and worn. Her eyes were wide and staring, her cheeks hollow, her lips parted in exhaustion and disbelief.

'You need fear no tricks or surprises, Mr Fairfax. Norberto would not dare to disobey me to my face. Take the girl back to her mother. It is time, I think, for us all to go home.'

'Sam?' said Derek, stepping into her path for fear she would otherwise walk straight past.

She pulled up. 'Yes. I'm Sam. Who . . . Who are you?'

'A friend of Charlotte's.'

She frowned. 'Don't I . . . Aren't you . . .'

'We met once. But that doesn't matter. Just carry on to the Land Rover. Another friend is waiting for you there. I'll follow.'

'All right.'

As she walked on, Derek glanced round at Delgado. But he had already turned and started back towards the other side of the bridge, where Galazarga stood waiting for him, his face icily expressionless. Soon, Derek would be alone on this narrow way across the water, this transitory meeting-point of half a dozen destinies. Delgado's secret was safe. But so was the gold. Nobody had won. Unless it was Beatrix. Only she had consistently wanted an end to the greeds and grudges of fifty years ago. And now she had had her way. It really was, as Delgado had said, time to go home. Eagerly, Derek swung on his heel and began to retrace his steps.

TWENTY-FOUR

MILLER AND GOLDING HAD evidently changed their minds by Saturday morning. After a largely sleepless night in a cell at Newbury Police Station, Charlotte was released without explanation immediately after breakfast. She was driven back to Tunbridge Wells in a panda car, monitoring on her wristwatch the gradual approach of nine o'clock while heading east along the M25. What was happening in Galicia she could only imagine. She knew, moreover, that she would have to go on *only imagining* until definite news reached her. A visit or telephone call to Colin Fairfax at this stage could be just the mistake her release was intended to provoke.

In such circumstances, her return to Ockham House was merely the exchange of one kind of cell for another. She could go nowhere in case word came while she was out. She could speak to nobody for fear of betraying herself. And she could think of nothing beyond all the reasons why Frank's plan might have miscarried, why he and Derek, especially Derek, might, thanks to her, be in mortal danger.

An hour of such agonizing made confinement unbearable. Leaving the French windows open to ensure she would hear the telephone if it rang, she walked out on to the lawn, where the autumn leaves had fallen thick and fast during the past distracted week. She remembered the hot day in June when the family had assembled there after Beatrix's funeral and Derek had burst in on them, levelling accusations they had all agreed were absurd. The only absurdity apparent to her now was their collective ignorance, their mutual unawareness of what the future held. It was not yet four months ago, but seemed in other ways as distant as her own childhood, when they had played French cricket on this same lawn, her father winking as he tossed the tennis ball towards her and Maurice smirking as he crouched by the holly-bush, preparing to catch her out. *'Hit it this way, Charlie. Go on. You can—'*

Suddenly, a car appeared up the drive, moving fast enough to throw a shower of gravel on to the lawn when it braked to a halt. It was a large rust-pocked old Jaguar, similar to a model Charlotte's father had once owned. Colin Fairfax climbed out, grinning from ear to ear.

'What is it?' Charlotte cried.

'Good news.'

'Really?'

'The best.' He lowered his voice as she approached. 'Derek rang me from a bar in Castro Caldelas about twenty minutes ago. I thought I'd come straight over in case you'd been released, which I'm glad to see you have. Well, so has your niece. Everything went according to plan. She's with Derek – safe and sound.'

'Oh, thank God.' Impulsively, Charlotte leant up and kissed him. For a moment, the car, his smile and her sudden elation made it seem as if her father had arrived home from work, armed as he often was with a present for her. 'And thank *you*, Colin. Without you, it wouldn't have been possible.'

'True.' His smile broadened. 'But, after what I've been through recently, pulling the wool over the old bill's eyes was a real pleasure.'

'What you've been through is the fault of my family – the family you've just placed hugely in your debt.'

'Freedom must be making me generous. How about a drink to celebrate?'

'Certainly. Come inside.'

It was over now. The uncertainty. The misery. The suffering Maurice had caused to one and all by meddling in matters he did not understand. Life could begin again, on a note not of triumph over the past but of liberation from it. Laughing at the simple joy of it, Charlotte led the way towards the house. There she poured

Colin a large scotch and herself a scarcely smaller gin to toast the success of their strange and fleeting alliance.

'How long before the news becomes official, do you think?'

'Several hours, I shouldn't wonder. Derek said they planned to drop Sam at the police station in Santiago de Compostela. God knows how long it'll take the Spanish authorities to sort things out from there.'

'Meanwhile, only we know she's safe. It seems a pity her mother should have to go on thinking the worst until . . . Do you know, I've half a mind to call her right now.' But, as soon as she had said it, Charlotte realized how unwise such an act would be. 'I can't, can I?'

'Not if you want to be sure of keeping our part in this secret.'

'If only Ursula were here. If only I could tell her without running the risk of being overheard.' The obvious solution flashed into her mind. 'Why don't I drive up and put her out of her agony?' Then another objection arose. 'But my car's still at Speldhurst. Colin, could you—'

'I'll take you the whole way,' said Colin, draining his scotch and gazing fondly at the bottle. 'Matter of fact, I wouldn't mind letting your sister-in-law know it was *me* who helped save her daughter.'

'All right,' said Charlotte decisively. 'Wait here while I change into something that doesn't smell of a standard issue police mattress.'

'Want a hand?'

'*Wait here!*'

When Charlotte returned to the lounge ten minutes later, she found Colin seated on the sofa, gazing benignly at Beatrix's old Tunbridge Ware work-table, which had stood empty in the corner of the room since Charlotte had removed it from Jackdaw Cottage shortly after the funeral.

'I've just been admiring it,' said Colin. 'Lovely marquetry. One of Russell's, I shouldn't wonder. Your aunt's, of course. I remember seeing it there – during my brief visit.'

'A brief visit with enduring consequences.'

'I should say so.' Colin sipped at his scotch and smiled gently, as if reflecting on the irony as well as the injustice of what he had endured.

'But they're nearly at an end now.'

'What are?'

'The consequences.'

'Ah. I see what you mean.'

'So, shall we go?'

'Yes.' Colin heaved himself up. 'Let's do that.'

TWENTY-FIVE

DRIVING SAMANTHA ABBERLEY FROM the Sil Gorge to Santiago de Compostela had not proved the carefree aftermath to his encounter with Delgado that Derek had anticipated. At first, she had been too confused and disorientated to say much. But a stop for breakfast near Orense had enabled her to order her thoughts and absorb the reality of her new-found freedom. From then on, the questions had flowed. And as Derek's answers had grown more evasive, so her demands for information had grown more strident.

'You're Derek Fairfax, aren't you?'

'Yes.'

'What are you doing here?'

'Helping you.'

'But why? You're no friend of mine.'

'I'm a friend of Charlotte's.'

'Charlie? What's she got to do with this?'

'She arranged it.'

'She did? Not my father?'

'No. Not your father.'

'But he knows about this, doesn't he?'

'Not exactly.'

'What do you mean?'

'I mean your family will explain everything. I can't.'

'Why not?'

'It's for your own good. It was part of the deal we struck with your kidnappers.'

'Who are they – the people who were holding me?'

'I can't tell you.'

'Why not?'

'I just can't. Isn't it enough to know you're safe?'

'No. I want to understand what happened to me. Why I had to go through all that.'

'And maybe you'll find out,' Frank had interrupted. 'But not from us.'

Frank's forbidding tone – and the baleful glare accompanying his remark – had subdued Samantha for a while. No doubt she had found him the greatest puzzle of all. She was not to know what Derek knew – that the circumstances of her release had cheated him of his chance to avenge the murder of a friend. How – or if – he had reconciled himself to seeing – but not challenging – Delgado there was no way of telling. His thoughts were hidden behind a well-worn mask.

At last they reached Santiago and eased their way through the Saturday morning traffic to the police station. It was located in a wide stretch of road, the centre of which functioned as a car park. Thus Frank was able to pull up exactly opposite the *Policía Nacional* building without attracting the least attention.

'This is as far as we go,' he baldly announced. 'You're on your own now.'

Samantha stared at him incredulously. 'You're not coming in with me?'

'We can't,' said Derek. 'It's part—'

'Part of the deal,' parroted Samantha sarcastically. 'What do you expect me to tell them?'

'Say the kidnappers let you go on the outskirts of the city after driving you blindfolded from wherever you'd been held. Say you've no idea where that is, who they are or why they decided to release you.'

'I haven't.'

'Then it shouldn't be difficult, should it?'

'But I'm to say nothing about you?'

'Nothing.'

'That's part of the deal as well?'

'Yes.'

She looked at him suspiciously. 'That man on the bridge – what did you give him? What was the ransom?'

Derek shook his head. There was no point in even trying to answer her question.

'Something belonging to my father? Something they wanted him to give up?'

'In a sense.'

'In what sense?'

'Sam, I—'

413

'Don't call me Sam!' She was angry now and close to tears. 'My friends call me Sam. And you're not a friend.'

'I'm sorry. Look—'

'I'll find out what it's all about. I'll say the right things to the police and the consul and Christ knows who else, but I'll still find out. My father will tell me.'

Her trust in Maurice Abberley moved Derek to the brink of an unwise disclosure. 'About your father, Samantha. Perhaps I ought—'

'Miss Abberley,' Frank cut in, 'we've risked our lives to rescue you. We've made sacrifices you can't possibly comprehend. Set against them, the lies we're asking you to tell are trivial – and lily-white. So, why not stop feeling sorry for yourself, walk into that building and ask them to call the British Embassy?'

His words were harsher than Samantha deserved. But their effect was salutary. The edge of hysteria in her voice vanished. 'All right,' she said, wiping her eyes. 'I am . . . grateful, you know. It's just—'

'We understand,' said Derek.

'And remember,' said Frank. 'You're free.'

'Yes.' Her face was suddenly lit up by a smile. 'I am, aren't I?' She rubbed her eyes and sighed, then announced: 'I think I'm ready to go now.'

'Good.' Derek opened the door and climbed out to let her pass. The policeman standing on the station steps was picking his teeth, oblivious to the significance of what was about to happen. Yet still Derek was eager to have done and be gone.

'Thank you, Mr Fairfax,' said Samantha. 'I'll thank you again when I know what you really did.' She started walking towards the police station and Derek climbed back into the Land Rover.

'Poor kid,' he murmured. 'None of this was her fault. When she finds out about her father—'

'But you're no friend of hers,' growled Frank. 'She said so herself. Save your concern for those who are – or were.'

Derek knew at once who he was referring to. But, in a perverse attempt to exorcise the ghosts still clustering around them, he asked: 'Who do you mean, Frank?'

Ahead of them, the policeman stopped picking his teeth and held the station door open for Samantha, who vanished inside without a backward glance. Frank started the engine. He offered no answer to Derek's question, unless it was the remark he made as they pulled out into the traffic and headed away from the centre of the city. 'It's time you told me what Delgado said, boy. I want to hear every word.'

TWENTY-SIX

THE MORNING GLOWED WITH autumnal refulgence, or seemed to, as Charlotte leant back in the cracked leather seat of Colin's Jaguar and watched the golden glades of Surrey flash by. What she felt was a vast multiple of the joyful irresponsibility the end of a school term had inspired in her as a child, but which adulthood had somehow driven out. As the cares and fetters of the recent past fell away, the sensation grew, filling her with confidence and generosity, convincing her that all disputes could be resolved, all wounds healed, all antagonisms ended. Samantha was safe and her mother should not be denied the pleasure and relief of knowing she was. If Charlotte and Ursula could share nothing else, they could share the happiness of this moment.

The sunlight was sparkling on the water as they crossed Cookham Bridge and casting its mellow balm across the lawn of Swans' Meadow. At Charlotte's direction, Colin slowed and turned into Riversdale. As he did so, Charlotte caught sight of Aliki, cycling towards them along the road. She asked Colin to pull up so that she could speak to her and leaned out of the window to attract the girl's attention.

'It's me, Aliki! Charlotte.'

'Charlie!' Aliki skidded to a halt beside her. 'I did not recognize the car. And . . . You look so 'appy.' She put her hand to her mouth. 'Is it . . . Is there . . .'

'There may be good news. But I must speak to Ursula first. Is she in?'

'Oh yes. She 'as 'ardly gone out since . . . since it 'appened. She is . . . so sad.'

'Are you going shopping?'

'Yes. But only in Bourne End.'

'Well, by the time you come back, Ursula may not be so sad.'

'Really?'

Charlotte held her finger to her lips. 'Wait and see.'

With a puzzled smile, Aliki cycled off, leaving Colin and Charlotte to head on along the road, then turn down the drive to Swans' Meadow.

'Quite a place,' said Colin, as he pulled up in front of the house. 'Your brother didn't stint himself, did he?'

'Let's not talk about Maurice, please.'

'All right.' Colin shrugged his shoulders and grinned indulgently. 'Shall we go in?'

'I think I'd better go in on my own to break the news. I'll come and fetch you when I've explained everything.'

'Suits me.'

Charlotte climbed out and hurried to the door, suppressing a desire to skip at every pace. She had expected a swift response to the bell, but there was none. She tried twice more with the same result. Yet Aliki had been quite specific. Ursula was there. She could not have left after Aliki without passing them. Could she be out of earshot in the garden? It seemed the only possible explanation. Miming her intentions to Colin, she walked round to the side of the house.

As she entered the garden, she saw at once that, short of hiding in the shrubbery, Ursula could not be there. At the same moment, she remembered the July afternoon when she had arrived in search of Emerson McKitrick and followed these same steps, only to find far more than she had bargained for. But she was now the one bearing surprises. There were surely none left to lie in wait for her. A little irritated by having to go to such lengths, she tried the kitchen door and was relieved to find it open. Yet she was also perplexed, since it suggested Ursula really was at home and had simply chosen not to respond to the bell. Calling out her name and receiving no reply, she walked through to the hall and turned into the lounge.

She saw Ursula, seated stiffly and expressionlessly on the sofa, a split-second before she saw the reason for her blank and staring silence. A man was standing near the window, dressed in jeans, short leather jacket and sweater. He was stockily built and bull-necked, with a craggy weather-beaten face and crew-cut hair. Charlotte recognized him instantly as Brian Spicer, Maurice's former chauffeur. He was holding a blunt-nosed revolver in his hand and it was pointing straight at her. She had never seen anything smaller than a shot-gun before and for a moment thought it might be a toy. But

Spicer's cold unblinking gaze and the nervous motion of his tongue between his lips told her it was not.

'Spicer,' she said numbly.

'*Miss* Ladram,' he sneered. 'Sit down beside her ladyship.' He waved her towards the sofa with his gun.

Ursula looked up at her. 'Do as he says, Charlie. He's quite capable of using that.'

Charlotte obeyed, moving slowly and cautiously. As she settled on the sofa, the frantic pace of Ursula's breathing became apparent to her. Then she realized her own was equally fast. Her heart was racing too, beating like a drum inside her head. 'What . . . What's going on?' she asked.

'We were having a private chat,' said Spicer. 'I'd waited for Aliki to go out so we wouldn't be disturbed. I didn't know you were going to barge in.'

'Why are you here, Charlie?' asked Ursula, clutching her hand for comfort.

'Never mind why,' snapped Spicer. 'Maybe she can be more *illuminating* than you.'

'About what?'

'He thinks Maurice stored a large quantity of cash here,' said Ursula. 'I've tried to convince him he didn't, but—'

'I *know* he had some stashed away here,' interrupted Spicer. 'Ready cash for the sort of transactions he specialized in. Ones that didn't go through the books. Pay-offs. Back-handers. Sweeteners. You know the kind of thing.'

'We don't,' said Ursula. 'Unless you mean the sort of work you did for him.'

Anger flared in Spicer's eyes. He moved closer to them, then stopped and said: 'Yeh. That sort of work – since you mention it. I'm still owed some. Which I intend to collect – plus enough to set me up abroad. Thanks to Maurice, I've got the police on my tail, trying to pin the old girl's murder on me. So, I need to make myself scarce. And I need spending money to do it with.'

'Take whatever you like,' said Ursula. 'But there's no hoard of cash.'

'Pull the other one. I want all of it. And I want it now.'

Could it be true? Had Maurice hidden money somewhere in the house? Was it the source of what he had foolishly offered Delgado's men at their meeting on Walbury Hill? If so, Ursula probably did not know where it was. But Spicer would never believe that. Desperate to distract him, Charlotte said: 'You *were* responsible for Beatrix's death, then?'

'What do you think?'

'And for the robbery at Hendre Gorfelen?'

'The Welsh job? Yeh, that too.'

'All at Maurice's bidding?'

'I did what I was paid to do.'

'Including planting the stolen Tunbridge Ware in Colin Fairfax's shop?'

'Yeh. So what?'

'Your dismissal for drunkenness was just a charade?'

'I didn't take much persuading. What Maurice had in mind was preferable to touching my forelock to this bitch.' He nodded at Ursula.

'Maurice must have paid you well.'

'Not well enough. I'm here to collect what's still due to me.'

'Unfortunately,' said Ursula, 'you're not going to be able to.'

'Want a bet? If you won't give it to me in cash, I'll have to take it in kind.'

'What do you mean?'

'I mean I'll get a life sentence if they do me for murder – which they will if I'm caught. But I can't serve life twice, can I? A second murder – or a third – wouldn't make much difference, would it?'

'Of course it would,' said Charlotte. 'You may be able to persuade the court you didn't mean to kill Beatrix. You may—'

'Shut up!' Spicer marched towards her and pushed the gun against her cheek. The coldness and the shock of it made her flinch. Tears started into her eyes. She had been so happy and carefree only a few minutes ago that the danger she was now in seemed monstrously unfair. She had thought it was all over, the last problem solved, the last risk run. But it was not. And this time there was absolutely nothing she could do.

When Spicer spoke again, Charlotte was aware he was talking to Ursula, not her. 'Listen to me, *Ursula*.' He stressed each syllable of her name equally in mockery of her accent. 'I'm glad your sister-in-law's turned up, because she makes this a whole lot simpler. She may not know where Maurice's loot is, but you bloody do. So, either you tell me now or I pull this trigger – and make a real mess of your sofa.'

'Spicer—'

'*Where is it?*'

'I don't know!'

'You're lying.'

'No. For God's sake—'

Ursula stopped speaking and a fraction of a second later Charlotte realized why. The front doorbell was ringing. And only she knew who was ringing it.

At the same moment, in Galicia, Derek emerged from the terminal building at Santiago Airport and walked across to the Land Rover, where Frank was waiting for him, seated at the wheel.

'Well?' the old man enquired.

'I'm booked on a flight to Madrid leaving in just over an hour. It connects with one to Heathrow. I should be home by early evening.'

'I'll leave you to it, then. It's a long drive back to Wales. I'd better make a start.' He turned the ignition and the engine spluttered into life.

'Frank—'

'What is it?'

'About Delgado . . .'

'Don't say it, boy. Whatever it is won't bring Vicente back to life – or his murderer to justice.'

'I know, but . . . well, Charlotte was worried you were coming for . . .'

'Revenge?' Frank nodded. 'It was in my mind.'

'Is it still?'

'Yes. But that's where it'll stay.'

'For Beatrix's sake?'

'For all our sakes – the living and the dead.'

'Would it have been different if you'd met him on the bridge instead of me?'

'Maybe. Maybe not. If he'd stood in front of me and admitted torturing Vicente to death, I might not have been able to keep my hands from his throat. But what then, eh? What about you and the girl? If I'd avenged Vicente, who would have avenged Delgado? In the end, somebody has to call a halt. I don't know whether I'd have been able to. And I never will now, will I? Nor will you.' He jerked the Land Rover into first gear. 'I must go. When you see Charlotte, send her my regards.'

'I will. But I'm sure she'll want to thank you in person.'

'What for? In the end, it was you who pulled it off. Pretty neatly, too.' One end of his mouth curled up in a concession to a smile. 'Go home and make her happy, Derek. It's good advice – for both of you.' With that, and the faintest of farewell nods, he released the clutch and moved off towards the exit road.

Derek stood watching the Land Rover until it had vanished from sight. It was, he rather thought, the first time Frank had addressed him by his Christian name. If the purpose was to emphasize his parting piece of advice, it was hardly necessary. One reason for flying home was to see Charlotte as soon as possible. And he did not intend to do so simply in order to say goodbye.

What was Charlotte doing now? he wondered as he made his way back into the terminal building. Colin would have conveyed the good news to her long since. Perhaps they were sharing a celebratory drink. Or perhaps not. Either way, he felt sure he would be able to persuade them to share one with him. There was, after all, a great deal to celebrate. For the first time in months, not a cloud was to be seen on any of their horizons.

'They're not going to give up, are they?' said Spicer, as the doorbell rang for the fifth or sixth time. 'Who the bloody hell is it?'

'I've no idea,' said Ursula. 'I'm not expecting anybody.'

'Well, you'd better get rid of them. Stand up, *Miss* Ladram. Very slowly.'

With the gun still only an inch or so from her face, Charlotte rose from the sofa. She did not know what to say or do and could only obey dumbly. There had to be a way out, surely. The conviction was almost as strong as her fear. After all that had happened, it made no sense for her life to end like this, snuffed out in a moment of panic and stupidity. Yet why should it make sense? To expect it to was perhaps her greatest fallacy. And perhaps also her last.

'Walk ahead of us into the hall,' Spicer said to Ursula, stepping behind Charlotte and twisting back her left arm with his own while pressing the gun into the nape of her neck, where she could feel the barrel cold and hard against her skin. Ursula moved past them and a prod of the gun told Charlotte to follow. The door-bell rang yet again as they edged out of the lounge. 'Open the damn thing! But only wide enough to tell whoever it is to sod off. Remember: try anything stupid and I'll put a bullet through your sister-in-law's head.'

Ursula hesitated momentarily, then started towards the door. A vague and bulky shape could be seen through the panel of frosted glass above the letter-box. There was no doubt in Charlotte's mind who it was. But Ursula would not recognize him. Nor would Spicer – unless he identified himself. The door was fitted with a chain, but Ursula left it hanging where it was as she turned the handle and moved to block the narrow opening.

'Mrs Abberley?' Charlotte heard Colin say.

'Yes, but—'

'Where's Charlotte?'

'She's not here. And I don't know who you are, but—'

'Colin Fairfax-Vane.'

'What?' Spicer's grip on Charlotte's arm tightened. He too had heard the name.

'Look, I know she's with you. I saw her go in. Why don't we stop playing games?'

'This isn't a game. Please leave.'

'I've no intention of leaving.' Ursula tried to close the door, but without success. Colin's weight was more than sufficient to prevent her. Then, as he pushed and she pulled, the handle slipped from her grasp and the door flew wide open, bouncing back against its stop. 'All I want to do is—' Colin's lips froze as he barged past Ursula and looked down the hall.

'I've got a gun,' said Spicer. 'And I'll use it if I have to.' He was frightened. Charlotte could tell as much by the panting of his breath in her ear and the vice-like intensity of his hold on her arm. He was frightened because the odds had changed, because events were running out of his control, because there was too much for him to watch and consider.

'Who . . . Who are you?' asked Colin.

'He's Brian Spicer,' said Ursula from close behind him. 'The man who framed you for Beatrix's murder.'

'What?' Colin's frown of incredulity changed as Charlotte watched, disbelief hardening into anger. And Spicer too was watching, reading the same emotion in his face. In as many seconds as it had taken Ursula to speak, Charlotte's frail hopes of a peaceful outcome had vanished. Why had Ursula done it? Why, unless she no longer cared what happened to anyone except herself?

Just as this conclusion entered Charlotte's mind, Ursula seized her chance. She pushed Colin hard between the shoulders. Caught off balance, he stumbled forward. As he did so, Spicer, clearly believing he was about to be charged, hurled Charlotte to his left and raised the gun. He fired as Charlotte fell. She heard the explosion somewhere above her as she struck the newel-post at the foot of the stairs and crumpled to the floor. Then, as she twisted round to look, she saw Colin spinning back against the opposite wall, clutching at his side, grimacing with shock and pain. Ursula had ducked out through the doorway and vanished. But Spicer, who must have realized she was the only one of them likely to know where Maurice's cash had been hidden, was making after her, running down the hall and swearing as he ran. Charlotte and Colin did not matter to him now. Only Ursula – and the money he had to believe she could still lead him to – figured in his thoughts.

As Spicer plunged out through the doorway, Charlotte scrambled to her feet and moved towards Colin, who had slid slowly down into a sitting position between the umbrella-stand and a console table, leaving a barometer swaying on its hook like a pendulum above him. There was blood oozing between his fingers where he was clutching his left side, but he seemed almost to be laughing as he gazed blearily up at her.

'Hello, Charlotte. Are you all right?'

'Of course I am.' She crouched beside him, consumed by a desperate wish that he should not die. It would make a bitter waste of all their efforts – hers and Derek's and Beatrix's as well – if Colin should die now, victimized by the Abberleys to the very end. 'Let me see the wound,' she said anxiously.

'No. Phone for an ambulance. Better . . . use of time. Where . . . Where's Spicer?'

'I don't know, but—'

The wail of a siren cut across her thoughts. It was near by and drawing nearer by the second. Colin heard it too and frowned at her. 'You . . . You've already phoned?'

'No. I don't understand.'

'Never mind.' His voice faltered as his concentration seemed to drift. 'Listen . . . There's something . . . I have to tell you . . .'

But his words were swamped by an invasion of noise. There were two sirens now, both very close, each wail distorting and amplifying the other. Then there was a crunch of braking tyres on gravel, a slamming of doors, followed by a shout of 'Put that down!' and other shouts Charlotte could not catch. A second later,

Chief Inspector Golding burst through the doorway, panting hard.

'Miss Ladram! Are you all right?' Then he saw Colin and shouted over his shoulder: 'Ambulance! Straightaway. One wounded. Val! Come and do what you can.'

D.C. Finch hurried past him and knelt beside Colin, waving Charlotte aside. She stood up slowly and looked at Golding, aware there was much to say and ask but too battered and confused by the rush of events to do more than gape at him.

'It's OK,' he said. 'Spicer's given himself up. We nearly ran him over in the drive. We moved in as soon as we heard the shot.'

'Moved in?'

'We've been tailing you since we let you go this morning to see if you'd contact the kidnappers. This isn't at all what we anticipated.' He nodded down at Colin. 'Why was he with you?'

'He was just . . . trying to help. How is he?'

D.C. Finch glanced up at her. 'Well, he isn't losing too much blood, but . . .' She shrugged. 'Don't worry. The ambulance will be here soon.'

'Hurts like buggery,' mumbled Colin. 'Not that . . .' He tried to grin. 'Not that I speak from experience.'

'Miss Ladram,' said Golding. 'What was Spicer doing here?'

She was about to reply when Ursula appeared in the doorway, smiling hesitantly, as if what she had done could be atoned for with a brisk apology and an ingratiating word. 'Thank God you're all right, Charlie,' she said softly.

'Ask *her* what Spicer wanted,' said Charlotte bleakly. 'Ask *her* how she got the better of him.'

Golding frowned. 'Mrs Abberley?'

Before Ursula could respond, an officer Charlotte recognized as Sergeant Barrett loomed up behind her. 'Sir!' he exclaimed. 'Important news from Divisional HQ.'

'What is it?' snapped Golding.

'Mrs Abberley's daughter's been released. She's in the hands of the Spanish police – safe and well.'

TWENTY-SEVEN

COLIN FAIRFAX – WHOSE ADDITIONAL surname the National Health Service declined to recognize – did not die of his wounds. Unlike Tristram Abberley, he was destined to make a complete recovery. Indeed, after an initial twenty-four hours of alternate agony and oblivion, he quite enjoyed being a patient in Wycombe General Hospital. He realized he was over the worst as soon as he stopped regarding the nurses as mother substitutes and began indulging in sexual fantasies about them. From then on, he positively revelled in the celebrity status conferred on him by the dramatic circumstances of his admission and, but for the management's puritan attitude towards drinking and smoking, could happily have contemplated a lengthy stay.

He decided at the outset to plead total ignorance where the events of 10 October were concerned, claiming to the police that he had driven Charlotte to Swans' Meadow at her request and without the first idea what might be happening there or in Spain. When she and Derek told him the whole story, he was confirmed in his judgement. The less of the truth the police knew the better. Not least because he was in sole possession of one vital fragment of it. Charlotte seemed to have forgotten his attempt to share it with her, which was understandable in view of all that she had on her mind. And now, as the future stretched out enticingly ahead of him, he began to think it might also be providential.

On the day Colin was discharged, Derek drove up from Tunbridge Wells to collect him and take him back to his flat above the Treasure Trove. An heroic effort on Charlotte's part had rendered this almost homely in his absence. She was waiting to greet him with champagne and canapés, which he deemed an ideal way to inaugurate a convalescence during which his surgeon had urged him to forego alcohol.

It was clear to Colin from the popping of the first cork that Charlotte and Derek had more to celebrate than his recovery or, indeed, the formal dropping of all charges against him by the police. Their faces glowed with conspiratorial happiness and, though they were too bashful to say as much, it was obvious that love had blossomed during his stay in hospital.

'So,' he innocently enquired halfway through his second glass, 'What are your plans?' Deliberately, he had failed to specify which of them he was addressing.

'Well,' Derek replied defensively, 'they're a bit up in the air, actually. As of the end of the month, I shall be joining the ranks of the unemployed.'

Colin choked. 'You mean Fithyan & Co. have sacked you?'

'Not exactly. We've agreed on a parting of the ways.'

'You mean they've sacked you.'

Derek grimaced. 'Chartered accountants don't use such expressions. I was . . . allowed to resign at short notice. But don't worry. With FCA after my name, I should be able to find somebody who wants my services.'

'But before he starts looking,' Charlotte interposed with a smile, 'we're going on holiday. A few recuperative weeks in the sun.'

Noting but not remarking on her use of the collective pronoun, Colin said: 'Splendid idea! No objections from the police, I trust?'

'I'm not being charged with anything, if that's what you mean. Sam's safe return seems to have defused their wrath. And Golding's given up asking questions. He knows we slipped something past him, but I don't think he's going to be allowed to spend any more time trying to find out what. The Spanish police are still investigating the matter, but Sam's given them so little to go on I imagine they'll soon lose interest.'

'And how is Sam?'

'Up and down. Ecstatic one minute, depressed the next. I told her as much as I could, but I'm not sure she can bring herself to believe the truth about her father. She's taking it out on Ursula, I'm afraid – refusing to talk to her, excluding her from her life. She's even staying with friends until she goes back to Nottingham. It'll be a long time before she trusts her mother again – if she ever does.'

'You aren't expecting me to sympathize with the wretched woman, are you?'

'Of course not. *I* certainly don't. In fact, I haven't spoken to her since . . . well, since you last spoke to her. And I don't plan to. I've decided to forget about my family – what's left of it – and concentrate on myself.' She glanced at Derek. 'And on those who I can be sure won't let me down.'

'A sound policy,' said Colin, holding out his glass for Derek to top up. 'I should have done the same long ago.'

Charlotte smiled. 'And what are your plans, Colin?'

'Mine? Oh, business as usual. Re-open the Treasure Trove ASAP. Scout around for new stock. Then sell it all at a huge profit in the run-up to Christmas. Some hopes, eh?'

'Nothing else?'

'What else should there be?'

'Oh, I don't know. It's just . . . When the police arrived, that day at Swans' Meadow, you were trying to tell me something. But you never finished and in the confusion I forgot to ask you what it was. I've been meaning to ever since.'

'Really?'

'Yes. It seemed to be something quite important.'

'I don't remember.' Colin grabbed at a cocktail sausage by way of distraction. 'If and when I do, I'll be sure to let you know.' He grinned uneasily and cast around for a change of subject. 'Where are you going on this holiday, then?'

'The Seychelles,' Derek replied.

'Perfect! And so appropriate for a pair of lovebirds.'

Charlotte arched her eyebrows. 'Who said anything about lovebirds?'

'Nobody. But I heard their distinctive song among the branches.'

Derek laughed to cover his blushes. 'Why so appropriate, may I ask?'

'Well, the Seychelles are home to the *coco de mer*, aren't they?'

'The what?'

'Haven't you heard of it? It's a species of palm unique to the islands. The nut of the female tree is shaped exactly like . . . But you'll find out for yourselves soon enough. Why should I spoil the fun? Just think of me sometimes, labouring away here, while you're . . . Well, just think of me.'

'We will,' said Charlotte. 'And when we come back—'

'You can tell me what date you've fixed for the wedding.'

By late afternoon, the party was over. Colin stood at the window, sipping at a last glass of champagne as he watched Charlotte and Derek walk away along Chapel Place. They were holding hands and Charlotte had leant her head on Derek's shoulder. Colin smiled indulgently at the sight and dismissed any lingering

426

doubts he might have had: he would soon be acquiring a sister-in-law.

Not that he objected. Quite the reverse, in fact. Charlotte was a likeable girl, just the spirited but sensible wife his brother needed. As for her curiosity about what he had been on the verge of telling her at Swans' Meadow, he reckoned he could deflect it for as long as it took to fade away completely. What else could he do? To tell her now would be to revive so much she wished earnestly to forget. It was kinder by far to guard his tongue. Indeed, he had only to imagine the words he would have to use to explain it to her to realize how unwise such an explanation would be.

'Well, Charlotte, it's like this. Remember when I called at Ockham House that morning to tell you Sam had been released – and we decided to drive up to Bourne End to put Ursula out of her misery? Of course you do. How could you forget? How could I? You went upstairs to change, leaving me in the lounge. While I was waiting, I gave your late aunt's Tunbridge Ware work-table the once over. A lovely piece, as I said at the time. And easier to examine because it was empty. Or almost empty. I noticed the lining in one of the drawers had become detached from the wood – or rather had been detached. And then I noticed the reason. A sheet of paper had been inserted under the lining. I pulled it out and took a look at it. It was pretty old and yellow at the edges: a hand-drawn map, with place-names and directions written in Spanish. I was still looking at it when I heard you coming down the stairs. There wasn't time to replace it, so I slipped it into my pocket, intending to mention it to you later. While I was waiting in the car at Swans' Meadow, I transferred it to my wallet for safe-keeping. Then, when I was lying on the hall floor with blood pouring out of me, wondering if I might actually be going to die, I tried to tell you about it – without success. Later, in hospital, thanks to what you and Derek told me, I realized what the map was. And how it came to be there. At least, I guessed. Beatrix must have stopped short of destroying it at the last moment and hidden it in the work-table. The irrevocability of what she'd planned to do must have stayed her hand. I can understand why. I couldn't bear to destroy it either.'

No, it would not do. It would not be fair. Charlotte believed it was all over. And so it was, as long as the existence of the map remained a secret. His secret. Worth the small matter of forty million pounds.

Colin took out his wallet, slid the map from behind a wad of old credit card receipts and examined it reflectively. The route from Cartagena to the abandoned copper mine was clearly shown.

It could be followed on any large-scale map of the locality. Or in a car, for that matter. If one wished to.

What was he to do with it? Post it to Delgado? Definitely not. Wait for the old fascist to die, then offer it to Galazarga? Hardly. Auction it at Sotheby's? Difficult, since he was not the rightful owner. Burn it? That would be a shame, after it had survived for so long. Donate it to the Spanish nation? Too philanthropic for his taste. What, then?

Colin put the map back in his wallet, drained his glass and wondered if there was another bottle somewhere. Perhaps tomorrow he would turn his mind to finding out where Spanish law stood in relation to treasure-trove. Yes, on balance, that would probably be the best thing to do. To begin with.